Can't Go Back

ALSO BY MARIE MEYER

Across the Distance

Can't Go Back

MARIE MEYER

FOREVER
YOURS

New York Boston

Forever Yours
Hachette Book Group
1290 Avenue of the Americas
New York, NY 10104

hachettebookgroup.com
twitter.com/foreverromance

First ebook and print on demand edition: August 2015

Forever Yours is an imprint of Grand Central Publishing.
The Forever Yours name and logo are trademarks of Hachette Book Group, Inc.

The publisher is not responsible for websites (or their content) that are not owned by the publisher.

The Hachette Speakers Bureau provides a wide range of authors for speaking events. To find out more, go to www.hachettespeakersbureau.com or call (866) 376-6591.

ISBN 978-1-4555-9097-1

For my Darlings.
Always follow your dreams.

Can't Go Back

Chapter One

The headlights flashed across the PENNSYLVANIA WELCOMES YOU sign just as my playlist ended. Reaching for my phone, I scanned through others. I needed music to fill the growing hollowness inside me. Moving my best friend, Jillian, to design school was one of the hardest damn things I'd ever had to do.

With the cruise set at eighty, I watched the odometer tack on mile after mile. Jillian snored away in the passenger seat, her head against the window, legs stretched out, bare feet resting on the dashboard. Every now and then, I'd sneak a quick peek at her and smile, years of friendship playing on a highlight reel in my head.

Twelve years ago, after Jillian's parents died during the 9/11 attacks, she came to live with her grandparents—my neighbors. The day she arrived, she refused to get out of the car. I climbed into the backseat with her, offered her my hand, and promised to always make her smile. I'd never leave her. Now I was driving her a thousand miles away, so *she* could leave *me*.

When she'd been offered a scholarship to an elite design school in Rhode Island, I was thrilled for her. Jillian had always dreamed of being a designer. After everything she'd been through, losing her parents at such a young age, and then blaming herself because she'd asked her parents for a souvenir, which in turn prompted them to meet a friend at the World Trade Center that morning. Not to mention her struggle to overcome her self-harm tendencies as she got older. It was time something positive came her way. But it wasn't until now that I'd realized just how many miles stood between Rhode Island and Illinois…between Jillian and me.

"Uhhh," I groaned, pressing my feet into the floorboard, stretching the best I could. I needed some tunes to liven up the drive. The lonely, dark road was fucking with my state of mind. With the pad of my thumb, I swiped through countless artists on my iPhone, finally deciding on the Red Hot Chili Peppers. I needed something heavy, loud, and bass-driven to pull me out of my current funk. Letting my head fall against the headrest, I fingered Flea's bass riffs along the steering wheel.

Jillian sighed and moved her head from the window, placing it back onto the seat. Wisps of blond and orange hair covered her face and her neck slumped at an odd angle. No way was she comfortable. Hell, I wasn't comfortable. It was almost eleven. I was tired and hungry, and I really needed a restroom.

Holding the wheel steady with my left hand, I used my right to rock her gently. "Jillian. Jillian, wake up."

She blinked a few times and sat up, still half asleep. Her hair was a tangled mess on top her head, like a pile of vanilla ice cream swirled with orange sherbet. I ran my palm over her head, smoothing some of the pieces back where they belonged.

Jillian looked out her window, then back to me. "I'm sorry," she croaked, her voice thick with sleep. "I didn't mean to fall asleep on you. What time is it?" She lowered her pale legs from the dash and raised her arms high, stretching.

She wore a faded t-shirt featuring the name of my band, Mine

Shaft, and as with any red-blooded male, it didn't escape my attention when the t-shirt rode up, exposing a small patch of skin above the waist of her yoga pants. She wasn't the scrawny little girl who used to play in the dirt with me.

I removed my hand from her head with a sigh and adjusted the volume knob, reducing Anthony Kiedis to background noise. "It's just after eleven."

"Ugh, I hope there's a good yoga class on campus." She yawned, arching her back. "Where are we?"

I took the next exit, getting off the turnpike, following the blue signs to the nearest hotel. "We're in Pennsylvania. Do you want to keep driving or call it a night?" It was up to her; if she wanted me to keep going, I would. But I hoped she didn't. I was beat.

"Shit, I'm sorry. I should have taken over the wheel a hundred miles ago."

"It's all right." I flashed her a smile. "You looked too peaceful to wake up." More than peaceful, she'd looked gorgeous. Many times throughout the night, I'd fought the urge to run my fingers through her hair, or touch her porcelain cheeks.

But then I'd reminded myself, friends didn't get to touch.

Three months ago I'd had my chance. Back in May, the easygoing friendship Jillian and I had had as children was obliterated the second she kissed me. In that moment I wanted to do a whole hell of a lot more than kiss her.

A light wind whistled through the doorway, causing Jillian's long hair to float on the breeze. Without a second thought, her hand came up and she swiftly tucked the flying strands behind her ears. I would have liked to do that for her…but it was too late. I kept my hands in my lap.

Stretching out my legs, I leaned my back against the wall of the little old cabin. Jillian did the same, resting her head against the dusty log walls. This cabin had been our place in high school. Off the beaten path, in a forested section of the state college campus, the miniature cabin had become the home to many late-night talks and songwriting sessions, and countless other memories. Where most childhood friends have tree houses, Jillian and I had a tiny cabin in the woods.

After having dinner with my parents and sister, Jillian had insisted on coming out here. Since she was leaving for college in three months, it seemed fitting that we say good-bye to "our cabin."

She'd been quiet since we'd gotten here. "What's on your mind, Jillibean?" I nudged her with my shoulder.

"Hmm," she hummed. "Nothing. Just enjoying the night. It's always so peaceful out here."

"Yeah, it is." I closed my eyes and listened to the crickets chirp. In the distance an owl hooted.

"Griffin?"

"Yeah?" I answered, but kept my eyes closed. I liked the way her voice mingled with the sound of the wind.

"Griff."

At a tap on my shoulder, I rolled my head in her direction and opened my eyes. Our faces were less than an inch apart. My pulse went from zero to erratic in a matter of seconds and the cabin grew stuffy. Jillian's midnight eyes searched my face.

My eyes fell to her mouth. As so many times before, I wanted to kiss her. What would her lips feel like on mine? What did she taste like?

I moved my head closer…the tips of our noses touched and Jillian sucked in a tiny breath.

What noises could I elicit from her? How loud could I make her scream my name?

And while my mind conjured a dozen and a half erotic scenarios, Jillian closed her mouth on mine.

I shivered at the memory and readjusted in the seat, trying to accommodate the bulge in my pants.

It had taken every ounce of energy I possessed not to push my hands through her long, rainbow-dyed hair, press her against the cabin wall, and show her exactly why she couldn't leave me at the end of the summer.

Her lips were hot and full, and I wanted to devour her. My hands itched to explore the curves of her tiny frame. With just one kiss, she'd released a flood of emotions I'd never felt for another woman.

And it scared the shit out of me.

Jillian was my friend…my best friend. If we ventured down that path, I feared she'd give up on her dream to stay with me. I didn't want her to blow off design school and stay in Illinois and end up at the junior college. She was too talented for community college. I wanted more for her. I'd spent so many years trying to protect her from every pain and sadness life threw her way, I worried she'd grown too reliant on me. She needed this opportunity to spread her wings and find herself.

With one infinitesimal nudge—all I could muster—I pushed her way. When our lips parted, I could still taste her, and like a starving man, I wanted more. Energy crackled between us. Jillian stared at me, desire and confusion pooling in her dark-chocolate eyes. Her expression begged me for an explanation. Then I told her the biggest lie of all: I only wanted to be friends.

And now she was leaving…without knowing the truth.

She yawned loudly, snapping me out of my thoughts. "I'm such a slacker." She scrubbed her hands along her face. "I don't think I can make it any farther tonight. Let's get a room."

That's my girl. "That's what I hoped you'd say. My ass hurts, and I really need to piss."

Not familiar with the area, I didn't travel too far into town, sticking close to the freeway. I pulled the car into the nearest hotel parking lot and killed the engine.

The second I got out, I stretched my hands above my head, rising onto the balls of my feet. My body was stiff. What I wouldn't give for a workout about now.

Jillian got out on her side and mimicked my stance. When she stretched, the bottom of her shirt came up again. My eyes were drawn to her tiny waist and flat stomach. *Damn it, Griffin.*

Attempting to keep my thoughts pure, I dropped my hands and went to check on the trailer carrying my motorcycle. Since Jillian was keeping her car at school, I'd need a set of wheels to get back home.

"Everything good?" she asked, coming to stand beside me.

I yanked on each of the chains securing my bike, checking for any weak links. "Yep. All good." I gave one last tug and turned to face her. She smiled up at me with droopy eyelids. Dusting my hands on my jeans, I brushed a wayward strand of hair out of her face.

"Thanks," she said sleepily.

I smiled. "I'll get our bags."

* * *

Once we checked in, the desk clerk handed over our key cards. I hefted Jillian's backpack onto my shoulder, and scooped my bag off the floor. "Ready?"

Jillian nodded.

I led the way, keeping watch for our room number as we walked down the hallway. Not too far from our room, I heard Jillian laughing behind me. I stopped and turned around. "What's so funny?"

Jillian pointed at the wall. "The wallpaper. It's the same stuff Jennifer has on the walls in the guest room...my room."

"Leave it to Jennifer to troll cheap hotels for interior design inspiration," I said, laughing.

Jennifer was Jillian's older sister and guardian. When the girls' grandparents had become too ill to care for them, Jennifer, being in her early twenties at the time, assumed guardianship of Jillian. Something Jennifer's resented ever since.

Jennifer was always cold and distant to Jillian, never kind. She wasn't a fan of me either, and the feeling was mutual.

Five years ago Jillian started cutting herself, a way to cope with the loss of her parents. She kept it a secret from everyone, until I found her unconscious and bleeding on her bathroom floor.

I stayed by Jillian's hospital bed all day long, praying for her to wake up. When visiting hours ended, Jennifer sent a nurse into Jillian's room and demanded that I leave. That night Jillian was all alone. Even thinking about her waking up scared and by herself made my blood boil. From then on I didn't give two fucks what Jennifer said or did, she'd never keep me from Jillian again.

Finding our door, I slid the plastic card into the handle and was denied access. The blinking red light taunted me. I tried again. Access denied.

I turned around. "Did I ever tell you how much I hate these things?"

"Scoot over, let me try." Jillian plucked the card from my hand, threw her hip into my leg, and pushed me out of the way. For a tiny thing, she wielded a lot of power in those hips.

She stuck the card into the handle and pulled it out quickly, just as I had done. But this time the light blinked green and the latch clicked. Access granted.

"It's OK. You can't help it." She patted my shoulder. "It's not your fault you lack rhythm."

I swallowed a laugh. *I lacked rhythm?* That was funny. She never said that when I played the bass or guitar for her. I shook my head and shouldered past her. "Definitely a smartass."

I walked into the dark room and tossed the bags on the bed, beating a quick path to the john. I took care of business and hopped in the shower.

The hot water loosened my tight, sore muscles. I made it quick, though, careful to save some hot water for Jillian.

Shutting the water off, I pulled the curtain open, realizing I'd left my bag on the bed. "Shit," I mumbled. Even though I'd known Jillian for years, things have been awkward between us since she kissed me. And I was certain my girlfriend wouldn't approve of my next move.

I yanked a towel from the rack and dried off. Wrapping it around my waist, I stepped out of the shower and opened the bathroom door.

Jillian was lying on the bed, right beside my bag. I crossed the room, doing my best to ignore her, but I felt her eyes on me. My pulse quickened. A bead of water rolled down my neck.

"Whoa," she said breathily. "Where did those come from?" She pointed to my arms.

Ignore her. Ignore her. Remember Erin, your girlfriend? I chanted in my head while I unzipped my bag.

I pulled out a t-shirt. "What?" My face heated. Being naked next to this girl was bad news. I was thankful she was fully clothed or I'd cross a serious line.

"You're looking good, Daniels. Real hottie material now."

"Shut up," I grumbled.

Keep it friendly, Daniels. Don't forget about Erin.

"I'm serious, Griff. Your tat looks amazing now that your arms are bigger."

At the mention of my arms, I flexed. My ink did look damn good. *Put it back in the friend-zone, Daniels.* "Enough, Jillian. I don't want to talk about my arms. The shower's all yours." I snapped my t-shirt at her. "Move over."

She slid off the bed, and I took up her spot. I fished a pair of boxer briefs from my bag.

"Touchy, touchy. Remind me not to give you any more compliments," she said with a pout. When she leaned over me, I caught a whiff of coconuts…her shampoo. She pulled her backpack off the bed and froze.

"You didn't tell me you got a new one." She leaned over me farther, trying to get a better look. Our close proximity wasn't helping matters. With my lack of clothing and her tropical scent, my blood went south, fast. "Turn around. I want to see it." Placing her hands on my shoulders, she guided me around, and I let her.

My back on display, she drew a hot finger over the lines of the griffin spanning from one shoulder to the other. I closed my eyes, memorizing the feel of her hands on my skin.

"Griff, this is amazing. When did you get it?" she asked.

"Um, it was finished up about a month ago." I wanted her to keep touching.

"And you didn't tell me?" Her hands left my back and she swung her backpack in my direction.

I threw my arms up as a shield. "Sorry, the band's been busy."

Cocking her head to the side, she put her hands on her hips. "Well, you certainly look the part now: Mr. Hardcore Rocker all tatted up and sexy." She emphasized the point with a little shimmy. *Me? Sexy?* She was one to talk.

I pulled my arms through the sleeves of my shirt and yanked it over my head. "I do have an image to uphold." I smirked.

One side of her mouth pulled up and she shook her head. "I'll be out in a bit." Turning, she headed for the shower.

I fell back onto the bed and growled, throwing an arm over my eyes. The next few days were going to be impossible.

While Jillian finished up, I climbed into bed, anticipating her body pressed to mine. I would behave myself. She and I cuddled all the time. We were just friends.

When she emerged from the bathroom I feigned sleep, wondering what she'd do about our sleeping situation.

She picked up a pillow and slowly dragged a blanket toward the foot of the bed. "What are you doing?" My voice broke the silence.

She froze. "Uh…getting ready for bed?"

"Get over here." I patted the space next to me.

She sighed. "Griff, I don't feel right about this. What about Erin?"

Yeah, this probably wasn't something Erin would approve of, but I didn't have much more time with Jillian. We were about to be separated by time and miles. Something neither of us was used to.

I would behave. Right now I just wanted to be close to my friend. "Jillibean, I'm tired and I want to go to sleep. Erin's fine. Now get over here, I'm not letting you sleep in a fucking chair."

Tossing the pillow next to mine, she spread the blanket out and climbed in beside me. "You're already in trouble, aren't you?" she asked, snuggling into the covers.

Damn, she smells good. Like the ocean. "Nothing I can't handle." Her scent was intoxicating. I needed a distraction. In my head I recited the starting lineup for the 2006 St. Louis Cardinals. *Number 4, Yadier Molina…number 29, Chris Carpenter…27, Scott Rolen…*I rolled over, putting her at my back. "Good night, Bean."

"Good night," she whispered, turning to face the other wall.

I listened to her breaths even out as she fell asleep. Staring at the wall, I forced myself to get my shit together. Jillian had too much going for her to throw it all away for me. I pushed all notions of us as a couple from my mind. Not only for my own sanity, but because I wouldn't jeopardize Jillian's dreams…her future…for my selfish desires. She deserved so much more than I could offer. I didn't have the best track record when it came to women and it scared the shit out of me to think Jillian and I could end badly. Maybe distance was what Jillian and I needed. A chance to reset our friendship.

Chapter Two

Once we made it to the college, the week flew by. During the day Jillian and I walked around campus, toured the city, and got her dorm set up the way she wanted. Evenings were spent binging on Netflix shows and on my giving Jillian pep talks. With my looming departure, Jillian was more on edge. I'd only planned to stay a few days, but when she asked me to stay until her roommate arrived, I couldn't say no.

And then I'd run out of days. One evening was all we had left.

Leaning against the bar, waiting for our beers, I watched her from across the room. Twelve years of watching out for that girl, and tomorrow I'd officially be off duty. It fucking hurt.

Sleeping next to her each night this week, I'd had to recall lots of baseball stats. I deserved an Oscar.

And then there was Erin. She kept me honest. Once I got home, things would be better. She was a great girl. I really liked her, and I hoped she'd fill the void in my life once Jillian was gone.

"Here, man," the bartender said. "Put it on your tab?"

I turned around and grabbed the two bottles he'd pushed in my direction. "Yeah, thanks."

Beers in hand, I walked back to Jillian and plastered a happy-ass grin on my face, even though I was dying inside.

Jillian looked up at me with her warm brown eyes and smiled. "Thanks." She held out her hand, waiting for me to pass over her beer.

I looked at the bottles and then back at her. "Oh, did you want one?" I loved giving her shit.

She cocked her head to the side and glared at me. "Yeah." She pointed to my right hand. "That one."

I laughed and held it out to her, but just beyond her reach. "This?"

Leaning over the table, she wrapped her hand over mine and pulled the bottle free. "Thanks." She flashed me a smile and took a long pull.

"Damn, that one was mine," I said, frowning. "This was yours." I held up the beer in my left hand and dragged the chair from underneath the table.

She took another drink, raising an eyebrow. "Sucks to be you."

She isn't lying.

"What time is your—" I was caught off guard when my phone vibrated in my pocket. I set my beer down and pulled my phone out. Erin's picture smiled back from the caller ID. I pressed "Decline" and stuffed the phone back into my pocket.

"Who was that?" Jillian asked.

"Erin. I'll call her later. When's your roommate supposed to get here?" I asked, hoping to change the subject.

"Tomorrow night," she answered, then gave me a sidelong glance. "Did you just send her to voice mail?"

"What?" I shrugged. "I said I'd call her back later." I offered Jillian the most innocent smile I could conjure. "This is our last night together, you have my undivided attention."

"I appreciate that, but I don't think it's smart to send your girl-friend to voice mail. You're going to be in trouble," she sang.

"Me and trouble," I said, crossing my fingers, "we're like this." I winked at her and took another drink.

"Well, that's the damn truth." She smiled.

"Speaking of truth, how 'bout we play a game?" I grinned, re-membering all the times we used to play that god-awful game she'd made up when we were kids.

"What game?" she asked, scrunching her face up.

"Do you remember how to play phony baloney?" I asked.

Jillian took a drink of her beer and nearly spit it out when I said the name. "Oh my goodness, I do!" she yelled. "We haven't played that in ages. What made you think of that?"

I shrugged. "Feeling nostalgic, I guess."

"If I recall, that really isn't a game meant to be played in public." Jillian looked around the bar. "As much as I would love to tickle you to death, I'm not sure this is the place."

"As much as I would love to get my ass tickled by you, college girl," I said, smirking, "why don't we make the rules a little more grown-up?"

She leaned forward, intrigued. "What'd you have in mind?"

"We'll play the game the way we used to, but instead of the tick-ling, the loser has to drink instead."

"A drinking game?" Her eyes twinkled. "You hate drinking games."

It wasn't that I hated drinking games, I just hated playing drink-ing games with Jillian. The knowledge that she took antidepressant meds coupled with my deep-seated urge to protect her—even from herself—always overruled the reckless tendencies I usually had. I didn't know what had prompted me to suggest this, but I'd already gotten her excited, so there was no backing out now.

"Yes, and if you get silly, I will cut you off." She couldn't hold her liquor worth shit. Drunk Jillian was incredibly goofy and completely adorable.

What am I doing? I can't leave her here. What if she gets drunk at a party and some asshat takes advantage of her?

"Griffin." Jillian called my name, pulling me from my spiraling dark thoughts. "Whatever. I do not get silly." She smirked. "Are we going to play? I'll go first." She bounced excitedly on the chair. "OK, I walked in on my sister and Matt having sex," she said with a straight face.

Bullshit. I knew her sister and there was no way in hell Jennifer would have been careless enough not to lock the door. "Phony baloney," I said confidently.

Jillian scowled. "Damn, how did you guess?"

"Seriously? Matt probably has to put it to her through a hole in the sheet. I highly doubt she'd forget to lock the door." I raised my beer. "Drink."

As the grown-up rules stated, if the person guessing answered correctly on a false statement, both players had to drink. "My turn," I said, swallowing.

I steepled my fingers, resting my elbows on the table. Since she'd started with a sex-related statement, I decided to keep the theme going. "I walked in on my parents having sex." I leaned in close and whispered, "Last week." I delivered the line with my best poker face.

Jillian gasped. Her eyes searched my face, trying to read me. "Phony baloney," she said, not sounding too confident.

I slowly lifted my beer to my mouth, but stopped before I tipped it back. She was wrong; I wasn't bullshitting. "Drink." I lowered the bottle and laughed.

Jillian's jaw dropped. "What?" she screeched. "Last week?"

I nodded, smiling. "I stopped by to raid the fridge before heading to my apartment one day last week. When I walked in, the house was quiet, except for the dog going crazy upstairs. I figured Mom had trapped him in one of the rooms and forgotten him. I followed the barking down the hall and opened the door."

"Oh." Jillian clapped a hand over her mouth.

I sighed. "Oh, it gets worse. I opened the door…" My phone buzzed again. Cursing under my breath, I pulled it out.

"Erin, again?" Jillian asked.

I shook my head. "Thor. The guys are going bug-nuts trying to plan the Sig Nu gig without me." I typed a quick response and hit "Send."

"Griff, I'm sorry. I should have never talked you into staying longer. I just…" She trailed off.

"Fuck them. They can handle shit for a few days." I waved off her comment and looked at her beer. "Since you got the answer wrong, I can't take a drink until you do. Bottoms up, Jillibean." I sat back and stretched my legs out.

She smiled at me, but it didn't reach her eyes. I'd seen that sad grin far too often and it stabbed my heart every time. She picked up her bottle and knocked it against mine before taking a sip. "You going to finish your story?" she asked quietly.

I took a swig of my beer and continued, "I opened the door and the dog came bounding out. It caught me off guard, and I threw the door open wider and stepped back. The second my eyes lifted from the ground, Mom screamed and dropped onto Dad, pulling the covers over the top of them."

"No way," Jillian said. "Dear God. I am *so* glad you didn't tell me that story a week ago. I don't think I could have looked them in the eye at my going-away party."

"It's funny, Mom still blushes when she sees me." I shook my head, smiling.

"And I'm sure there's no way you'll let them forget, right?" Jillian smiled. For real this time. Her dark-chocolate eyes warmed, melting away the sadness that had haunted her a few minutes before. *That* was the smile I'd do anything for.

"Damn straight." I killed my beer and slammed it on the table. "I've got those two right where I want them."

"Your poor parents," Jillian said, shaking her head.

Jillian loved my parents and they adored her; she was like a second daughter to them. When we were younger, Jillian had spent more time at my house than at her own.

"Oh, whatever." I rolled my eyes and stood, stretching.

Jillian looked up at me. "Where are you going?"

"I'm going to find the bathroom and get another beer. You need anything?"

Jillian drained the rest of her bottle and smiled at me. "I'll take another. We aren't finished with our game yet," she said, wagging her eyebrows.

Dear Lord, What did I get myself into? The last thing I'd planned to do was get her wasted. I swallowed my better judgment and said, "Sure thing. I'll be right back."

* * *

I woke when I felt the bed shift, but I remained still, not eager to start the day. When Jillian's door was pulled open, I heard her step out.

Rolling onto my back, I stared at the ceiling. "Fuck," I sighed. "Get it together, Daniels."

I sat up, thinking about how far Jillian had come. She wasn't the sad, fragile girl of a few years ago. She was resilient, confident, and ready to carve out her own path. I was so proud of her.

I kicked off the hideous lime-green comforter she'd bought and went to work gathering my belongings. As I pulled on my clothes and folded the others into my bag, I resolved to follow Jillian's lead. I needed to set down my own tracks: Mine Shaft, Erin, school…in that order.

The door was pulled open and I looked over my shoulder. "I've been dreading this part since we left Illinois last Friday," Jillian said, tossing her bathroom things into the closet. Her wet hair stuck to the sides of her face.

I rose, coming to stand beside her. "Me too." Her dark eyes were sad. Hugging her to my side, I loosened some of the strands from her face. "I am going to miss you so damn much." I choked on the words. I'd told myself I wasn't going to get emotional, but watching her fall apart wasn't making it any easier for me.

I wiped a tear from her cheek with my thumb, pressing my palm to her face. "Come on, Jillibean. This is too fucking hard when you're sad. We'll talk every day. Especially this coming week." She leaned into my hand and drew in a sharp breath.

"Promise?" Her voice was thick with tears.

Brushing her hair behind her ear, I cupped the back of her head and brought her close, kissing her forehead. Lingering longer than I should have, I finally found the willpower to let go. I stepped back and looked her in the eyes. "Have I ever deserted you on that day?"

She shook her head. "No."

I hefted my bag off the ground, shouldering it as we walked slowly to the parking lot.

Standing beside my bike, Jillian sniffled. "I miss you already."

She threw her arms around my middle and squeezed as hard as her small frame would allow.

My arms went around her and I kissed her forehead. It felt as if a knife had been plunged into my chest. "I miss you, too." If I didn't let go now, I feared I never would. A clean break. I swung my leg over the seat and started the engine.

I reached for her and she put her hand in mine. "We'll get through this together."

"Promise?" she asked, the way she always did.

I winked. "Forever."

She smiled and stepped right up next to me. She lifted my arm and fit herself perfectly to my side. "Where's your helmet?" she asked.

"You know I don't like those things." She'd always been on me to get one.

"Damn it, Griffin." She pushed off me and stared. Her black-brown eyes screamed. "You better start wearing a goddamn helmet."

"I'll buy one just for you when I get home." I pinched her chin and smiled.

She pushed me away. "Damn right you will."

"I gotta go, Jillibean. I'll check in all day. Keep your phone close," I said.

Her tears were coming fast and furious now. I hated to see her cry, but I couldn't fix this. "OK."

"Have fun this year. You're going to rock those design classes." I hugged her one last time before I took off for Illinois. "Bye, Jillibean." I waved as I pulled out of the parking lot.

Chapter Three

"What the fuck, man." My roommate burst into my bedroom. "You going to sleep all day?"

Without opening my eyes, I skimmed my hand across the small table beside my bed, latched on to the bulkiest object I could find, and hurled it in his direction. "Get the fuck out, Thor," I mumbled into my pillow.

The book I'd thrown landed with a thud and an expletive from Thor's mouth. "It's already after one. We have a show tonight, Griff. Get your ass up," he demanded.

I rolled onto my back and looked at my pissed-off roommate and bandmate standing in the doorway. "It's after one?" I asked groggily. "Shit." Pushing myself up, I scrubbed my hands over my face.

"When did you get back?" Thor asked, leaning his broad shoulder against my doorframe and crossing his colorfully tattooed arms over his chest.

Swinging my feet over the side of the bed, I stood up. "Around three a.m."

"Well, at least you're dressed," Thor said.

I extended my middle finger in his direction and looked down at the boots on my feet. "I was too tired to change when I got home." But that was only a half-truth. I had been tired from the eighteen-hour drive, but I hadn't slept a wink. From the moment I'd fallen into bed, I hadn't been able to stop thinking about Jillian. I'd left her there, all alone.

"Griffin...dude," Thor shouted, waving his hands above his shaved head. "What's with you?"

I shook my head, trying to chase away exhaustion and a heavy heart. "Sorry."

"You going to be OK for the gig tonight?" he asked.

I shrugged off my jacket. "Yeah. I'm going to hit the shower. I'll be down in a minute."

"All right," he sighed, shutting my bedroom door as he left.

I pulled my shirt over my head and headed for the shower. In the bathroom mirror I caught a glimpse of the cursive script circling my right bicep: *Always protects. Always trusts. Always hopes. Always perseveres. Never fails.* Out of frustration I flexed my arm and watched the words shift as my muscles contracted. My tattoo felt like a lie; I couldn't protect her anymore. She was on her own.

I hated feeling so inept. I needed to get over this. Jillian would be fine. She needed to do this. I showered quickly and made an appointment with my tattoo artist, knowing exactly what would make me feel better.

Downstairs, in the living room, I heard Thor plunking out chords on his guitar. As I walked through the kitchen, the guitar grew louder; he was really working it over.

"Save something for the show tonight," I quipped, coming around the corner.

Thor played a dissonant chord and left it unresolved. "Better now?" he asked, over the fading atonal triad.

I shook my head. "No, but I will be. I made an appointment with Angelo." I leaned against the wall and waited for his reply.

He didn't say anything, just resolved the earlier chord.

"You know I wouldn't be late for a gig if it wasn't important. The ink won't take long, it's small," I added.

"It's cool," he said, looking up from his strings.

"Thanks." I pushed off the wall and brushed my hair back from my forehead. "I'll meet you at the bar."

He lifted his chin in acknowledgement.

"Later." I turned and walked back down the hallway on my way out the back door, to where my bike was parked.

The steamy September air barreled into me the second I opened the door, as if I had walked into a steaming wall of water. I mounted my bike and pushed the fuel valve down, tickling the carburetor before I hit the choke blade. My vintage Triumph never failed to calm my nerves. I turned the key in the ignition and tromped on the kick starter. The engine roared to life beneath me. I slipped on my sunglasses and tore out of my parking space.

* * *

I pulled the door open and stepped into the tattoo studio. Greeted by the familiar buzz of the artists' tools, I already felt more relaxed.

Angelo Castell glanced up from the girl he was working on and nodded. "Hey, Griff."

"Angelo." I nodded in reply.

"I'm just about finished, have a seat. I'll be ready for you in a few." He returned his attention to the client in front of him.

"Cool," I said, sitting down on the black leather couch that served as the waiting area.

While I waited for Angelo, I toyed with the idea of calling Jillian. I'd texted her earlier that morning, when I'd gotten home at around three a.m., but hadn't talked to her since I'd left her dorm yesterday. Her tearstained face in my rearview mirror was an image I wouldn't soon forget.

I traced my thumb over her illuminated name on the screen. I wanted very much to hear her voice, but she was starting a new life on the East Coast, and she needed for me to give her space and let her live.

"Griff, you ready?" Angelo asked, standing in front of me.

I clicked my phone off and stood, shoving it into my pocket. "Yeah."

He nodded to his workstation and led the way. "I've got your sketch over here. You said small, right?"

"Yeah, I want it to be subtle. Barely noticeable." Jillian would kill me if she knew what I was about to do.

"Here you go." He passed me the sketch. He'd done every one of my pieces and he knew what I liked. Jillian's nickname filled a tiny droplet that matched the others I already had on my chest.

Five years before, when my friend Thor and I started our band, Mine Shaft, I'd promised myself that I would get a full chest piece when we booked our first paid gig. I'd settled on a likeness of my bass guitar, broken and bleeding song titles from the fracture. Now I was about to add one more "drop" falling from the guitar: Jillian's nickname.

"It's perfect. Let's do it." I handed the sketch back to him with a smile.

"All right then." He clapped his hands together, ready to get to work. "You know the drill. I'll get my stuff together and we'll get started."

"Sounds good." I pulled my shirt over my head and got comfortable in the chair. A little smile crept to my lips and a thrill went through me. There was nothing like getting a tattoo. Since I'd gotten my first one, I'd become addicted. Plus the ink I was about to get was something I'd wanted for a long time, and now that Jillian wasn't there, it only seemed fitting.

"Got the stencil," Angelo said, walking over to the chair.

"Cool."

He prepped my skin and laid the stencil near the top of my left pec, right where the bass cracked open. When he peeled the paper away, the tiny drop bearing Jillian's name clung to the edge of the guitar.

"Look good?" he asked.

I sat up to glance in the mirror near the chair. "Yeah," I replied, looking down at her name clinging to the edge of my bass.

"Cool." He smiled and grabbed his machine from the tray.

I lay back down and Angelo leaned in, ready to begin. I closed my eyes and sighed, ready for the welcome burn of the needles.

While Angelo worked I ran through the melody I'd written during my eighteen-hour drive home from Rhode Island. By the time I'd pulled into my apartment complex, I had written a whole new song.

With my eyes still closed, I could hear the chords Thor would play on his guitar, Adam's steady drumbeat, and Pauly's keyboard. I layered each instrument, finally adding the bass line, breathing life into the song. The only thing missing was the lyrics, which in my opinion were the most difficult part of songwriting. For me they always came last. I had to hear the music—feel it—in order to write something meaningful.

Concentrating on the scratching sensation of Angelo's machine against my chest, I allowed the vibration of the needles to provide the rhythm I needed as I worked through some lyrics.

"That's it, man," Angelo announced, wiping my chest one final time and silencing his machine.

I hadn't come up with anything useful before he finished. I pulled my eyes open, squinting through the bright lights of the room, and looked down at my chest. Although the droplet was only a little over an inch long and "Jillibean" was barely visible, it was already my favorite.

"What do you think?" he asked as I admired his work.

"It's perfect." I held up my fist and he knocked his knuckles into mine. "Thanks, man."

"Sure thing." He rubbed some Vaseline over Jillian's name and bandaged it up. "Leave the bandage on until morning, wash it real good, then lotion it up."

Once the small bandage was in place, he handed me an aftercare card. I stood up from the chair and folded the card into my back pocket before I slipped on my shirt. "Thanks again, man. I appreciate you getting me in on such short notice."

"Anytime, dude." Angelo looked me in the eyes and gave me a small smile. "She's gone, huh?" he asked.

I nodded. Jillian had come to the shop with me when Angelo did the script on my bicep and the guitar on my chest, so he knew her well.

"She'll be back for Christmas and summer, though," I sighed. *My best friend leaves for college, and I turn into fucking pussy. What's wrong with me?* "Thanks. I'll see you around, man."

"Looking forward to it. Hang in there, she'll be back before you know it."

I smiled. "Yeah, you're right."

I settled up with Angelo and walked the couple of blocks to where I'd parked my bike. Before I got on, I checked my phone: four missed texts and one voice mail. Thor and Erin, but no word from Jillian. *What is she up to?* I had the feeling I'd be thinking that a lot from here on out.

Chapter Four

I shot Thor a quick text, *Be there in 30*, then mounted my bike, putting a call in to Erin before I hit the road. Scrolling through my contacts, I hit Erin's name and waited for her to answer.

"Hey, Griffin." Erin's honeyed voice met my ears. "What have you been up to?"

I couldn't tell her about my new ink. She wouldn't understand. "Not much. Sorry I didn't call earlier. I got in around three a.m. and slept most of the day."

"It's no problem. I had volleyball practice today anyway. Are you at the bar yet?"

I leaned back on my seat and slid the keys into the ignition, waiting to start the engine. "Not yet. I'm on my way, though. Meet me there?"

"You bet," she said. "Griffin?" Her voice dropped into a hush.

"Yeah?" I answered.

"I missed you." The statement was a whisper slipping from her mouth, barely audible from my end of the line, almost as if she were afraid I would hear.

In the back of my mind, I could hear Jillian telling me to give

Erin a chance, and she was right, I did need to give her a chance. That was the whole reason I'd asked her out in the first place, to erase any notions I had about being with Jillian. I needed a distraction. Erin was cool and we always had a great time together. If I let myself believe it, she was someone I could fall for…in time. She was strong, smart, a damn good athlete, funny as hell, not to mention gorgeous. Images of her long, sculpted legs came to mind.

I only had to give her a chance.

I scrubbed a hand over my face. "I missed you, too."

"I'll see you soon." The twang of her Georgia accent came alive.

"See you." I ended our conversation there. If I didn't get a move on, Thor would have a coronary.

* * *

By the time I got to the bar, Pauly, Thor, and Adam were already there. I pulled the door open and took off my sunglasses.

"Hey, man," Pauly said, looking up from his keyboard. He was busy taping down wires and getting his keyboard situated in the confined space the local bar called a stage. "Where have you been?"

Thor must have kept my detour to himself. "I had something I needed to take care of." I shrugged and joined him on stage, grabbing the roll of tape from his hand and tearing off a piece. "Where's Thor?"

"Out back." Pauly gestured with his head. "He's bringing in the last cabinet."

"Cool." I tossed the tape to Pauly and headed toward the rear exit. "Gonna see if he needs help." I'd made it halfway down the hall when Thor came in, hauling the speaker in his arms.

"Got your shit straightened out now?" he asked, walking in my direction.

I followed him into the main room and onto the stage. "Yeah. Better now." I rubbed my hands on my jeans, ready to pull the gig together.

Thor placed the speaker on the floor and got it set up before standing back up. "Good to hear." He slapped my back and smirked.

I smiled, thankful he understood. "The set list still the same?" I asked while I shoved my keys and sunglasses into the backpack we kept on stage.

"Pretty much." Thor finished hooking the cabinet to the amp and plugged in his guitar. "Adam was bitching about something, but he can piss off. We're not changing shit now."

I reached for my bass and plugged it into my amp. Systematically I worked my thumb along each knuckle of my right hand, then my left. Each joint gave a loud pop as I pressed down. "Agreed." I shook out my hands and adjusted the volume and tone before I walked my fingers across the strings.

The rich, deep sound vibrated through my body, and I instantly relaxed. No matter what kind of mood I was in, my bass always pulled me out of my head and into the music. I took a deep breath and played some scales, tuning as I went along. Reaching over to the amplifier head, I adjusted the EQ knobs and found my tonal sweet spot. I stood back up and started plunking out a few lines of the first song on our set list. Thor grinned and added his guitar riff to my bass line, beginning a mini jam session for the few bar patrons perched on their stools.

Our tune quickly evolved into an improv session, each of us playing off of what the other was feeling. I relished organic moments like these, getting lost in the music. Thor and I had been playing together since we were fifteen and knew each other's style like it was our own.

I guided my hands across the taut strings, bringing out the bass line to Thor's melody. I let the music wash over me, fill me. I anchored my heavyheartedness due to Jillian's absence on the lowest notes of my bass, drowning my feelings beneath the music.

"If I didn't know better, I'd think you two were trying to get rid of us," Pauly said, coming back into the room with Adam following behind.

I slapped a few more notes and quieted my instrument. Thor did the same. My blood was pumping and my breath came fast. With music running through my veins, I was amped up for the show, even though it would be small.

"You didn't get the memo?" Thor said, punching Pauly in the shoulder.

Pauly flipped Thor off and took his stance by the keyboard. I laughed, shaking my head while I watched Adam mount his drum kit.

"You guys ready to hit this?" Adam asked.

Thor made some minor adjustments on his amp and said, "Count us in, dude."

Adam counted and we came in on the downbeat. I listened intently to Adam's kick drum, making sure we both stayed in sync. With the small venue, we didn't need much extra equipment in order to hear each other.

Still thumping out the bass line, I stepped closer to the mic, ready to rock this gig.

* * *

Sweat rolled down the sides of my face and my hair stuck to my forehead and cheeks. Despite the heat and cramped quarters, this was what I lived for. The crowd bobbed up and down, an undulating mass controlled only by our music. I knew the effect music had on me, how it consumed me wholly, and here it was doing the same thing to complete strangers. Who knew my lyrics and music held that kind of power? *God, I love this.*

Exhausted and rocking on pure adrenaline, I sang loudly into the mic and the crowd cheered, raising their hands above their heads, beer bottles and all. Thor hit two fast chords, I laid into the bass, Pauly struck the keys, and Adam pounded a steady beat as I brought the neck of my bass down, cutting them off.

The crowd stilled, unsure if the song was finished.

I loved writing songs that messed with the audience. The guys and I remained still, giving no hint of whether we would resume playing. Then, very quietly, Adam picked up the beat with his kick drum. Pauly played a few dissonant chords on the keyboard, and I sang the last line just before Thor wrapped up the song with his guitar.

Once again the house went crazy. The crowd had grown exponentially. There wasn't a seat left. Hot, sweaty, and out of breath, I spoke into the mic: "Thank you." I took a little bow and winked at Erin standing in the front row. I could easily pick her out of the crowd; her long legs went on for miles. Her blond hair was swept back into a ponytail and her cheeks were flushed from dancing. She looked beautiful.

I held up my index finger, letting her know I'd join her in a minute. She winked, a huge smile blooming across her face. Nodding her understanding, she went back to talking to the friend she'd brought along.

I pulled the towel off my shoulder and wiped the sweat from my face. My cell phone buzzed in my pocket. Reaching back, I yanked it free, and noticed it said *UNKNOWN CALLER.*

"Hello?" I answered.

"Hello? Mr. Daniels?" a man replied.

"Yes?"

"My name is Leo Dane. I heard your band play about a month ago," he said.

I brushed my damp hair away from my forehead and took another deep breath. "Um, yeah?" I shouted over the din of the noisy bar.

"Is this a bad time?" he asked.

"Uh, no. Sorry, we just finished a show. Give me a sec, and I'll find someplace quieter." I made my way to the front entrance.

As I pushed my way through the crush of people, Leo Dane continued. "Like I said before, I had the pleasure of catching a Mine Shaft show last month. You've got a great sound."

I opened the front door and stepped into the crowd of smokers who'd been relegated to the outdoor seating. Shouldering through them and their haze, I walked a few steps down the street. "That's good to hear. When do you need us to play?" I asked.

"Thursday morning," he answered without hesitation.

"I'll have to—" I snapped my mouth closed when Mr. Dane started speaking, cutting me off completely. *What a dick.* This was not the way to get me to agree to a gig.

"Not only did I catch your show last month, Mr. Daniels, but I've also listened to the demo you sent."

Wait. What? "You have my demo?" I sucked in a breath and held it.

"Mr. Daniels, I work for Amphion Productions. We'd like to talk to you about Mine Shaft's future."

My mouth fell open. I was speechless.

"Is that a yes?" he asked, breaking the silence.

Snapping back to reality, I remembered to breathe, stumbling over my words as I spoke. "I…uh." I couldn't think. "Uh, yeah." God, I sounded like a bumbling idiot. "Yes, Thursday morning is great."

"Cool. Mine Shaft's name has been buzzing around the music scene for a while. I'm looking forward to meeting the band, Mr. Daniels."

"What time did you say you wanted to meet?" I paced up and down the sidewalk, savoring the moment. I was blown away. *Is this for real?*

Over the past year, I'd sent out handfuls of demos and hoped that something would come of it, but I'd never gotten any responses. Jillian had been the one who spurred me on, always telling me to keep going. She'd be flipping out about this phone call.

"Does seven thirty work for you guys?" Leo asked.

"Seven thirty's great," I confirmed. "We'll be there."

"Cool. I'm looking forward to hearing you guys again."

"Yes, sir. See you then," I said, and then the line went dead.

I dropped my hands to my sides, still reeling. *Holy. Fucking. Shit. Did that really happen?* I was ready to jump out of my own skin.

"Who was that?" Erin's Southern accent came up behind me.

I spun around with a big-ass grin on my face. In that moment it was nice to see a beautiful blonde walking toward me. She looked a lot like Jillian, except for their considerable difference in height. Where Jillian was barely over five feet, Erin stood about a foot taller.

I wished Jillian were the one standing in front of me, but she wasn't. Erin was here. My inner voice chimed in, *Give her a chance.*

Her bright-blue eyes were darkened by the night sky, yet they sparkled in the light of the street lamps. "That, my dear, was a record producer." I grabbed her waist and spun us around.

She laughed, wrapping her arms around my neck. "A producer?" she squealed. "What did he want?"

I set her down and planted a quick kiss on her lips. "We have a meeting with Amphion Productions. They want to discuss the band's future."

"What?" she exclaimed, a wide smile blooming across her face. "Griffin, that's amazing," she yelled.

I folded my arms around her back, drawing her closer. Because I was only about four inches taller, our faces were always perfectly aligned. I kissed her again, trying to convince myself that her kiss was all I needed in this moment. Her lips were soft and sweet on mine. "Mmm," I hummed against her mouth. "You taste like peaches."

Not wanting to back away from our kiss, she answered, "Peach schnapps." Then she slid her tongue past my lips and into my mouth.

She was a damn good kisser. I enjoyed kissing her. With her killer body pressed to mine, I was ready to do more than just kiss.

Slowing down, I pulled away just enough to see her swollen lips stretch into a playful smile. "I've got to tell the guys about the phone call," I said, sliding my hands down her arms and threading my fingers between hers.

"All right," she sighed.

I smiled, kissed her one more time, and pulled her along as I ran down the sidewalk, eager to tell the guys our good news.

Chapter Five

After the call from the producer, the party really got underway. For an hour we celebrated our good news at the bar. Erin, Pauly, and Adam did shots while Thor and I stuck to one victory dance beer each—sometimes it sucked being the designated drivers.

With her third shot sitting on the bar, Erin grabbed my wrist and slicked her tongue over it.

"Woo, you go, girl!" Pauly shouted, throwing back his shot.

She smirked at him, sprinkling granules of salt onto my skin, and licked my wrist again. This was damn hot. Her heated gaze locked onto mine as she grabbed the shot glass, threw the tequila into her mouth, and swiped a lemon wedge from the bowl on the bar. With the lemon between her lips, I took the opportunity to kiss the corner of her mouth. She didn't taste like peaches this time. With a couple of drinks, her sweet Southern charm morphed into sexy Southern sass.

Erin pulled the lemon from her mouth, licking her lips.

I put my mouth to her ear. "Ready to get out of here?"

As I leaned back, she nodded. "Yes, please."

"Well, gents. It's time I took the lady home," I said in an affected Southern drawl.

Thor stood just as I did, holding his arm up. I clamped my palm against his and he pulled me into a one-armed hug. "This is it, man." He slapped my back a few times, and I did the same to him.

"So close I can taste it," I said, stepping back, and looping my arm around Erin's waist. I saluted the table. "Night, boys."

"Night, Griff. See ya, Erin," they all slurred.

Erin waved. "Bye, guys!"

I led her toward the exit, and we stepped onto the sidewalk. The street was quiet. Nothing happened in our small town beyond midnight. The hint of fall was in the air as a cool September breeze blew, sending escaped strands of her ponytail into my face.

I brushed them away and she giggled. "Sorry."

I looked at her and smiled. "No reason to be sorry, peach."

"Peach?" Her eyes tightened.

"It suits you." I winked and brought her closer so I could kiss her. It was a quick kiss, but playful. With a flick of my tongue against her mouth, I watched her eyes widen. Since she'd licked salt off my wrist, I wasn't thinking with the head on top of my shoulders.

I reached in my jeans pocket and pulled Erin's car keys out. I punched the key fob with my thumb and her blue Mustang chirped, headlights winking.

I opened the passenger side door and Erin climbed inside. Before I closed her inside, she asked, "What about your bike?"

"It'll be OK." At least I hoped it would. "I'll get it tomorrow." I waved it away like it was no big deal, smiled, and shut her door, making my way to the driver's seat.

Folding myself behind the wheel, I started the car and pulled out onto the empty street, pointing the car toward Erin's place.

For a few blocks, neither of us said a word. Even without the heater blasting, the car still managed to fill with heat. The tension between us was combustible. I threw a quick glance in her direction, wondering just how drunk she was. "How are you feeling?" I asked, trying to gauge her level of sobriety. The last thing I wanted to do was start something she wouldn't remember in the morning.

Her head snapped in my direction. A quirky smile on her face, she bit her bottom lip. "I'm good. Soon to be a whole lot better." She reached over and put her hand on my leg and squeezed.

Two involuntary reactions happened at the same time: My jeans became a hell of a lot tighter and my foot pressed down on the accelerator in my eagerness to get back to her apartment.

I cleared my throat, trying to concentrate on the road and not her hand working its way up and down my right leg. Each time her hand came a little closer to where I wanted it, I was tempted to pull the car over and seal the deal in the backseat.

It was an excruciating twenty minutes back to her apartment. I pulled up to the curb and shut off the engine. Neither of us wasted a second getting out of the car.

I slammed my door shut, rounded the car, and hopped up on the curb. Grabbing her hand before she walked away, I yanked her to my side. Pressing her against the cool blue metal, I kissed her hard.

Her lips still wore the tang of salt from the tequila shots, coupled with a hint of citrus. With frenzy, our tongues swept over each other's. She put her hands against my chest and pushed me backward, but kept her mouth squarely on mine. Together we stumbled up the walk, devouring each other with a hungry need.

At the door Erin broke away from my mouth long enough to turn around and let us inside. She made quick work of the lock and pulled me into her place. Not a second later, our mouths came back together with equal ferocity. Rough and wet.

Erin kicked the door shut, and I pushed her against it with a thud. She dug her fingers into my back and I leaned my weight into her, raking my lips across her cheek and down her neck.

"Roommates home," she breathed, tapping her palms on my back. "Bedroom."

I nipped at her earlobe and pulled back, my chest heaving. "Lead the way."

She smiled widely and laced her fingers through mine, practically dragging me down the hallway.

The second the door was shut, we crashed into each other, tearing at each other's clothes. Erin pulled my shirt up and over my head, her eyes landing on the bandage that covered my new ink.

"What happened here?" she asked, running her fingers over the gauze.

"Nothing, just some new ink."

"What'd you get?" Her eyes flashed with curiosity.

"Some new script to match the other drops." I shrugged off the answer, wanting to get back to undressing. "Where were we?" I fingered the hem of her shirt and whipped it over her.

"Oh!" she squealed. I captured her mouth with mine, sucking her bottom lip between my teeth. My hands smoothed over her back and up her neck, while her fingers skimmed over the skin at the waist of my jeans.

Still holding her body to mine with one hand, I worked the other up to her ponytail, pulling the hair tie out in a swift motion. I opened my eyes in time to see her long curtain of blond hair spill over her shoulders.

Then images of Jillian's blond hair flashed through my mind. Like white light separated into its individual colors, Jillian's hair usually resembled a rainbow. My eyes fell shut. I ran my hands gently through her hair…so soft against my fingers.

Jillian's hands worked at the button of my jeans…pulling down the zipper…her fingers dipping beneath the waistband of my boxers…lower, until she…

The world froze…I froze.

"Griffin?"

A raspy Southern drawl scattered my illusion into a million pieces.

What the hell am I doing?

I blinked.

In a sexy black bra, one strap hanging low on her upper arm, Erin stood in front of me. "You OK?" Her eyebrows rose, sending lines of worry across her forehead.

I shook my head and blew out a breath. No. No, I wasn't OK. "Uh…yeah." I didn't sound very convincing. Reaching for her arm, I fixed her strap. "Sorry. I don't know what came over me." The room swayed. I raked my hands through my hair and looked up at the ceiling for a second, trying to center my thoughts.

Erin bent over, retrieving her shirt from the floor. As she stood back up, she held the shirt to her chest, uncomfortable with her lack of clothing and the awkward situation I'd put us in. "You look like you've seen a ghost," she drawled.

You don't know how right you are, Peach. Why can't I get Jillian out of my head?

I took a step closer and wrapped my hands around the backs of her upper arms, running my palms over her soft skin. Looking into her blue eyes, I noticed their usual sparkle was gone. "I'm sorry, peach."

I was sorry. I hadn't meant for tonight to end like this. I didn't know what my fucking problem was. No, that was a lie. I did know what my problem was. I needed to get my act together and get the hell over my *friend*. Erin was my girlfriend...not Jillian.

"It's just been a long day," she said, pressing her lips into a tight smile. She fed her arms through the sleeves of her shirt and tossed it over her head.

"Yeah." I stepped backward and grabbed my shirt off the floor, putting it back on, too. "It's late. I should let you get some sleep. Got some extra blankets? I'll just crash on the couch." I hooked a thumb over my shoulder, motioning toward the living room.

"My roommates are pretty loud in the morning. You can sleep in here, Griffin." She walked over to the bed and turned down the sheets. "I'm going to brush my teeth. I'll be right back." With a quick smile, she turned on her heel and made her way to the door.

Alone in Erin's bedroom, this wasn't exactly the kind of sleepover I had planned. *Fuck, Daniels. What is wrong with you?*

I ditched my jeans and climbed into Erin's queen-size bed. The mattress contoured itself to the shape of my body. I was in memory foam heaven. Laying my head back on the pillow, I closed my eyes and drew in a deep breath. Erin's fruity scent clung to the sheets. In the quiet of the room, my mind tried to decipher what had happened. The last thing I wanted to do was hurt Erin.

"I'm back," she called, coming into the room.

I pulled my eyes open and clasped my hands behind my head, looking at her standing in the doorway. "Forgive me?" I asked.

She smiled and tilted her head, shutting the door. "There's nothing to forgive."

Yes there was. My head was not in the right place at the moment and that was inexcusable.

"I'm sorry just the same."

Erin walked around to the other side of the bed and hopped in beside me. She lowered her head slightly, placing a gentle kiss on my lips. Her hand came to my jaw, holding my face to hers.

Erin's lips were soft, yet there was a firm, strong presence to her kisses. She was a woman who knew what she wanted. Erin wasn't afraid to take charge.

Jillian's lips were soft and delicate, like a flower petal. Though I'd only kissed Jillian once, and very briefly, the sensation was seared into my memory. Jillian might have initiated the kiss, but the moment our lips touched, she'd given me permission to take the lead.

Erin was a good kisser, but very different from Jillian.

And once again, I'm comparing Erin to Jillian. Give it a rest, Daniels!

Erin pulled back, removing her hand as well. "What was that for?" I asked, knowing I didn't deserve her kisses.

"Just a good-night kiss. It'll give you good dreams." She winked and snuggled down into the blanket.

"I'm sure it will." I took my arm from underneath the pillow, inviting her to cuddle up next to me. "Good night, Peach."

"Night, Griffin."

With Erin's head on my shoulder, I closed my eyes. Her tall body was stretched out next to mine, and I couldn't keep my tired thoughts from drifting again…she didn't fit next to me the way Jillian did.

Chapter Six

The next four days flew by. The guys and I squeezed in as much rehearsal time as possible. We were determined to sound our absolute best on Thursday morning...tomorrow. But first I had to suffer through my econ class.

I hated wasting precious rehearsal time on school. Over the last few years, I'd taken the fewest classes possible. I hated school with a passion. It always got in the way of my music. I'd only continued with the college charade to appease my parents. But now, with graduation upon me, Mom was up my ass to enroll at a four-year university. I wasn't sure I could pull off the "studious college guy" act any longer. It wasn't me. I had never been good at school, and I dreaded the idea of suffering through another couple of years at a university.

I glanced at my phone, checking the time: twenty more minutes. With my phone still in hand, I swiped through some old pictures. Most of them were from the summer. Jillian was always taking my phone and telling me that I needed more pictures, so I wouldn't forget about her. *As if that were possible*. I smiled at the ridiculous selfies she had planted on my phone.

I wondered what she was doing right now. Since I'd gotten back to Illinois, we hadn't talked. I'd texted her a few times and she'd responded, but nothing too detailed. She did mention that she'd won the roommate lottery, which I was glad to hear.

"Griffin," a female voice whispered beside me.

I turned to look at the woman next to me. "Yeah?"

She passed a stack of papers in my direction, just as the prof told us to turn to page six.

I grabbed the bunch. "Thanks." Pulling a sheaf off the top, I passed the stack to my left.

"On page six," the prof continued, "you'll find a comprehensive list of assignments that will need to be completed in order to pass this course."

My eyes skimmed down the page, noticing the small notation at the bottom: "continued on reverse side."

I flipped the page with my thumb. Dread pooled in my gut. It might as well have been written in Greek, because I didn't understand a word of it. And where the hell was I going to find time to finish this shit? Leo Dane needed to come through tomorrow. I needed a good reason to leave school behind, and in my opinion, a recording contract fit the bill.

* * *

I pulled up at the Sigma Nu house and saw Adam's van parked outside. I killed the engine and closed off the fuel line before getting off. I headed for the front door and knocked. A guy the size of a linebacker answered. "Yeah?"

I was not fond of frat guys. After what my sister went through with a couple of fucking frat boys, I couldn't tolerate them. But I had to remember that they were paying customers tonight. I pulled my sunglasses off to make direct eye contact and offered my hand in greeting, like a reputable businessman. "Griffin Daniels. I'm with Mine Shaft, the band you hired for your party tonight."

"Oh, yeah," he said, shaking my hand. "The rest of your boys are downstairs. Come in. I'm Tucker, by the way. If you need anything, just ask."

Our amicable handshake came to an end and he pushed the door open wider, stepping aside to let me through. "Nice to meet you, Tucker." I nodded and walked past him.

"You too. I heard you guys a few months back. You rocked. I was stoked when we were able to book you for tonight." Tucker nodded with a goofy smile, his head bobbing.

I raked my hand through my hair, pushing it off my forehead. "Thanks for looking us up, man. You said the guys were downstairs?"

"Oh, yeah. Just go straight down the hall and make a left at the end. You'll run right into the staircase." Tucker closed the door and pointed me in the right direction.

"Thanks, man."

Opening the door to the basement, I could hear the guys banging shit around and a few guffaws. My boots clomped down the wooden stairs and I eyed up the acoustics we'd have to account for tonight.

"You made it," Adam said, walking over and slamming his hand on my back. "After tomorrow, dude, you won't need that college gig anymore."

God, I hope he's right. "Are we set up?" I asked.

"Yep," Thor said, picking up his guitar. "We wanted to be ready as soon as you got here."

I smiled and shrugged off my jacket. "Cool." I stepped over to the lead mic and Pauly handed my bass over. Before I even had a chance to adjust the knobs on my instrument, my phone buzzed in my pocket. I pulled it out quickly and saw Erin's name on the screen.

When I accepted the call, there was a collective groan from the guys. I flipped them off and said, "Hey, Peach, what's up?" I liked calling her Peach. It was the perfect nickname for her, being that she was from Georgia and she'd tasted like peach schnapps when I kissed her a few nights ago. *See, you're making it work, Daniels.*

"You guys still playing the Sig Nu party tonight?" she asked.

"Yep. I'm at the house now. We're getting ready to run through our set."

"I'll see you later then." The twang in her voice made even the simplest of phrases seem suggestive. Damn, she was hot.

"Say good-bye, lover boy," Pauly hounded me.

"We go on at nine. Come find me when you get here." I scuffed my boot on the floor, not liking that she'd be alone in the crowd during the show. Sadly, girls who attended frat parties alone were likely to end up with shit mixed into their drinks and a morning of fear and humiliation to follow. My sister knew that all too well. I hated playing for frat parties, but living in a college town, frats were our number one source of income. We didn't have the luxury of turning down gigs. We had to pay the rent.

"I will. I'll see you soon," Erin said.

"Bye." I pressed "End" and pocketed my phone. I worked my knuckles over and they popped loudly. "Count us in, Adam."

Adam followed my directive and we spent the next couple of hours ironing out the kinks in the show.

* * *

Standing by the speakers, I adjusted a few settings on the head. I was having trouble getting the sound I wanted.

"Hey, Rock Star."

I turned around and smiled, seeing Erin standing behind me. "Hey, Peach," I said, reaching for her.

She grabbed my hand and I pulled her close. The only thing keeping our bodies from touching was my bass.

"Ready for your show?" she asked, a mischievous gleam in her eye.

"Yeah." I leaned my forehead to hers. It still felt strange not having to bend lower. Typically I had to accommodate Jillian's diminutive stature, but not Erin's; she and I were practically face-to-face.

"I'm glad you're here," I intoned. And I was. I pressed my lips to hers. She returned my affection, running her tongue along the seam of my mouth. I separated my lips and my tongue met hers as I pushed into her mouth, tasting her. She was always sweet, but every time we kissed, I had to force myself not to compare her lips to Jillian's.

Erin worked her arms around my neck, pulling me closer, deepening the kiss.

"I don't recall that on the set list." Pauly snickered beside me.

Erin's lips curled into a smile against mine, but she didn't pull away. "Haters gonna hate," she drawled.

I nodded and kissed her again, ignoring my douchebag of a friend. She got the idea. Our tongues resumed their fevered rhythm, and my blood pumped faster.

"I'm still here," Pauly sang, standing beside us.

And there it was, his voice like ice water pouring over my head. I was going to murder him. I pulled away from Erin and shot daggers at Pauly. "Enjoy the show?" I asked, acid in my voice.

"Yeah," he scoffed. "Hardly. We're about to go on, you ready?"

I held up my bass, answering his asinine question. I was more than ready.

I turned my attention back to Erin. "Sorry, Peach. Time to go to work. See you later?"

"Absolutely." She winked and leaned in for one last kiss, sweeping her tongue across my mouth. *Holy shit.* I shivered as she pulled away, trying to keep my mind focused on business and not pleasure. "I'll catch you after the show." She tapped my nose and spun on her heels.

"Be careful out there," I yelled. "Don't accept drinks from anyone."

She craned her neck around and the little strap of her shirt fell from her shoulder. Once again my mind was not on business. She pushed it back up and smiled. "Don't you worry about me, I'll be fine. Knock 'em dead."

The second the words left her mouth, Erin's image morphed into Jillian's before my eyes. That was Jillian's thing, she always told me to "knock 'em dead" before a show. Then panic washed over me. "What day is it?"

Erin looked at me in confusion. "Wednesday, why?"

I shook my head. "No, what's the date?"

"September eleventh," she answered.

Fuck me. "Shit. I forgot to call Jillian."

Erin's eyes pinched together, darkening her expression just a little. I could tell she was annoyed by my declaration. Erin didn't know how to interpret my relationship with Jillian, even though I'd told her repeatedly that we were just friends.

"I'm sure she's not waiting by the phone, Griffin," she said. "Call her tomorrow."

I bit my tongue, trying hard not to get angry. Erin didn't understand. It wasn't her fault she didn't know that today was the anniversary of Jillian's parents' death.

And I was absolutely certain Jillian was waiting for my call.

Chapter Seven

Hey guys, give me two minutes. I have to call Jillian." I was the worst friend in the world…of all days not to make calling her a priority.

"Dude, we're ready to go on. Call her later," Thor chided.

Erin kissed my cheek and said, "I'll see you after the show." She turned around and shrugged her shoulders, giving Thor an apologetic look. "Good luck."

I watched her walk away, trying to remind myself it wasn't her fault she didn't know, that I shouldn't be angry with her.

Once Erin was gone, I gave Thor a don't-fuck-with-me look; after all, he *did* know. "I have to call her. You know what today is." His expression turned somber and he nodded. "I have to hear her voice before I can go on. I have to make sure she's OK."

I pulled my phone from my back pocket and touched the screen by her name. The guys busied themselves while I listened to Jillian's phone ring. I lifted a bottle of water from the cooler sitting against the wall and pulled the cap off, taking a long drink. *Why isn't she answering?*

After three rings Jillian's voice filled the line. "You buy a helmet yet?" she shouted, her end of the line just as noisy as mine.

Aw, shit! With everything going on, I'd completely forgotten. If she knew, she'd leave school just to come home and kick my ass for not buying one yet. Honestly, I didn't want a helmet. I liked the sound of the wind, the rush of open air blowing over me as I rode. But I understood why she was so insistent. With all the loss she'd endured over the years, it was her way of keeping me safe. I couldn't fault her for that. I'd spent so many years trying to do the same thing for her.

"Hello to you, too," I admonished playfully, trying to redirect her question. I didn't have time to argue about a helmet right now. "Where the hell are you?"

"Hi, Griffin," she replied sweetly this time. The noise dissipated, and I could hear her clearly now. "Thanks for saving me. Even eleven hundred miles away, your timing is impeccable."

Impeccable my ass. My timing sucked. I should have called first thing that morning. But I did wonder what I was supposedly *saving* her from.

I set the water bottle on a small table, my insides knotting due to her comment. "Where are you? Saving you from what?" I hated being this far away from her; nothing about it was right or natural. I needed her near me as much as I hoped she needed me.

"My roommate, Sarah, talked me into going to the Phi Psi party tonight. I'm here now," she sighed.

Damn it all to hell. What was she doing at a frat party? "Be careful, Jillibean, fucking frat boys can't be trusted."

"Don't worry, I will."

"How are you?" I asked, trying to calm my nerves. I needed her to tell me she was all right. I prayed no one hurt her, today of all days.

"I'm OK." Her answer was quiet. I could hear the sadness in her voice. "But I'm not going to lie, it completely sucked ass having to start classes today."

My heart pinched at the palpable grief in her voice. "I'm sorry, Bean. I wish I could be there with you, but I know how strong you are. You're going to do great."

"I appreciate the vote of confidence." She sighed.

I needed to turn this conversation around. She needed to know how amazing she was. "Damn right I have confidence in you. You're the strongest person I know."

"Thanks, Griff," she replied.

"I don't need thanks for telling the truth," I said. "Are you alone? Where's Sarah?" Thor gestured for me to speed things up. The guys were ready to go on. I wanted to tell her about Leo Dane and our meeting tomorrow, but I didn't have time. Besides, she needed *me* right now. I had to be there for her.

"She's off somewhere with her boyfriend. Did you start classes today?" she asked.

"Yeah, I had one. The guys and I spent the rest of the day rehearsing." I nodded to Thor and held up one finger. I just needed a minute.

"Do you have a show tonight?" she asked quietly.

"Yeah, but I wanted to call you before we went on."

"I miss you, Griff," she said. The pinch in the middle of my chest, right beneath the tattoo of her name, grew even tighter. I missed her so goddamned much.

"I miss you, too." I could barely get the words out, but I managed. "I may not be physically there, but I'm still with you, Bean."

Adam was already at his drum kit and my attention shifted to the steady beat of his kick drum.

"Promise?" Jillian said quietly.

Thor put my bass in my empty hand and mouthed, "Let's go."

"I'm sorry, Bean, I've got to go." Thor was practically pushing me toward the pseudo-stage.

"That's OK. Knock 'em dead." Even through her sadness, she found it in her to cheer me on, the way she always did. If it hadn't been for her confidence in me and my music, I would have given up a long time ago. Damn, I missed her.

"Be careful, Jillibean. I mean it," I said.

Thor was still at my side, getting more pissed by the minute.

"I will. I promise. Bye, Griff."

"Bye, Bean." I clicked my phone off and slipped it back into my pocket.

Thor walked toward the stage, ready to add his guitar melody to Adam's drumbeat. "Jesus, Griff," was all he said.

I followed Thor onto the stage and over to the mic, cracking my knuckles before I laid my fingers on the strings. I opened my mouth and sang the first word of our opener, "Forever." It was then that I realized that I hadn't said "forever" to Jillian. Now I was officially the worst best friend ever.

How could I've forgotten to answer her? It was our "thing." It had been our thing since the day she came to live with her grandparents—the day I told her that I would always be there for her. She'd been a petrified six-year-old, silently begging for a small sliver of hope to cling to after she'd lost her whole world. Even at nine years old, I knew what she wanted, and always wondered why the adults could never figure it out. I promised I'd always be there for her…forever.

We were just two kids, sitting in the back of her grandfather's station wagon on that dark, stormy day twelve years before, when I promised I'd always make her smile…and I meant every word.

The words of the song came from my lips and my hands played the notes, but it was all muscle memory, my mind was eleven hundred miles away, with Jillian. It was a good thing that Adam, Thor, Pauly, and I were so used to playing with each other, years of practice having made us a well-oiled machine.

I knew what Jillian was thinking right then. I could feel her disappointment like a second skin. Of all the days not to give her the comforting reply she'd grown accustomed to hearing from me. I hated myself right about now. I had to fix this.

The lyrics I'd written so long ago—that I sang with practiced stage presence now—made the guilt in my stomach curdle. Nausea ate me with each line.

> *Forever wipe the tears away and pocket your sadness for another day.*
> *I'll make you smile, just wait and see. Hide your pain inside of me.*
> *Keep it there. Hidden away.*
> *Never to see the light of day.*
> *Forever is a long way away.*

I sang each line and by the end of the song, I was numb. I silenced my instrument and Thor and Pauly did the same, it was Adam who kept the song alive for a few more beats, his drum the heartbeat.

When he pounded the tom one last time, the crowd erupted into applause. Whistles and squeals traveled from the partygoers, but I couldn't enjoy their appreciation. My stomach was twisted in knots. The euphoria I usually felt onstage was gone, replaced by disquiet and tension. The last thing I wanted to do was let Jillian down. My mind was solely focused on Jillian and sending her a one-word text.

The guys and I smiled and nodded our heads in gratitude. As

front man, I had to engage the crowd and make them feel important. I was the mouthpiece of our group.

My mind worked double time, trying to figure out a way I could incorporate a text to Jillian into our show. If I deviated from our set, the guys would not be happy with me, but what choice did I have?

I turned to Thor and said, "They liked that one."

He nodded and smiled, thrown by my off-the-rails improv. But he went along with it. "We have a hot crowd tonight, Griff," he said, laying down a distorted sound on his guitar.

The small crowd went wild.

Now that Thor was playing along, I took my chances. "What do you say we have a little fun, guys?" I addressed the crowd and my bandmates, pulling more applause from the crowd with my hand gestures.

"What'd ya have in mind?" Thor asked, smiling.

I turned to the crowd and said, "Tonight's a good night and I'm feeling generous."

The assembly erupted into cheers and whoops.

"I'd like to host a contest. How many of you follow us on Instagram?" I asked.

Again, everyone hollered.

"Fuck yeah!" I shouted, punching my fist in the air, eliciting more exuberance from them. Adam started in on the kick drum.

I reached in my pocket and pulled out my phone, holding it up to the mass of college students before me. Adam sped up the beat, getting the crowd more amped. "We want to see your pics from the show," I said. "Use the hashtag Mine Shaft."

I looked at my phone and pretended to open my Instagram app, but instead I opened my text messages. I quickly found Jillian's name and typed her word, "Forever," and hit "Send" before anyone was the wiser.

Adam changed up his beat and segued into the rhythm of the next song on our set. Thor also quietly added his guitar riff, looping it to give me a few more minutes to wrap up my bogus contest. When Pauly got in the mix, I knew it was their subtle way of telling me it was time to move on.

I joined with the trio, adding the bottom to the song before I spoke. "We'll randomly choose a photo from tonight's concert. The winner will receive my undivided attention." I spoke in a throaty voice. As suspected, a few females couldn't contain themselves and answered my practiced bedroom voice with catcalls. "Oh, that's not all," I teased. "Along with my undivided attention, I will give the winner bass lessons for one week," I shouted.

The crowd erupted and we took that as our cue to rip into the next song on our list.

This time I fell into the song the way I usually did. I let the music speak for me, bleeding my heart and soul into each note I played and each syllable I sang. The party was in full swing now and I loved every minute I was on stage. With any luck, Leo Dane was going to change our lives tomorrow and I couldn't wait.

Chapter Eight

"Hey, you!" Adam shouted from behind the drum kit.

What the fuck is he doing? We're in the middle of a song. I turned around and gave him my best pissed face, turned back to the mic, and continued singing.

> *I scream into the void, swallowed up whole*
> *Alone. I'm afraid. Too scared to lose control.*

"Fuck," Adam screamed. "Get your hands off of her!" He stopped drumming and stood up from behind the kit, launching one of his sticks into the audience.

Thor, Pauly, and I quit playing, and stood in complete shock at the scene unraveling before us. Adam had never gone ape-shit like this before. *Is he fucking high?*

Adam stormed from behind the drums and headed into the crowd, in the same direction his drumstick had gone two beats earlier.

The rest of us watched in horror as Adam elbowed his way through the crowd and landed a punch to some guy's jaw.

"You guys better get your boy before that dude beats the shit out of him," said a dude from the front row.

Standing next to a live mic, I shouted, "Adam!" as loud as I could. The crowd went still. *Who knew I had that kind of power?* I set my bass down next to the drum kit and walked through the crowd to where Adam was sprawled out on the floor, clutching his left hand to his chest. He was a mess. His shaggy dark hair stuck to his face, falling over his clenched eyes.

In no time Pauly and Thor flanked me. Even Erin made her way through the crowd to stand beside me. "What the fuck are you doing, Adam?" I spit.

Adam winced, lying on the ground, rocking from side to side. "Ugh," he groaned. "That fucking prick had his hands all over Trina's ass." He pointed to the guy rubbing his jaw, standing beside Trina—Adam's flavor of the month.

"Are you fucking kidding me?" Thor yelled. "You go ape-shit in the middle of a goddamn show because of some girl?"

"Hey," Trina whined, insulted by Thor's comment. "I was just dancing with him, Adam. You don't have to be such an overbearing asshole."

I reached down, offering Adam my hand. He latched on with the hand that didn't appear to be hurt, and I pulled him up.

"Fuck me," he shouted, standing up. "I think I broke my wrist. Frat Boy has a jaw made of fucking steel."

"That ain't all, little drummer boy," the guy taunted. "Sure you don't want to go home with me tonight, sugar?" Frat Boy asked, turning to Trina. "I'll show you what kind of steel I'm packing." And as if Adam needed any more of a reason to kick this dude's ass, he added a few pelvic thrusts to punctuate his statement.

"That's it," Adam said, bouncing on the balls of his feet. His breath came fast and loud, pushing through his teeth. "I'm going to lay you out, fucker."

I angled my body, putting Erin behind me. I didn't want her getting caught in the middle of Adam's tirade. "Oh, no, you're not. We're done here," I said, blocking Adam from Frat Boy's line of sight. Sometimes being six foot four had its advantages. "Let's get our shit cleaned up, boys, and get the hell out." I walked forward, forcing Adam to shuffle backward, away from any more humiliation. Erin put her hand on my shoulder and walked behind me. I glanced back at her and shrugged, confused. *What the hell happened tonight?* Pauly and Thor followed too and we all marched our asses back to the stage. The quicker we got out of here the better.

"Trina?" Adam called, watching her as he backed away. "You're coming with me, right?"

I couldn't see Trina, and I didn't hear an answer, so I could only assume her curiosity about steel-dick Frat Boy had gotten the better of her.

I watched Adam visibly deflate at her rejection. *Damn, that girl is cold.* "Turn around," I told Adam. "You don't need her shit." I placed my hands on his shoulders and forced him to look away. "She's not worth it, Adam."

Adam didn't argue back, but looked down at the hand he clutched to his chest. "Shit," he groaned. His wrist was already swelling and turning fifty shades of purple.

* * *

Once Adam's van was packed up, I went to find Tucker—the guy who had answered the door when I arrived. "Sorry, man," I said, offering my hand. Thor and I always prided ourselves on being good businessmen. I hoped Tucker proved me wrong about my frat boy stereotype (steel-dick sure the hell hadn't) and would accept my apology on Adam's behalf.

"I'm sorry, too. Blaine is such a tool sometimes," he said, shaking my hand.

"There's no charge for tonight's show. Not after what happened. I do hope that this incident hasn't turned you off of Mine Shaft, though. This is the first time anything like this has happened, I assure you."

"No worries. You guys are cool in my book," Tucker said, shaking his head and smiling.

"Thanks." I returned his smile.

"Hope your boy isn't too hurt," he added.

Yeah, me too. "He'll be fine," I said, trying to convince myself more than Tucker. "See you around." I nodded and turned toward the front door.

Outside, Erin and Thor waited near Adam's van. "Pauly drove Adam to the hospital. I'm going to drive the van back to our place. I'll pick up my car sometime tomorrow," Thor said.

"We have to figure out what the fuck we're going to do in the morning," I sighed, running my hand through my hair.

"No shit," Thor added.

"I'm following Erin back to her place. I'll meet you back at the apartment. Maybe by then we'll have more news on whether or not Adam can play."

"Griffin," Erin said, "You don't have to follow me home. If you guys need to get things sorted out, I understand."

I reached for her hand, lacing my fingers between hers. "Nonsense. I want to make sure you get home OK." I squeezed our interlocked fingers reassuringly.

"All right, then. I'll see you back at the apartment," Thor said, swinging the van keys around his index finger. "Oh, and what was up with you tonight?"

I cocked my head in confusion. "What do you mean?"

His eyebrow shot up. "A week-long bass lesson?"

I grinned sheepishly. "Sorry, dude. It was a spur-of-the-moment decision. The crowd was turned on and it just seemed like a good idea at the time."

He nodded his head and then smiled. "That was brilliant, man. Way to keep us relevant."

"You're not pissed?" I asked, stunned by his reaction.

"Hell no. I trust you. You always know what's hot. I bet over half of the university's student body was at the show. We probably more than doubled our followers and gained a shitload of new fans. Or did, at least…until Adam."

I did not deserve his trust. If he knew my true motives behind that scam, he'd be planting his fist in my jaw. "That was the idea." I shrugged.

Erin stretched her arm around my waist and squeezed. "That's Griffin, always knows what's up."

"Brilliant, man. Fucking brilliant." He clapped me on the shoulder and laughed. "But I'm only voting for the pictures of chicks with really big tits."

I laughed. "I'll put you in charge of choosing the winner, then."

"I think that's a great idea." Erin smiled. "I don't think I want my boyfriend looking at pictures of a bunch of drunk college girls. That has *Girls Gone Wild* written all over it."

"Fuck yeah, it does." Thor chuckled and opened the van door, climbing inside. "See you, man." He pulled the door shut and started the engine.

"Bye." I tapped the door and gave him a wave as he drove away.

I looked at Erin and frowned; this was not how I'd pictured this night ending. "I'm sorry, peach."

Still holding hands, we walked down the side of the street to her car. "It's fine."

When we got to her car she unlocked it, but before she had a chance to open the door, I pulled her toward me and kissed her. She melted into my arms.

With the palm of my hand, I brushed her long blond hair away from her cheek, feeling her smooth skin against my callused fingers. "I hate that I have to spend my evening with Thor and not you," I said against her mouth. I had entertained high hopes for tonight. Hopes for Erin and me finally getting between the sheets. After what had happened the other night, I needed to make things up to her. And from the vibes she had been sending earlier, I got the idea she was thinking along the same lines.

"That would have been nice," she moaned, biting gently at my lip.

I pressed my body closer to hers. "Screw it. Thor's on his own tonight." I kissed her harder, biting her lip less gently than she had mine. My fingers worked their way into her hair as I moved my mouth to her cheek…down her jaw. She smelled fruity and so damn *sweet*. In my mind, the epitome of a Southern belle. Tilting her head invitingly, she worked her hands beneath the hem of my shirt. With ample pressure, her strong fingers raked over my back…up and down.

I brought my lips back to hers and thrust my tongue into her mouth, matching the rhythmic pulse of her fingers on my skin.

"Griffin," she whispered after a beat.

"Hmm?" I smiled, but refusing to take my mouth off hers.

She pulled away and looked up at me with her dark eyes, and for a split second I saw Jillian in my arms, again. I blinked hard and I shook my head, trying to clear the image.

"Everything all right, Griffin?" Erin asked, taking her hands from beneath my shirt and running them over my arms.

I am losing it. I took a step backward. How the hell could I be so caught up in Erin one moment and think of Jillian in the next? Sighing, I pushed my hand through my own hair. *Get your shit together, Daniels. Erin's a great woman, you're lucky to have her.*

"Yeah, fine. Sorry." I shivered, the picture of Jillian still in my head. "Just stressed, I guess." I played off the sudden change in my demeanor, but not very well.

I looked at Erin, the sexual tension from a second ago replaced with an awkward strain. This was becoming a problem. Disappointment softened the look in her eyes. "Tonight was really messed up," she said, standing up straight.

"Yeah," I agreed. She turned and opened the car door.

Over her shoulder she smiled. "You sure you can't come over tonight?" An attempt to rekindle what we'd just shared. A very tempting offer. She had no idea how much I wanted to take her to bed. But with Jillian suddenly on my mind…always on my mind, that wouldn't be fair to Erin. My head was too crowded.

I shook my head. "I wish I could tonight." I gripped the frame of the car door in my left hand as she climbed inside. "Wait for me, I'll follow you back."

"Griffin," she sighed. "It's not that late." Her eyebrows pinched together as she gave me a stern look. "I know you and Thor have a lot to do tonight, especially if Adam can't play. You go home. I'll text when I get back to my apartment."

"You sure?" I asked. Erin lived in the campus apartments, which were notorious for their lack of safety when it came to the female residents, especially at night.

"Of course." She cocked her head. "I come and go all the time. I'll be fine."

"Text me the minute you're home?" Since Jillian wasn't here, Erin had to put up with my overprotective nature. Jillian had always needed that from me, but Erin was different. She always seemed to balk when I flexed my protective muscles. It was almost as if she found that personality trait annoying.

"I will. Go home and figure out what you guys are going to do. And get some sleep, you're going to need it."

"All right," I reluctantly agreed. Was I making the right decision? Should I go home with Erin? Would that help me get over my feelings for Jillian? I was so tired of the uncertainty swirling around in my head.

"Good luck tonight." She winked.

"Thanks." I let out a long, frustrated breath. "Feel like making a trip into the city with me tomorrow?"

"Really? You want me to go?"

I could hear Jillian in my head telling me to make an effort with Erin. "Yep. An unbiased opinion, if you will." Someone to fill in for Jillian. Even though no one could fill her void, I still liked to pretend. Erin was a nice substitute.

"Sure," she drawled, a wide smile spreading across her face. "What time should I come over?"

"The meeting's at seven thirty a.m., so we'll have to leave around six, traffic and all."

"Not a problem. I'll be there at five forty-five," she said, grinning from ear to ear. She started the car, and I pushed the door shut. Erin rolled down the window and folded her arms on the window frame, resting her head on top of her hands.

I crouched down and put my hands on each side of her face. She closed her eyes, and I kissed her lightly. "See you in the morning," I whispered.

Erin's lips parted in a smile. "Yes you will."

Sliding my hands from her cheeks, I rocked back on the balls of my feet and stood up. "Text me when you get home."

"I will," she said as she rolled up the window.

I stepped back a few feet, into the road, and Erin blew me a kiss as she pulled away from the curb. I watched her taillights grow smaller as she drove down the street.

Walking back toward the front of the frat house, I thought about giving Jillian a call, but once was enough tonight. I didn't want to interfere with the life she was making for herself at college. Before she left, we had seen each other every day. Now it was doing well for us to talk once a week. I was happy she'd found her niche. This separation was good for both of us. I couldn't speak for Jillian, but the distance was exactly what I needed to sort out my feelings, get my head and heart in the right place. Jillian was my friend and there could never be anything more.

Chapter Nine

When I got home, Thor was on the phone. He mouthed Pauly's name and shook his head. It didn't take a rocket scientist to figure out what that meant, Adam was on the DL. *God damn him.*

"Yeah, uh-huh," Thor said, nodding his head. "See you in the morning." He pulled the phone from his ear and threw it at the couch. "Damn it!"

I fell into my recliner, letting the momentum of my fall rock me back and forth. "How bad?" I scrubbed my hand over my face, preparing for the worst. I wanted to know, but I didn't want to know.

"A broken fucking wrist," Thor growled. "He's going to be out for at least six weeks, maybe longer." Thor plopped down on the coach, next to his phone.

We sat in the living room, neither of us knowing what the fuck we were going to do. I stared at the blank television as if the answer to our problem would flash across a ticker at the bottom of the screen.

I stared for so long, my contacts dried out. Blinking out of my stupor, I pressed the heels of my palms into my eyes and rubbed while I mentally ran through a list of guys I knew who played the drums. "What about Murphy?" I said, throwing out a name.

Thor stood up from the couch, pointed at me, and snapped his fingers. "This is good. We need to come up with a list of everyone we know that could fill in for us." He clapped his hands together and took a few long strides in the direction of the kitchen.

"Where are you going?" I asked, getting up to follow him.

In the kitchen Thor was rooting around in a drawer. "Murph doesn't know our material well enough to help us out tomorrow, but with some practice, he might work for some of our later gigs." Thor turned around with a pocket-size notebook and a pencil, flipping the notebook open.

I pulled a chair away from the kitchen table and turned it backward, straddling it before I sat. Thor joined me at the table with his notebook. "Jim," I offered.

Thor wrote the name down, but shook his head. "Not good enough. What about Sebastian?"

"Didn't he go into the Marine Corps? I don't think he lives here anymore."

"Oh, yeah." Thor wrote his name on the paper and drew a line through it. "Well, shit." Tipping his chair onto two legs, Thor dropped the pencil onto the paper and blew out a breath. "What are we going to do?" He looked at me, lacing his fingers behind his head.

I stood up and went to the fridge. Pulling it open, I grabbed two beers and slammed the door shut with my foot. "Drink."

He held his hand out for a bottle and I walked it over to him.

For five minutes we spitballed names back and forth, but couldn't come up with one person who knew our material well enough. Tomorrow we'd be at Leo Dane's mercy. Hopefully, Adam's condition wouldn't be a deal breaker.

I stretched my legs out and took a long drink. "I'm sure this isn't the first time Dane has had to deal with an injured musician. The studio has to have some sort of protocol for a situation like this."

"A 'your bandmate is a moron' clause?" Thor said. "Yeah, I'm sure they do." He burped and placed his bottle back on the table with a thud.

"Let's hope so." I swallowed the dregs of my beer and pounded the table with my fist, looking at the microwave clock. "I'm going to bed. My head hurts." Standing, I headed for the stairs.

"Night," Thor said.

"See ya, dude."

From halfway up the stairs, I heard Thor ask, "How's Jill?" Even through all of the Adam shit, Thor still remembered that today was hell for her.

I stopped. She hadn't sounded good on the phone, and I was worried. I backpedaled down a few steps and looked at him, shaking my head. "She sounded miserable." I could still hear the sadness in her voice and it was killing me.

"She's strong, Griffin. She'll be all right," he said, pressing his lips into a tight smile.

I nodded. I knew she was strong…a real fighter. But as long as I lived, I would never forget the day she had almost given up the fight, and I hoped the stress of college didn't drive her back to that dark place. "You get some sleep," I said, changing the subject. "Big day tomorrow."

"Yeah." He stood up and pushed his chair and mine under the table. "You know, I've dreamed of this day since I was fifteen, and now that it's here, I'm sorry to say that I'm not that excited." He shook his head. "Fucking Adam."

"You can say that again." Between worrying about Jillian and dealing with Adam's shenanigans, the meeting with Leo Dane had gotten buried beneath a heap of shit.

* * *

My iPad came to life way too early the next morning. I hated mornings. Pulling the blaring tablet off my nightstand, I silenced it and rolled out of bed. I had purposely set my alarm to go off earlier than I needed. I wanted to leave some time to FaceTime Jillian. I needed to see her, my sanity depended on it. She'd always been a calming presence in my life.

I showered quickly and got dressed, excited by the prospect of some time with Jillibean. Hearing Thor's heavy footfalls between his room and the bathroom, I decided to take the call someplace quieter. I grabbed my iPad off the bed and headed downstairs.

Flopping into my recliner, I tapped the FaceTime app and then her name. I anxiously listened to each high-pitched trill as I waited for her answer. After what seemed like forever—which was probably only thirty seconds—I glanced at the clock, not even knowing what time it was. Maybe she wasn't answering because she'd partied too much last night and was sleeping it off. Maybe she'd met someone and hadn't gone back to her dorm. These unsavory thoughts ramped up my pulse.

My mind went through a laundry list of reasons why she wasn't picking up the call, each thought worse than the one that preceded it.

And then her face filled the screen.

"Jillibean," I said. Seeing her face was exactly what I needed. My eyes roamed over all her features: Her golden hair was a wild blue mess, her brown eyes sparkled, and her lips were pressed into a gorgeous smile. God, I loved her smile. When the corners of her lips pulled up, the warmth spread through her cheeks and radiated out of her eyes. I'd kill for that smile.

"Hey, Griff," she said groggily. I must have woken her.

Despite all her loveliness, I couldn't help but notice the dark circles under her eyes. Her lids were red and swollen. Faint traces of old makeup ran down her cheeks. "You OK? You don't look so good."

Her picture bounced around the screen as she opened doors and traveled downstairs. "Well gee, thanks." She ran her hand through her hair, showing off more of the blue. "You're one to talk, Daniels. Trying to grow a beard?" The smile she flashed right then would get me through any shit that happened today.

Damn, I missed her.

Playing along, I rubbed my stubbly jaw and gave her a better view, turning my head from side to side. "What? I thought you liked my scruffy look."

"You're looking more like a rock star every day." She smiled.

I kicked out the footrest on the recliner and rested my iPad on my chest, right above my new tattoo. Her screen wobbled again and a door opened and then closed behind her. "How was your party last night?"

She sighed and her smile disappeared. "After I talked to you, some sleazeball hit on me, and I convinced Sarah to leave. I wasn't in the party mood."

My legs folded the footrest back down, and I sat at attention. Hearing that some asshole had hit on her sent fire coursing through my veins. And the worst part was that I couldn't protect her…she was on her own. I reined in my worry and asked, "Did the sleazeball hurt you?"

"No." She shook her head. "But I wasn't so good last night. Like I said before, starting classes this week sucked."

This was not what I wanted to hear. Inwardly I kept praying she hadn't hurt herself. I could tell she'd spent the night crying and that killed me. I wanted nothing more than to wrap her in my arms and hold her tight, so nothing could hurt her…not even herself. "Your eyes are swollen," I said. "You spent the whole night crying, didn't you?"

"I did," she whispered.

I was dying. *How the hell am I supposed to do this?* She was the most important person in my life and she was the farthest away from me. I took a deep breath. I had to be calm. I wouldn't let her see how much this separation was affecting me. I also needed some reassurance that she hadn't resorted to cutting again. "Bean, you need to call Dr. Hoffman."

She shifted and her image wiggled on the screen. "I'm fine, Griff. When Sarah and I got back to the dorm, I talked to her. I told her what happened to Mom and Dad."

I scrubbed my hand over my face and bit the inside of my lip. She'd opened up to someone. That was huge. My heart clenched in my chest. "How do you feel?" I was cautious. I didn't want to push too much and have her melting in a puddle of tears if her room-mate hadn't been supportive. I didn't know if I was strong enough to see her cry when she was so far away.

"Better," she said reassuringly.

"Really? I don't want you to start hurting yourself again."

Jillian sat up straighter. "I'm not. The thought never even crossed my mind. It actually felt good to open up to Sarah. She's amazing."

Relief washed over me. I felt as if a weight had been lifted from my shoulders, and I smiled. She was making it on her own. "I'm so proud of you, Jillibean. That took a lot of fucking courage to let her in."

"Thanks," she said. Her eyes sparkled and the smile on her lips took my breath away.

Despite the bravery it had taken for her talk to Sarah, I felt she needed to check in with her therapist. "But I still think you should call Dr. Hoffman. I worry that you're not meeting with her on a regular basis. College is stressful."

She pressed her lips together and cocked her head to the side—classic smarty-pants Jillian. "If things get crazy, I promise to call her."

I shrugged, feeling tension in my shoulders. "OK." I wasn't happy with this answer, but I trusted her judgment. It would have to do.

"What are you doing up this early? Didn't you have a show last night?" she asked, changing the subject.

"The guys and I have a meeting with a producer this morning. But I'm not sure how that's going to work. Fucking Adam broke his wrist at the show last night. We didn't even play the full set."

"Whoa, back up a minute. A producer?" she asked, shifting her iPad again.

"Yeah, the day I got back from taking you to school, I got a call from a guy who heard Mine Shaft play about a month ago. He was interested in our sound and wants to meet with us."

Her image on the screen shifted violently and then focused back in. "Are you kidding?" she squealed. "Griffin, that's awesome. Why didn't you tell me?"

"I was going to tell you, but things have been so busy. And now all this shit with Adam. Besides, I knew you were starting school this week and I didn't want to distract you," I said quietly. She didn't need to worry about my shit on top of her own.

She pursed her lips together, a telltale sign that she was pissed. "That's bullshit and you know it. I always want to know what's going on with you. No matter what."

She was so stinking cute when she was mad. Her cheeks turned a dark shade of pink and her lips…don't even get me started on those. It was probably best I didn't think about her lips. They were lethal.

If I played my cards right, I knew she couldn't stay mad at me if I gave her one of my I'm-sorry-I-fucked-up smiles. "Forgive me?" I asked sweetly, turning the corners of my smile into a pout.

"Yes," she grumbled. "But you better not do it again. You better fucking call me the instant something happens." She pointed a finger at the screen in warning.

"Yes, ma'am." I saluted.

Changing the subject again, she asked, "You said Adam broke his wrist? How did that happen?"

I relaxed into the chair and gave her the highlights. "We were at the Sig Nu house last night, and according to Adam, he saw a frat boy with his hands all over Trina."

"Uh-oh," she breathed.

"Yeah, Adam went ballistic. He chucked his drumstick at the guy's head and went after him. Adam said the dude had a jaw made of fucking steel. Needless to say, he couldn't finish the set and we had to pack up and leave."

She listened intently, nodding as she absorbed the ugly story. "Ugh, I'm sorry."

"We can't afford to cancel the rest of our shows. And there's no way in hell I'm going to miss out on what this producer wants just because Adam can't control his fucking temper. We're going to have to replace him until he can play again," I said.

"Anyone in mind?" she asked.

"Not off the top of my head. We'll figure something out, though. I don't want to talk about Adam, it just pisses me off." I shoved my hair off of my forehead and pulled a tactic from her book: It was time to change the subject. "You said some jackass was hitting on you last night?" I needed to know more about this clown, because when it came time for me to visit her, I wanted to know his name.

"Yeah, but don't worry about it. He knew I was not interested," she said, shrugging it off.

I was just about to ask her how she gotten rid of him, when my doorbell rang. "Hold on a second, Bean." I set my iPad down and went to the door.

I pulled it open, and Erin stood on the other side. She looked incredible, dressed in tight bright-blue pants and a white lacy top that revealed another blue shirt underneath. Having been around Jillian and her love of clothing for so many years, it astounded me how much work girls put into their wardrobes. But I certainly appreciated the effort.

"Hey, Peach." I stepped aside to let her in.

She leaned close, kissing me. I gave her a quick peck, not wanting Jillian to see or hear Erin and me lip-locked. Strange, I know. Over the years Jillian had seen me with plenty of girls. I couldn't explain my reaction. Unease settled in the pit of my stomach, a feeling I wasn't used to.

"Hey, Rock Star. You look nice," she drawled, giving me two thumbs up. "You ready?"

"Yep." I stepped back, heading over to the recliner, where I'd left my iPad. "I was just talking to Jillian while I waited for you." I picked it up and sat back down, centering myself in the frame. Erin sat on the arm of the chair, leaning over my shoulder. Awkward didn't even begin to describe this situation. Showing any kind of affection toward Erin felt wrong in Jillian's presence, and I didn't feel like I could be myself with Jillian while Erin was in the room.

My heart tapped out a staccato beat that I felt in my temples. A headache was on the horizon.

"Hi, Jillian," Erin said, waving.

Jillian smiled and waved back. "Hi, Erin."

This was awkward on so many levels. I needed to wrap things up. "Hey, Bean, we need to get going. I'll call you later and let you know what the producer said."

"Sounds good." I could see sadness clouding her eyes, making them darker.

"Bye, Jillian," Erin shouted over my shoulder.

"Bye, guys," she said.

"Bye, Bean." I smiled and disconnected the call. I hated to end our conversation so abruptly, but now that Erin was here, things didn't feel right. I didn't want Jillian to see me with Erin.

"Well, that was a nice surprise, getting to talk to Jillian this morning," Erin said, trying to relieve some of the awkward tension in the room.

I shrugged and stood up, trying to ignore the weird vibes coursing through me. "Um, yeah, it was."

Erin stood, too. "You all right?"

I gave her an awkward smile. "Yeah. Just nervous." I looked back toward the kitchen and said, "What the fuck is Thor doing? We need to leave." I turned back to Erin and held up my index finger. "Be right back."

She nodded. "Sure thing."

I walked into the kitchen and yelled up the stairs. "Yo, Thor, we going to do this thing?"

Seconds later he stomped down the stairs looking pissed off. "It is too fucking early."

"Get over it, dude. Let's go."

Thor flipped me off and walked over to the counter, grabbing the keys to the van. "You ready?"

"Yeah, but I'm riding with Erin," I said, heading back into the living room.

Thor opened the back door. "Meet you there."

I rounded the corner and saw Erin sitting in my recliner, messing around on her phone. "Mind if we take your car?" I asked.

"Not at all." She tossed me the keys.

I caught them and let out a giant breath. This meeting had the potential to launch Mine Shaft into the world or bury us alive, and it all hinged on how much mercy Leo Dane was willing to grant us.

Chapter Ten

On our way into the city, Erin messed with the radio every three minutes. I could feel a headache coming on. I was tense, on edge, and in a piss-poor mood by the time we were stopped in traffic on the bridge. When Erin went to change the radio station for the tenth time, I put my hand on hers and shook my head. "Please don't." Maybe it had been a mistake asking her to come along.

She turned her eyes to me and smiled. "You like the 'Cups' song?"

"No." I shook my head. "But I can't take the channel surfing right now." I reached for the volume dial and turned it down.

"Aw, come on. It's got a catchy tune."

I didn't play along and put my attention back on the road.

Erin sat back in her seat and gave me a defeated look. "OK, then…" She trailed off and turned her head toward the passenger side window.

I blew out a frustrated breath and reached for her hand. "I'm sorry. Just nervous," I lied. It wasn't nerves. I'd been waiting for this day since I was fifteen. I had played through every scenario in my head and none of them had ever gone down like this. Nothing about this day felt right. Yet despite all the shit with Adam, the one thing that felt the most fucked up was the fact that Erin was sitting beside me and not Jillian. I couldn't shake my discontentment.

Erin looked at me. "Everything is going to be fine. Don't worry." She squeezed my shoulder reassuringly.

Inching along through the traffic on the bridge, I stole a quick look, flashing her a smile before turning my attention back to the parking lot in front of me. That was Erin, always so positive. I had to give her credit, she tried. But I didn't think I'd ever stop comparing her to Jillian. Jillian got me. She understood. I could hear her now: *Yeah, Adam fucked up. There's nothing you can do to change that. You're going to go into that meeting today and show Leo Dane how much he needs Mine Shaft.*

Jillian was my cheerleader. Without her, my life didn't have the same verve.

* * *

At Amphion Productions, I parked Erin's blue Mustang near the back of the parking lot, hoping to avoid some asshole's planting their door into the side of her beautiful automobile.

I turned off the ignition and got out, walking around the front of the car to open Erin's door. I offered my hand, and she placed hers into mine, standing. Side by side, she and I were almost the same height. It was very different from how Jillian fit to my side—I could tuck Jillian safely under my arm, where she fit perfectly. Not Erin, though. She was all legs, which made her an outstanding volleyball player.

"Well," I said. "This is it." I sucked in a huge breath and blew it out. With my free hand, I put Erin's car keys in my pocket and brushed my hair away from my forehead. Everything would work out fine. I just had to keep telling myself that.

Erin squeezed my hand. "You got this," she said reassuringly.

I scanned the parking lot, looking for the guys, just as Thor pulled in, followed by Pauly and Adam.

Erin and I walked over to the van as Thor was climbing down.

"Hey, Erin," Thor said, with a nod in her direction.

"Morning, Thor," she replied, adjusting her purse strap and stepping closer to my side.

"Well, dudes. This is it." Adam rounded the van, practically skipping. "We finally made it."

"Let's not get ahead of ourselves." I laced my fingers with Erin's and pulled her with me toward the door. "Let's not be late for our first meeting either."

The guys followed. We crossed the parking lot, coming to a glass door with the record studio's logo etched in white. I pulled it open and ushered Erin in before me.

The studio was a refurbished antique home, at odds with all the high-end recording equipment filling each room. Even the back wall, behind the reception desk, was lined with dozens of different kinds of guitars, some acoustic, others electric. It was an impressive display. It seemed the house itself was an anachronism with all the technology living inside it.

My eyes were scanning the wall, taking in the different instruments, when a tall, lanky hipster came around the corner. "May I help you?"

I stepped to the front, taking up my role as the band's spokesperson. "We have a seven thirty meeting with Leo Dane," I said.

"You're Mine Shaft?" he asked, pushing his thick black-framed glasses up on his nose.

"Yes." I nodded.

"I'm Leo. Pleased to meet you." He held out his hand. I shook it, then he made the rounds, introducing himself to the rest of the guys.

After we exchanged pleasantries, Leo said, "Why don't we head to the conference room, it's a little more comfortable."

"Sure," Thor answered.

Adam, Pauly, and Thor followed Leo, and I brought up the rear. But as soon as I started down the hall with Erin by my side, it didn't feel right. I needed Jillian right now and if Jillian couldn't do this with me, then I didn't want a stand-in.

I stopped abruptly and Erin bumped into my shoulder. "Griffin?" she said.

I felt terrible. I'd asked her to come and now I was going to ask her to wait in the lobby. *Why do I keep trying to turn her into Jillian?* It wasn't fair to Erin. I shook my head before I spoke. "I'm sorry, peach. But I think it should just be the band that goes back." I wrapped my arm around her shoulder and turned us toward the reception area. I felt her shoulders slump in disappointment. "I want to come off as professional as possible with this guy. I'm sorry," I said again.

Erin shook her head, but the look on her face said something else. "I'm thrilled that you asked me to come to this meeting. I don't mind waiting, Griffin." She pulled her lips into a smile and sat down on the couch near the door.

"I'm sorry," I said again.

"Knock it off. Get in there and make Mine Shaft a household name." She winked, pulling her purse onto her lap. "I'll be right here when you're finished."

I leaned down and kissed her quickly. "Thank you for understanding." I smiled and jogged down the hall just as Adam was closing the door.

"Well, gentlemen," Leo said, rounding a large mahogany table in the center of the room. "Please, take a seat." He gestured to the numerous chairs pushed in around the table. "Thanks for coming in this morning."

The four of us followed Leo's cue and found chairs across from him, sitting down.

"Thank you for meeting with us," I said.

Leo nodded. "So, guys. I'll get right to the point. I've had your demo for a few months and I've been to a couple of your shows. I'm impressed with your sound and from what I've seen, you've got a solid fan base with the college students. Have you gotten much airplay?" he asked.

I smoothed my hands across my lap, trying to play it cool. "Yes. We get quite a lot of airplay at State. We're booked solid for the next few months: frat parties, bar gigs, and some smaller festivals here in the city. I know the radio station manager at the university and he's been very helpful in getting us prime exposure." I took a deep breath, starting to relax into my role as Mine Shaft's mouthpiece. Since Mine Shaft was my baby, I'd always taken the reins and the guys never complained. But this meeting would make or break us, and I did not want to fuck anything up. "State isn't the only school that has Mine Shaft on their radar either. We've been picked up by a dozen college stations here in the city, too."

Leo listened and nodded while he took notes. "Well, from the looks of it, it sounds like you guys have done your homework. And I must say, I'm impressed with the quality of your demo. Very professional."

Thor looked at me and grinned. "That's all Griffin," he said. "He's a perfectionist."

"And perfection is what gets you noticed in this business, gentlemen," Leo added.

In one sentence Leo Dane justified all my idiosyncrasies, all the arguments I'd had with the guys, trying to get them to be better. "Thank you, Mr. Dane," I said, feeling vindicated.

"So here's what I have to offer," Leo said, pushing a document across the table toward the guys and me.

Excitement boiled in my veins. It took every ounce of my concentration to keep from pacing the room. "OK." I took the paper from the table and glanced at the bold-faced letters at the top: "Amphion Productions Recording Contract."

Holy shit. Is this really happening?

"Amphion Productions would like to sign Mine Shaft to a record deal." Leo pushed his glasses up onto his nose. "This contract outlines the all the details in regards to terms, services, recording, production, and marketing."

I listened intently to what Leo was saying, but the words "recording contract" reverberated in my head, making the rest of my body hum with excitement. I glanced at the document, my eyes scanning each section. Words like "exclusivity" and "work product" made me nervous. Passing the paper to Thor, I said, "This is a fantastic opportunity. We're very excited. When would you need our answer?"

"I would advise you to take a week or two to look over the contract," Leo said. "After you sign, it's full steam ahead. We want your first album finished by the New Year."

Adam raised his casted arm. "Uh, I won't be able to play for a while."

"Adam was injured last night. We haven't had time to find someone to fill in yet." Thor clapped Adam on the back.

"I see." Leo's demeanor went from chummy to callous in an instant. "That does pose a problem."

I shifted in my seat. I had been afraid this might happen. Leo wasn't cool with Adam's being out of the picture for a while. "I understand that Amphion wants to get us out quickly, but we're at our best with Adam." I brushed my hair back and took a deep breath. "I feel it would be in the best interest of Mine Shaft to wait until he's ready to play before we move forward."

Leo acknowledged me with a dip of his head. "I'm not going to mince words, gentlemen. You have a great band. Once I sign you, I have to deliver a product and there isn't time for any of you to be convalescing. You sign, we get to work." Leo stood up from the table. "But, Mr. Daniels, I'd be willing to rework the contract for you." He stared me down, no humor in his eyes.

"Awesome. I knew something could be worked out." I smiled. Maybe Leo wasn't so much of an ass to work with. The guys looked happy with Leo's response, too.

"I think you may have misunderstood me, Mr. Daniels."

As I brought my attention back to Leo, my forehead creased in confusion.

"Have you thought about a solo career?" he asked.

What? I stared back. *Did I hear him correctly? He couldn't be insinuating that I should leave my band.* I shook my head. "Umm...no, sir." I challenged his stare.

"That's too bad. Amphion is looking for someone with your caliber of talent."

The air in the room became very thin, making it hard to breathe. I couldn't focus on any one conversation because there were too many happening at once. Hushed whispers passed between Thor, Pauly, and Adam while Leo waited for me to pull the biggest douchebag move ever and leave my bandmates in the dust.

Someone knocked into my shoulder and I turned. Thor eyeballed me, demanding that I tell Leo to get fucked. Drawing on some of the rage pouring from Thor's eyes, I found my voice. "I'm sorry, Mr. Dane, but I'm not a solo artist. I've worked with these guys for five years. I would never abandon them."

"Of course." Like a switch, he flipped on the practiced camaraderie he'd shown moments earlier. He reminded me of a car salesman. "It was worth a shot." He smiled, fake as hell. "I had to ask. But that does leave us with a problem. I can't wait for Mr. Long's injury to heal. The studio is expecting a quick turnaround on their investment. Like I said earlier, I'll give you two weeks max to look over the contract I've presented to you today. I will need a hard-and-fast decision by September twenty-sixth. However, you will have to produce a competent drummer within the next forty-eight hours, or I'll have to withdraw the contract before the two weeks is up. Sorry, guys, I can't sign a band without a drummer."

At this moment I really wanted to think of Leo as the bad guy, but I knew he was only looking out for Amphion's bottom line. He had no reason to show us any loyalty, we hadn't proven shit. This turn of events rested squarely on Adam's fucking shoulders.

"Well, gentlemen." Leo passed me a manila folder and stood. I placed the contract into the folder and stood as well. "I am looking forward to hearing from you," Leo said, walking to the end of the table. "Mr. Daniels, if you change your mind, you have my number. I know talent when I see it."

Shit. This was so fucked up.

Leo shook hands with the guys, none of whom said a word to him. "It's been a pleasure meeting you." His voice remained pleasant even though he'd basically just told my friends they sucked ass.

When Leo made his way to me, he proffered his hand, waiting for me to offer mine. I took it, giving it a firm shake even though I really wanted to tell him to fuck off.

"Think about what I said, Mr. Daniels. You're talented enough to make it on your own."

I let go of Leo's hand. "In all honesty, Mr. Dane," I responded with the same amount of artificial warmth, "If I can't work with these guys, I don't want a recording contract. We'll find someone to help us out. You get Mine Shaft or you don't get any of us."

Turning my back on him, I followed Adam out the door.

Erin uncrossed her legs and stood as we came into the lobby, a huge smile spreading across her face.

"Thank you again, gentlemen. I really am looking forward to working with you. I'm hopeful everything will work out." Leo shook hands with each of us one more time. "Here's to Mine Shaft and Amphion, and a promising future together."

"Thanks," Thor mumbled, reluctant to give him any kind of gratitude.

Leo nodded and walked back down the hall.

"Well?" Erin asked. "How'd it go?"

I wrapped my arm around her waist and drew her to my side. "I'll tell you later," I whispered.

Her expression clouded over. "OK?"

Pauly, Adam, and Thor gathered behind me while I ushered Erin toward the door. With the recording contract in hand, I stepped out into the humid September air, feeling like I was drowning.

Chapter Eleven

W hat the fuck was that?" Adam shouted in the parking lot. "The Griffin Show? What? Are we your bitches now?" Adam got right in my face, not even considering Erin standing beside me.

"Whoa, calm down, man," Thor said, stepping between Adam and me.

I had no intention of starting something with Adam, especially with Erin there. I knew he was hurt. Hell, I'd have been hurt if I had just been tossed aside like yesterday's garbage. His anger was meant for Leo, and I made the perfect substitute.

Stepping back, I put myself in front of Erin. I didn't want her hurt in the event that Adam did lose his temper. "I'm sorry, Adam. I had no idea he'd do that. You know how I feel about Mine Shaft. I'd never fuck you over like that."

Adam growled and turned, kicking the tire of the van in the process.

"Dude, don't go breaking your foot, too. We can't afford any more injuries," Pauly said.

It was quiet for a minute. None of us knew what to say or do.

There'd never been this much tension between us, but now it was as thick as the St. Louis air.

I stared at the ground, shoving a rock with the toe of my boot. It was in my best interest to stay quiet. Erin still stood behind me, a firm grip on my hand.

"Why don't we get something to eat and figure shit out?" Pauly suggested, pulling at his beard nervously. "The usual?"

"Yeah, whatever." Adam dismissed us and walked back to Pauly's car.

Thor nodded his answer as he turned to unlock the van.

I looked at Erin. "Want to go?"

Her lips pressed into a frown and she shook her head, checking her watch. "Sorry, Griffin, I have practice, and then I have to get to class."

"No problem. I'll hitch a ride with Thor." I looked at Thor and held up a finger for him to wait, then locked my eyes back onto Erin's. "Call me later?" I pulled her over to the passenger side of the Mustang, away from the guys.

"The guys are really pissed. What happened in there?" she asked when we were out of earshot.

I shook my head. "I'll tell you later." I didn't feel like rehashing what Leo had said at the moment. Adam's reaction had me worried about what the rest of the guys were thinking, and it wasn't something Erin or I could fix by talking about it in the parking lot.

"OK." The corners of her lips turned downward. "I'll text you when I get out of class?"

I gave her a halfhearted smile and pushed a strand of hair behind her ear, bringing her into my arms. Even though I hadn't told her what had happened, her presence helped ease some of the discord I felt. In the end I was glad she'd come.

I gently kissed the corner of her frown. "Sounds good. I'm not sure where I'll be, or what I'll be doing, but you can meet up with us later, if you want."

She kissed me back, then put both hands on my chest and pushed away. "I will. I've got to get to practice. I can't be late, or Coach will kick my ass. Whatever happened in there, Griffin, you guys will work it out."

Taking a step back, I reached around her body to open the car door. "Yeah, we will."

She smiled and got in. "See you, Rock Star."

I waved as she backed out of the parking space. Walking back to the van, I climbed in the front seat and slammed the door. Thor didn't say a word, just started the van and pulled out behind Erin.

As I sat in the passenger seat, beside Thor, the silence was excruciating. Of all the guys, I knew he was probably the most hurt by what Leo had offered. He and I had started Mine Shaft. For Leo to offer me a contract and not Thor too was inconceivable. We were a team.

"You know I'd never…" I couldn't finish the sentence.

For the first time since we'd left the conference room, Thor looked me in the eye. "Yeah, I know." He nodded and turned his attention back to the road.

Uncomfortable in my own skin at the moment, I shifted in the seat. "We need to find someone."

Thor pulled out of the parking lot, the tires squealing in protest. "No shit."

Watching the trees blur outside the passenger side window, I ran through the list we'd made last night. There had to be someone talented enough to pick up Adam's sticks and help us out.

I leaned back and closed my eyes, resting my pounding head on the seat. In a million years, this was not how I'd envisioned our big break.

Thor's voice broke through the thrum of the tires against the road. "What about an open audition?"

I opened my eyes and turned my head, not bothering to lift it; it weighed too much. "An audition?"

"Yeah, we can hold an audition at Fifth's. Bax will let us use the party room in the back of the bar, I'm sure of it. He'd even advertise for us." Thor pounded the steering wheel with his fist.

I raised my head. My mind skipped over the party room at Fifth's. It could work. "Think we can pull it off on such short notice?"

"The second we get to the Waffle House, I'll put a call in to Bax."

"You think Adam and Pauly will be down with an audition?"

Thor glanced my way. "As far as I'm concerned, Adam's opinion means shit. We wouldn't be in this mess if it wasn't for him."

"Good point, my friend. An audition it is." I sat up, clapping my hands together. "We need to start auditioning people tonight. As soon as we get a yea or nay from Bax, I'll post info on our website and social media sites."

"You do realize we're going to have every Tom, Dick, and Harry coming out of the woodwork for this," Thor grumbled.

"If this contract"—I swiped it off the dash and held it up—"is something we're serious about, an audition is our best shot."

"You're right. We'll get it worked out."

I let out a big breath and hoped that something would go right for us today.

* * *

Inside the Waffle House, the air smelled like stale bacon and maple syrup. My boots slid easily across the grease-coated linoleum. We'd spent countless nights stuck in our booth, drafting songs, working on set lists, and doing other tedious band-related shit, all the while packing away mounds of bacon and stacks of waffles.

We took our usual seat at the booth in back of the restaurant. I slid in first and then Adam plopped down beside me. Thor and Pauly took up the other side, like they always did.

Pauly drummed his fingers on the yellow envelope sitting in the middle of the table. "So what's the plan, dudes?"

"Forty-eight hours doesn't buy us a whole lot of options," Adam said.

Thor ran a hand over the stubble on his head and sighed. "Griff and I think we need to hold an audition."

I tore at a napkin sitting in front of me and nodded. "It'll bring the talent to us."

Pauly nodded in agreement. "Cool. Where and when?"

Thor lifted his phone into the air, ready to give Bax a call, when Maggie, one of the waitresses who regularly worked our table, stepped up, balancing a tray of water glasses over Adam's head. I wished she'd drop it. But, being a seasoned professional, she juggled her note pad, pen, and full tray like a champion. "Hi, guys. What are you having this morning?" she asked, passing out the glasses.

Adam ordered the All Star Special, Pauly ordered chocolate chip waffles and a double order of bacon, Thor stuck to a heaping mound of scrambled eggs, and I ordered my usual—cheese 'n eggs with bacon and raisin toast. My thoughts instantly went to Jillian, because she always ordered the same thing. But, with her quirky eating habits, she'd always douse her cheesy eggs with syrup. Jillian was known for putting the strangest food combinations together.

Not that I'd ever admit it, because I loved giving her shit about ruining food, but it was one of her most endearing qualities.

Maggie smacked her gum and wrote down our orders. "I'll have this right out for you guys."

"Thanks," we replied in unison.

With her sneakers squeaking on the linoleum, she turned to go.

"I'll call Bax." Thor held up his phone just as it lit up with an incoming call. He turned it around, quickly swiping a finger across the screen. Pressing the phone to his ear, he stood. "Hey, let me take this outside. Hold on." Lowering the phone, he looked at us. "Be right back."

"Who was that?" I asked, smirking.

Thor cleared his throat and straightened his back. "Just a girl I met the other day."

"A new woman?" Adam asked, wagging his eyebrows. "What'd she do, steal your number before she took the walk of shame?"

Thor stared Adam down. "Harper. And no, I gave her my number." He motioned toward the door. "I'll be back."

I threw a pile of shredded napkin onto the table. "Back to the audition," I said loudly, calling order to our meeting. "Adam, we're out of time. Stop screwing around."

"Fuck you, Griffin." Adam turned toward me, holding up his middle finger. "What do you care anyway? You have a record contract with or without us."

My fist itched, begging to be planted into Adam's jaw. I bit my lip, trying to rein in my temper. "You're the reason we're in this goddamn mess," I growled through gritted teeth. Like a balloon deflating, Adam sank farther into the booth and averted his eyes. "Yeah, that's what I thought."

The three of us sat in silence. Our plan hinged on Bax's answer, and until we had his approval, there was nothing more to discuss.

Leaning against the wall, I pulled my phone from my back pocket, hoping Jillian had called. Nothing new popped up when I opened up my text messages. It was almost ten a.m. in Rhode Island. I wanted to call her, but I knew she was in class. I had no interest in typing out a lengthy text message detailing the meeting with Leo. I'd call her between auditions tonight.

"Hey, we need to pick a winner for that damn contest you made up last night," Pauly said, breaking the silence.

"Yeah, you're right." I swirled a finger through my pile of shredded napkin. "Let's see what we got."

I clicked on the Instagram app, my feed loading sluggishly. Once the app fully loaded, I clicked on the small starburst at the bottom and typed *#mineshaft* into the search box. Instantly hundreds of pictures filled my screen.

More pictures came into view as I swiped my finger up the page. "Shit, guys. There's a ton."

Adam opened his palm. "Let's see."

I placed my phone in his hand. He scrolled some more, whistling when a picture met his approval. "This one gets my vote." He turned the phone around so Pauly and I could see. Someone had taken a picture of two girls making out.

"Now this is what I'm talking about," Adam said. "You could give one a bass lesson and I could give the other a drum lesson. Then the two of them could get together and make beautiful music and we could watch." Adam's head bobbed up and down as the fantasy took shape in his head.

"Yeah, only one problem, dipshit. You had to go and hurt yourself." I held my hand out for my phone, waving my fingers for him to pass it over.

Adam laid it in my palm and I took it back, scrolling through more pictures. "How are we going to choose a winner?"

Just then Maggie arrived with a huge tray of food. "Here you go, guys."

She passed out the plates, refilled our drinks, and asked if we needed anything else. We shook our heads and mumbled, "No."

Not waiting for Thor, we dug in. My stomach growled. We sat quietly for a while, enjoying our breakfast. I shoveled another bite of eggs into my mouth while I continued to scroll through the Instagram feed. "Isn't there a way for us to choose a random photo?" I asked.

"What are we talking about?" Thor asked, sliding back into the booth.

We stared at him. "Did you talk to Bax? What's the verdict?" Pauly asked.

"Everything's good, gents," Thor said with a smile. "Bax is letting us have the back room for the next two days. As long as we want it."

"Nice," Adam muttered around a mouthful of food.

Thor piled his fork with eggs and took a huge bite, not speaking until he swallowed. "Soon as we're done here, we're headed to Fifth's. Bax is spreading the word. What were you saying about random photos?" he asked, shoveling in another bite.

Pauly, with a large amount of waffle in his mouth, said, "That contest Griffin started last night. What about that random website?" he asked, turning to me.

"Dude, chew your damn food." Thor punched him in the shoulder. "No wonder you can't keep a lady around."

"Hey." Pauly rubbed his arm and swallowed. "I was just trying to help."

Thor held up his index finger and chewed his bite of eggs before he spoke. "Are you talking about random.org?"

Pauly took another bite of chocolate chip waffles and nodded.

"Yeah, that's the one," he said, opening his mouth real wide, giving Thor a nice look at his masticated waffles.

I picked up my phone and opened the web browser, typing in the address. On the page was a number generator. "How many pictures do we want to include?" I asked. "Don't make it too high, though. Someone's going to have to count the pictures until we get to the winning number."

"Uh, that someone would be you." Thor said, pointing in my direction. "This was your brainchild, I'm giving you full control."

"Touché." I nodded. "Fifty it is."

"That's not really fair to those who come after fifty, is it?" Adam asked.

"You want to count?" I held my phone out for him.

Adam shook his head and chomped on a piece of bacon. "It's all you, big guy."

"Looks like we have a winner." I held up my phone, showing Thor, Pauly, and Adam the number seventeen.

"Count it up. Who's the lucky winner?" Pauly asked.

I pulled my phone back and clicked on Instagram again. I counted to seventeen and stopped. An older woman smiled back at me. "What the hell?" I said.

"What? Let me see." Pauly grabbed my phone and winced. "What was she doing at our concert?"

Pauly passed the phone around the table so the other guys could see. "Here it says, 'Perks of being a house mom.'" Thor read the comment below the picture. "Looks like Carol Hall will be getting your 'undivided attention', Griff," he laughed.

Adam had just taken a drink and nearly sprayed Thor and Pauly, only clapping a hand over his mouth at the last minute. He swallowed and then burst into laughter. "House mom? Shit." He set his glass down and turned his body in my direction. He placed his hand on my shoulder and pressed his lips together before he spoke. "I didn't know what you were doing when you came up with that idea, but I'm glad it's working out for you, bud. Don't worry, I won't tell Erin." He patted my shoulder and turned back to face the table, laughing.

I rolled my eyes. "Whatever. It's just a week. Who knows? She may not even want the damn lessons." I shrugged. The contest had served its purpose…I got my text to Jillian.

Chapter Twelve

By the time auditions rolled around, I was already beat. It had been a long damn day. After breakfast with the guys, I went to work, spending the afternoon giving private guitar and bass lessons to wannabe teenage musicians who thought they were the second coming of Kurt Cobain. I already had the headache from hell and it was about to get worse.

Opening the back door to Fifth's, I pulled off my sunglasses and walked down the hall. I followed Adam's voice, stepping into the room Bax had set up for our auditions. Adam sat behind the kit tapping out eighths on the hats with his good hand.

"Do we really have to go through with this?" I asked, sliding a chair out from under a table so I could sit down. "Just play one-handed."

Adam silenced the cymbal, then raised his middle finger. "I'm not Rick Allen."

"Ain't that the truth," I mumbled, pulling my phone out of my pocket.

"You got a problem with me, Griff?" Adam shouted, smashing the cymbal and standing up.

Lifting my gaze from my phone to Adam, I refused to react to his temper tantrum.

"Leo Dane offers you a contract and all of a sudden you're some fucking rock 'n' roll god? Things are always good in Griffin's world, huh?" he shouted, walking to stand right in front of me.

"Excuse me?" I stood, glaring down at him. Once again my size came in handy. "I don't recall accepting Dane's offer. As a matter of fact, he wouldn't have made me a fucking offer if you hadn't decided to act like a dumbshit. This"—I gestured around the room, shoving my chest into his—"is all because you are a fucking idiot." If he knew what was good for him, he'd back the hell off.

"Whoa, boys!" Bax yelled, pushing between us. "Not in my bar. Griffin, take a walk. Adam, sit down."

I backed away and turned toward the door. Rounding the corner, I bumped into Thor, clipping his shoulder with mine.

"Dude? Where are you going?" he called after me.

"I need some air." I marched down the hall, not bothering to look back. Throwing the back door open, I kicked it wider with my foot. It flew against the brick wall outside and recoiled, almost snapping shut in my face. Catching it, I pushed it open again and stepped through.

Walking over to the side of the building, I pressed my back against the sun-scorched brick and looked skyward. Adam had no right to be pissed at me. I was not the one who had put Mine Shaft's future in jeopardy. I was so tired of his goddamned jealousy.

"Hey, man. Is there a band audition happening here?"

I turned my head in the direction of the screechy voice. A pimply-faced boy smiled at me, tapping sticks against his leg.

I sized him up. "How old are you?"

"Sixteen. Just got my driver's license yesterday." He grinned, flashing a mouth full of metal.

I shoved off the wall, rising to my full height, towering over the newly pubescent teen. "You play the drums?"

"Yeah." He held up his sticks and smiled wider. "My parents hate when I practice. I thought if I got a real gig, they'd take my music seriously. And it would totally increase my chances of scoring a hottie for the homecoming dance."

"Right," I grumbled. "Come on, auditions are inside."

The kid followed me to the audition room.

"Here's our first tryout, boys." I turned around and looked at him. "What's your name?"

"Derek," he replied.

Thor nodded. "Hey, Derek."

"Let's see what you got." Adam rounded the drum set and came to sit at the table with Thor and me.

"Cool." Derek lumbered to the drum set, taking up residence on the throne. "Uh, is there anything you want to hear?" His voice cracked.

Thor let out a low, irritated breath and sat up in his seat. "Play whatever you want. Just play something."

"Yeah. Uh-huh. OK," he said, nodding like an idiot. For a long minute, he fiddled with the cymbals, adjusting their heights and angles. When he seemed comfortable with the setup in front of him, he looked over at us and smiled. "This is one of my favorite beats," he offered as a precursor.

Derek tapped out a simple 5/4 pattern on the snare and toms, but struggled to keep the fifth beat steady with each repeat of the cadence. I looked to Adam, wondering if it was me or if he'd picked up on the kid's terrible sense of rhythm. Adam's face pulled together and his head nodded in time with the beat, trying to help the kid out with the bob of his head.

Over the years I'd become attuned to the drummer. As a bassist

I relied on the steady beat to be the backbone to my bass rhythms. Watching Derek attempt to rock out on Adam's high hats and throw a stick into the crash cymbal every now and then was painful. The only thing that made this audition worthwhile was that I was calling it over.

I held my hand high and shouted, "Thanks, Derek. That's good." I waited another beat and Derek kept on playing, oblivious to my voice. "Derek," I called louder. "That's enough!"

Derek plowed his stick through the crash cymbal and looked up. Sweat dripped down the sides of his face and his shoulders moved up and down from exertion. "Wow," he breathed, a metallic grin spreading across his face. "That was awesome."

Adam typed something on his iPad, not bothering to look up. "Thanks, Derek. You have a number we can reach you at? In case we need to get in touch with you?"

I sat back down beside Thor just as Derek got up and walked over to the table. "Uh, yeah." Derek set his sticks on the table and reached into his back pocket. Removing his wallet, he pulled a business card free and tossed it on the table.

Thor picked up the card and smirked, handing it over to me. "Derek's Drums" was printed across the top of store-bought perforated card stock. Along with his contact information, his home-made business card also sported a cartoon clip art image of a drum kit. Holding the card between my index and middle fingers, I passed it to Adam so he could type Derek's number into the iPad.

"Thanks, man," Adam said, holding the card back for him to take.

Derek waved his hands in protest. "You keep it. I've got tons." He smiled and picked up his sticks. "When do you think you'll make your decision?"

I shrugged. "Probably within the next day or two." Leo's voice popped into my head: *Forty-eight hours.* If every audition was as promising as Derek's, we were in some serious shit. Mine Shaft would never see the light of day.

"Cool." Derek saluted with his sticks and said, "Talk to you soon." As he headed for the door, the next starry-eyed teenager strutted into the room.

"Fuck me," Thor mumbled under his breath.

* * *

For three hours Adam, Thor, and I listened to a dozen and a half mediocre-to-downright-terrible drummers. By hour four Pauly had gotten off of work and joined us for another round of torture.

"I'll be right back," I said, standing up. "I'm gonna hit the head."

As I was on my way out the door, a petite redhead passed by me and entered the audition room. Her height reminded me of Jillian and for a second, I thought about turning around and heading back in there. If I knew my bandmates, she'd need some protection. They'd be all over her like cheap cologne. But I really needed to hit the john.

Taking large strides down the hall, I made it to the restroom and finished up quickly. By the time I returned to the audition room, the guys were circled around the poor girl like a pack of horny wolves.

"Why don't you give the lady some room?" I spoke loudly, walking over to their meet-and-greet circle.

"Thanks, man," the redhead said, acknowledging me with a nod. "But I can handle these douchebags."

I laughed, having not expected her bold comment. "It sounds like it."

"Griff," Adam said, "this is Stephanie." A dopey grin was plastered over his face.

I offered my hand and Stephanie smiled, shaking it. "Nice to meet you, Griff. It's Nee." She looked to Adam, stressing her nickname.

"Likewise, Nee," I said. I already liked this chick.

She let go of my hand, clapping hers together. "Well, guys, as much as I love all this cozy get-to-know-you slumber party shit, I'm here for a drum audition." Laying her hands on Thor's and Pauly's shoulders, she pushed them to the sides and made her way to the drum set.

Speechless, the four of us watched as the diminutive but hard-as-nails pixie sauntered her way to the throne.

Sitting down, she tinkered with the height of the seat and made some minor adjustments to the toms and cymbals.

"Holy shit. I'm in love," Adam muttered.

"Uh-huh," Pauly added, wistfully.

Shaking my head, I went to sit down. "You two are idiots." Thor followed me, but Pauly and Adam didn't move. They watched in awe, as if she were performing the best striptease they'd ever seen. "Guys, come on." I waved them over, irritated by their unprofessionalism.

As Pauly and Adam walked to the table, Nee didn't wait for a go-ahead from us, but instead ripped into a groove.

Owning the kit, she played hard. She knew her way around a drum set—a rock goddess sitting upon her throne. "Damn," I whispered to Thor.

"No shit. This chick is hard-core." Thor reached for the iPad, adding her name to our list.

For ten minutes Nee disappeared into her own world, rocking out a gorgeous beat. My fingers itched to pick up my bass and jam with her. She was seriously talented. Better than Adam, but I'd never tell him. By the time she finished, her skin glistened with a layer of sweat. Watching the way Pauly and Adam eyed her, I worried they might try to lick her.

Nee stood and walked over to us. I followed her lead, as did Thor and the two dumbasses. We met in front of the table. Adam regarded her the way a toddler would a lollipop and Pauly blurted, "Marry me."

Chuckling, Nee said, "I'm pretty sure my boyfriend would have a problem with that. But you're free to ask him."

"What's his number? I'll call him now," Adam challenged.

Nee pulled out her phone, made a few quick swipes across the screen, and handed it over to Adam. He studied the screen and looked back at Nee. "Your boyfriend is Keshawn Fischer? The MMA fighter Keshawn Fischer?"

"Yep." She nodded. "Want me to dial?"

Adam grinned and handed her phone back. The spell she'd held over him was broken. Thankfully, he knew when to back off. "He's a hell of a fighter."

"Yeah. He's pretty kick-ass." She grinned, glancing at the picture on her phone. "He's actually part of the reason I'm here," she continued. "There's a UFC training facility in Vegas. Keshawn wants to train there, so we're saving up as much as we can and heading for Vegas right before the New Year. I'm only looking for a part-time gig."

Was this girl for real? She looked the part, she was uber-talented, and she only needed a part-time gig? I was convinced she was an angel sent to rescue Mine Shaft from record label purgatory.

"Give us a minute?" I asked, motioning for the guys to join me in the hall.

"Sure." She nodded her approval and walked around the table, sitting down in Thor's vacated seat. She propped her feet on the table and leaned back in the chair, making herself comfortable.

The four of us walked into the hallway to make our deliberation seem more legit, even though I was sure everyone was on the same page. We'd found Adam's replacement.

Chapter Thirteen

Yes, everything's squared away." I shoved a hand through my hair, feeling nervous. I didn't usually get nervous, but since everyone was ready to climb into bed with Amphion Productions, there wasn't much left to do but seal the deal with Leo and sign the contract. I think my nerves were warranted.

Everything was falling into place. Nee had practiced with us for about a week and a half and was un-fucking-believable. The girl oozed talent. And while we pulled all-nighters, bringing Nee up to speed, my dad's lawyer friend looked over our contract.

It was time for Mine Shaft to move up to the big leagues.

"Great," Leo said over the speaker. "Let's meet at the studio in an hour. We'll get the technicalities finalized and you guys into the studio for a pre-prod session. I want to get a track sheet started."

"Cool." Pauly passed a coin over and under the knuckles of his right hand, something he did when he had a lot of nervous energy to let off. I was glad to see I wasn't the only one affected by this decision.

Nee cleared her throat. "Excuse me?" she corrected, her hands on her hips.

We all stared at Nee. In the short time we'd worked with her, we'd learned she didn't take shit off of anyone, and she didn't mince words. She was a straight shooter, not afraid to give someone a piece of her mind. Each one of us had been on the receiving end of one of Nee's verbal lashings.

Adam was still completely lovestruck. Even the promise of a beating from Keshawn Fischer didn't deter him from professing his undying love every time the girl played cross-rhythms and triplets in different time signatures.

Once Pauly learned of Nee's relationship status, he wasn't so enthusiastic about getting into her pants, but he still liked to rile her up. They got along like long-lost siblings. And then there was Thor. Thor's reaction to Nee surprised me the most. Typically he'd have been all over her, boyfriend or not—that never stopped him from a potential hookup. And Nee was definitely his type: tiny, curvy, and heavy on top. I knew he was still talking to that Harper chick, but I had yet to meet her. His disinterest in Nee meant that Harper was something special, and that was huge for Thor because he didn't do relationships.

Nee smacked her palms on the table and brought me back to the present. She leaned in close to the phone's speaker. "This band isn't just penises anymore, dude. At least until Drummer Dumbass is healed."

"Ah yes, thank you, Nee. *And lady*," he revised.

Smiles went around the table. "That's what I thought," Nee laughed. "I may not be a permanent fixture, but while I'm on that throne, you're going to know it."

"Yes, ma'am," Leo said.

"See you in a few, Leo," I replied, ready to get things moving.

"Nice to have you aboard…gentlemen."

The way he said "gentlemen" didn't possess any of his usual "all business" intonation. He almost sounded playful. And again, he'd neglected to include our saucy dash of estrogen.

Nee cocked her head. "Dude!" she yelled.

"Nee, you're going to be so much fun to work with." He laughed this time. "I'm just shitting you."

"Bring it, mister," Nee challenged. She pounded her fist into the palm of her hand, but the smile on her face made her appear less intimidating.

Still laughing, Leo said, "See you soon, Nee," then ended the call.

"Well, gentlemen," Thor said, staring right at Nee, smirking, "I don't know about you, but I'm ready to sign a fucking recording contract." His hand hit the table and a round of whoops hit the air.

Nee moved her index finger back and forth in front of her face as she said, "Thor, Thor, Thor." She sauntered around the table, swinging her hips seductively. *Damn, is this chick for real?* They did not grow women like her in the Midwest.

Stretching onto her tiptoes, she looped her arm around Thor's neck. Despite their significant height difference (which reminded me of the way Jillian and I looked standing side by side) Nee sidled up close to him, pouting her lips. She crooked a finger and batted her black lashes, beckoning him closer.

Thor complied warily, unsure of what she was about to do. He leaned in.

In a breathy, come-hither whisper we could all hear, she put her mouth to his ear, licking her lips. "I've got more balls than any of you douchebags, combined. Don't forget it." She dropped her arm from around his neck and smacked his ass. "All right, ladies," she said, with too much enthusiasm. "Let's get the fuck out of here."

The look of shock on Thor's face was laughable. I didn't doubt that Nee had some serious *mucho grande cojones*. She was a force to be reckoned with and a breath of fresh air for Mine Shaft. She'd only been with us for a little longer than a week and I was already going to miss her when she decided to pack up and move to Vegas.

"Damn, Nee," Adam said, "I've never been so turned on and insulted at the same time."

"No shit," Thor grunted, grabbing his phone off the table. He reached for the doorknob and pulled it open. "Ladies first," he said, ushering Nee through the doorway.

"Now you're getting it." She smiled up at him and winked.

If anything, Nee's presence was about to make Mine Shaft a hell of a lot more interesting.

Chapter Fourteen

After all the paperwork was signed, and we were officially under Amphion's wing, Leo set us up with the studio engineer to get our track sheet started. We had been playing for almost two hours when Leo stepped back into the recording room. He held up his hand, a gesture meant to silence us.

I laid a hand across the strings and Thor followed suit. Mid-strike, Nee opted for flipping her stick instead of making contact with the tom. She caught it cleanly and gave Leo her full attention just as Pauly let up off the keys.

"That's it for today, everyone. Luis has enough to work with." Leo smiled. "We're working on the track sheet this weekend. Next week I want Nee and Griffin in studio. We'll be putting your tracks down first." Turning toward us, Leo pointed his finger at Nee and then me, raising his eyebrow like a stern father. "Be prepared to put in a full day's work. Six…maybe eight hours each day."

Shit. Where does that leave time for school? I'd skipped class that day because signing a recording contract was a pretty big deal, but skipping indefinitely was going to be an issue. Rock star and college student didn't make great bedfellows.

I lowered my bass, careful not to hit the mic in front of me. There had to be some sort of backup plan when the musicians were also going to school. "Is it possible to record around our work and school schedules?" I asked, not just for me, but for everyone.

Leo shook his head. "Sorry, man. This is your first priority. You're in the big leagues now. Everything else will have to fit in around the band's commitments."

I nodded. "Got it." He was right. I was a professional musician now. This was my *career*, not a hobby. Whatever plans my parents had for me would have to wait. *But how to break the news to them?*

Leo clapped his hands together. "Go on, get out of here. See you two on Monday." Again he pointed to Nee and me.

"You got it, boss man." Nee played through the pass that had been cut off earlier and struck the crash hard.

We broke down our set and got our shit packed into the van. Pauly threw the back door shut and spun around, throwing a fist in the air. "Party time, motherfuckers!" he shouted and then looked at Nee, having forgotten she was there. "No offense." He bowed his head apologetically.

Nee smiled and patted his bicep. "He's right, where's the party, motherfuckers?" Her bright-green eyes sparkled in the fading sunlight.

Pauly shrugged and hooked his arm around her shoulders. "Yeah, what she said."

I was down to party, but Thor and I didn't have the room, so I kept my mouth shut.

"What about Fifth's?" Nee suggested.

"I like it." I leaned against the van, waiting for everyone else to respond. I was ready to get shit-faced, be loud, and hopefully have a moment to call Jillian. God, I missed her.

"Fifth's. Cool. Let's hit it," Thor added. He swung the van's keys around his finger, making his way to the driver's side door. "Who's riding shotgun?"

"Um, that'd be me." Nee raised her hand and gave a little skip on her way around to the passenger door.

I nodded with a salute to the rest of the crew and walked to my bike. "See you there."

I kicked my leg over the seat and put the key in the ignition, the bike rumbling to life. Squeezing the throttle, I leaned to the right and picked my feet up off the ground, ripping out of the parking lot, past Adam and Pauly.

Traffic was light on the freeway, and I made it to Illinois in record time. Fifth's was a different story. The small parking lot was full, which forced me to park a block down the street.

Pulling into a parking space between a Porsche Cayenne and a beat-up F-150, I killed the engine and stepped off. As soon as both my feet hit the sidewalk, my phone buzzed in my pocket. Pulling it out, I saw *Dad* spelled across the top of the screen. I tapped the green button and put the phone to my ear.

"Hey, Pop."

"Hey, Son. You have your big meeting today?" he asked gruffly.

Dad wasn't a conversationalist. For twenty-plus years he'd coached high school football. He was more comfortable barking orders than shooting the shit.

The day I started high school, Dad couldn't wait to get me on the field. I went to a few practices and got my ass handed to me, along with several organs, it felt like.

As a freshman I still hadn't grown into my body. I was tall and lanky, freakishly so. I was better suited for basketball—a sport I enjoyed playing far more than football—but since Dad was the coach, I wasn't given the choice. To Dad there was only one sport and that was football.

It nearly killed him when I quit the team to start a band. If Jillian hadn't been there to smooth things over, he'd still be giving me the silent treatment. Jillian had the unique ability to make people see things differently, to accept someone else's choices. No matter what I chose to do, she was always there to support me.

Though Dad accepted my choice to quit the team, disappointment bled from his eyes like tears every time he drove me to Thor's house to practice. I hated feeling like I'd let him down, but I knew I'd never make it as a football player. In the end I was sure Dad realized the same thing. I guess that's why he gave up the fight when I traded the pigskin for a Rickenbacker. I saved him from having to cut his own son during team tryouts.

"Your big meeting was today, right?" he asked again.

"Uh, yeah." I stuffed the keys to the bike in my jacket and headed down the sidewalk toward Fifth's. "Everything's said and done. We signed the contract this morning."

"So what happens now?" he asked. He sounded genuinely curious, which wasn't really like Dad. Mom asked the questions for the two of them.

I reached for the door, pinning my phone to my ear with my shoulder as I walked into the bar. "We had a preproduction session today, with the sound engineer. I start recording Monday, along with Nee, the girl who's filling in for Adam." I glanced at my watch, making my way to the bar, wondering why the place was so crowded at four o'clock in the afternoon.

"Well, that's great news, Son!" Dad's enthusiasm was good to hear. "Here's your mom, she wants to talk."

I could hear Mom's impatient voice in the background as Dad passed her the phone.

Bax smiled and threw a rag over his shoulder. "Hey, Griff. You alone?" He glanced at the door and then back at me.

I shook my head and held up my index finger. Through the shuffling noises on the other end of the line, I shouted, "Mom, one sec." I pulled the phone away from my ear to give Bax an answer.

"They're right behind me. We're celebrating tonight, Bax. We signed our recording contract."

"No shit?" He pulled the rag from his shoulder and snapped it on the bar top. "Drinks on the house, my friend. What'll it be?"

"Griffin!" I heard Mom shout through the phone.

I picked it back up in a hurry, just in time to hear Mom saying, "What's happening? Dad won't tell me anything. Are you still there?"

I swallowed. "Yes, Ma, I'm still here. Sorry about that, trying to talk to too many people at once. Mine Shaft has a record deal," I said, smiling.

"Ahhhhhh!" she screamed. I pulled the phone away from my ear, wincing. "Oh, Griffin, sweetie, that's wonderful news! We have to celebrate tonight. Come over to the house and I will make your favorite dinner. Have you told Ren yet? What about Jillian?" Mom went from one question to the next, barely pausing to breathe.

"You and Dad are the first to know. I just left the studio. Haven't had time to call anyone yet."

"I'll call Ren and tell her to come over, but I won't tell her your news. I'll let you do that.
Get your butt over here, I'm making your favorite, lasagna."

"Mom!" I shouted. It was nearly impossible to get her attention when she started rambling on and on like that.

"What?" she hollered, stunned by the sharp bite of my voice.

"I'm sorry, Ma, I can't tonight. We're all celebrating at Fifth's."

"Oh, of course you're busy tonight. How about tomorrow night, then?"

I sat at the bar, waiting until everyone showed up. "Yeah, tomorrow works better."

"Tomorrow, then," she continued. "I'm so proud of you! I'll have dinner ready around five thirty."

"Thanks. Love you, Ma. Gotta go." Bax set a beer down in front of me.

"Don't forget to tell Jillian the good news. I bet she's dying to find out how things went." I was fairly certain Jillian was going out of her mind waiting to hear from me.

"I won't forget. She's next on my call list." My parents loved Jillian like a daughter. They opened their hearts and home to her. Like Mom, I wished she were here. More than anyone else, Jillian was the one I wanted to tell in person. I wanted to see the look on her face. I wanted to wrap my arms around her so fucking bad, it hurt. But I'd have to settle for FaceTime. "Oh, Ma?"

"Yeah?"

"You're making the Buffalo chicken lasagna, right?" I thought she was, but I wanted to make sure. My mom's culinary skills were impressive, but her Buffalo chicken lasagna was by far my favorite.

"Well, duh," she said.

"Ma, only kids say that." I chuckled, taking a sip of my beer.

"Oh, knock it off and go have fun with your friends."

Laughing, I said, "Yes, ma'am. Bye, Ma. Love you."

"I love you, too, baby boy. See you soon. Oh, and tell Jillian I said hi. It's been over a week since we last talked."

Huh? Jillian must be really swamped at school. Even Mom was having a difficult time keeping in touch. "I will. See you tomorrow."

"Oh, Griff," Mom said, right before I was about to hang up. "Are you still seeing that Erin girl?"

Oh, shit. With everything going on today, I'd completely forgotten about Erin. "Um, yeah," I said. "Why?"

"You should bring her over. And any of the guys, if they aren't busy. You know I always make enough food for an army."

That was true. My mom didn't know how to cook small. "I'll see what everyone's doing."

"Wonderful. Be safe tonight. I'll see you tomorrow." She disconnected the call.

I took a long pull on my beer. *Damn, that tastes good.* With my thumb I scrolled through my favorites list. I hovered over Jillian's name. A pull like gravity had me ready to tap on her name. I wanted to tell her my good news, hear her voice. But then I saw Erin's name a few entries below. Shouldn't I tell my girlfriend first?

Forcing my thumb downward, I hit her name. After a couple of rings, she answered.

"Well? What's the news?" she drawled excitedly.

"It's official." I took another drink and looked around the teeming room. "We signed."

"Hot damn!" she squealed. "How exciting is this? I...I just...I'm just so happy for you, Griffin!"

"Thanks, Peach." I swallowed another gulp. "I'm up at Fifth's. You busy? We're celebrating tonight."

"Hell yeah. I'm on my way."

"Cool. See you soon."

I hung up with Erin, ready to give Jillian a call, just as the guys came rolling in. I'd have to call her later. I slipped the phone into my pocket and picked up my beer. "Took long enough. I started without you."

Nee came over and snatched the beer from my hand. "Well, we'll just have to catch up then." She threw it back, draining half of it.

Behind her an enormous black man had his hands at her waist. He must be Keshawn. I raised my hand in greeting and nodded in his direction, before I scolded his girlfriend for stealing my drink. "Damn, girl," I groaned. "I was working on that."

Keshawn nodded back and pulled Nee closer, snaking his arms around her waist. "Work faster," she jeered.

"Gotta watch out for this one." He kissed her cheek. "She's feisty."

I laughed, snatching my beer from her hand. "That's an understatement." I spun on the stool and offered my hand to Keshawn. "Griffin Daniels."

He reached around Nee. "Keshawn. Nice to meet you, man." He gripped my hand and shook it enthusiastically. "My girl's real excited about this gig. Says you guys are cool."

Nee rounded on him. "Dude!" she shouted. "You're going to ruin my rep."

Cupping a hand around his mouth, he pretended to whisper, "Don't let her fool you. She's all piss and vinegar on the outside, sweet as candy on the inside."

I raised an eyebrow. "I'll remember that." Over my shoulder I waved Bax in our direction. "Yo, Bax." I lifted my beer to get his attention. "We need a round over here." He acknowledged me and went to work gathering our drinks.

From the corner of my eye, I could see Nee trying to land a solid punch to Keshawn's bicep, doing little damage.

I stood and drained what was left of my beer, noticing Thor had grabbed an open table. "Come on, you two." I tilted my chin in Thor's direction. "Thor's looking lonely over there."

Beside me Nee was leaned in close to Keshawn, giggling. *Giggling*. I hadn't thought she had it in her to giggle…at least in public.

I led the way, with Nee towing Keshawn behind her. The three of us pulled out chairs and plopped our asses into the seats. From under heavy lids, Thor stared at us. "Can I help you?" His phone was pressed to his ear.

"Harper?" I smirked. I loved giving him shit about her. He was so far out of his comfort zone.

"I'll call you later." He nodded. "Yeah. You too."

Bax came over with a trayful of drinks, setting them down between us. "For my boys," he called.

"And girl," Nee added politely.

"And girl," he corrected himself, patting her on the head as he returned to the bar.

We divided the drinks up and relaxed, letting reality soak in…we were contracted recording artists. A dream come true.

"Hey, Rock Star." A breathy twang tickled my ear, followed by a pair of arms twining around my neck.

I glanced up. Erin stood over me. "Hey, Peach."

She stepped around my chair and sat on my lap, looping her arm around my shoulders. Pauly and Adam joined the rest of us at the table. The whole gang was here. And then my heart clenched…not *everyone*.

Erin's closeness suddenly felt *too close*. I wanted Jillian here.

Stretching behind me, I clamped my hand on a chair at a nearby table and dragged it over. With a pat on Erin's back, I motioned for her to slide over. She complied, sliding off my legs and onto the chair.

"Hi, I'm Erin," she said, extending her hand to Nee.

"Nee. This is Keshawn." She thumbed over her shoulder.

"Nee, how'd you and Mr. Fischer meet?" Pauly asked, breaking up the introductions.

Keshawn covered his mouth, failing to stifle a laugh. "Good luck getting that story out of her."

Nee threw an elbow into his ribs.

He put a bottle to his mouth. "What?"

I enjoyed watching the two of them interact. Their easy comfort with each other had me thinking of Jillian again.

"Start talking, girl," I commanded, leaning back in my chair to get comfortable. Erin inched her chair closer and put her hand on my knee, stroking slowly up and down the length of my thigh.

As of late she'd been pushing to get closer, doing all she could to seduce me. But every time we had the opportunity to take our relationship further, something stopped me. The last few times had been the worst. We'd be going at each other, clothes shed, fingernails scratching down my back, her legs wrapped around me...then all of a sudden, it wasn't Erin beneath me, it was Jillian. Jillian's teeth biting...her lips sucking, and...

That's when I'd slam on the brakes.

Erin was feeling it, too. I could tell. The more I pulled away, the harder she pressed. She wasn't an easy woman to say no to.

When a beer bottle hit the table, I snapped back to the conversation.

"Can I show 'em the pictures?" Keshawn asked.

At the prospect of pictures featuring Nee, Adam livened up. "Pictures? What kind of pictures? I want to see pictures."

Keshawn dug in his pocket and brought out his phone. Quickly tapping something, he pulled up a picture and turned the phone around, giving us a better look. A chick wearing a blue string bikini and red fuck-me heels stood at the center of a ring, holding a sign above her head.

Nee's head hit the table with a thud. "I'm ruined," she mumbled.

Adam grabbed Keshawn's phone and flipped through the other

pictures. "Fuck. Me." His mouth dropped open. "You were a MMA ring bunny?"

"Oh, yeah. And a damn hot one, too," Keshawn growled.

Nee lifted her head and glared at him. "Don't even think you're getting a blow job tonight."

Erin sprayed her beer, quickly clamping a hand over her mouth. "Sorry," she choked, wiping the back of her hand across her mouth. "Went down the wrong tube." She laughed nervously.

I rubbed a hand over her back. "All right?"

She nodded and took another drink.

"Mighty pretty there, Nee." Even Thor jumped at the chance to ruffle her feathers a little.

Nee flipped him off. "OK, douchebags, the hazing ritual's over. Yep, Stephanie Hamilton was a ring bunny. It paid the bills. But that chick is long gone. Don't forget it." With each sentence she pointed at us, driving home the point.

"Thor, was that Harper on the phone?" I couldn't resist getting him riled up, too.

Thor sat back and took a drink.

"When do we get to meet the girl who has tamed 'the Hammer'?" I asked dramatically, using the nickname he'd given himself in high school.

He shrugged. "I need to get this relationship shit figured out before I bring her around you asshats." He spit the word "relationship." "I'm out of my league with this girl."

Pauly landed a heavy hand to Thor's back. "A girlfriend?"

"Maybe?" Thor nodded. "Probably."

"Ha! Never thought I'd see the day when Thorin Kline went and got himself a girlfriend." Pauly laughed.

He sneered. "Me either."

"That's great, man. I'm happy for you." I held up my bottle of

Schlafly. I looked around the table; I'd been through so much with this crew. Things were changing so fast…we were changing. "To new beginnings," I said.

Joining in, everyone clinked their bottles together. "To new beginnings!"

Chapter Fifteen

Three hundred and ninety-eight...three hundred and ninety-nine...four hundred. My abdominal muscles protested as I pulled myself off the sweaty mat. As I reached for my water bottle, my abs screamed. After a lightning round of four hundred crunches, they were pissed. Biting my lip, I pushed through the pain and stood, wiping sweat from my face with my bicep. Breathing hard, I drained my water bottle and then bent over to pick up my phone and keys.

In the month since we'd signed with Amphion, I hadn't been able to find a balance between my personal life and Mine Shaft. Everything was Mine Shaft. Hours spent at the studio, gig after gig, rehearsals, press junkets, and now Amphion had started talking about a spring tour. Hell, I barely made it to class, which pissed my parents off considerably.

I was thankful for the couple of hours of gym time I squeezed in each day. It was the only time I could think. Or not, as the case may be.

Today was a day I wished I could turn off my brain. I didn't want to think. But even after a two-hour workout, I still couldn't stop mulling over the last e-mail I'd gotten from Jillian. I tried to work my body to a point where all I could concentrate on was the burn in my muscles. But Jillian's words, coupled with our distance, burned more.

She'd written a lengthy message about struggling to find her groove at school. The e-mail had reeked of self-doubt. I wanted more than anything to take her by the shoulders, stare her in the eyes, and tell her she was ridiculous. The raw talent that girl possessed was mind-boggling. She could take a cardboard box and turn it into something runway-worthy. But, being so far away, I couldn't do that. I was limited to words, instead of actions—something I was not used to when it came to her. Not to mention that her schedule and mine were polar opposites. When she was free to talk, I was working, and vice versa. We were forced into an unfamiliar routine of e-mails, texts, and somber voice messages—always playing phone tag. I never had liked playing tag, and I loathed it now.

Weaving between the rows of Nautilus equipment, I made my way to the door. I had an hour and a half before I needed to pick Erin up for the Amphion party tonight. Leo was excited to show us off to the higher-ups at the record label. He'd wanted to host a party in our honor sooner, but we'd held him off; Nee needed time to get comfortable with our music. Leo gave her a month. We rehearsed our asses off, leaving only a few hours for sleep, work, and school. Every other aspect of our lives was filled with Mine Shaft obligations. We weren't individuals anymore, but fractions of a whole.

A cool fall breeze blew across my damp skin as I pushed open the door. It was days like this that made owning a motorcycle worth it. I anticipated the ride home.

As I crossed the parking lot, I shot Erin a quick text, *See you at*

7. After two steps I already had a reply: *Can't wait. Soooooooooooo excited!! :)*

I shook my head at her fondness for the letter "o." Erin was yet another casualty of Mine Shaft's newfound success. I didn't have much free time, which meant she and I didn't have many opportunities to go out. My new lifestyle wasn't conducive to fostering a new romantic endeavor, and Erin was getting the short end of the stick. I didn't have the time or energy to worry about our relationship at the moment. Honestly, my heart wasn't in it. I knew it, and I was pretty sure Erin did, too. That's why she tried so hard, for the both of us. At least the party tonight would get her off my back for a couple of days.

Stowing my gym pass and wallet, I mounted my bike and started her up. She purred to life between my legs, and I gave her a good rev before pulling out of the parking space.

Traffic was light, and I was able to sail through town. The wind blew across my face and through my hair, quickly drying the sweat from my body. I relished the twenty minutes of travel time between the gym and my apartment. If anyone tried to call, I couldn't hear the phone over the roar of the engine. It was just me, the wind, and my bike—a blissful trio.

* * *

Arriving home, I showered quickly and was ready for Amphion's party. Looking at the clock, I saw I had enough time to give Jillian a call before I needed to be at Erin's place. Jillian and I hadn't had a meaningful conversation in more than two weeks, and it was wearing on me, bleeding into my music. I was so sick of writing shit. I needed to talk to her, hear her voice. Find my inspiration again.

She brought so much light and color into my life; it was no wonder things seemed so bleak right now. Damn, I missed her.

Resting my back against the headboard of my bed, I pressed Jillian's name and listened to a series of rings. I closed my eyes and let out a deep breath, ready for the next round of tag to begin. "Hi, it's Jillian. Leave a message."

I squeezed my fingers around the phone, resisting the urge to launch it across the room. I bit down on my lower lip and yanked the phone away from my ear, ending the call. "God damn it, Bean. Where are you?" I shouted.

I kicked my legs off the side of the bed and stood, sliding the phone into my back pocket, walking out of my room. In the hallway I knocked on Thor's door.

"Yeah?" He opened the door and poked his head out.

I kicked the doorframe with my boot. "I'm heading out," I said in a low growl. I hadn't meant to sound pissed off, but I couldn't help it.

He threw a quick look over his shoulder and turned back to me. "For the party? Already?" He opened the door just enough to fit his body through and closed it quickly. He was wearing only boxers, and I knew I'd interrupted something.

"Shit. I'm sorry, man. I'll leave alone." I turned toward the stairs.

"I'll meet you there," he said, rubbing his shaved head.

I stopped and looked over my shoulder. "Bringing Harper tonight?" I nodded to his closed door.

"Maybe." He glanced over his shoulder.

I held up my hands. "I'll be on my best behavior."

Thor chuckled. "It's not you I'm worried about, man."

With a nod I headed for the stairs. "Later."

* * *

Amphion had spared no expense. The party rocked. The old Victorian mansion and sprawling estate offered a nice counterpoint to Mine Shaft's alt-rock sound filtering through the state-of-the-art sound system. The house belonged to one of the Amphion investors. From the looks of it, Amphion artists were making someone a hell of a lot of money.

Yet despite the vastness the mansion offered, I still felt like the walls were closing in. It was imperative that I talk to Jillian. In my current mood, someone was bound to get hurt.

I pressed my lips to Erin's ear and whispered, "I'll be right back." I kissed her cheek and excused myself from the conversation we were having with Leo.

"Everything OK?" she asked.

I nodded. "Just need some fresh air."

"I'll go with you." She reached for my hand, but didn't catch it before I pushed it through my hair.

"No, stay. Enjoy the party." I touched her shoulder and smiled at Leo. "I'll be back in a minute."

"You sure?" She pressed close, concern hiding her usual smile.

"Yeah."

"OK." The corners of her lips turned up in a halfhearted smile. "I'll be right here when you get back."

"I'll keep her company," Leo chimed in.

"Sounds good." I nodded, regarding him. "Be back in a few." I planted a quick kiss on her cheek and turned to navigate my way through the suits.

I walked through the crowded house and out onto the deck in the back. The sun was just about to set below the horizon. A stiff wind blew through the trees, stripping the last of the leaves from the branches.

Through the rustle of the leaves, a few lonely cicadas filled the early evening with a song. I exhaled. Being here tonight, I wished more than anything that Jillian were, too. We'd always talked about the day Mine Shaft would hit it big, how we'd celebrate. I'd never dreamed I'd be celebrating without her. It felt wrong on so many levels.

I glanced behind me. The glow of the party's lights filtered through the glass patio doors. Dozens of strangers had vied for my attention all night, kissing my ass, in order to keep Mine Shaft happy and make more money for the already well-off producers. Hell, a few of the producers didn't even try to hide the fact that they would have been happier if I'd signed as a solo artist. Regardless, none of the pomp and circumstance inside the mansion meant shit to me. All I wanted was to hear Jillian's voice. To tell her everything.

To have her here.

I tapped the toe of my boot against the stair railing and pressed Jillian's name on my phone for the second time tonight. I willed her to pick up.

"Hi, it's Jillian. Leave a message."

Defeated and worried as hell, I closed my eyes and waited for the beep this time. "Hey, Bean. Sorry I didn't leave a message earlier. I just get so tired of hearing your voice message instead of you. Call me. I need to talk to you." I pressed "End" and rested my elbows on the railing.

I did need to talk to her. With Amphion getting the ball rolling with a spring tour, I had a huge decision to make…one that could jeopardize my relationship with my parents. They were supportive of my music as long as it didn't interfere with what they felt was more important…school. If the tour was green-lit, we'd head out in May, which meant I'd have a legit reason to quit school. Which also meant I'd let my parents down. I knew what I wanted, but I didn't know if it was the right thing. I needed Jillian's perspective…her guidance.

"Hey, everything good?"

Behind me Erin's accent drowned out the mating call of the cicadas. I turned and watched her close the patio door.

No, everything wasn't good. I shook my head. "I still can't get ahold of Jillian."

Her heeled boots clicked a steady beat on the deck. "Seems like she's adjusting well to college life, if you ask me."

I didn't ask. A flare of anger kindled at my center. *Why is she out here?* I'd told her to stay inside.

Erin nudged me with her shoulder. "I'm sure she's out with her roommate or at a study session."

"Yeah." I forced myself to believe her words.

Erin didn't say anything else. We stood side by side on the deck and gave the cicadas a chance to drown the awkward tension. I knew Erin was trying her best to be comforting, but she didn't understand the connection Jillian and I had…what we'd been through in the last twelve years. She was my *best friend.* I needed her right now. But more than anything, I needed to know she was all right. And playing phone tag was shit.

Erin turned toward me, lifted my arm, and fit herself to my side. I flashed her a quick smile. A fake smile. "Come on, lighten up." She pressed, jostling me. "Jillian's fine. You're missing out on a great party in there."

"Not really into partying right now."

Erin sighed heavily and pulled away. Turning to face me head on, she crossed her arms and stared me down. "I'm trying here, Griffin. I'm trying to understand what it is that you have with her.

But I don't get it. She's been gone a little over a month and all you've done is sulk."

Erin's ice-blue eyes and cold words stung. I didn't expect her to understand my relationship with Jillian. Hell, since Jillian kissed me, I'd been trying to figure it out myself. Now that she was gone, I didn't know what I wanted.

Wrong. Yes I did. But I couldn't have what I wanted.

I challenged Erin, returning her stare. I knew she was waiting for an apology, or reassurance that everything was all right between us. But I couldn't offer any consolations. I knew I was being an ass, but right now…at this very moment…all I wanted was to hear Jillian's fucking voice. Jillian was all that mattered.

"I'll be inside," she said. She left without giving me a second glance.

Yep. I deserved that. I was being a dick, but the worst part was, I didn't care.

"Fuck." I walked down the stairs and out into the yard. Lyrics to a song itched in the back of my mind, something about being lost in the dark. I envisioned the darkness as a living, breathing creature—a thing that swallowed memories and cries for help, until there was nothing left for it to consume but the souls trapped within it. I had to laugh. Since late August, my songwriting had taking on a much darker tone.

Erin was right. I needed to lighten the fuck up or no one would buy a Mine Shaft album.

Skirting the perimeter of the yard, where the forest lined the freshly mown grass, I turned and made my way along the side of the house. Inside, the sound system's bass pounded, sending vibrations through the walls and across the yard. I could feel it. It's what I loved most about the bass—the way it got under my skin. The music fused with every cell of my body, while my heart pumped, keeping it alive. I lived off of that feeling, like my heart couldn't beat without the force of the music behind it. In a lot of ways, Jillian had the same effect on me. She made me feel alive. I hid it well, but without her I was sinking beneath the weight of the recording contract, school, and Erin. I couldn't breathe anymore.

I made my way toward the front of the house, still concentrating on the faint thump of the sound system. Following the walkway to the porch, I made the conscious decision to go back inside before I pissed anyone else off.

The second I opened the door, Pauly shouted, "Where the fuck have you been? We've been looking all over for you."

"I needed some air." I hooked my thumb over my shoulder and pushed past him, through the doorway.

Pauly stared at me, holding a beer in one hand and an electrical cord in the other. "What the hell are you doing?" I asked.

"We're setting up. Here, help me with this." He thrust the cord into my hand. "Follow me." He turned, expecting me to comply, but I didn't.

"We can't. Nee's not here yet."

Pauly turned around slowly and swung his arm around my neck, careful not to spill his beer. "Nee just got here, and now the producers want their show."

"Damn." I wasn't in the right frame of mind to play.

"Come on." Pauly lifted his arm off of me and held his beer high. "Welcome to the world of corporate music, Griffin, my man. They say, 'Play,' we say, 'How loud?'"

"Yo, Pauly, what's the holdup?" Thor asked, coming around the corner. "We need that extension cord. Glad you could join us." Thor walked over and yanked the cord away from me. "You going to help, or what?"

I closed my eyes and shoved my fingers through my hair. Sucking in a deep breath, I let it out slowly, trying my damnedest to be professional. It was time to show these rich assholes what Mine Shaft was made of.

"Fuck it," I said, beating a path to the room where all the investors and producers mingled. "Let's do this."

* * *

I closed my eyes, listening as the drums helped steady my bass line. With the mic at my lips, I didn't concentrate on anything but the music.

I let it override my system.

Sweat rolled down my neck. My fingers walked over the strings of my bass. My body absorbed every note.

Nee gave one final thump to the bass drum, and the lifeblood of the song vibrated throughout the room even after we finished playing. The small crowd of wealthy record producers erupted into applause. I looked to the guys and Nee, making eye contact with each one of them, and I smiled. No matter how stressed I was, music always had a way of setting me straight…just like Jillian.

"Thank you," I said into the mic. I was out of breath.

Leo Dane pushed his way through the audience and came to stand beside me. He leaned close to the microphone. "The future of Amphion Productions," he said, clapping louder. Pride oozed from his words.

I grinned, tossing the wet strands of hair off my forehead with a flick of my head. *The future of Amphion Productions. The future?* We had a lot riding on us.

"Mine Shaft," Leo shouted. The rich suits whistled and

whooped. It was actually comical seeing a bunch of rich old men pretending to be teenagers.

As I soaked in the sounds of the appreciative crowd, my eyes scanned the room, looking for Erin. Our eyes met, and I mouthed the words, "I'm sorry."

A subdued smile pulled at the corners of her lips. She was careful not to give me a full one. I'd have to work for that. I needed to make it up to her. I had been a dick outside. Never once had I considered her feelings when it came to what Jillian and I had. As much as I'd tried to explain to Erin that Jillian and I were nothing more than very close friends, I was sure our relationship looked to be something more to an outsider. But who was I kidding? There was something more, I just refused to let it happen.

I was ready to leave. I needed to make things right with Erin. She was a kick-ass girl who deserved so much more than she was getting from me. Setting my bass into the gig bag, I turned to the microphone so I could wrap up this celebration and take my girlfriend home.

"We'd like to thank Amphion for this opportunity. We're happy to be part of the family and we're ready to rock!" I shouted, and another thunderous round of applause filled the house.

I stepped away from the mic and made my way through the crowd. Strangers shook my hand and patted my back, but I didn't stop until I reached Erin.

When I was two feet from holding her in my arms, my phone beeped, signaling a new voice message. Still pushing through the crush of people, I pulled my phone out and looked at the missed call. Staring at Jillian's name, without a second thought, I knew who I wanted at my side.

Chapter Sixteen

With my ass parked in a chair in the back row of the econ lecture hall, I tapped a quiet beat on the small desktop with my pencil. Down front, Professor Dewley rambled on about numerical representations of preferences. I listened to the lecture and took notes, but my mind kept wandering back to the argument Erin and I had had last night.

October had been a good month for us. November...not so much. When I mentioned traveling to Rhode Island for Thanksgiving, she'd thrown an all-out temper tantrum. I'd never seen anything like it, and I certainly hadn't been expecting her reaction.

I was trying to make things work with her. She was fun, kind, and drop-dead gorgeous. But with each passing day, I knew I was grasping at nonexistent heartstrings. Erin wasn't who I wanted. I was being unfair to her by not ending things. If I was honest with myself, I knew why I kept Erin around. With the cover of a girlfriend, no one tried to push Jillian on me. It kept me honest and Jillian safely on track to following her dreams. She didn't need me derailing something she'd wanted and waited for her whole life.

Professor Dewley waved a long pointing stick in his hand and tapped it against the ancient chalkboard at the front of the room. The two-sided board teetered and threatened to roll over to the side he hadn't written on. "This is important, people. Make sure you have it written down. It will be on the test next week."

I was jotting down the notes he'd pointed out when my phone buzzed in my pocket. I left my pencil on the notebook and pulled it free, my heart giving an extra thump when I saw Jillian's picture and name on the screen.

Standing up, I answered the call and walked toward the glowing exit sign. "Jillibean!" I shouted a little too loudly, but I didn't care. I pushed through the door, unable to contain the smile that spread across my face. I missed her so much my body ached, literally. The Jillian-size hole that had been produced in my life two months ago had festered to the point that it just fucking hurt. Although it had only been four days since we'd last talked, it felt like an eternity.

"Jillibean?" I said again, still waiting to hear her voice. "Jillian, you're scaring the shit out of me. Say something," I demanded. My heart beat hard against my ribs. Something was wrong.

"I'm…here," she croaked.

I paced up and down the sidewalk, taking long strides in an attempt to keep from getting on my bike and driving to Rhode Island right that second. "What's wrong?"

"I just wanted to hear your voice."

She was too quiet. I knew this girl too well, and I could tell she was hiding something. "That's bullshit. I can tell something's wrong." I pulled in a deep breath, trying to remain calm. Jillian didn't need me freaking out on her. "Just tell me what it is, so I can help you."

I could hear her deep breaths on the other end, followed by the words I feared the most. "I hurt myself."

I sank onto the bench near the edge of the sidewalk. Terrible images of the day I found Jillian covered in blood and nearly dead in her bathroom flooded my vision.

I pulled in a long breath. She needed me calm right now. I had to pull myself together, for her sake. "How did you hurt yourself?"

Sounding like a robot, she recounted the events that had led to this phone call. "In the studio, I was cutting fabric…I sliced my finger."

I hadn't realized I had been holding my breath that whole time, but a long whoosh of air escaped my lungs, passing loudly over my lips. I ran my free hand through my hair, clutching a fistful, giving myself something to hold on to. If I could have stood, I would have, but the fact that she was hurt and I wasn't there with her was a stronger punch to the gut than one of the guys nailing me with his fist.

I drew in another breath, slowly letting it out, giving the oxygen time to make it to my brain. I needed a level head right now. She needed me to be strong…to help her. I'd done it once, I could do it again.

I would do it again. *I'd do any goddamned thing for this girl.*

"It's OK, Bean," I said on an exhalation. "It was an accident, right?" I prayed it had been an accident. *Let it have been an accident. These things are bound to happen, right? She's around sharp objects all the time. She's going to cut herself. Fashion people cut themselves all the time, right?*

I couldn't stop speculating. I couldn't stop worrying. I wanted to fucking scream. If she were here, I could fix this.

A quiet sound broke through my silent ranting. "Mmm-hmm," Jillian answered.

"Is your finger all right?" Truthfully, I wasn't worried about her finger. She'd survived worse cuts than this little one. I wanted her to talk to me. I was worried about her frame of mind. She didn't sound good. Why had this cut freaked her out so badly?

"It felt…good, Griffin. For a split second, I thought about…"

And there it was. A relapse was staring her in the face. I needed to get to her. But the miles between us prevented me from getting there as quickly as either of us would have preferred. She needed help now. When I'd found out she was cutting five years ago, I'd seen to it that she talked to someone. Even with all of her ranting and hateful words, I sucked it up because her well-being was more important than what she thought of me at the time. Now was no different.

"Jillian, you need to call Dr. Hoffman. You promised if things got too crazy, you'd call her."

"I'm so stressed, Griff. I'm not cut out for this." Her voice gave a little hitch and I could tell she was holding back tears. What I wouldn't give right now to wrap her up and hold her tight. *God, this hurts.*

"Will you please call Dr. Hoffman? At least talk to her until I get there."

"What? You're coming here?" she choked.

There was no way in hell I wasn't going to visit her now. Erin would just have to fucking deal. "I was planning on visiting you for Thanksgiving, since I knew you weren't coming home. It was supposed to be a surprise."

"Griffin…"

By the way my name fell from her lips, I knew I'd just made her smile. I already felt better. I'd kept one of my promises. I would always do what I could to make her smile.

"But," I continued, not giving her a chance to finish her exclamation, "I'll only come on one condition. You have to call Dr. Hoffman. Promise me," I demanded.

And just like that, the sun rose in her voice. "I will. I promise." If she hadn't been smiling before, I knew she was now. I could feel the smile in her words, like warm rays of sunshine on my face.

"Good." A sigh of relief washed over me, and I basked in the incandescence of her words. The cold pang of fear that had wrapped around my heart loosened its vise grip, and I could breathe again. But she still needed a distraction from the cut on her finger. The last thing I wanted was for her to fall back into those old habits. "So you're cooking me a Thanksgiving feast, right?" I joked, changing the subject.

"Um…no." A breathy laugh touched my ears, followed by a sniffle.

Feeling came back into my legs, and I stood. "Wow. You treat all of your guests like that? Or do you save your top-notch hostessing skills just for me?"

"I'm not in culinary school, Griff."

OK, this was good. She sounded like my Jillibean again. "Damn." I gave a teasing groan. "And here I thought you'd be so happy to see me, I'd get a five-course feast out of the deal."

"How does pizza sound?" she asked playfully.

I couldn't help but laugh. It wasn't a secret that Jillian couldn't cook worth shit, and she had terrible taste in food. "Now that's a Thanksgiving feast I can't resist. But," I warned, "none of that shitty fancy pizza. Normal pizza, just meat and cheese."

"And pineapple," she added.

"Ugh. Being a sophisticated college woman hasn't refined your palate any." I walked up and down the sidewalk, kicking rocks to the grass.

"Nope." She giggled. An effervescent sound. I could listen to her laugh forever. With her happiness still echoing through my ears, I'd forgotten to how to speak. "Griff? You still there?" she asked.

"Yeah." All the tension from minutes before melted away in that moment. Just a small giggle from her had set my world back on its axis. "It's just good to hear you laugh. You feel better now?" I asked quietly, fearing I'd ruin the lightness of the conversation we were having now. But I needed to know. If she wasn't right, I'd leave for Providence tonight. Eighteen hours wouldn't stand in my way when it came to her well-being.

Before she answered, there was a lot of shifting and rustling on her end of the line. Then she said, "Yeah, thanks to you." Her voice trailed off, wavering at the end. "You always have a way of making everything OK."

With a strong voice, I reiterated what I'd told her so many years ago. "I promised you a long time ago that I'd always try to make you feel better...I'm just glad I still can."

Quietly she added, "Forever."

Again there was sadness in her voice that knocked the breath out of my lungs.

"I should probably get back to class," she said.

"Don't forget to call Dr. Hoffman." I spoke up, clearing my throat. "I'll be there in a couple of days. Take care of yourself, do you hear me?"

"I will, I promise." There was a slight tremble in her voice. "Night, Griff."

"Night, Bean," I replied softly.

Then the line was quiet and she was gone.

Chapter Seventeen

The roar of a wild crowd filled the living room the second Thor's wide receiver passed into the end zone. He spiked the controller between his legs and stood up, arms raised above his head. "Aw, yeah. Take that, Daniels." He pointed at me, a smug grin on his face. "The season is mine," he bellowed. He pumped his hands up and down as if to spur on his simulated fans.

I rested my elbows on my knees and let the controller slip through my fingers, dropping my head in defeat. "Shit."

"I ran all over your bitch ass," he continued to gloat. "You're off your game, man."

And he wasn't wrong. The last couple days had been hell. I'd been a nervous wreck since Jillian had called about the cut she'd gotten in class. And the blowup I'd had with Erin earlier tonight hadn't helped matters. She was furious when I confirmed I'd be spending Thanksgiving in Rhode Island. I tried to explain the situation to her, but she didn't want to hear it. Before I left tonight, she told me not to call her until I had my shit figured out.

I hoped this trip would help me do that.

I shook off my loss and looked up. Thor rubbed a hand over his shaved head, flashing a shit-eating grin.

"You have no idea," I muttered.

"Rematch?" Thor asked, bending over to retrieve his controller.

I lowered my hand and snagged mine off the carpet. "Nah. Long day tomorrow." I pushed out of my favorite black leather recliner, sending it rocking back and forth. I tossed the controller in the chair and headed for the kitchen. I needed a drink.

"Daniels," Thor called, after he verbally told the Xbox to shut down. He came up behind me. "What's up with you, man?" he asked. "I thought you'd be excited about this trip."

I went to the refrigerator and pulled a bottle of water from the door. Twisting off the cap, I kicked the door closed. I took a long swig, wishing it were beer. *Why do women have to be so complicated?*

Sucking down the last of the water, I chucked the empty bottle across the room, missing the garbage can entirely.

Thor went to the fridge and took the beer I wanted. "I don't get you, man." He placed the cap at the edge of the counter and slammed his free hand down, popping off the top with ease. "You've been testy all week. I thought a trip east would set you right." Thor took a long pull on the bottle and leaned against the counter.

I watched Thor put away one beer and then go for a second. "It's complicated," I said.

"Well, whatever the fuck it is, you have to pull it together, man." Thor set his half-empty bottle on the counter and walked toward me.

He slapped his hands down on my shoulders and looked me square in the eyes. "Who do you want, man?" he asked, point-blank.

I shrugged him off and started for the stairs. I was not having this conversation with him.

"When you heading out?" he called after me.

"Early."

Despite my being halfway up the stairs, he continued the conversation. "Your girlfriend know you're going?"

"None of your business," I called down the stairs.

"If you ask me, you're with the wrong one."

"Didn't ask. Night, Thor."

I opened the door to my room and waded through piles of dirty clothes and discarded pages of sheet music on my way to the bed. Peeling my t-shirt off, I added it to the collection on the floor before stepping out of my jeans. The ceiling fan whirled overhead, blowing cool air onto my bare chest and legs. I fell onto the mattress, the old king-size bed frame groaning from the force. I didn't bother with the blankets, I enjoyed the chill.

I stole a look at the clock: one a.m. I exhaled in frustration and flopped onto my stomach. I needed to get some shut-eye. Bunching the pillow into a ball under my head, I closed my eyes just in time to hear my phone play a Mark Sandman bass riff.

I shifted to the side of the bed and reached for my jeans. Mark worked his bass over as I freed my phone from the pocket. As soon as I had a grip on it, I rolled onto my back and answered. "Hey."

"Hey." Erin was quiet…reticent.

For an awkward moment neither of us spoke. The faint sound of her slow breathing filled the silence.

Then she whispered, "Sorry I called so late." Her Southern drawl touched my ears.

"No problem." I was surprised, though; she'd been pissed off when I left.

"You still planning on going tomorrow?" Her question was equal parts sad and irritated.

I understood Erin's complaint about me visiting Jillian. I'd tried to explain how important it was that I go, especially after that damn phone call on Monday.

I closed my eyes and sighed. "Yeah."

There was a long pause before she spoke again. "Griffin, after you left, I got to thinking."

"About what?" I massaged my forehead, trying to relieve the building pressure.

"I think this trip is a good thing."

I stilled my fingers. "Really?" She hadn't been thinking that a few hours ago.

"Yeah. I really like you, Griffin. You're smart, kind, respectful, fun." She paused for a beat. "Andreallyfreakingsexy." Her words came out in a breathy jumble.

"Erin," I intoned. She didn't have to shower me with compliments.

"No, wait. Let me finish." She took a deep breath and jumped back in. "I like us...a lot. We're good together. We have fun. But we need to use this little break to figure things out. I want more, Griffin. More than just having fun together. When you get back, it needs to be all or nothing."

I agreed. "You're a peach, you know that, right?"

She gave a humorless laugh. "Just honest."

"Thank you, Erin."

She let out a long breath. "OK. See you in a few days. Be careful."

"I will. Bye, Peach."

"Bye."

The line went dead.

With the phone still in hand, I set the alarm for five a.m. and put it on the bedside table. I rolled back onto my stomach and shoved my arms beneath the pillow. My eyes fell to the tattoo circling my right bicep. *Always protects. Always trusts. Always hopes. Always perseveres. Never fails.* Each line was how I felt about Jillian.

Erin was right, I needed to figure shit out. I shook my head, searching for the clear answer. Erin or Jillian.

The way I saw it, I had only two options: work things out with Erin and shut down my feelings for Jillian, or end things with Erin and shut down my feelings for Jillian.

No matter the scenario, Jillian was off-limits.

Chapter Eighteen

Pulling into the well-lit gas station, I unlatched the driver's side door and unfolded my legs from the sardine can that Ren called a car. *God, I miss my bike.* As soon as I had extricated myself from the vehicle, I stood and stretched. My back snapped in protest. Miatas were not made for people over six feet tall.

Shutting the car door, I walked over to the pump and swiped my credit card. I read and answered several questions as they popped up on the screen, becoming more irritated by the minute. *No, I don't want a goddamned car wash! It's fucking freezing outside!*

After my game of twenty questions with the pump, the attendant finally clicked it on and I could fill up my car.

I set the pump to fill automatically, shoved my hands into the small pockets of my leather jacket, and bounced on the balls of my feet to keep warm.

As I waited, I wondered what Jillian was up to. *How does she occupy her time?* It was so strange not knowing the girl I used to know so well. A lot had changed in two months.

The gas pump clicked off and snapped me back to reality. I shivered as I dislodged the pump and screwed on the gas cap. Once I folded myself back into the car, I fired her up and headed back to I-95 North.

I set the cruise and let off the accelerator. With the car on autopilot, I peeled my ass off the seat and retrieved my phone from my back pocket. I laid it in my lap and fumbled around the passenger seat for Ren's aux cable. Once I had the cord, I carefully plugged my phone in while trying to keep the car on the road. Soon The National's newest album blared from the speakers.

I adjusted Ren's EQ settings, cranking the bass so Scott Devendorf's sound would fill the car. I listened. My fingers danced on the steering wheel as if it were the neck of my bass.

When the song came to the bridge, I belted the lyrics along with Matt Berninger. These guys were fucking amazing. Gearing up for the chorus, I took in a huge breath and let my voice go, just like I would at a gig. But Matt's voice didn't back me up, instead it was my own voice coming through the speakers—Jillian's ringtone.

Grabbing my phone from my lap, I glanced at the screen and pressed "Answer."

"Where are you?" she shouted. Her voice filled the car, coming through the stereo speakers.

I couldn't stop the smile that spread across my face. "I just had to stop for gas. I'll be there in about thirty minutes."

"Well, hurry up!" she demanded.

"I am." I laughed. She was so damn cute when she was excited and the fact that she was excited to see me made her that much fucking cuter. "I'm—" The line went dead and Matt's voice filtered through the speakers again. I shook my head. Typical Jillian, she always had trouble focusing on one task at a time when she was excited about something.

I tossed my phone on the passenger seat, tried my best to get comfortable (even though the damn wheel was in my chest), and focused on the next song on The National's album.

After I'd listened to a couple of songs twice, my exit crept up sooner than I'd thought. I turned onto the off-ramp and stayed alert, knowing a turn was coming up. Once I made it into the heart of Providence, I would be on campus before I knew it.

Having only driven this route once, I surprised myself by how well I'd remembered the directions when I turned into the back parking lot of Jillian's dorm. I killed the engine and got out of the car as best I could without looking like a total dumbass. I hated Ren's car with a passion. I pulled the lever that brought the seat forward, grabbed my duffel bag from the backseat, and headed toward the dorm's rear entrance. I dialed Jillian's number and waited for her to pick up.

On the first ring, I heard her voice. "Griff?" she shouted.

I smiled. "Are you going to let me in or what?"

"Ahh! You're early!" she screamed. I pulled the phone away, worried her squealing would bust my eardrum. "I'm on my way down!" And once again the line went dead.

I slipped my phone into my back pocket and waited in the freezing cold. Seconds later Jillian emerged from the staircase and ran toward the door, crashing into it at full speed. I gave her a casual wave and stepped out of the way before the door took me out. But it wasn't the door that threatened to knock me on my ass, it was Jillian, leaping into my arms.

My arms were around her instantly. I bowed my head and took a deep breath, letting the familiar scent of *her* fill my lungs. I would have stayed like this forever, but it was fucking cold outside. I pulled her closer, wrapped her tighter in an effort to make her warm, and moved my mouth to her ear. "Jillibean," I whispered. "You going to let me through the door? It's freezing out here."

Like she'd been struck by lightning, she jumped and pulled away from me. "Oh, sorry." She grimaced and stepped aside so I could come in.

Once I was through the door, I had to have her back in my arms. It'd been too fucking long. Without a word I pulled her to my side, where she belonged. In seconds I realized I fucking loved this girl with every fiber of my being. I didn't want to live another second without her fucking knowing it. The two options I'd thought about last night went by the wayside, making room for a third option: Jillian was the one. As much as I'd tried to stay away, I couldn't anymore. I had to have her.

But I couldn't hurt Erin like that, so until I was able to break things off with her, I would have to restrain myself. *Goddamn, this visit is going to be hard.*

I looked down and smiled and when her eyes met mine, I could have gotten on one knee and proposed marriage right then and there, but now wasn't the right time, so I resorted to jokes. "Have you always been this short? I don't remember you being this short." She laughed and I pulled her closer to my side. *But really, has she always been this short?*

"You have no idea how happy I am to see you," she whispered.

Wanna bet, sweetheart? "Oh, I'm pretty sure I do," I answered quietly.

Jillian led the way to the top floor and opened the door to her room. I'd just driven eighteen hours with minimal breaks, I was tired, and her bed looked as inviting as ever. I dropped my arm from her shoulder, left my shit in the middle of the floor, and stretched out on her green comforter.

"You're tired," she mumbled.

I lifted my head off her pillow, kicked my boots off, and held out my hands. *Why the hell is she standing by the door looking at me as if*

I were a goddamned stranger? I let out a sigh and said, "Come here."

She walked toward me and sat on the very edge of the bed. *Seriously, what is going on with her? She's acting so strangely.* Her telltale fidgeting gave her away; my Jillibean was nervous. *But why?*

Reaching across her lap, I stilled her busy fingers with my hand. I pulled her hand to my chest and relaxed back onto her pillow. I trailed my fingers in lazy paths over her skin, until they rested on the Band-Aid covering the wound from earlier that week. *Maybe this is why she's nervous? Or scared?*

I wanted to her ease her anxiety, so I shifted my body over, making room for her to curl up beside me. I tugged her down onto the bed and wrapped my arms around her. "Now I can rest." I smiled through a yawn, loving how perfectly we fit together. We'd slept like this hundreds of times over the years and I'd taken each one for granted. Well, not anymore.

Jillian let out of deep breath and relaxed further. I closed my eyes, reveling in the feeling of her pressed against me, my world set to rights.

* * *

"What is that god-awful noise?" I groaned. It sounded like the wail of a hundred dying cats. I shook Jillian's shoulder.

"Ugh," she moaned. "That's my alarm." She rolled off the bed and stood up, stretching her hands above her head before she walked to her desk and turned the alarm off.

I rolled onto my back, taking up the entirety of her bed. I tried to move my right arm, but because Jillian had slept on it all night, it was asleep. I forced my fingers to wiggle a little and eventually the pins-and-needles feeling spread from the palm, all the way to my shoulder. "What time is it?" I asked, throwing my left arm over my eyes to shield them from the light Jillian had flipped on.

"Six thirty," she said with a yawn.

I turned my head and stared at her from under my elbow. "Are you kidding?"

"Nope." She flashed me a pretty grin and walked toward the bed. "Come on, Daniels. I only get you for a couple of days. There's no way I'm letting you spend them in bed."

Spending the next couple of days in bed didn't sound half bad, but I wouldn't want to spend them sleeping. *Shit! What am I thinking?* There was no way in hell that Jillian and I could be together. I wouldn't ruin this for her, and I wouldn't hurt Erin.

Jillian pushed on my shoulder, rocking me back and forth. "Dude, get up!"

As much as I wanted to pull her down on the bed with me, I fought that urge and pushed myself up to rest on my elbows. "All right, all right. I'm up." Sitting the rest of the way, I scrubbed my hands over my face and blinked away the fatigue from driving eighteen hours straight.

Jillian stood beside me, her hands resting on her hips. I lifted my tired eyes, wanting to get a better look at her. She was dressed in a long orange sweater, tights, and furry boots, and I once again fought the temptation to pull her to me and lose myself in all that softness. *This is going to be a long fucking weekend.* "You got a plan, Bean?" I gave her a lopsided grin, hoping to distract her from the growing situation in my pants. I had to pull myself together.

"Yes," she beamed back at me. "It snowed last night. We're going to be the first ones to put tracks in the snow. And we need to find an open coffee shop. I need caffeine."

All I could do was smile at her plan. This time her words elicited only good memories. Memories of when Jillian and I were kids and living next door to each other. With each newly fallen snow, Jillian wanted to be the first to put down tracks. She'd stand on her porch and yell my name until I came outside.

"*Griffin! Hey, Griff! It snowed, get your butt out here! Griffffi-innn!*"

I pushed open the screen door, slipping on a coat. "Jillibean, it's so early. What are you yelling about?"

"*It snowed! Come on, let's make tracks before it gets messed up.*"

"*What is it with you and making tracks in the snow?" I asked, irritated that she'd woken me up so early.*

"*I don't know." She shrugged, bouncing up and down, barely able to contain her excitement. "It's like the world's been erased and you can make it look any way you want. You can make a path go anywhere." She stepped off the porch and onto the first step. "Come on." Bounding down the last two steps, she placed her foot into the ankle-deep snow.*

I followed suit. I made careful, deliberate steps, cutting a curved path toward Jillibean. She did the same, until we stood toe-to-toe.

She looked up at me, beaming. She had such a pretty smile. I wished I saw it more. Few things made her smile like this.

"*See," she said, pointing to our footprints. "We made our own path. We can make it look however we want."*

I nodded. "Yeah." Then I pushed her shoulder just enough to make her teeter and fall backward into the powdery snow.

"*Griffin!" she yelled, lying flat on her back.*

I burst into laughter.

But instead of getting mad at me and stomping back into the house, she began moving her arms and legs, giggling.

I shrugged and lay down, too, making my snow angel right beside hers.

I felt the bed bounce and I shook my head, the memory blowing away like flakes of snow.

"Griff? Everything OK?" she asked.

Pulling my legs off the bed, I sat beside her, smiling. Lifting my arm around her shoulders, I hugged her to my side. "Never better."

She scrunched her eyes, small lines creasing her forehead. "You're acting strange."

With one last squeeze of her shoulders, I stood up. My back popped and creaked in protest. "Nope. No strange here. We better get to that snow before someone else does."

Jillian watched as I took a few steps toward the door, where I'd left my duffel bag. I was so stiff after being crammed in Ren's car, and then sleeping on a bed that was meant for a toddler. The world was unforgiving of people who were taller than six feet.

I stretched my hands above my head and leaned from one side to the other, my back snapping loudly. "Ahh…," I groaned.

"You all right there, Daniels?" Jillian asked, her eyebrow pulling up.

"Uhh…" I sighed. "Yeah, just stiff." What I wouldn't give for a workout. "Do I have time to do a couple sets of push-ups?" I asked her. "I need to loosen up."

"Make 'em quick," she demanded with a wink. "My snow and coffee await."

"Yes, ma'am." I saluted and dropped to the ground.

Jillian shook her head, smiling, and walked to stand in front of the mirror.

I pounded out a set of push-ups, loving the strain I felt in my arms and shoulders. The stiffness from moments ago dissipating.

Occasionally I'd catch myself stealing a glance at Jillian. She pulled some orange stuff through her hair, turning it into something that resembled a Dreamsicle. To me Jillian had always been pretty, but after the two months we'd been apart, she wasn't just pretty anymore, she was fucking gorgeous. The way that sweater dress clung to her curves did things to me that it shouldn't.

When she caught me watching her, I looked away and quickened my pace, breathing harder, trying my best to keep my mind from wandering to places it wasn't allowed to go. Set two was almost finished. "Ninety-eight...ninety-nine...," I grunted, "one hundred." I extended my forearms and pulled myself up. *Damn, that felt good.* I was breathing hard and a thin layer of sweat beaded on my forehead.

Lifting one arm above my head, I bent it back, using my other hand to press down on my elbow. While I held the stretch, I watched Jillian in the mirror again.

She caught my stare and our eyes locked. I didn't avert my gaze this time. I couldn't have even if I'd wanted to. An inexplicable force had a hold on us. Neither of us spoke. There was something different in the way she watched me.

"Better now?" She pulled the orange color through another strand of hair and smirked, breaking the connection.

I switched arms. "Absolutely."

"Good. You ready to go?" She sprayed some stuff in her hair, turned around, and leaned on the little dresser, folding her arms across her chest.

I glanced down at my sweat-soaked t-shirt and held up a finger. "Quick shower, I promise." I spun around and picked up my duffel bag and ran out the door before she had a chance to protest.

Before the door clicked shut, I heard her laughing, a sound I'd missed more than I realized.

Chapter Nineteen

We found an open Starbucks, drank coffee, and caught up on each other's lives. I still hadn't grown accustomed to Jillian being the stranger in my life, not knowing every small detail like she always used to. I didn't like it.

By the time our drinks were gone, it was time to head back out into the cold. We were both more than ready to hunker down in her room, eat pizza, and enjoy each other's company. I even promised her I would help with one of her design projects.

"You're really going to help me with my designs while you're here?" she asked.

"Victoria told me all of her secrets before I left." I tapped a finger on my temple. I had no idea what the hell I was getting myself into, but for Jillian, I'd do it.

"Well, shit, too bad I'm not designing a line of lingerie. And how did you get Vicky to share her secrets?" She grinned.

"You probably don't want to know." It was a damn shame she wasn't designing a lingerie line. Now *that* would have been fun. I'd have her modeling that shit all night. I winked at her as my imagination conjured some naughty designs of my own. Standing, I pulled my jacket from the back of the chair.

She stood too and grabbed her coat. "You're incorrigible."

She has no idea. I reached over and took the coat from her hands, holding it out for her. "Damn right I am."

A small chuckle fell from her lips as she tucked her arms into the sleeves of her coat. I brought the collar up, resting it on her back, and with my other hand lifted her blond-and-orange hair from beneath it. She turned her head and stared up at me. "Thanks."

"My pleasure." And it was.

* * *

Like old times, we spent most of the afternoon playing in the snow. After a pretty wicked snowball fight, and Jillian thoroughly kicking my ass, I fell over and cried, "Uncle!" I lay on the cold ground, staring up at the fading blue Providence sky, trying to catch my breath.

Jillian plopped down beside me, laughing, out of breath, too.

Out of the corner of my eye I watched her, our chests rising and falling heavily to the same beat as we both stared into space. The fingers of my left hand just barely touched the outstretched fingertips of her right hand. I wasn't quite sure how long we stayed like this, all I knew was I didn't want to move. When we shared silent moments like this, my heart threatened to stop beating altogether. She was so much a part of my life that I had a hard time recognizing myself without her.

She turned her head in my direction and I did the same, meeting her eyes. She smiled. "That was fun."

"It's been a long time since I've had any of that."

"Me too," she sighed. "My ass is cold."

"Mine, too," I agreed, but didn't move a muscle.

"We should go in."

"Yeah." I still didn't move. I liked the quiet. I liked that it was just the two of us.

Jillian didn't move either. I held her eyes, the dark brown of her irises drew me in. She blinked and sighed, but didn't look away. "You going to get up?" She challenged me to be the one to break away first.

"After you, Bean." I gave her a little nod.

"I don't want to move," she whispered.

I felt the same way. There was a kind of magic surrounding us. I could feel it. If either of us moved, the magic holding us in this moment would disappear.

"Neither do I."

"But we have to get up." Her smile faded. "It's getting dark."

"Here, I'll help you up." I stretched my hand out farther, grasping her fingers and pulling her hand into mine. I lifted my back off the ground and hopped up, pulling Jillian with me.

Her arms went around my waist. "Whoa!" she gasped, having not expected to be yanked off the ground.

Now that I was standing, my brain registered how fucking cold it really was. A shiver went down my spine and my teeth began to chatter. "It's damn cold out here, I'm going in."

Reaching behind my back, I latched her hand in mine, and we ran back to the dorm. Jillian swiped her keycard at the main doors and we rushed inside. Jillian was shivering uncontrollably, her shoulders shaking. My arms were around her instantly, wrapping her against my body, sharing what little warmth I had to offer.

I ran my hands up and down her back, holding her as close to me as I could. I didn't want to let her go. "You're so cold."

"Yyyyeeeess." Her teeth chattered as she spoke.

Even though I was freezing, too, my first priority was getting her warmed up. "You need dry clothes and hot chocolate."

Still keeping her folded against me, I angled my body so I could walk us up the flight of stairs to her room.

Once we made it to her floor, I pulled open the heavy steel door and Jillian stepped through. She yanked a lanyard from the inside of her coat and unlocked her door.

Once inside, we clomped over to the bed and collapsed beside each other. My eyes slid closed, and I reveled in the quiet once again. Nothing was quiet at home anymore. I missed those quiet days with the band.

I missed my quiet times with Bean.

Letting my head flop to the side, I opened my eyes. She stared back at me, the corners of her mouth lifted into a lazy smile. Her eyes, the color of a deep, rich espresso, were warm and inviting. I wanted to take in every last drop, but I couldn't keep my gaze from drifting and settling on her lips.

Those lips. The same lips that had tested the boundary of our friendship three months ago. The same lips I'd pushed away. It would be the easiest thing in the world to stretch my neck another inch or two and our lips would meet again. I wanted to taste her. I wanted to tell her I was an idiot for pushing her away.

Despite my racing heart, I relaxed my head, letting it fall a little farther to the side, my temple resting against hers.

She inhaled slowly. Our lips a breath away…

Damn, I want her.

Inwardly I was screaming, fighting with every last cell in my body to resist that last half inch, because if I didn't, I knew I wouldn't be able to push her away this time. And I had to. I had to give her a chance at the life she'd dreamed about.

I wouldn't fuck this up for her.

Before I steeled myself to break our connection, I paused to memorize the way her lips parted. The way her heated breath felt when it kissed my lips. Then, with all the strength I could muster, I gritted my teeth, grabbed her hand, and sat up. "So, what about that pizza?" I said with a little too much enthusiasm.

"Oh!" she shrieked, startled.

"You promised me pizza." I pulled my eyebrows down, giving her my best attempt at a serious face, anything to disguise how I was really feeling.

Sitting up, she took a big breath and let it out loudly. Her shoulders followed suit, rising and then lowering before she spoke. "Yeah." Letting go of my hand, she clapped hers together. "Pizza. Right." She pushed a hand through her hair and sighed again.

I could tell by her reaction that she'd felt the pull, too.

Digging into her pocket, she freed her phone and tapped the screen a few times before she put it to her ear. She gave me a toothless smile, not saying a word. Things felt so fucking awkward between us. I hated it.

The second someone answered on the other line, Jillian stood, pacing while she ordered.

I got up and walked around, too, an attempt to lower my pulse rate and return my thoughts to those of someone in the friend-zone.

"Uh, yeah." Jillian said, nodding her head. "Pepperoni and pineapple. You heard correctly."

With my back to her, I craned my neck and looked over my shoulder, shaking my head in disgust. Her food combinations sucked.

And like everything else, I loved that about her.

* * *

After we annihilated our pizzas and me trying my damnedest not to cross the line and fucking kiss her, I tossed my pizza crust into the box and sat back, nursing what was left of my beer. "So, what is this Spring Showcase thing that has you doubting your mad skills?" I asked.

Standing, she brushed her hands on her knees and walked to the mini fridge. "Every year, the apparel design department hosts a student-led runway show. All fashion majors must design an original, themed collection to be presented at the show. Most of my classmates already sketched their designs and have begun to put them together." Turning around to face me, she took a long pull on the beer she'd just opened.

"How far are you?" I stretched my legs out and sat back against her bed. Jillian watched me get comfortable and then began to laugh. "What's so funny?" I held up my hands.

"You," she replied bluntly, pointing her beer bottle at me.

I pointed my bottle at her. "I'm cutting you off. I forgot how wacky you get when you drink." Shaking my head, I leaned back and rested against her mattress.

"I do not get wacky." She stuck my tongue out at me.

She actually stuck her tongue out at me. Dear God, the thoughts that had just run through my head. I bit my tongue to keep from tackling her to the ground, sucking her tongue into my mouth, and...*Shit! No! I cannot get carried away.* "I rest my case." I chuckled. I needed to change the subject, too many images of tongues and our bodies pressed together were making things way too hard. "How far have you gotten on your Showcase stuff?"

She frowned. "Not very."

"When is the show?"

Joining me back on the carpet, she pushed my feet out of the way and said, "Not until May, but we're required to have a minimum of five different pieces, so it takes a while to sketch the ideas and turn them into wearable clothes."

I lifted my head and set my beer down. "Well, let's get on it, then." I clapped my hands together, ready for her to put me to work. "You said the collection has to be themed? What does that mean?"

As if reciting something she'd heard a billion times that semester, she dove right into her explanation. "All the pieces must be different, yet similar enough to tell a story. There has to be something that ties all the pieces together."

I pulled my legs up and rested my elbows on my knees. "Get your stuff. Let's see what you've got."

"Really, Griffin, you don't have to do this." She sighed, set her beer down, and fell onto her back. Shielding her eyes from the light, she dropped her arm onto her face. "I'm sure an up-and-coming rock star has better things to do with his time."

This kind of talk had to stop. She knew I'd do anything for her. I knocked my boot against the side of her foot, forcing her to look at me. "Seriously, Jillian, go get your shit. I don't know one thing about designing clothes, but I can certainly watch you do it. Get up." I held my hand out for her to take. Placing her fingers in my palm, I wrapped my hand around hers and pulled us both up so we sat face-to-face. I stared her down, all joking aside. "Where's your stuff?"

She blinked and tilted her head toward the desk. "On the floor over there."

I tapped my finger against her nose and smiled. "Well, go get it."

With a little groan she got up and trudged over to her desk, leaned down beside it, and pulled two large duffel bags and a book bag from the floor. "I've got dozens of different fabrics and embellishments in these two bags," she said, holding them up.

"Embellishments?" I raised an eyebrow in confusion. "What the hell is an embellishment?"

A little smile bloomed across her face, her cheeks the color of a light-pink rose. She was so beautiful when she smiled.

Tossing the bags into the center of the room, she sat down with a thud beside the bags and me. "I have my sketchbooks in here," she said, pulling the bag onto her lap.

I took a swig of beer and swallowed. "Do me a favor." I stretched behind her and set my beer on the desk. "Never mention this to the guys."

"Your secret's safe with me." Pretending to seal her lips, she pantomimed locking them up and tossing the key over her shoulder.

I pulled the purple duffel to my lap and unzipped it. Turning it upside down, I emptied the contents onto the floor. Tons of shiny shit fell out. I ran my hand over the mess, with not a clue what the purpose of any of this stuff was. I stared at Jillian.

"What?" She giggled, unzipping the other duffel bag. "You wanted to know what embellishments were…well, there you go." Jillian grabbed a fistful of beads and playfully tossed them at my head.

Shielding my face from the attack, I mumbled, "I think I'm going to need another beer for this." I leaned over and pulled another from the mini fridge.

We stared at the small pile. "Any ideas?" I asked, twisting the cap off my beer. I sure as hell didn't have any.

"None. I'm telling you, the second I got here, every ounce of my artistic ability disappeared."

I looked at her, irritated that my eccentric, creative Jillibean's self-esteem had tanked. "Fuck that." I took a drink and reached backward to set my beer beside the empty one. "Come on, there's got to be something in here you can use." I pieced through the pile, finding some lacy circles and a couple of graduation-tassel-looking things.

"Here, what about this?" I put the circle on my head and batted my eyelashes. A swell of laughter rose from inside Jillian, pure music. "Or this," I continued, not wanting her laughter to fade. I held the tassels to my chest and twirled them around suggestively.

"Stop...stop," she cried, punching my shoulder, laughing. I playfully pushed her backward and she fell onto her back with a sigh. I tossed the tassels into the pile and sat up on my knees. I wanted a better look at my girl.

Still laughing, she wrapped her arms around her stomach and looked at me. "If the guys could see you now." She smirked.

"Uh-uh," I said, waving my index finger back and forth. On my knees I shuffled through the glittery mess and hovered over her. I loved the way her hair fanned out around her face, like an orange-golden sunset. "You promised." I pressed a finger to my lips like a secret. "You locked it and threw away the key." Moving my leg over her small body, I straddled her and leaned in close, easily pinning her beneath me. My eyes lingered on the swell of her breasts, then grazed along her slender neckline. I licked my lips, wanting to the trail my tongue along the same path my eyes followed. She looked so fucking hot between my legs.

Her breathing grew shallow and her eyes blazed as she anticipated my next move. Slowly I slid my arms down hers, stopping to grip her waist firmly in my hands. Her body felt incredible in my hands. Too incredible. I shouldn't be touching her like this. Damn, she took my breath away.

Staring at her, I struggled to keep my heartbeat steady. I needed a reason to keep my hands on her, because I couldn't let go. It took every last bit of my resolve not to seize her mouth.

With a sly smile, I wiggled my fingers at her sides, tickling the hell out of her. "You promised," I whispered in her ear.

She laughed uncontrollably and squirmed beneath me. She had my dick's attention immediately. *Fuck! This was a bad idea.*

"OK! OK!" she squealed, and tried to wiggle out from underneath me. Did she feel my body's reaction to her? *God, I hope not!* "I give!" She giggled.

I needed to get off her, but if I got up now, there wouldn't be much left to the imagination. Just then the door flew open, making the decision for me, and I shot up like I'd been caught with my hand in the cookie jar, pulling Jillian off the ground with me.

A girl stood in the doorway, her jaw dropped in shock. "I'm sorry…I didn't mean to interrupt," she stuttered.

Jillian ran a hand through her hair, trying to straighten it. "Sarah, no…it's fine," she said in between heavy breaths.

"Yeah, no problem," I added, also out of breath. "Hi, I'm Griffin." I reached around Jillian, who was thankfully standing in front of me, and offered Sarah my hand.

Sarah stepped closer and took my hand and Jillian stepped aside, giving her a full view of the growing situation in my pants. I cleared my throat and prayed she'd keep her eyes on my face.

"It's nice to finally meet you, Griffin. I've heard so much about you." Sarah looked from me to Jillian and smiled. I think she may have even winked at Jillian. *What did that mean?*

"Is everything OK?" Jillian asked, kicking an empty duffel bag to her side of the room. "Aren't you staying at Brandon's brother's house?" Jillian fidgeted with the hem of her shirt, something she did when she was nervous. *Why is she nervous?*

Jesus, I'm a wreck. I need to pull myself together or this trip is going to end in disaster.

Sarah stepped over the pile of shit on the floor, took a couple steps in my direction, and pressed her lips into a thin smile. "Excuse me," she said kindly, pointing to the dresser behind me.

"Oh, sorry." I took one giant step and went to sit on Jillian's bed, running my hand through my hair.

"No, no, it's fine," she said, pulling open one of her dresser drawers. "I just forgot…something." She looked at me over her shoulder and smirked.

It felt strange watching Jillian interact with another close friend. I had always been that person, but now she had Sarah. I liked that Sarah had taken on the role of best friend. *Does that leave room for me to be something more?*

Jillian cleared her throat. "How was your Thanksgiving?" she asked.

Sarah claimed her forgotten item and stood, pushing the drawer shut with her foot. "Good," she drawled. "But apparently the party is here tonight." Her eyes scanned the mess on the floor, and then the two of us.

"Griffin was just—" Jillian stuttered.

"Helping Jillian find her muse." I finished her sentence, trying to ease the tension in the room.

"I can see that," she intoned, her eyes scanning the length of my body. "Well, Brandon's waiting in the car," she said, turning to leave. "Good luck finding your muse." Giving Jillian a smirk, she pulled the door open.

"Good night, Sarah," Jillian groaned, pushing her out the door. "I'll talk to you tomorrow."

"Good night. Nice to meet you, Griffin," Sarah called over my shoulder in a singsong voice.

"You too, Sarah." I craned my neck to see her around the door and waved.

Jillian slammed the door shut and turned around. "Well, that was weird."

I nodded, running my hand through my hair. "Yeah." I looked at Jillian, who was still worrying the hem of her shirt.

Jillian collapsed on the bed beside me, groaning. She buried her head in the mattress. "It's late and my head feels fuzzy. I need to go to bed," she mumbled.

"Scoot over." I pushed her tiny frame toward the wall and kicked my boots off, lying down.

"Thanks for putting up with me," she whispered.

Dear God, after all these years, doesn't she know what she means to me? What I'd do for her? I stretched my arm up, forcing her to lift her head.

I felt her body relax as she used my arm as a pillow. Tilting her head up, she unleashed the full force of her dark eyes. Like black holes, they pulled me in and refused to let me go.

I brushed my fingers across her cheek, smoothing away a few strands of colorful hair. "Jillibean," I whispered, fearing the emotions I felt right now wouldn't allow me to speak. "I will always be here for you." I tucked an orange strand of hair behind her ear. Lowering my head, I was determined to kiss her...in some way. I placed my lips on her forehead, leaving them there longer than any friend should.

Chapter Twenty

Even after countless prayers, the sun rose early on Saturday morning. I hadn't wanted my weekend to end. I wasn't ready to leave Jillian…and go home to Erin.

God, what am I doing with Erin? I had to end it.

Since August I had tried to turn Erin into Jillian. Tried to make her the part of my life that was missing, and it wasn't working.

There was no denying that Erin was a wonderful, beautiful person. She was kind, considerate, and a blast to hang out with, but that was all I had. Erin was *now*. That was it. No history…no future.

That wasn't love.

I shook my head, disgusted with the way I was treating both girls. I'd gotten so good at pushing them away, albeit for different reasons. I was an asshole.

Jillian was snuggled close to my side and breathing deeply, still fast asleep. I watched her. The sun shining through the slats of the blinds lit Jillian's face.

I trailed my fingers over the rays of sunlight splayed on her cheeks. The warmth carried from her skin to mine. Jillian stirred beside me, a slight hum vibrating at her mouth. I pressed my fingers to her lips, wishing I could kiss them.

The months we'd been apart were supposed to reset our friendship. But that's not what had happened. Wasn't love supposed to be all-encompassing? All-consuming? Jillian was my past, my present, and I wanted more than anything for her to be my future. I couldn't live without her. She brought balance, order, color, and warmth to my otherwise chaotic black-and-white life. She was so much more than a friend. She was my reason for being.

I shook my head, in awe of her. I didn't want a fleeting *now*. I wanted a lifetime. I wanted to be consumed.

With my face pressed to the top of her head, I drew in her familiar scent. Her hair smelled faintly of coconuts, while her body reminded me of the scent of flowers drifting along an ocean breeze.

It was so hard to leave her. Her absence felt like being caught in an ocean wave. It crashed down on me with such force, holding me under the surface of the water, my body begging for oxygen, my lungs burning. And just like the fury of the ocean, my life without Jillian tossed me around like a rag doll until I was beaten and broken. Until there was nothing left. Not even her.

Drawing in one last Jillian-scented breath, I held her inside me, refusing to exhale. Slowly, sliding my arm from beneath her head, I rolled my body off the bed. Jillian shifted a little, snuggled deeper into her pillow, and pulled the comforter under her chin, never opening her eyes.

I let out my breath and stood. I'd let her sleep a little longer while I showered and packed. Walking over to my duffel bag, which lay on her roommate's bed, I removed my shower items and headed for the bathroom down the hall.

* * *

Wrapping a towel around my waist, I pulled the door open a smidge and stuck my head through, hoping the ladies on this floor were still on vacation. I made a mad dash back to Jillian's room, quietly pulling open her propped door.

Still asleep, she'd rolled onto her stomach and put a pillow over her head. I smiled. Every little thing she did got to me like no one else was able to do.

I tiptoed over to my bag and pulled out a pair of jeans, a t-shirt, and some boxer briefs. Dropping the towel, I quickly stepped into my underwear, pulled on my shirt, and sat to put my jeans on. Standing, I gave the jeans one last tug before I buttoned and zipped them closed.

I looked around and gathered the clothes I'd worn on previous days. Kneeling, I rolled up a couple of shirts and another pair of jeans and stuffed them into my bag.

"You know what I'd love to have right now?"

Jillian's groggy voice floated from the bed and landed at my ears. I lifted my head and smiled, laying my eyes on her. With her dark bedroom eyes and mussed hair, she was too damn sexy for words. It took my brain a second longer to register what she'd said. "What's that?"

"A bright-blue police box that can transport me back to Tuesday night," she sighed, her lips turning downward.

Jillian had always loved that strange *Doctor Who* show. When we were younger, she'd held me hostage many nights, forcing me to watch an alien time lord magically fix things with a screwdriver.

Unable to resist her pout, I left my things on the floor and walked over to the bed. I pushed her over and fell down beside her. Instantly Jillian rolled onto her side to face me. I did the same, inches separating our noses.

I smiled even though I wasn't happy. I was anything but. Needing to touch her, I brushed my fingers along her cheek, pushing a few strands of hair behind her ears. "All you've ever talked about was getting the hell out of Jennifer's house and going to design school. But..." My throat caught, and I couldn't finish my sentence. I needed to get a grip on my emotions.

I pushed my hands beneath the pillow we shared and sought out her hands. Wrapping my fingers over her fists, I held them tightly. "Now you're sad all the time," I croaked. "Isn't this what you want anymore?"

She shook her head infinitesimally, and I hated that she wasn't happy here. Everything she'd ever talked about...dreamed about...and now that the dream was realized, yet she still seemed lost...sad. More than anything, I wanted to fix that for her. I wanted to make her happy.

"I feel like a failure here. Everything feels...forced." Her words were quiet, emotionless. My heart hurt. But I knew how she felt.

"Except for these last few days," she continued.

Her eyes roamed over my face, and then she turned them away, refusing to make eye contact. Her gaze fell on my arm, specifically my scripture tattoo. She pulled her hand free of my grasp beneath the pillow and brushed my shirt sleeve up to reveal more of the dark script winding its way around my bicep. With the slightest bit of pressure, she traced the cursive writing. My arm flexed involuntarily at her touch, which sent a shiver down my spine and blood rushing elsewhere. If she didn't stop, I wouldn't be able to stop myself from starting something that would alter our friendship forever.

"Can I tell you something?" I spoke, trying to mask the groan of pleasure she elicited.

"What?" she whispered, still tracing the lines of my tattoo. Still driving me insane.

"I feel the same way."

Sliding her hand beneath my arm, she wrapped her fingers around my bicep and squeezed. "You do?"

I tightened my grip around her hand that was still under the pillow, anything to keep my mind on the conversation and not what I really wanted to do with her. "'Forced' is the perfect way to describe everything." An unbelievable amount of force. I knew if I just gave in to the force acting on us, pushing us together, everything would be easier. But I couldn't. I had Erin's feelings to consider.

Jillian blinked a few times, almost as if she were shocked by my answer. Her eyebrows pulled close together when she scrunched her face. "The same can be said for you. You're following your dream. The band's doing well and you've got Erin, what's not right?"

I didn't like the confusion on her face, the worry. I let go of her hand and with my fingers smoothed the creases between her eyes. "None of the band's success feels right without you there to share it with. And Erin…" With all the seriousness I could muster, I stared at Jillian. I wanted her to read between the lines, to know how much I'd fucked up in May, when I'd pushed her away. "She's not who I want."

Tears fell from her eyes and she gripped my arm harder, refusing to let go. "Who do you want?" she choked.

With my thumb I brushed her cheek. Then a loud beeping sound blared from my pocket. "Fuck," I mumbled, and shot up, pulling my phone out.

Jillian sat up, too. "Who is it?"

I gave the screen a quick glance and saw my sister's name and picture. I didn't answer the call, but quieted it instead. "It's Ren. I've got her car."

"Oh." Her voice was hoarse.

I held my hand out to her. When she placed her tiny palm in mine, I yanked her into my arms. Instantly her arms went around my waist, and she buried her head between my arm and chest, refusing to let go.

I couldn't lie to myself anymore. These last few months had been torture. With Jillian pressed against me, my arms enveloping her, I couldn't go back to the way things had been before she kissed me. No matter how hard I tried, Erin would never fit into my heart like Jillian did.

My pulse beat loudly in my ears and my throat was thick. I didn't want to leave her. Every fiber of my being screamed *stay*. Things had changed between us this weekend, and I knew Jillian felt it, too.

* * *

On a steady diet of Monster Energy drinks and chips, and with a few stops for gas, I managed to shave two and a half hours off an otherwise eighteen-hour road trip. Not to mention the fact that Ren's car was most comfortable sailing down the interstate at eighty-five; that seemed to help ease some of the tension I'd felt since leaving Jillian crying in the parking lot.

Once I hit exit thirteen, I took the ramp and made a left to drop in on my parents instead of heading right to go to my apartment. I pressed the hands-free dialing feature on Ren's steering wheel and

let the car dial her number for me. After three rings Ren's voice
came through the speakers. "Dude, you home yet?"

I adjusted the volume, bringing it down a notch before I spoke.
"Yeah, I'm on my way to Mom and Dad's. Be there in ten."

"Cool. I'm here. Did you have a nice visit?"

"Yep."

"Sooo," she drawled. "Give me details. How is Jill?"

I rolled my eyes. Whatever she was fishing for, she wasn't going
to get it. "She's good."

"Good? You've got to give me more than that! What did you
guys do?"

"Um…hung out?" I offered.

"When you get here, I expect a better answer than 'good,' baby
bro," she scolded.

Irritation got the better of me, and I snapped, "I don't know
what more you want. Jillian's fine. I helped her with some
school project, we ate pizza, did some shopping, and now I'm
home."

"Well, aren't you just a ray of sunshine. I thought a weekend
with Jillian would have at least put you in a better mood."

Yeah, I thought so, too. Now I'm more at odds with myself. "Whatever," I groaned. At times my sister could be as annoying as a
housefly. "I'm here."

Pulling into the gravel drive, I pushed a button on the steering
wheel to disconnect the call. The radio resumed playing Morphine
as I shut off the engine.

I pushed open the car door and freed myself from the confines
of Ren's glorified tin can. God, I missed my bike.

"Hey, big guy," Ren yelled from the porch. She pulled the front
door shut behind her and ran down the steps. With open arms she
wrapped me in a hug. "Glad you're back."

I closed my arms around her shoulders and squeezed. As annoying as she was, we were really close. I'd do anything for her.

"Thanks for the wheels." I clapped a hand on her back and she pulled away, smiling.

"Anytime, Bro. Besides, it was fun…and cold, riding around town on your bike." She giggled.

I stepped back, jaw dropped in horror. "You didn't."

She shrugged, still laughing.

I was about to take off running for the garage, where I'd left my baby, but Ren squeezed my arm.

"Whoa, don't have a heart attack. You know I'd never get on that thing. I was just messing with you."

I relaxed my shoulders and swung my arm around her neck, securing her in a headlock. "Don't mess with the bike," I warned playfully. Even though she was my older sister, I was still bigger than her.

I dragged Ren toward the house. "Mom and Dad home?"

She nodded her head, still anchored between my forearm and bicep. "Yep."

We walked to the side of the house, and I let go of her head so I could open the door. Ren stepped into the house, and I followed.

"Baby boy," Mom crooned. "How was your trip?" She stood at the sink, loading the dishwasher.

"Hey, Ma." Taking two steps in her direction, I folded her into a hug. She and Jillian were just about the same size.

Without missing a beat, Awesomesauce came barreling around the corner into the kitchen, barking and wagging his tail at my feet. I let go of Mom and bent down to pet him. "Hey, little buddy." I scratched behind his big ears and he was putty in my hands, rolling over so I would scratch his belly, too.

"How is Jillian?" Mom asked, turning and wiping her hands on a dish towel. "It's been a little over a week since I've spoken with her."

"Yeah," Ren added in a sassy tone. "How is she?"

I sighed, knowing that I wasn't getting out of this kitchen without telling them something. "She's good. School's keeping her busy. She also told me to tell you she misses you both." Jillian hadn't really, but I knew she did. She loved my mom and sister like they were her own.

"I'm so glad she wasn't alone on Thanksgiving," Mom said.

So was I.

Ren sat down at the kitchen table and Awesomesauce scrambled to his feet and waddled over to her. She leaned over to pet him, and I stood up.

"Has she made any progress on that project that's been giving her fits?" Mom asked.

"A little." In my head I could still hear her laughing at my attempts to help her. "It's definitely challenging her."

"That's great. Now, if only I could get you to follow Jillian's example."

I groaned and looked at the ceiling, pushing my hands through my hair. "Mom, don't start."

"Seriously, Griffin, it's time to start taking school more seriously. You have wasted so much time piddling around at the junior college. Have you even applied to the university? Graduation isn't that far off."

The last thing on my mind right now was going to a four-year university after I graduated from the junior college. I was banking on the spring tour Dane was putting together. If that went through, I was done with school.

I dropped my hands and looked my Mom in the eyes. "Mom, I'm doing what I want to do right now. The band is my first priority."

Exasperated, Mom threw the dish towel on the counter. "Griffin," she shouted, "I've seen it a hundred times. How many of those American Idols or *Voice* winners actually make it in the music business? They're famous for a while, but then everyone forgets about them. Well, except for that Underwood girl, she's really good. And pretty."

Jesus, now she's comparing me to people who've won a fucking talent show? "What I've got going, Mom, is a little different from what you watch on TV." I threw Ren a silent plea for help. She shrugged and returned her attention to Awesomesauce, who was now curled into a comfortable ball on her lap.

Thanks a lot, Sis!

This was bullshit. I was twenty-one goddamned years old. My parents needed to understand that I wasn't their *baby boy* anymore; I was a man. It was time I started living my life the way I wanted. "Mom, I'm not finishing school." There. I'd dropped the bomb.

Mom froze.

I looked at Ren. Her face matched Mom's.

"Excuse me?" she whispered, still reeling.

I leaned against the counter and folded my arms across my chest. "There's a good possibility Mine Shaft is going out on tour in May. I won't have time to finish out the semester. I'm a recording artist, Ma. That's my chosen profession. Not business. We all know school has never come easy to me. Music is something I'm good at. Mine Shaft needs my full attention right now." I kept my stance firm. She needed to know I was serious, and I wasn't going to change my mind. "I have to take this chance, Mom. School will always be there, but this opportunity may not." I begged her to understand where I was coming from, that this was my dream.

Without a word she walked past me, out of the room.

I'd known she wouldn't understand. I turned to Ren. "Thanks for the car." I tossed the keys onto the table and stormed out the back door. Why was everything so black-and-white with her? Not everyone was cut out for school.

From outside I heard Dad calling, "Griffin, wait. Come back here. We need to talk about this."

I kept walking. I was done talking.

Standing next to my bike, I swung my leg over and gave it a start. I revved the engine a couple of times and shot down the driveway faster than I should have, checking for oncoming traffic a second before I flew into the street.

"Fuck!" It felt good to scream. I felt liberated.

Chapter Twenty-One

For the next week and a half, I dodged calls from my parents and my sister—whom I was sure Mom had recruited into calling on her behalf. I couldn't take any more talk about what a fuckup I was, and how I was ruining my life by pursuing a music career. If anything, the time I'd spent with Jillian had helped me put things in perspective. It was time I manned up and took control of my life.

I buried myself in music. I lived at the studio. When I wasn't recording, I was in the booth with Leo, mixing. I loved the production side of things, turning raw, uncut music into something radio-playable.

I found it easy to hide from everyone when I was at the studio. It was even easy to pretend that I wasn't in a weird place when it came to Jillian. Right now music was the only thing that made sense.

Sitting in the booth, I listened to Nee pound out the rhythm to "Home," the song slated to be the third track on our album. She'd done a couple of other sessions, but didn't feel like she'd nailed this piece. She was a musical perfectionist, like me.

When she finished she stood up, twirled her sticks, and slid them into her back pocket before giving me a thumbs-up and a smile.

I held up my thumbs and switched on the comm mic. "You nailed it that time."

"Yeah, that felt good," she said, out of breath. Stepping away from the set, she made her way to the booth. Inside she held out her fist to me.

I knocked it back and said, "That's it for you, girl."

She plopped into the chair beside mine and exhaled. She listened while I played back her tracks. I adjusted some settings and cleaned up the sound on the toms and the bass drum.

"Wait, wait," she said, sitting up. "Play that back a sec."

I backed up the track and trained an ear, trying to catch the "off" sound.

"You hear that?" Nee leaned over me and adjusted a few settings. "The sound coming from the toms isn't right." She shook her head, scrunching up her nose. "There, play it back again."

I backed up the track once more. Neither of us dared to breathe as we listened to the slight adjustments Nee had made. "Bingo," she said, clapping and sending her office chair spinning. "That's better." The chair came to rest and she sat back with a beatific smile.

"Feeling pretty good about yourself, huh?" I laughed.

"Fuck yeah. That song is complicated. Whoever wrote it *obviously* never sat behind a drum set." She winked and gave me a sidelong glance.

I flipped her off and grinned back. "I'll take that as a compliment…I think? And I'll have you know Adam contributed heavily on that project."

"I'm sure he did." She rolled her eyes and leaned closer, nudging my arm with her shoulder. "Anyway," she sighed. "You spending the night here, or something? All work and no play makes Griffin a dull boy," she sang.

"Shit! What time is it?" I searched for my phone, not remembering where I'd left it when I came into the booth. "I have to be at Erin's at six."

"You'd better get a move on, then." Nee held my phone out to me. "You got like twenty minutes."

"Shit." I grabbed my phone from her hand and my jacket off the back of the chair, and raced out of the booth.

"Good luck, big guy," Nee shouted after me.

On my way out of the studio, I texted Erin, *Sorry, Peach, ran late @ the studio. OMW.*

Since I'd gotten back from Rhode Island, I'd put Erin off, too. I knew I had to end things, there just hadn't been a good time. So tonight was going to be it. She wasn't busy, and I'd asked if I could come over. She'd sounded excited about the prospect of hanging out together, which made me feel like shit, knowing what I planned to do.

Traffic wasn't too heavy on the way back into Illinois, and I went straight to her apartment. I pulled into her lot and killed the engine, shoving down the kickstand with my foot. Erin's front door opened and one of her roommates came skipping down the sidewalk.

"Hi, Griffin. Erin's inside. You can go on in."

"Thanks." I stepped onto the sidewalk, giving her a wide berth. I'd only met her once before, and I couldn't for the life of me remember her name.

"I can't believe Erin's dating a rock star." She grinned widely and batted her eyelashes. "I bet you look really good when you're onstage."

Her words hit me like a ton of bricks, and I couldn't ignore the look on her face, a look that screamed, *I'm a desperate groupie and I'll do ANYTHING you want.*

For some this look would have brought on the "Hell yes!" response, but it did the exact opposite for me—I hadn't signed up for the popularity that came with a record deal, and I probably wouldn't ever be comfortable with it.

"Um…," I sputtered. "Yeah, live shows are way better than working in the studio." I tried to deflect her attention to something other than how I looked on stage.

"When does your album come out?" she asked, ducking her head to drape her purse strap across her body and cinch up her coat. It was beyond cold outside, and I was frozen after a thirty-minute ride from St. Louis. Not even my winter riding gear held up against single-digit temps.

"January." I kept my answers short, hoping to end the conversation quickly.

"Well, let me know when it does. I'll totally buy it," she giggled.

I pressed my lips into a tight smile. "I'll keep you posted." I took a slight step toward the porch and lowered my chin. "I shouldn't keep Erin waiting." I hitched my thumb in the direction of the door.

"Oh, yeah. Sorry," she said hurriedly. "See you later."

"Yeah. Later." I took a deep breath, exhaling on my way up to the small concrete patio.

I knocked on the door and a beat later Erin's smiling face approached. She opened the door and I stepped inside. Erin stepped back toward the center of the living room and twirled, showing off a short denim skirt, a sparkly tank top, and black cowboy boots. She looked like she'd just stepped out of a *Dukes of Hazzard* rerun. She looked hot.

While my eyes swept over every inch of her, she shimmied and said, "Whaddaya think?" Her accent controlling each syllable.

"I…uh…" I couldn't talk; she'd knocked the words clear out of me. I wanted to tell her she looked hot, but that would be totally inappropriate considering the fact that I was about to break up with her. Instead I opted for something much more tame: "It's awfully cold out there if you're planning on going somewhere. You might want to wear something a little warmer."

Her face went from playful to serious as she put a hand on her hip. "Dude, that was not the reaction I was after."

Damn, this sucks. I ran my hand through my hair and blew out a breath as I went to sit on the couch.

"Griffin," she whispered. "Is everything all right?" She picked up on my strange behavior right away. Sitting down beside me, she rested her hand on my leg.

I patted her hand with mine, but didn't look at her. I couldn't. I didn't want to hurt her. She was a smart, considerate, beautiful woman. She just wasn't…Jillian.

Erin lifted her hand and placed it on my jaw, a gentle touch to shift my eyes in her direction.

"Griffin, hear me out," she said, dropping her hand once our eyes locked. "I get it."

I opened my mouth to say something, but she shook her head and pressed a finger to my lips.

"Uh-uh." She shook her head. "I've needed to say this for a while, let me finish, please."

I nodded.

She took a deep breath, closed her eyes for a second, and then focused them back on me. "These last four months have been a blast. But this isn't working, Griffin. I can't compete with everything you have going on right now."

With a subtle nod, I agreed. "I know, I'm sorry." Leaning forward, I rested my elbows on my knees, dropping my head against my folded hands.

"And come on, let's face it, I'm not who you really want to be with." She nudged me with her shoulder and laughed dryly.

I glanced up at her. "What do you mean?" I'd never said anything to her about how I felt about Jillian. I hadn't told anyone.

Erin cocked her head, pressing her lips tight. "Oh, come on. She's a thousand miles away and yet I feel like she's standing right between us."

I dropped my head again. I didn't know what else to say.

"Griffin." Erin put her hand on my shoulder to get my attention, but I continued looking at the floor. "Griffin," she said again, a little louder.

Reluctantly I looked up.

"It's OK." She smiled. "We had fun for a while. I can tell everyone I dated Griffin Daniels." She said my name with dramatic flair. "But we both know that this"—she gestured between us—"isn't meant to be. You're meant to be with her."

I wanted to be with *her*, but Erin didn't know that wasn't meant to be either.

"Friends?" she offered.

I smiled, sitting up. I wrapped my arm around her shoulder, drawing her into my side. "Damn straight."

With a big grin on her face, she lifted an eyebrow, "And friends still get backstage VIP access at Mine Shaft shows?"

"My friends? Always. Not Adam's, though. You're not a friend of Adam's, are you?" I teased.

"Nope. I am a card-carrying fan of Griffin Daniels, only."

"Thank you, Erin." I squeezed her in a friendly hug. "You are by far the coolest girl I've ever dated."

She laughed. "I can say the same. I haven't dated many rock stars."

I scoffed. "Rock star."

"What? You make it sound like a dirty word." She tossed my arm off her shoulder and stood up, making her way toward the kitchen. "I don't know about you, but I need a drink," she called over her shoulder.

"God, yes," I answered.

She rounded the corner and disappeared. From the other room, I could hear her rooting around in the fridge, and then a couple of drawers opened and shut. A minute later Erin came back into the room with two bottles and an opener. She set the Bud Lights down on the small table beside the couch and handed me the opener. "I suck at these. Help a girl out?"

I took the bottle opener from her hand and set it on the table. "Watch this." I reached for one of the beers, setting the lip of the cap at the edge of the table. I slammed my left hand down and the top popped right off.

"Oh!" Erin shouted. "Where on earth did you learn to do that?"

I handed her the first one and went to work on the second. "In high school. Thor and I needed a cool trick to impress the ladies. Are you impressed?" I slammed my hand down hard a second time, sending the cap skidding across the table. I didn't waste any time sucking down the cold courage-in-a-bottle. "Damn, that's good." I swallowed the large gulp.

"Well, color me impressed." Erin plopped on the couch beside me, falling back into the cushions. "Oh, dear Lord," she sighed, savoring her drink. "It is, damn good."

We enjoyed our drinks in companionable silence. When I threw back the last dregs of my bottle, I kicked my feet out in front of me, throwing my body forward to stand up. I bent down and placed my empty bottle beside the opener on the table. "Again, thank you, Erin," I said with a nod in her direction.

She took a dainty sip of her beer and set it down beside my empty, standing up. "You don't need to thank me, Griffin. I didn't do anything that deserves thanks."

Without any reservation or forethought, I pulled her into a hug. "You're a peach," I said.

She hugged me back, holding on longer than I'd expected. "You know, I've always hated that nickname."

I pulled away, my hands on her shoulders. "That's all right, the women in my life rarely like the names I give them, but they always seem to stick." I cocked my head and shrugged.

"You're such a smug asshole, you know that, right?" A huge smile spread across her face.

"Damn straight." I winked.

"Well, Griffin Daniels, I'm glad we had this talk." She took a step back and held out her hand for me to shake.

Placing my palm against hers, I shook her hand. "Me too."

"Glad to hear it. Now if you'll excuse me, friend, I'm kicking you out. My roomies are waitin' for me at that country line dance place."

"Line dancing?" I wrinkled my nose. "No offense, Peach, but we broke up just in time."

She punched my arm. "Oh, shut up. But sadly," she pouted, "I do regret not getting you out on the dance floor sooner. I would have loved to show you a move or two."

"Oh really?" I laughed. "I don't know, I think you might have missed out on something. Back in the day, I used to be quite the line dancer." I shrugged.

"Uh-uh." She shook her head. "You're so full of it."

"No, seriously, in high school, Jillian would drag me line dancing every Thursday night. They have TV cameras recording everyone stomping and kicking, and then they air the 'performance' on Saturday night. I think they still do, if I'm not mistaken."

"You? Line dancing?" She looked me up and down. "That I'd pay to see. You busy tonight, Rock Star? One last hurrah together?"

"As tempting as that sounds, I'm going to pass."

"You sure?" She batted her eyelashes and shimmied a little.

"Yes, I'm sure." I laughed, heading for the door. "I've had enough line dancing to last me a lifetime."

Erin followed me to the door. "Your loss."

Turning the knob, I pulled open the door and stepped out onto the little porch. "I'll live," I said, facing her.

Hopping back and forth, she wrapped her arms across her torso. "Hot damn, is it cold out there."

Chin raised, I cocked my eyebrow. "I told you that when I got here."

"I'm gonna go change," she said through chattering teeth. "See you, Rock Star."

"Bye, Peach." I smiled with a salute as I turned down the sidewalk.

"Griffin?"

I halted when I heard my name. I spun around on my heel. "Yeah?"

"Get your head out of your ass. Don't wait until it's too late. You deserve happiness, too."

She smiled and shut the door.

I walked the rest of the way to my bike. *Happy?* I knew what I needed to be happy, but I still wasn't sure I could have her and risk compromising her happiness and future.

Chapter Twenty-Two

Since the breakup I'd kept to myself. I didn't want to field a bunch of questions from the guys and Nee. I made sure I was in the studio when I knew they wouldn't be. Lately even working with them felt strained. Like I'd told Jillian at Thanksgiving, nothing felt right; nothing was working out the way it was supposed to. And it all stemmed back to Jillian...what I wanted and what I couldn't have.

It was Friday night, and I was sitting on my bed, cradling my guitar like some sappy country singer. Next thing I knew, I'd be writing fucking song lyrics about crying into my beer.

Someone pounded on my door. "Yo, Griff. You in there, dude?" Thor called from the other side.

"Yeah." I had a pencil shoved between my teeth and my fingers on the guitar.

My door opened and Thor stuck his head in. "We're partying tonight. You coming?"

I shook my head. "Nah." I wasn't in the mood to party.

"What is with you, man? You used to be a fun motherfucker. Now you're just a moody, punk-ass bitch."

I lifted my left hand off the strings and extended my middle finger.

"Thanks for proving my point." Thor saluted my silent gesture. "When's Jill come home? Hopefully she can do something to set you right."

"This weekend." I put my hand back on the strings, adjusting my right-hand fingering. "I'm working on something. I need to get it down before I lose it." Once my hands were positioned, I glanced back up at Thor. "Close the door when you leave."

Thor sighed. "Whatever, dude. I'm hanging with Harper tonight, so don't wait up."

Not looking up, I said, "I never do, man."

He shut the door harder than necessary, causing the change on my dresser to rattle. "Dick," I shouted. Hopefully, he heard me.

Shaking off the interruption, I tapped out a rhythm on the wood before bringing my fingers over to the strings. This wasn't a song for Mine Shaft, but a song for me, to Jillian.

I was just getting into the groove of the song when my phone buzzed on my nightstand. "God damn it," I growled. "Why won't people leave me the fuck alone?"

Tossing my guitar to the end of the bed, I reached over to the small table and looked at the screen. It was Jillian. Instantly my mind was racing. I hit "Accept." "Jillibean?"

"Holy shit, you answered. Don't you have a show tonight?"

I breathed a sigh of relief. She sounded fine. "Nope." I relaxed at the sound of her voice and leaned over and grabbed my guitar, settling it back in my lap. "We have the night off."

"Uh…can you talk?" she asked hesitantly.

"To you? Fuck yeah. What kind of question is that?" I shook my head. She was acting weird again.

"Oh, well, you just sounded busy. I didn't want to interrupt anything," she laughed dryly. "You're not hanging with Erin tonight? I thought she'd be all over your downtime."

I balanced the phone between my shoulder and ear, putting my fingers back into place on the strings. "We broke up. And Thor has a date, so he most likely won't be home before sunrise."

"You broke up?" Her voice rose at the end.

I had to smile. Did I sense a little excitement in her tone? I shook my head and silently worked my fingers over the keys. "Yeah."

"What happened?"

I paused my fingers, resting them on the strings. "Nothing really. We just weren't that into each other."

"Is everything all right?" she asked. She sounded worried.

"Mmm-hmm," I mumbled, picking up my pencil to jot down a chord progression. "Just working on…a new song. We have a gig on New Year's Eve, and I want it ready for that night." Not really, though. This song wasn't on the New Year's Eve set list, but I held out hope that I'd get to perform it for her, one day.

Even though the song wasn't finished, I still had the scene worked out in my head…how I would play this song for her.

Up on stage, just me, a stool, and my acoustic guitar. I'd perch myself atop the stool, cradle the guitar in my arms—just the way I'd hold her, if I were allowed that privilege. A single spot would be trained on me. I'd start to play slowly, caressing the music from my instrument as I kissed the mic. I'd seek out her face in the crowd, knowing I wouldn't be able to see her, but that wouldn't stop me from trying. Once I could feel her presence, I'd sing…only for her.

"That's awesome, Griff." Her exuberance brought me out of the fantasy. "Where's the show?"

I shook off the dream and leaned back against the headboard. "At the Pageant."

"What? That's huge! Why aren't you more excited?"

"I guess I'm just a little nervous. I don't want any fuckups." I was nervous about the show. It was Adam's first gig since his injury and he hadn't had much rehearsal time. Not to mention this was the biggest fucking show of our lives. The Pageant was huge. And our spring tour hinged on the turnout.

"Griffin!" she cheered. "I'm so proud of you! You guys are great, you have nothing to worry about."

"You'll be there, right?" I asked, hoping she hadn't made New Year's Eve plans. I needed her there like I needed air in my lungs.

"Uh…yeah," she scoffed. "What? You think I'd miss your biggest gig yet? Someone would have to chain me to a cinder-block wall to keep me away."

I sighed, relieved. "Good."

"Will you sing me the song you're working on?"

Her voice was home, wrapping my body in warmth. I just listened, luxuriating in the rise and fall of her natural cadence.

"Please, Griff?" she asked again, adding a musical lilt to her voice. I couldn't deny her now.

I was no longer the musician, but the instrument she played. I'd do anything she asked of me. "All right, but if I'm going to do this, I need to play it, too," I said. "Hang up, and we can FaceTime. I'll test what I've got out on you. Sound good?"

"Hell yeah."

I laughed at her excitement. "I'll get my shit together here, and I'll call you back. Give me a minute."

"OK," she said, and then wasted no time disconnecting the line.

I stood up, stretched, and went to find a couple of books to prop my iPad on while I played. God, I wasn't ready to sing this song to her. How was I going to hide all my feelings I didn't want her to know?

Stacking the books in a pile on my bed, I rested the iPad against them. Testing out the angle, I sat back on my bed, my guitar in hand. My face filled the screen, but if I kept my head down, concentrating on the strings, I could avoid making eye contact. Getting through the song would be hard enough. I didn't need the allure of her dark eyes making things more difficult.

I reached over my guitar and tapped her name on the screen.

She answered. A giddy smile pulled at her lips, and my heart dropped into my stomach. *God, she is beautiful.* I wanted to tell her. I wanted to tell her how much I loved her. I wanted her to hear it in my song. But then I remembered her, and her dreams. And I hoped she didn't hear my heart.

I steadied my voice, trying to pretend she had no effect on me, when clearly that wasn't the case. I cleared my throat. "OK, I'm set up here. Can you hear me all right?"

She nodded, a brilliant smile lighting her face. "Perfectly."

I smiled, too. I couldn't help it. My body ached, I missed her so much. "It's good to see you, Bean."

"Ditto." She exhaled.

I held her smiling eyes with mine for one more second, then looked down at my fingers. Strumming a couple of slow, steady chords, I returned my eyes to her, something I'd told myself I wouldn't do. But her stare was magnetic, a pull I couldn't withstand. She was my north, my way home.

I took a deep breath, ready to sing for her.

The words poured out of me. I prayed for her to understand what I felt for her. With our eyes locked on each other's, my song bridged the thousand miles separating us. She rested her chin in the palm of her hand, a quiet, contented smile playing at her lips as she watched and listened. My body swayed with each strum, my fingers knew exactly where to be. And my mouth sang the words

I'd never dared to speak. It was always easier to put my feelings into a song and bury my true emotions in metaphors.

On the screen Jillian swayed to the beat of the music, soaking in every note…every word. When my fingers rounded out the last chord, I didn't dampen the strings right away. Instead I let them wrap around us, sealing us away from the rest of the world.

* * *

Are you busy tonight? I REALLY want to see you.

I read the words on the screen and my heart sank. Her winter break was in full swing; she'd been home for four days already. We hadn't gotten to see each other at all. I wanted to see her more than anything, but I knew I wouldn't be able to hold back how I felt. I would be selfish and take what I wanted…*her*. But if I could keep her at a distance, I wouldn't ruin everything she'd accomplished. I couldn't have that on my shoulders. So I made us both miserable and hid behind my work. I typed back, *Jillibean, I'm so sorry. I can't come over tonight. I'm at the studio until late.*

I hit "Send," hating myself.

In the recording room, Adam worked out the stiffness in his wrist. I hit the switch and the mics on the kit went live. Adam always liked to hear the playback. My phone buzzed with an incoming text. Jillian: *No problem. I miss you.*

I kept my response short. I didn't want to run the risk of saying something that would cross the line. Because damn, I was so close to crossing that fucking line. *I know. I miss you, too. I'm sorry.*

Don't be sorry. I'm proud of you!

Thanks, Bean. I'll talk to you later.

Just as I hit "Send," Adam finished playing, quieting the crash.

He insisted on practicing in the recording booth, hoping Dane would change his mind and let him rerecord some of the tracks Nee had already finished. But Dane shot him down—not with the album coming out in two and a half weeks, a week after our NYE gig.

The album was finished and well into the postproduction stages. Dane hoped to create enough local buzz to boost album sales in the coming weeks. With Mine Shaft having released its first single a month ago—which was already sitting in the top twenty on iTunes—and a second scheduled for right before the concert, things were happening faster than Adam healed. When I played the acoustic song I'd written for Jillian, Dane had gone ape-shit, already lining up an acoustic EP to put out a month after our debut.

I was glad Dane knocked down Adam's pleas to redo his tracks. My head was already spinning with the concert, the albums, and songwriting. Nee was by far the superior drummer and she'd done a hell of a job. But now that Adam's wrist was healed, and Nee was packing to move out west, it was time for Adam to return to the throne.

He came into the booth, sweating like a pig. Nee made sweat look hot, Adam looked fucking disgusting. "Dude, I think there's a puddle under the kit. Is it hot in there or something?"

Adam flipped me off. "I'm giving it all I got, man. Lay off," he said, wiping a towel across his forehead and breathing heavily. "I think I'm ready, though."

"You're doing fine. How's the wrist?" I kicked my feet down off the desk in the booth and spun the chair around to face him.

Adam twisted his hand around, testing it out. "Feels good." He nodded. "I can tell you it feels *damn* good getting back behind my drums. Uhhh," he sighed, throwing his head back. A moment later he looked back at me and smiled, snapping his towel at my chair.

"What are you doing here so late? I figured you'd be hanging with Jill, now that she's back."

I glanced at my phone, wondering if she'd texted back. Nothing. I shook my head. "Too much going on here."

Adam shook his head. "I don't get you, man. Why do you insist on making her miserable?"

"Excuse me?" I was thrown off by his comment. I've always striven to do the exact opposite.

Adam tossed his towel across the room like a basketball. "Who are you shitting? You two look at each other and Cupid throws up. I just don't get why you're so worried about screwing things up with her. You're the golden boy, Griff. Good things just happen for you."

I wanted to laugh. He really had no idea. "Whatever, dude."

"If you say so." He knelt, shoving his sticks into a backpack. Standing up, he swung the strap onto his shoulder. "Well, I'm out, man. See you."

"Yeah."

As he left, the door didn't latch shut, but stayed open just a little. I shrugged it off, too lazy to get up and pull it closed. Reaching for my guitar, sitting beside the mixing board, I picked a few strings and adjusted the tuning pegs.

Enjoying the quiet darkness, I strummed miscellaneous chords, seeing what I could come up with. I hummed a melody over the chords, lyrics igniting like a wildfire in my head.

Lost and lonely in a crowded room
Can't shake the dread I know will loom
When I'm surrounded by a million faces
But not yours 'cause time erases.

"Pretty haunting tune."

Startled, I slid my hand down the strings, the discordant sound killing my mojo. "Oh, hey, Nee." I leaned my guitar against the desk and turned to face her. "I thought I was the only one here."

"Nope. Since I'm finished with Mine Shaft, Leo's looking into getting me a solo gig. I was working on some vocals."

"Is there anything you can't do?"

"Ride a bicycle."

I stared at her. If there was one thing I'd learned about Nee in the last four months, it was that she was brutally honest. "You can't ride a bike?"

"Nope. I fall off every time." She propped herself against the doorframe and folded her arms across her chest.

I laughed. "Sorry, I've just never heard of a grown person not being able to ride a bike. I mean, it's like a rite of passage. Every kid picks it up eventually."

She shook her head. "Laugh it up, pretty boy." She came into the room and sat beside me, smiling.

"I'm sorry. I shouldn't laugh."

Smacking my leg with the back of her hand, she said. "It's fine. I'm over it. Most people have parents to teach them shit like that. Let's just say my parents wouldn't win any 'Parent of the Year' awards."

That sobered me. "Sorry, Nee."

She waved off my apology and rolled her eyes. "I'm cool. Who needs to know how to ride a lame-ass bike when you've got a car?"

"You got a point."

"Why are you here so late?" She sat back and curled herself into the chair. Her pint-size frame reminded me of Jillian; they were both so tiny.

"Just messing around." I tapped my toe against my guitar. "I like it here when everyone's gone. It's quiet. I can hear myself think." I looked back up at her. "Lately, that's been impossible."

She nodded. "I hate to tell you, but it's about to get more fucked up, dude. Especially if you keep writing songs like the one you were just singing. That one sounded personal."

"Yeah," I mumbled. "Most everything I write is personal. Song-writing is my therapy. I'm not good at talking about feelings, so I put them to music instead."

Nee smiled and her eyes softened. "Was that song for Erin?" Her voice did that weird, girly, pitchy thing.

I wrinkled my nose and shook my head. "Erin and I broke up."

"Oh, no. What happened?" Her playful demeanor disappeared.

"Nothing really. We just didn't click." I propped my boot up on the desk next to the mixing board and rested my other foot on top. It felt good to stretch out.

"So tell me who the song's about, then." She held my eyes, daring me to spill my guts.

Strangely enough, I kind of wanted to tell her everything. If I couldn't tell Jillian how I really felt, I wanted someone to know…someone to hear how much I was dying inside. "It's about my best friend…Jillian."

She sat forward. "You have a best friend that doesn't have a dick, and you've never introduced me? And here I've had to deal with your dickhead friends for the last few months."

I gave her a sidelong glance. "You love those guys, and you know it."

She softened. "Yeah, I do. I just like fucking with you. So, tell me more about this Jillian."

"How long you got?" I reclined my head on the back of the chair, staring up at the ceiling. "That could take all night."

She shrugged. "Keshawn's at a fight. He won't be home until late. Lay it on me, big guy."

A dry laugh punched its way out of my chest. "Jillian's my best friend. I've known her forever. She's been through a lot of shit over the years, and I've been right there by her side. She always had my back, too. Whenever I doubted my music, she never let me give up. She's my biggest cheerleader."

"And why haven't I met this chick?" Erin kicked my chair.

"She's off living her dream."

"Which is?" Erin asked.

"Design school. She's always wanted to be a fashion designer." Pride swelled inside me.

"Cool," Nee said. "But why the melancholy song, then?"

I swayed the chair back and forth. "You don't miss anything, do you?"

She shook her head and smiled.

"A few weeks before Jillian left for school—which by the way is in Rhode fucking Island, eleven hundred fucking miles away—"

"You sound pleased about that." Nee's head bobbed up and down.

"Oh, yeah. It's great." I matched her level of sarcasm with my own.

Nee leaned forward. "So what happened before she left?"

Racking a hand through my hair, I continued, "She kissed me."

"What?" Her mouthed formed an O shape. "I thought you two were just friends?"

"We were…we are," I corrected. "But for some reason, Jillian pushed the issue that night." I let out a breath, remembering exactly how her smooth, hot lips had felt pressed to mine.

"Did you kiss her back?"

I felt a pinch inside my chest, right where her name was etched into my skin. I rubbed it. "No. I pushed her away," I said somberly. "But I wanted to. *God*, I wanted to. The second her lips touched mine, it took every ounce of willpower I possessed not to take her home and show her exactly how much I loved her. I love that girl so much it hurts." My chest clenched.

Nee stood up and the office chair went sliding across the small room. "Are you an idiot? Why the hell did you push her away?" She smacked the backside of my head. For such a tiny person, she hit hard.

"Ow." I rubbed my head, forgetting about the pinch in my chest. "What was that for?"

"Asshat, pay attention," she said, talking with her hands. "When the girl you're in love with kisses you, DON'T PUSH HER AWAY!" she yelled. "Why?" She threw her hands up, waiting for my answer.

"I had to. I know Jillian. If I had told her then that I loved her, she wouldn't have gone away to school. She would have given up on her dream—something she'd talked about for years—and for what, me? I couldn't let her throw everything she'd worked for away. So I lied. I pushed her away and told her I only wanted to be her friend. And there you have it"—I waved my hand—"the catalyst for my melancholy music."

"Ugh, men are so stupid," Nee grumbled, walking over to retrieve her chair. She pulled it behind her and parked right in front of mine before plopping down. "Listen, I'm going to give it to you straight, man. Jillian put herself out there. That took balls. Now, I'm going out on a limb here, but I'd bet my house in Vegas—and you know how much I love my new house in Vegas"—she pointed her finger in my face and cocked an eyebrow—"Jillian fucking loves you as much as you love her. What you're doing isn't fair. You didn't even give her the chance to make the decision between you and school. What if she had chosen both? What? You too much of a coward to make a long-distance relationship work? Give me a break." She took a deep breath and sighed.

I was afraid to say anything; Nee was scary when she was pissed.

Still talking animatedly with her hands, she continued. "You may know her well, but I guarantee you don't know everything. There are secrets women keep that are only known to God. And now"—she moved her hand, gesturing toward me—"you're miserable, and I bet she is, too. It's time to grow a pair, Griffin, and tell your woman you were fucking wrong."

"What if it's too late?" I whispered.

She pursed her lips. "Then you'll know, and you can move on. But you'll never know if you don't tell her how you really feel. Give her a choice. Relationships, friendships, for any of them to work, everyone needs a voice…not one person calling the shots."

I was speechless at the moment, my mind soaking up all of Nee's wisdom.

After a minute or two, I asked, "What do I do? How do I fix this?"

Nee smiled like she'd just solved all the world's problems. "What you do best…sing to her."

Chapter Twenty-Three

*M*erry Christmas, Bean! I texted, stretched out in bed, thankful to have the day off. I had big plans for the day: doing whatever the hell Jillian wanted to do. I missed her so goddamned much, and after taking Nee's beatdown that she called advice, I had things in the works for the New Year's Eve concert...something special for Jillian...so she'd finally know how I felt. But right now I just wanted to see her.

Merry Christmas, Griff! Please say I get to see you tonight?

I smiled when her reply came through, then typed back, *You bet your ass, it's Christmas.*

Remind me to thank baby Jesus for giving you a reason to hang with me!

That hurt. And it should. I'd been deliberately avoiding her, trying to figure out what my next move would be. *Damn, that's harsh. I'll see you later!*

I sprang out of bed, ready to hit the shower before I went to get her. Outside my bedroom door, I rummaged around the hall closet for a clean towel. I couldn't remember the last time I'd done laundry. "Yo, Thor." I banged my fist on his door. "Dude."

He tore his door open and stuck his head out. "What the fuck, man?"

"Merry Christmas to you, too," I snapped. "Are there any clean towels anywhere?"

"How the hell should I know?" He shrugged and glanced over his shoulder. "Can't talk," he said, looking back. "Company."

"Sorry, man. Go." I waved him back into his room.

Thor didn't stick around to hear my dismissal, and I didn't blame him. Chuckling under my breath, I went downstairs in search of clean towels.

I opened the washer. Empty. Next I moved to the dryer and pulled the handle. The stench of wet, mildewed towels assaulted my nostrils. "Fuck me," I growled. I couldn't remember if I'd thrown them in the dryer without starting it, or if it had been Thor. Regardless, they smelled like death.

I held my breath and began pulling out the cold, smelly towels, tossing them back into the empty washer. I threw in a couple of those pod things and started it up.

With more time on my hands than I wanted, I grabbed a slice of cold pizza and a glass of milk and headed back up to my room.

I opened my door and heard my phone buzzing. Taking two large steps, I glanced at the name on the screen and saw it was my mother. Ever since I'd told her I was quitting school, she'd pussyfooted around the issue, refusing to acknowledge that I was following my dreams just like Jillian. If she was happier with her head in the sand, then so be it. At least my announcement had gotten her off my back.

Setting the glass down on my nightstand, I answered the call. "Hey, Ma, merry Christmas."

"Merry Christmas. Did I wake you?"

I took a bite of pizza, speaking through a mouthful. "Uh-uh. Just got up."

"Oh, good. We're eating around five. You're coming over, right?" She sounded leery, unsure if I was still pissed or not.

"Yeah. I'm bringing Jillibean, too."

"Great. I was going to tell you to bring her. See you both then. Love you."

"Love you, too, Ma."

She disconnected the call. I folded the rest of my pizza in half and stuffed it into my mouth before dropping onto my bed. I snatched a notebook and pencil from my bedside table. With the notebook in my lap, I took a hefty drink, finishing the tall glass of milk in one gulp. I slammed the glass back onto the table.

I focused my attention on the song I'd been working on the night Nee kicked my ass about Jillian. I leaned against the headboard and closed my eyes, calling on Jillian to be my muse. Her image rested behind my eyelids.

My eyes fixed on hers. She stared back, a mischievous smile on her lips, daring me to make a move. Her nearly black eyes held a mysterious quality—a gravitational pull that refused to free me.

If it were up to me, I'd gladly get lost in those eyes and never return, as long as I could look at her, touch her, and hold her in my arms forever.

God, I want her.

I wanted to run my hands over every inch of her tiny, curvy frame. My mouth trailed behind, tasting her…drinking her in. My lips savored the warmth of her skin, memorizing each hill and valley of her body.

I wanted more.

The desire to fold my body around hers, to bury myself deep inside her, was almost too much.

With the image of Jillian and me locked together, my hand skimmed the waistband of my jogging pants before plunging inside. The vivid picture of Jillian and me lost in each other was enough to leave me panting and gritting my teeth together. It didn't take long. My legs went weak, and the image I'd conjured blurred as I pressed my eyes closed tighter, finding my release.

* * *

By the time I'd finished the small load of laundry, showered, and headed over to Jillian's sister's house, it was nearing four o'clock.

Pulling into the driveway, I revved the engine a few extra times for Jennifer's sake and parked my bike in the driveway for all the neighbors to see. I hopped off and went up the sidewalk, resisting the urge to tromp through Jennifer's still ridiculously green lawn. It was fucking December, how in the hell did she keep her grass so green?

I rang the doorbell and heard a flurry of activity inside before the door opened.

"Giff-in!" yelled Mitchell, one of Jillian's twin nephews.

I crouched down, putting myself at eye level with him. I palmed his head, giving his white-blond curls a good muss. "Mitchell, my man, how are you?" I brought my hand down in a fist and he bumped it back.

Coming up behind Mitchell, his brother Michael sailed down the hall. "Griff!"

Before I could stand up, the two boys launched themselves onto me, practically knocking me over.

"Boys, boys, boys." Matthew Barrett, their dad, followed after them. "Come on." He pulled Michael off me. "Let Griffin in the door, will you?"

I stood up, scooping Mitchell into my arms. "It's all right, I missed them, too." These boys were the one part of Jennifer I did like. I could never figure out how she'd had such amazing kids. They definitely took after their dad. Matthew Barrett was a great guy. What he saw in Jennifer I didn't know, and I didn't really care to find out.

"Where have you been?" Mitchell asked.

I turned around and shut the door. "Well, I've been working a lot." I bounced him a couple of times and he giggled.

"My turn!" Michael shouted, jumping at my feet.

I bent down and lifted him into my other arm. Even with both of them in my arms, they weighed nothing.

Over the twins' giggles, Matthew asked, "How's it going, man?" He patted my shoulder, directing me into the living room.

"Good, the album's in postproduction. Comes out January seventh." I brought the twins over to the couch and made a show of dropping them onto the cushions, WWE style. They rolled over each other, belly laughs ripping free from deep inside them. I couldn't help but laugh, too.

"Great. I'll have to check it out," Matthew said.

"Yeah, that'd be cool. Is Jillian around?" I looked toward the stairs leading to her room.

"Oh, yeah. Upstairs." He tilted his head in that direction. "Go on up. I'll keep the wrecking crew down here." He winked at me and then looked at the boys wrestling together on the couch.

I shook my head. It astounded me that such a prim and proper woman as Jennifer had given birth to those rough-and-tumble boys. "Thanks, man."

I left the guys alone in the living room and made my way up the stairs. Strangely, I was both nervous and excited. It was time to quit playing games. I wanted Jillian to know that things were going to be different now. At least I hoped.

I knocked on her door and waited. No answer. I knocked again. There was still no answer. Not wanting to startle her, I turned the knob and slowly opened the door.

Lying on her stomach, her feet crossed in the air, she looked so peaceful, happily sketching, not a care in the world. She was breathtaking.

I sneaked into her room, quietly shutting the door behind me. As I crept toward the bed, I saw earbuds pressed into her ears and heard the faint sound of a very familiar song blasting from her iPhone.

Carefully I crawled my way onto the bed, resting beside her.

She turned toward me, her dark eyes widening in surprise…pulling me in.

Without a word she rolled her body in my direction. On my outstretched arm she laid her head, still holding me captive with her eyes.

Entranced by this woman, my best friend, I reached to touch her. My fingers brushed over her soft cheeks, moving some loose strands of blond hair away from her face. This close, I could feel her warm breath on my face, and I'd have given anything to kiss her. But I resisted, not wanting to ruin my carefully constructed plan for New Year's Eve. However, if she kept staring at me the way she was, her eyes soft and glowing…her sexy lips parted slightly…I'd have to reconsider.

She leaned in a little more.

This is going to be a long fucking week! She was not making this easy.

A new song came through her earbuds, another Mine Shaft

song. Her eyes still on mine, she moved her right arm between us, causing some of her pencils to fall to the floor. I couldn't help it, I wanted her closer. I grabbed her hand, using it to pull her toward me. I draped my arm over her waist, breathing in the scent of her. She smelled so fresh, like flowers in the wind.

With only inches between us, Jillian remained still in my arms. She had to know how I felt about her. How much I loved her. Just as in my daydream earlier, my eyes skimmed over her features. I also knew how this would end if my gaze kept roaming, and I had to do this right. Jillian wasn't just some woman. She was *the* woman…my woman.

Lifting my hand from her waist, I rested it behind her neck, feeling her soft hair beneath my callused fingers. It seemed disgraceful to touch her with my roughened, bass-torn hands. She was so delicate and soft, I feared my touch would mar her tenderness. But she didn't shy away, and I was thankful.

My fingers trailed along her jaw, over to her ear. Pulling gently, I grasped the wire to her earbuds. The earpiece fell out. "Whatcha drawing?" I whispered.

Her cheeks flushed in response to my question. That piqued my interest. It wasn't like her to withhold her creations. I brought my arm up, bearing the weight of my head on my elbow. "Jillibean? You OK?"

Then, like a bolt of lightning, Jillian was out of the bed. The rest of her pencils fell on the floor, along with her sketch pad. "What? Yeah…fine. I'm fine," she stuttered.

What the hell is wrong with her? I ran a hand through my hair and down my face, the stubble scratching against my calluses. Blowing out a breath, I stretched over the side of the bed, trying to get a glimpse of this drawing that was making her spastic. "Let's see what masterpiece you've created today," I drawled.

My fingers brushed against the spirals and the pages, struggling to get a firm grasp on it. I didn't know why she was being so weird. It wasn't like her not to show me her work; she showed me everything.

I lifted it from the ground. Just as my eyes landed on the lower half of the paper, the sketchbook went sailing from my fingers, hitting the door across the room. "What the fuck! Why'd you do that?" I sat up on the bed, shocked.

"I…I'm sorry," she stuttered. Her eyes were as wide as mine.

Pulling my feet to my chest, I rolled to the side of the bed where she stood, and I got up. Half a step, and I towered over her. She followed me with her eyes, but refused to really look at me. If I didn't know better, she would have seemed scared. *But why?* I didn't like it. The subtle fear on her face was out of place when it came to me. She *never* needed to fear me.

I lightly pinched her chin between my thumb and forefinger and drew her head up, forcing her dark eyes to look at me. "You better start talking. What's wrong?"

She stared at me. The color of her eyes intensified, turning from dark brown to almost black. But she remained quiet.

I didn't press. She'd tell me what was on her mind when she was ready. Instead I held her. Closing the physical distance between us, I wrapped my arms around her, folding her to my chest.

She let out a long breath and relaxed against my chest. I held her, breathed her in, and tried my damnedest to take away all her worries.

"Come on, get changed," I said close to her ear. "We've got somewhere to be." I pulled her away and smiled, hoping to lighten the heavy gravity surrounding us.

Chapter Twenty-Four

I pulled Jillian's tiny Honda Civic into my parents' gravel drive and glanced over at her. She looked back at me and smiled. "Your parents' house is the big surprise?"

"They've been dying to see you." I pushed open the door and got out at the same time Jillian opened hers. She'd beaten me to it. Taking a couple steps around the front of the car, I noticed Jillian hadn't budged. "You coming?" Behind the open car door, she stood frozen in front of the house.

Startled, she jumped and shut the car door. "Yeah," she answered, an air of excitement in her voice.

I made my way around the car and held my hand out for hers, craving her touch like a starving man craves the smallest scrap of food. With our fingers intertwined, I pulled her up the sidewalk. Jillian marveled at my mother's over-the-top light display. Since Mom bought her dream house three years ago, Pop has had some major decorative feats to accomplish. I didn't envy him.

Once we hit the front porch, I went right in, not bothering to knock. Awesomesauce came barreling down the stairs, barking gruffly, announcing our arrival. "Hey, buddy," I crooned, bending over to pet the dog, but refusing to let go of Jillian. I scratched behind his ears. Awesomesauce rolled over onto his back, begging me to scratch his belly. I stood back up and rubbed his belly with the toe of my boot. "Come on, boy." I tapped my leg. "Let's go see what that amazing smell is." I turned to Bean and smiled, nodding toward the kitchen, and reaching for her hand.

"Everything smells heavenly," she said with a contented sigh.

Walking down the hallway, I tapped my leg again, encouraging Awesomesauce to follow along as we started for the kitchen. "Mom insisted we have a late Christmas dinner, so I could pick you up." I glanced over my shoulder and noticed how her face softened into a relaxed smile. She was finally home.

"Mom, we're here," I called. My boots clomped on the shiny floor and Awesomesauce trotted at my heels. "Mom?"

"I'll be down in a minute!" Her voice came from upstairs. I shrugged and continued toward the kitchen. The cold pizza I'd had for breakfast hadn't filled me up, and I was fucking hungry.

Once we were in the kitchen, Jillian let go of my hand and walked around, taking in all the decorations, her fingers brushing gently over Mom's "Santas from around the World" figurine collection that sat on the tall rectangular table near the pantry.

I let her go, wanting her to feel at home. No pressures here—just family and people who loved her. I wanted the fear and apprehension I had seen in her eyes at Jennifer's house to disappear. I wanted the awkward tension between us to melt away.

I went to the oven and pulled it open, peeking inside. I hummed and breathed in a giant whiff of turkey. "Now that's what I'm talking about." I closed the oven door and turned around, still drunk on the smell of poultry.

"Thank you," Jillian said, turning to face me.

My eyebrows pinched together. "For what?" I walked toward

her, desperate to have her back in my arms. She'd been away from me for too long. *God, she has to know how much I want her...how much I need her.*

I lifted her purse from her shoulder, gently guiding it over her head, careful not to bump her. I didn't remove my eyes from her once, spilling the contents of my heart with just a look. Slowly I pushed back her coat, dragging my hands down her arms as the coat slipped off. "I'll put these up for you." I winked, kneeling down to pick her purse up from the floor. As I knelt, my nose brushed against hers, sending ripples of pleasure through my body.

"Jillian!" Mom sang, entering the kitchen. *Damn! Things were just getting interesting.*

Jillian spun around like she'd been caught doing something naughty. "Mrs. Daniels," she said, walking over to my mom's open arms.

"It's so good to see you, sweetie." Mom hugged her tightly, rocking her back and forth. "We've missed you so much."

I leaned against the island in the middle of the kitchen, watching the exchange between the two most important women in my life. I loved how much my parents loved Jillian. Nee was so right. I was a fucking idiot to keep Jillian so far away. What was I thinking? I was more convinced than ever that Jillian belonged with me. I just hoped it wasn't too late, and that I hadn't missed my chance. One more week, then Jillian would know exactly how I felt about her. But I prayed she already knew.

"I've missed you, too," Jillian said, hugging my mom in return.

Mom stepped back and slipped her arm though Jillian's, leading her in my direction. Ignoring my presence, Mom stepped around me and Awesomesauce and led Jillian to a chair on the opposite side. As they walked by, I caught Jillian's eye and shook my head, grinning.

"Hey, Ma," I piped up. "Remember me? Your son?" I tapped her on the shoulder. Now that Bean was here, I was forgotten. And I loved it. I loved how Jillian fit right in with us.

"Oh, shoo," Mom said, waving her free hand, brushing me out of the way. "You're here at least three times a week raiding my refrigerator." Or I used to be, at least. Mom was keeping our argument quiet, and I was thankful. I smiled and stepped out of her way.

"I don't know," I sighed, "I've always suspected you liked her better than me." I played along.

Mom cocked an eyebrow at me. Had I taken the charade too far? "Well, duh, she's much easier on the eyes."

I laughed, shaking my head. "I can't disagree with you there, Ma."

Jillian giggled, her cheeks reddening. I would have given anything to taste the sound of that laughter on her lips. It took every ounce of willpower not to snatch her away from my mom and capture her mouth with mine.

Mom pulled out a barstool and Jillian sat as Mom took up a small knife and went to work chopping the vegetables that were spread out on the countertop.

I stared at Jillian. The more I watched, the harder it was not to kiss her. I needed space to clear my head. She consumed me. "I'm gonna go find Pop," I said, knocking a fist against the island. "Don't talk about me too much while I'm gone."

Mom sent a piece of broccoli sailing across the island, hitting me in the head. "Didn't I tell you to shoo?"

I held up my hands to block any other flying vegetables. "I'm shooing!" I walked backward in the direction of the living room, keeping my eye on Mom…and Jillian.

Even with Jillian in the next room, I could feel her like a magnetic force. The living room was quiet and empty. "Dad?" I called, wondering what he was up to.

He didn't answer.

I walked through the living room and back to the front of the house, stepping outside. It was so fucking cold outside. Adjusting my flimsy leather jacket, I pulled it closed as best I could before I headed down the porch steps.

"Hey, Pop? You out here?" I called again, turning up the drive, toward the garage.

The garage lights were on. I twisted the doorknob and let myself in. A rush of warm air greeted me, and I saw Dad reclined in his favorite camo chair, watching a football game.

"Can you believe it?" he said, not bothering to turn around and see who came in. "Not one stinking football game on today."

"What do you mean?" I sat down on the ragged old couch beside his chair and stretched my legs out wide. "What's that?" I pointed to the screen.

"Just tape from earlier in the season," he growled, still scowling at the television screen.

I rested my head on the back cushion and closed my eyes. I blew out a big breath and relaxed. My Jillian-induced fog lifted slightly.

We were quiet for a long time. Dad remained absorbed in his game, and I welcomed the familiar sounds, which helped to clear my head. Even though I'd never enjoyed playing football, there was a soothing quality to the cheering crowd, the whistle, and the crunch of the pads as the players demolished one another. I'd grown up watching these films. It reminded me of being younger, a time when life was less complicated.

"What's on your mind, Son?" Dad asked, lowering the volume.

I lifted my head. I could never articulate what my problems were, that's why I wrote songs. It was easier to put emotions to music. I shook my head. "Just a lot going on." I scrubbed my hands over my face.

"You look like hell."

"Thanks," I spit back, annoyed.

"Jillian here?" He set the recliner rocking.

"Yep." I glanced at the ceiling for a second, organizing my thoughts. "Pop, can I ask you something?"

"Reconsider your decision about school?"

I gave my old man a sidelong glance. "Don't start, Pop."

"It was worth a try. But you're a man. I respect your choice."

I harrumphed. "Tell that to Mom."

"Just give her some time." Dad smiled.

"At least she's not making a fuss in front of Jillian. That's a start, huh?"

Dad considered my words but didn't voice his thoughts. "I know you didn't come out here to rehash this old discussion. What'd you want to ask me?"

I lifted my head, looking my father in the eye. "It's about Jillian."

"She all right?" Concern glossed over his features as he remembered back to a time when Jillian wasn't OK.

I nodded. "She's fine. It has to do with me…and her."

"What do you mean?" Dad sat forward in his chair, resting his elbows on his knees.

I took a deep breath and started in. "I'm tired of playing around, Dad. I can't pretend to hide my feelings for her anymore."

A smile cracked my Dad's tough exterior. "Well, it's about damn time." He reached over and smacked my knee, his smile giving way to laughter.

I shook my head. "What if I am too late?"

"There you go again, making excuses. I've watched you dance around that girl for years. Everyone that knows you two knows you're supposed to be together. Hell, the only two people that don't are you and her." He laughed dryly. "It's fourth down, Son, time to make your move. The only way you're going to know if it's too late is to put it all on the line. Tell her how you feel."

"I plan to. I just worry I've pushed her away so much, I can't get her back." I leaned forward, matching my father's stance.

"Son, throw the ball, send up your Hail Mary, knowing your Jillibean, she'll be there to catch it." He winked at me.

Inwardly I cringed. My dad and his ridiculous football analogies. But he had a point, just like Nee. Even though they used different phrases, their message was the same: I had to tell her how I felt, regardless of the outcome. I was cheating us both out of happiness.

I felt better now, more resolved. I would tell her everything on New Year's Eve, in front of a thousand fucking people.

"I don't know about you, but I'm hungry," Dad said, shoving my knee again. He stood up and groaned. "I'm going in the house."

"Right behind you, Pop." I stood, too, following Dad out of the garage and toward the house.

Dad put his arm around my shoulder, wrestling me to his side. "I know you've loved that girl for a long time. For years I've watched the way you look at her." He squeezed his arm, shaking me as he laughed. "I'm glad you finally figured it out."

My mind flashed back to Nee and the night she'd talked some sense into me. "I had some help."

"Course you did. Us men, we can be pretty dense when it comes to women."

"Ain't that the fucking truth," I sighed. Together we climbed the pack porch.

Before he pulled open the door, he squeezed my shoulder and smiled. "Don't let your momma hear you talking like that."

I smiled, pleased that Dad didn't regard my college-dropout status as grounds to quit speaking to me. I appreciated his candor. "No, sir."

* * *

By late evening we'd eaten and opened gifts. It was a great night, and I wasn't ready for it to end. Throughout the evening I flirted subtly with Jillian, finding ways to touch her when I could.

We said our good-byes and I ushered her back to the car. I pulled open her door, she sat down, and I sealed her away. Rounding the car, I climbed into the driver's seat.

Jillian sat back, a contented smile on her face, as I started the car and backed down the driveway.

"Thank you, Griffin. That was exactly what I needed." Her eyes closed and she relaxed farther into the seat.

A wicked smile spread across my face. Now that I had her alone, I was dying to turn things up a notch. I couldn't fight it any longer, I *needed* to touch her.

I rested my hand on her leg, like I'd done at dinner, but instead of a quick pat, I trailed my fingers up the length of her thigh. Lingering near the top of her leg, I dipped my fingertips between her legs, cursing the pants she'd worn. Heat rolled off her in waves.

She sucked in a breath. I threw a momentary glance in her direction just to see her bottom lip sucked between her teeth. *God damn it. I am losing my mind.* I was ready to fuck my New Year's Eve plan and turn it into a Christmas confession. I sat up in my seat, readjusting. My dick didn't care what day it was.

I pulled in a silent breath and put my eyes back on the road, holding on by a thread. Even though it was torture, I couldn't stop touching her. Occasionally I'd glance at her long enough to issue a silent dare, begging her to make the next move.

Does she want me the way I want her? Why does she keep quiet? I tried to gauge her body's reactions to my touch, but she was so guarded. *Have I done this to her? Made her scared to open up?*

For fifteen minutes my fingers traced lazy circuits up and down her leg, soaking in her warmth and inwardly dying for more. Neither of us spoke, the tension palpable. But when I saw taillights ahead, I reluctantly placed my hand back on the cold wheel.

Traffic slowed to a halt. Up ahead cop cars lined the street and another emergency vehicle flashed a bright-yellow arrow, directing people to the left lane.

We crept along, finally passing by the scene of the accident. Some unlucky bastard on a bike had eaten pavement. The bike, a tangled mess of metal, was being loaded onto a flatbed tow truck. There was no sign of the driver.

I looked over at Jillian. Her body was completely turned toward the window, held captive by the morbid scene. "Did you get a helmet yet?" she asked, coming back around to face me.

Uh-oh. This is not good. I bit my lip. I could feel her fury building as she anticipated my answer. "Not yet," I said sheepishly, trying my best to keep her calm.

"WHAT?" she roared. "You haven't gotten a fucking helmet yet?" She was pissed.

Even angry, she still lit a fire inside me. Her passion made her irresistible. I wondered how she'd respond if I kissed her. Just as I'd wanted to taste the laughter on her lips earlier, I'd have given anything to drink the anger right now. She was so fucking sexy when she was mad, and that wasn't helping the situation in my pants.

Taking a deep breath, centering my thoughts, I gave her an honest reply. "I haven't really had time. I eat and breathe Mine Shaft right now."

"Ugggh!" she growled. "I am so pissed at you right now!" She crossed her arms over her chest and sat back in the seat, fuming.

I made the left turn, heading into town toward Jennifer's house.

"Where are you going?" she asked indignantly, unleashing a murderous stare on me.

Confused by her question, I cut a quick glance in her direction. "To Jennifer's?"

"Uh-uh." She shook her head. "Go to your place. I'll drop you off and drive myself back to Jennifer's."

That was bullshit. No fucking way. "Jillian, that's ridiculous. I'm not leaving my bike parked at your sister's house."

"All right." She turned her whole body around, facing me. "We'll go get your bike, but I'm following you home." From the corner of my eye, I saw her lips press together as she gave me her meanest, toughest glare.

I dared a peek at her and shook my head. I knew better than to say anything.

It was quiet the rest of the way to Jennifer's, the hot sexual tension from earlier gone, replaced with Jillian's angry vibes.

I pulled into the drive, but the second the car came to a stop, Jillian got out and stomped around to the driver's side.

I pushed the door open and got out, leaving the car running. "Bean."

"Don't," she interrupted. "I'm following you home, and you're not going to change my mind."

There was no reasoning with her when she got this way. "I'll see you at my place, then." I sighed and walked to my bike while she got into her car.

A ten-minute drive home. I couldn't believe she had thrown a temper tantrum over a ten-minute drive. Now I was pissed. She had no right to treat me like an errant child. What was with the women in my life telling me what to do? First Mom and all the school shit, and now Jillian with the helmet.

I pulled into the back parking lot, and she followed, sliding into the space next to me. She turned off the ignition. I sat with the bike rumbling between my legs, loud and angry.

I wanted to hold on to my anger, but the second she stepped out of the car, it was gone. I killed the bike's engine and stared at her, face-to-face. All the passion expelled from us over the last few hours—the love, the lust, the anger…I swung my leg around, coming to stand beside her. "It's late, Bean. Why don't you just stay?"

She shook her head. "I've got to go." Without another word she turned to leave.

"Jillian, wait!" I raised my voice. I wanted her to stop.

She halted, reaching for the handle on her car door. I walked over and met her, pressing my hands into her shoulders.

I stared into her eyes, refusing to let her look away. "I'm really sorry, Bean. I've just been so busy."

"Since September!" she spit.

I cringed. I didn't want her to leave when she was this angry. "Will you go with me to get one?" I pouted, hoping to diffuse some of her rage. Even though I hated helmets, I'd put the damn thing on my head for her.

She nodded infinitesimally, and I could feel her letting go of the anger. "I'm still pissed at you, though."

I didn't answer; instead I ran my finger lightly along the side of her face.

"I should go," she sighed, leaning into my touch.

"You sure?" I cupped her cheek, dying to kiss her. *Fuck it. My willpower's shot.* I bent down, our mouths less than an inch apart.

My eyes slid closed. The moment I anticipated her warm lips on mine, she stepped away.

I opened my eyes, unable to read the expression on her face as she pulled the car door open and got in.

Standing in the cold, I watched her pull away, certain I was too late.

Chapter Twenty-Five

I unlocked the back door and kicked it open. I stomped to the fridge, yanking a Schlafly from the shelf. Popping the top off on the counter, I drained the bottle in record time and went back for another.

With the lip of my second beer pressed to my mouth, I heard Thor's heavy footfalls on the stairs. He peered over the half wall, his eyes squinting against the light. "What's with all the racket, dude? Some of us are trying to fucking sleep."

"Sorry, man." I downed another generous gulp. "Did I wake Harper?"

"Nah, she's out. What's with you?" he asked, making his way into the kitchen.

I kicked the chair away from the table and fell onto it, just about ready for another drink. "We got anything stronger?"

Thor grabbed himself a beer and opened the freezer, pulling out a bottle of Jack Daniel's. On the counter sat several shot glasses, and he grabbed two of the tallest and joined me at the table. "What gives?"

I shook my head. I didn't want to talk. I wanted to get shit-faced. I threw back the dregs of my beer and pulled the bottle of Jack closer, screwing off the lid. Thor slid a glass my way.

I poured liberally, so that a bit sloshed out of the glass, onto the table. I brought the liquor to my mouth, inhaling the woody scent. Tossing it back, I savored the frigid burn down the back of my throat. I closed my eyes and slammed the glass down. "Damn, that's good," I moaned.

"That bad, huh?" Thor said again, nursing his beer.

I poured myself another shot, not forgetting Thor this time. "You have no fucking idea." I used the toe of my right boot to pry the left one off. Once my left foot was free, I dug my toes into the heel of my right boot, repeating the process.

Wiping a hand over my face, I took the next shot. "Thanks, dude," I said, standing up.

"For what?" He rubbed his shorn head and looked up at me. "I didn't do anything."

"For drinking with me." I snatched the bottle of Jack off the table and headed for the stairs.

"Sure that's a good idea?" Thor sat forward, rested his elbows on his knees, and nodded to the Jack.

I looked at the bottle. "Yeah." I started up the stairs. "Night."

"Night, dude."

Inside my room, I shrugged my jacket off and threw it against the opposite wall. I wanted to scream, but I couldn't, not with Harper sleeping next door. I took a large swig of whiskey right from the bottle and fell onto my bed, waiting for the alcohol to numb the pain I felt inside.

Lying there, I closed my eyes. I thought of Jillian driving back to her sister's house alone. Despite the rejection—which I'd deserved—I pulled myself up and walked across the room to find my cell phone. I needed to text her, make sure she'd made it home all right. I dug the phone out of my pocket and my fingers slipped clumsily over the on-screen keyboard: *Bean, I'm sorry. Please let me know when you're home.*

I took another drink, just beginning to feel the cold whiskey freeze the rejection inside.

I fell onto my bed again. My eyes slid closed, my mind drifting as I waited for Jillibean to text back.

I ascended the small porch with a gift for Jillian. Knocking on the screen door with my foot, I watched her grandmother approach. "Oh, hi, Griffin." She wiped her hands on a dishtowel and pushed the door open.

"Can Jillian come out to play? I've got Popsicles." I help up the wrapped sticks and smiled.

"I'll see if she wants to come out. Hold on a second." Grandma Pat walked away from the door. "Jillian. Jillian, come down here, please. Griffin's at the door."

A couple of minutes later, Jillian appeared. Her eyes were puffy and red. She'd been crying again. She always cried. I wished I could make her happy, make her smile so she didn't have to cry anymore. "Hey, Jillibean, I brought Popsicles."

"Why do you call me that stupid name? And what if I don't like Popsicles," she snapped.

My heart sank. I didn't want to make her sad…I wanted to see her smile. "I call you Jillibean because I think you are sweet and colorful like a jelly bean. I love jelly beans, who doesn't?" I smiled widely, hoping it was contagious. "And I know for a fact that you like Popsicles because we used to eat them like crazy when you used to visit your grandparents. I recall a little girl wearing a Cinderella dress, sitting on top of that mound of dirt in the backyard, covered in rainbow-colored Popsicle juice."

She smiled. Just a little. But it was a smile nonetheless, and I'd put it there. "Come on, they're melting," I said, tempting her to come outside.

Jillian opened the screen door and shouted back into the house, "Grandma, I'm going outside with Griffin."

"OK," her grandma shouted back.

I handed Jillian the red one, because I knew it was her favorite. I'd eat the green one.

"Thanks." She took the sticky paper in her hand and started to peel it back from the treat inside. I did the same.

We sat down on the porch and slurped our Popsicles in silence. I didn't know what to do to make her happy, but if eating Popsicles quietly on her front porch did the trick, I'd do it.

"Hey, you two, turn around."

I looked over my shoulder. "Hi, Grandpa Earl," I said, returning his smile. He stood at the screen door, smiling down at us.

"Those good?" he asked.

"They're all right," Jillian said, turning around to look at him. "Hi, Grandpa."

"You two need your picture taken."

I turned all the way around and put my arm around Jillian. She scooted around too and threw her arm around my shoulder. "Smile, you two," Grandpa Earl crooned.

Click.

"Got it," he said.

Her smile retreated. Without a word Jillian turned and went back to her red Popsicle, shutting Grandpa Earl and me outside, while she disappeared into her sadness.

I tried to make her feel warm and happy inside…the way she made me feel.

I'd never stop trying.

* * *

Over the next week, I called and texted Jillian at least a hundred times. I apologized profusely to her voice mail. And still nothing. She'd disappeared, just like when we were young. I'd push too hard, and she'd retreat.

"It's Jillian, leave me a message."

"Bean, please don't be pissed," I said into the receiver. "Look, I need to know if you're coming tonight. I'm leaving you a VIP pass at the bar. Please call me back." I looked at the phone and pressed "End," stuffing it into my back pocket.

"Griff, we need you for a sound check," Leo said, walking in my direction. He waved me toward the stage, where the guys were taking their places.

"Cool." I grabbed my bass and jogged up the metal stairs. Even though we'd rehearsed night and day for a solid week, I was anxious to get our shit straightened out in the big arena. There was a lot riding on tonight. It had to be perfect.

I ran my hand over the mic and glanced back at the guys. "Ready?"

Adam nodded, twirled his sticks, and laid into his groove. With my well-trained ear, I easily heard the kick drum and the snare, concentrating on the backbeats to round out the rhythm. Masterfully Thor introduced the melody, along with Pauly, and I settled into the music.

I kept time with my body, the notes bleeding out of me with every slap and pop of my fingers. I stepped up to the mic and took a deep breath, ready to leave my soul on the stage. I'd learned a long time ago that it didn't matter if the performance was for one person or a thousand, a sound check or the real fucking deal, every musician played like it was the performance of a lifetime.

By the time the sound engineer had tweaked the PAs, adjusted our EQs, and worked out the sound quality onstage and out front, we'd played through half our set.

"That's it, boys," said Robins, the front-of-house engineer. He lowered his headset around his neck and used his hands to cut off our song. "We're good to go. Go take a breather." From the middle of the venue, he gave us a thumbs-up, and then jotted something down on the clipboard in his hand.

I was feeling more confident about the cohesiveness of our group stuff, but I still hadn't gone through my solo piece and that worried me. I was a perfectionist by nature, but that one song had to be beyond perfection.

Thor, Adam, and Pauly rested their instruments onstage and started toward the exit.

"You coming, man?" Pauly asked me over his shoulder.

I nodded. "Yeah, be there in a sec." I leaned into the mic, "Robins," I said, getting his attention.

He looked up from his clipboard.

"Mind if we run through the solo?" I squinted and put my hand up, shielding my eyes from the spot.

He checked his clipboard again. "Yeah, not a problem."

About a dozen engineers tooled about the venue in preparation for my solo, since it would be me and an acoustic guitar—very different from the rest of our set.

While everyone got set up, I traded my bass for my guitar, careful not to make too much noise while the mics were being set.

"OK, Griffin, it's all you." Robins took a seat at the mixer in the back of the room and the house lights went down, leaving only a single spotlight on me.

Just like I'd do that night, I sat on the stool and delivered my message to Jillian.

* * *

Hey Griff, I'm here. Headed for the dance floor. I read her text and was filled with equal parts relief and worry, relieved that she'd come and completely ill at ease that she was alone in the sea of people out there.

Be careful down there. I hate that you're alone, I wrote back.

Her response came quickly. *I'm fine. Don't worry about me.*

I always worry about you, Bean. Go to the main bar area, I left a VIP pass for you.

Thanks! Can't wait for the show!

The guys and I waited quietly backstage. Tonight's concert was the largest we'd ever played, not to mention the fact that we were headlining. It if went well, Dane said the tour was a go. Before he put in the final calls, he wanted to see how we could handle a show of this scale. The Pageant was a huge fucking venue.

The guys and I lined up just offstage, our bodies swaying to the beat of the music being piped through the PA as the sound techs set mics. My hand ran over the fret board of my bass, silently fingering different chord roots. I could feel the roar of the crowd in every one of my nerve endings, which were sparking with electricity. My fingers twitched with pent-up energy.

I closed my eyes and listened to the crowd, popping the joints in my hands like I always did before I played. The crowd was on—loud, engaged, and ready. Then my mind zeroed in on Jillian in the middle of that crowd…and everything that could go wrong.

I dug my phone from my pocket and typed out a quick text.

Bean, I don't like that you're on the floor alone. Come backstage for the show. You can watch from the wings.

"You're on, guys," one of the stage managers said, pointing at us. "Rock 'em into next year."

I panicked. I hadn't gotten a response from her, and it was up to me to start the show. I took a deep breath and tried to relax; she'd be fine. I nodded at Pauly, Thor, and Adam. "Let's do this."

I tucked my phone back into my pocket and walked up the steps first, getting set in front of the mic that was just offstage. I'd slap a few notes before walking out, just to tease the crowd a little.

My hand smoothed over the tightly wound strings and then my phone vibrated.

I had to look.

I pulled it out. *I'm fine. Stop worrying and start your show!*

That was all the motivation I needed. My hands fell into position, and I struck the first note.

Adam walked onstage and the crowd exploded. I watched from the side, slapping out a rhythmic sequence, waiting for Adam to start in on the kick drum.

One by one, each of us added his instrument, our sound filling every space of the massive hall. Finally I joined my boys on stage and the crowd lost their shit. Images of playing in Thor's garage came rushing back. All those late-night jam sessions when we'd pretended to have a crowd that sounded like this. All our hard work and dedication had paid off.

I soaked up the passion from the crowd and gave them a fucking show they wouldn't forget.

* * *

We played the hell out of the first half of our set—the best we'd ever played. But now it was time for my confessional.

After our last song ended, I ran a hand through the sweaty hair sticking to my face. "You're awesome," I breathed into the mic. "We'll be right back."

A massive cheer went up as we walked offstage.

Once I was clear, I grabbed a bottle of water and downed it, having worked up a thirst. Thor came up and slapped me on the back. "She's going to hear you," he said confidently.

I raised my chin in acknowledgment. "I fucking hope so. I can't play this game anymore."

He clipped my shoulder with a fake punch and smiled, picking up a water bottle of his own. "Go get your girl."

Tossing my empty bottle into the recycling bin, I blew out a large breath and headed back toward the stage.

Walking out there alone felt strange. I was exposed and vulnerable. The crowd watched me mount the lonesome stool like a pack of wolves eager to devour me. Just as during the sound check, a single spotlight was my only shield from the mass of people waiting for me to entertain them.

I squinted, hoping to catch a glimpse of Jillian, but I couldn't see anything. "We're going to slow it down a bit," I breathed into the mic.

"I love you, Griffin!"

The words came from the dark recesses of the hall, somewhere on my left. I knew instantly it hadn't been Jillian. But I'd learned how to seduce a crowd—especially a crowd of females. Fans who loved you bought more albums.

In my practiced bedroom voice, I answered my enamored fan, "Well, I love you, too."

The rasp in my voice elicited whistles and catcalls. Of the hundreds showing me their appreciation, I only cared about one.

I adjusted my stool and pulled my guitar over my shoulder. "This song is our brand-new single, debuting tonight. It's called 'About Time.'" I strummed a few chords, making minor adjustments to the tuning knobs until the strings fell into the right key. The crowd bellowed in anticipation. I loved teasing them.

I took a deep breath, strummed the chords, and looked up, pressing my lips to the mic.

> *Once upon a time I pushed you away*
> *Looked into your heart and begged you to stay*
> *I sang of words I couldn't speak*
> *You tried to taste them, but I was too weak*

I closed my eyes, picturing Jillian as I bared my soul to the hundreds of people in the room. She'd always been my inspiration…my muse.

> *And it's about time I bury the lie*
> *Speak the words and let them fly*
> *Grab hold and pull you close*
> *It's always been you I needed the most*

> *Pulled in every direction, but never near you*
> *I thought this would be easy, it's time I got a clue.*
> *My words run dry, my song unsung*
> *My actions a lie, and I know they stung*

The words on my lips…this song was hers. And I prayed she heard it.

I'll fight like hell, and make up for the past
A kiss to break the lie, I want to make this last
Taste the words on my lips
It's about time I let the truth slip.

And it's about time I bury the lie
Speak the words and let them fly
Grab hold and pull you close
It's always been you I needed the most
It's always been you I needed the most

I stroked the last chord until it melted into the back row of the hall and disappeared. The crowd remained still and quiet. No one dared make a sound. *Do they hate it? Why aren't they moving?*

In the dead center of the hall, a taxi whistle pierced the awkward silence. I knew it was her. I could feel her.

Then half a beat passed before the crowd erupted into thunderous applause. Torrents of screams and whistles flooded the stage. I stood from the stool and bowed. I pointed straight out into the mass of people, knowing Jillian was dead ahead. The connection we had was stronger than ever.

She'd heard me.

Chapter Twenty-Six

"Happy New Year, St. Louis!" I shouted before running offstage with the rest of the guys. The crowd went insane. Backstage I handed my bass over to Dan, part of our road crew and a good friend.

"You guys fucking rocked," he said, filling my hand with a bottle of water.

I uncapped that bad boy and drank heavily before accepting his compliment. "Thanks, man." I still hadn't caught my breath.

I ran the towel over my face and neck, drying off. I was a mess, covered in sweat. I needed a damn shower, but that would have to wait. The urge to find Jillian trumped everything else.

My eyes scoured the assembly backstage, desperate to find her. And when I did, my mouth would be on hers before she had a chance to say a word.

"Griffin!"

I heard my name. I searched harder, trying to pinpoint her location.

"Griffin." The voice called again, but this time it was different…closer.

Turning around, I saw Erin pushing through the crowd.

I smiled. "Hey, Peach."

She opened her arms and stepped closer, wrapping me in a hug. "You ever going to stop calling me that?" she asked, her Southern drawl melting over the words like syrup.

I pulled away, resting my hands on her shoulders. "Never."

She shook her head, a dubious smile at her lips. "You were fabulous."

I ran the towel over my head a few times, uncomfortable with all the kudos. "Thanks. I'm glad you made it tonight, friend." I tapped her lightly on the shoulder with my fist.

"No way in hell I would have missed this. Not too often I get to use the line, 'I'm with the band.' But don't be getting a big head now, thinking I'm going to turn into some groupie and follow you around the country."

"You'll always have an in with me." I winked at her, and then did another quick scan of the room. *Where the hell is Jillian?* I looked back to Erin. "You haven't seen Jillian, have you?"

She looked around, too. "No, I haven't."

"I'm sorry, but I need to find her." I hugged her one last time and kissed her cheek. "Thanks for being here, Erin. I appreciate it."

"My pleasure."

Leaving Erin standing just off the stage, I darted down the stairs, my anxiety growing with each passing second. Thoughts of Ren flooded my mind…the night she'd been slipped a roofie at a frat party.

What if someone fucked with Jillian's drink? Shit. Bile rose in my throat. I rounded the corner, coming up to the side door that led to the back alley. I punched the wall, my worry and anger taking over. I'd known it was bad idea to let her watch the concert from out there.

Ripping my phone out of my back pocket, I tapped her name on my contacts list. "Jillian, pick up the phone," I growled over the ringing.

No answer.

"God damn it!" I tapped her name again.

"Hi, it's Jillian. Leave a message."

"Fuck!" I screamed. "Jillian. Where are you?" I said to her voice mail. "Call me as soon as you get this message." I ended the call and switched tactics, opening the message app.

Jillian! Where are you? I'm losing my shit here. Are you ok? Call or text back ASAP!

I sent another one, not even giving her time to respond. *9-1-1! Jillian call or text now!*

I ran back toward the stage, maybe she was with one of the guys.

"Thor," I shouted, coming back into the crowded room. Thor was across the room. Since I towered over most people, I waved both hands above my head to get his attention. "Yo, Thor!"

He looked up and pushed through the crowd, coming in my direction. "What's up, man?"

"Have you seen Jillian?"

He thought about it for a second and shook his head, his face screwing up. "Can't say that I have."

"I can't find her and she's not answering her phone." I raked a hand through my hair, scanning the crowd again. She wasn't here.

* * *

Once Thor had convinced me to settle down and get my head on straight, I put a call in to Jennifer. It was a long shot, but maybe her sister knew where she was.

After I had called four times with no answer, my patience wore thin. The only thing that kept me from sending my phone across the room was the off chance that Jillian might need to get ahold of me.

"Hello?" Jennifer answered.

Relief shot through me. "Jennifer, it's Griffin. Is Jillian there?"

"I'm sure you're aware of the hour?"

I gritted my teeth to keep from spewing the names I wanted to call her. "Well aware. Have you seen Jillian?"

"Wasn't she supposed to be out with you tonight?" she asked smugly. Her haughtiness boiled my blood.

"She was, but we got separated at the concert. She won't answer her phone. Did she come home?" I raised my voice, fed up with her games.

"Hmmm…" She paused for a beat. "Seems to me Jillian's resolving to keep better company this year."

"Jennifer," I barked. "Don't fuck with me." She gasped, surprised by my tone and word choice. "Where is your sister?"

"I heard her come in a few minutes ago."

And then the line went dead.

"Well?" Thor asked. He leaned casually against the wall to my left, arms folded across his chest.

"She's home," I breathed. My reply was more of a reassurance to me than an answer for him.

"Is she OK?"

I shook my head, the fight in me gone. "It's over, dude." I rubbed my face and blew out a breath as I stood. "I guess it is true what they say…" I looked him in the eye. "You can't go back." I stepped past him to walk away.

"Go back to what, man?"

I kept walking.

"Hey." Thor grabbed my shoulder, forcing me to turn around. "What do you want to go back to? Being her *friend*? What do you want?" he asked again.

I wanted *her*. She pumped through my veins like a bass line…she was a part of me, the beat that kept my blood flowing. Our lives were so intricately woven, I didn't know where I ended and she began.

"You love her?"

I nodded.

"Then you're goddamn right, you can't go back."

"I fucked up, Thor. It really is too late. And now we can't even go back to being friends. I've ruined that, too. I laid it all out there tonight"—I gestured to the stage—"and she ran the fuck away."

"I've never known Griffin Daniels to back away from anything." He swung his arm around my shoulder. "Let's get the hell out of here. I'm beat. Text Jillian good night, because tomorrow you're going to show that girl she's more than a goddamned friend."

Following Thor's advice, I sent Jillian a text. *Hey Bean, what happened tonight? You scared the shit out of me when you didn't come backstage. For once, your sister was marginally helpful. She told me you made it home. Whatever's wrong right now, it will be better in the morning. I fucking promise. It's a new year, Bean. Time to shake things up.*

* * *

I pushed her door open and tiptoed over to the bed. She lay on her stomach, her blond-and-red-streaked hair fanned out, hiding her face. The natural yellow of her hair blended with the dull red she'd added, created a sunset on her pillow. Her warmth and vibrancy always conjured images of the sun. She was my sun…the center of my universe.

She looked peaceful.

I bent down and lightly pressed my lips to her ear. "Bean…," I whispered.

She lifted her arm, swiping it over her ear.

A laugh caught in my throat. "Jillibean," I sang. "Time to wakey-wakey."

"Ugh…" Pulling the blanket over her head, she rolled away from me. "No," she growled.

I was getting really tired of her running (or rolling, as the case may be) away from me. Shoving her over a bit, I climbed into bed beside her. I purposefully dropped my arm around her waist, and squeezed her close to my body. I'd like to see her get away now.

"You awake?" I asked.

She jerked her head a few times. I'd take that as a yes.

"You gonna talk to me?"

This time it was a definite shake. A no.

"OK, then." I kicked off my boots, pulled the comforter from under her perfect little ass, and threw it over my legs. "Might as well make myself comfortable, then." I snuggled down into her blanket. The light, sweet scent of her perfume clung to the blanket, and I pulled it tighter around me, clinging to her for dear life.

She let me hold her. I didn't speak, fearing she'd get spooked again. I let the quiet seal us together.

Minutes of the New Year ticked by, but it didn't matter, Jillian was in my arms. I listened to her breaths…in…out…in…out… My fingers trailed up her arm, testing the waters. *Would she let me touch her like this? Did she want me to touch her like this?*

I smoothed my fingers over her tangled hair. "Red, huh? I like it." My fingers plucked a dark-red strip from the bunch. "I bet there was no shortage of guys trying to get with you last night."

With her back pressed along the length of my body, she still opted for gestures instead of words. She shook her head no.

"Please, Bean. Talk to me. I've tried reaching you all day. You probably have fifty text messages from me by now."

Working her body around, she finally faced me. The space between our noses probably measured just over two inches. My eyes touched every part of her face. Even with tearstains and runny makeup, she looked like an angel.

The need too great, I moved my hand up her arm, touching her shoulder lightly as I worked my way to the sensitive skin of her neck. I couldn't stop, the growing pink flush in her cheeks begged to be touched.

My thumb circled over the warmest part of her cheek. Even my bass-callused fingers felt the heat rising from her skin. I craved that warmth, imagining how the rest of her incendiary body would have felt crushed against mine.

She wormed her hand through the blanket, bringing it up between us, and stilled my thumb with her dainty fingers.

I held her stare.

Her dark-chocolate eyes were rimmed with red, remnants of mascara blackened tears that had streamed down her cheeks. Passion and want bled from my eyes. When I looked at her, I wanted her to feel it…like the most intricately played music…music you can feel in your bones.

She moved her hand from mine, then to my chin…over my cheeks. The stubble on my face prickled beneath her scorching touch. *Heaven.*

She moved closer.

Then her lips touched mine and she froze.

No going back. No retreating. I grabbed her shoulders, spun her around, and pinned her tiny body beneath mine, devouring her with the kiss I should have given her months ago.

Our bodies lined up perfectly, and the feel of her beneath me took my breath away…literally. My body took stock of every curve she owned. My hands yearned to roam the landscape of her body. I wanted to memorize every inch of her. Starting with the crown of her head, my fingers slipped through her hair, down her neck…her shoulders…her sides. I needed to be closer, to feel her skin on mine.

Resting my fingers at the bottom of her tank top, I gave it a little flick and slipped beneath the hem. She responded to my touch, arching her back, begging to be held. I planted tiny kisses up and down the side of her neck. I tasted her skin on my lips and tongue—salty and sweet, while my ears soaked up the breathy moans that fell from her mouth.

Our friendship burst into flames of passion. She was my undoing.

Her teeth grazed my lower lip, pulling it into her mouth, and I nearly lost it. A groan rumbled in my chest. I deepened the kiss, opening my mouth wider. My tongue met hers, twisting and tasting, making up for lost time.

This was new territory. I'd never touched Jillian like this, but it felt right…so right. Each touch, every kiss, our bodies knew how to please each other.

The tips of my fingers skimmed along her waist, trailing up her rib cage as I kissed the delicate skin below her ear. She fit perfectly into my hands and I wanted nothing more than to keep her there forever. My fingers played over her soft, warm, splendid skin, coaxing a sensual melody of groans from her lips. Recapturing her mouth with mine, I tasted her song. Jillian returned my kiss with unrestrained passion. Everything in this moment was perfect. I'd promise her the world, give her forever, and never look back...if she'd let me.

Chapter Twenty-Seven

Jillian rested her head on my arm, and I seized the opportunity to touch her, smoothing away the loose strands of hair that covered her lightly freckled cheeks. "It's about fucking time," I whispered in her ear. "I could kiss you forever."

"Promise?" She smiled, her eyes shining like polished onyx.

"Forever." I folded my arm, drawing her to my side, determined to show her exactly what forever would be like.

I was on fire. Jillian's touch was like a sparkler on the Fourth of July, my skin bathed in sparks...heat...light. My lungs burned, yet I refused to pull away.

When our bodies demanded air, I growled my displeasure, collapsing beside her. She sidled up next to me, and I pulled her close, staring into her eyes. *God, I love her*.

"What's this?" she asked, brushing her fingers from the outer corner of my eye to my temple.

I played with a few strands of her red hair, running them through my fingers. "What do you mean?"

"You're sad about something. I can see it right here." With a light pressure, she ran the pad of her thumb over the thin skin.

I closed my eyes, drunk from her touch. "You know me so well," I whispered.

Her hands moved to my forehead, and I opened my eyes to see another question on her face. "What's the matter?"

"Did you hear my song last night?" I asked.

"Yes." She nodded.

"I wrote that for you." I looked her in the eyes, unblinking. "And you ran away."

"Griff," she said, running her fingers over my cheek and through my hair. I never wanted her to stop.

"No, Jillian, wait. I need to say this." I sat up on the bed and crossed my legs. Jillian did the same, mirroring my body. "I've waited a lifetime to say so much to you that I don't know where to start. Last year, when you kissed me, it scared the hell out of me. I freaked and pushed you away, because I didn't know what else to do."

So many long-forgotten thoughts and emotions surfaced at once. They tripped and stumbled over one another, each vying for its chance to spew from my mouth. My brain and heart weren't in sync, and I felt like a bumbling idiot. "When we were kids, you were my best friend. Because I was older, I felt like your protector. I loved that." I reached across and grabbed her hands. If I was going to bare my soul, I needed to be anchored to her. "Do you remember when we got caught drawing fake tattoos on each other's arms?"

"Mmm-hmm." She nodded. "My grandma wouldn't let us near each other for a month. She thought you were a bad influence on me. Body art was definitely not her thing. What was I? Twelve?"

"And I was fifteen," I added. "Do you remember what I wanted you to draw on my arm?" Like a movie, my brain played the scene.

I'd just bought a brand new pack of Sharpie pens. A bunch of dif-

ferent colors for Jillian. She loved Sharpies. Excitement spurred me on, and I raced over to her house.

Sitting together on the porch, we dumped the pack of twelve colors between us. Suggesting we give each other tattoos, I picked up one of the pens and twirled it between my fingers like a drumstick. Without skipping a beat, Jillian lifted up her shirt sleeve and flexed a nonexistent bicep, insisting I slap a rainbow on her arm. I tried to change her mind, said that tattoos were supposed to mean something, but no, she wanted a rainbow. Who was I to deny Jillian anything? I bent over her arm, determined to give her the best twelve-colored rainbow known to man.

As I finished her rainbow, I told Jillian what I wanted. But my words were buried beneath the rants of Grandma Pat, when she saw that I had "marked" her little Jillian.

"I don't remember, Griff," Jillian said, squeezing my hand. "By the time you finished with that rainbow on my arm, Grandma found us and started throwing an old-lady tantrum."

I smiled at the memory of Grandma Pat turning red in the face and doing her little tiptoe-shuffle dance number when she was angry. Grandma Pat had been small, but mighty…very much like Jillian. "I wanted you to write 'Jillibean.'"

She frowned. "I'm sorry, I don't remember."

I needed that frown to disappear. "I knew even back then how special you are, how much having you in my life meant."

"How? We were so young." She scooted closer.

"I knew because when I asked you to ink your name onto me, I was prepared to defend you and protect you from *anything*. But every time I looked in your eyes I could see things I couldn't protect you from. The way you blamed yourself for your parents' death, the heartache you wore like a second skin. You'd put a wall up, and I was trapped on the outside. But I still wanted to save you from all that." My eyes drifted over her face, begging her to understand how I felt. She was it for me.

"There was no light in your eyes anymore." I let go of her hand to brush my thumb over her eye. She closed them and leaned her head into my hand. Neither of us dared move. Then she placed a kiss in my palm, recaptured it, and laced her fingers through mine.

I firmed up my hold on her. "I told myself all the time that I'd be there for you, to hold your hand in the storm. I'd always be your friend. It was the best way I could think to protect you. I prayed that one day the storm would pass, and that light in your eyes would come back."

"Griffin—" My name caught in her throat.

"Bean, please. I'm getting my chance now. Let me finish."

She exhaled loudly and nodded, squaring her shoulders.

"In high school, you were in no shape to be in a relationship, and I knew that. And then you kissed me last year." I took a breath. "I got scared. Don't get me wrong, I wanted it…*God*, I wanted it." Needing to drive home how much I fucking wanted her, I leaned in and pressed our foreheads together, cradling her head between my hands. "But I didn't want to hurt you. You were doing so well, and finally getting your chance at a new life, doing what you wanted. That overwhelming urge to protect kicked in, and I pushed you away. I didn't want to stand in your way, and I didn't want to add any more stress to your life."

"So what changed?" she asked. "Why is *now* OK?"

"Being without you fucking hurts," I whispered, pulling away to hold her hands in my lap. "All these years, a day never passed that I didn't get to see you. But man, these last few months, not seeing your face every day…it was like part of me was missing."

She nodded. "I know what you mean."

"I know it's selfish, but I need you. I know you're leaving for school again, and we're going to be apart, but I can't let you go back believing a lie. I love you so damn much, Jillian." I cupped her face again, running my thumbs over her cheeks.

I was so consumed by her…by the fact that I could touch her and hold her. It wasn't a dream anymore, but reality. I reached for her arms, gently trailing my fingers toward her shoulders. The skimpy tank top she wore showcased her curves beautifully, but didn't do so much to hide the scars. The ghosts she carried and tried hard to keep hidden. I knew how self-conscious she was about her body, how she hated for people to see the cracks in her porcelain skin. She was beautiful, and I wanted her to know it…to feel it.

My fingers traced along her neck, continuing their slow decent before stopping at the top of a scar peeking out of her tank top. I lowered my head and placed a kiss on the barely visible scar. Jillian tilted her head back, relaxed, placing her body and soul in my care.

I massaged a finger over the scar, settling my eyes back on hers. "Jillian, why did you run last night?"

It took her a minute for her to answer. "Uh…I was backstage watching you finish up. When you came off the stage…" She glanced down. "Erin was there."

"Seriously?" I was shocked. "She was just saying hi, and she wished me a happy New Year." A relieved chuckle rumbled in my chest. What a colossal misunderstanding. I gripped her chin between my thumb and forefinger, and lifted her head, forcing her to look at me. "She broke up with me, Jillian. She knew I was in love with you. She was the one of the many people that told me to get my head out of my ass and tell you how I felt."

"Really?" she muttered. "Since I hadn't seen you in a few days, I just thought…"

I needed to rectify this fuckup. Jillian needed to know just how much I was into her. "Well." I kissed her neck. "You." And then her jaw. "Thought." And her cheek. "Wrong." Finally I pressed my lips to hers and pushed her onto her back. "I will *never* get tired of doing this."

"Me neither," she sighed, reaching up to lock her hands behind my neck. She used her leverage on me, and pulled my face to hers.

Lying on Jillian's bed, I savored her. Tiny kisses gave way to fevered, hungry groans. The feel of her hands beneath my shirt was irresistible. But she didn't stop there, moving the shirt up to my shoulders and pulling it off in one swift motion. I reclaimed her mouth, hooked an arm around her, and flipped us. She sat up, breathless. It was such a turn-on to see her legs straddling me. Her lips were swollen, eyes bright, cheeks flushed. *I did that to her. Fucking sexy as hell.*

One corner of her mouth turned up in a sexy, mischievous grin. Her dark eyes lingered on mine for a second before they drifted over my body. It was nothing Jillian hadn't seen before—except for the ink with her nickname—but it was so small, I doubted she'd notice.

Jillian gave me her full attention, trailing her hands over my shoulders…down my biceps. I flexed, her fingers like live wires sending jolts of electricity through me. "This feels fucking awesome," I exhaled.

She traced the lines of my ink with her finger. *Always protects. Always trusts. Always hopes. Always perseveres. Never fails.* Her touch was light…teasing, then punctuated by the heat of her mouth on each line of script, like a prayer.

As she moved her body sinuously down mine, her fingers continued their relentless pursuit, working over the tuning heads of my bass guitar tat. I sucked in a breath when her fingers teasingly dipped beneath the waistband of my jeans. *Fuck me.*

Moving diagonally across my chest, Jillian fingered the strings, working her hand toward the body of the guitar. My breath came faster every time she put her lips to my skin, kissing each of the drops that bled from the shattered bass over my heart. *Will she notice her droplet?*

Her lips kissed the tattoo bearing her name and she paused. Her scorching mouth branded me. I opened my eyes in time to see her sliding up my body. "When?" she asked.

I shifted to accommodate her and she rested her head back on my arm.

"When I got back from taking you to school. I told you, it felt like a part of me was missing. I had to do something."

"Thank you," she whispered.

"For what?" I smoothed my fingers over her shoulder, making up for lost time.

"For never giving up on me. For *always* being there for me. For everything."

"Ditto." I smiled and pulled her closer, kissing her. Not wanting to pull away, I spoke against her mouth. "Kissing you makes me want to write a song."

"Sing to me," she breathed.

Who was I to deny her? I'd done that once and almost lost her. There was no way in hell I was ever going back. She wasn't just a *now* (even though now was pretty fucking amazing), she was my future. My whole song.

I'd spend the rest of my life giving this girl her heart's desires. She didn't have to ask twice. I drew in a breath and rasped a much more intimate version of the song I'd sung for her last night. She wasn't getting away from me this time.

Chapter Twenty-Eight

After the concert at the Pageant, things really started heating up, with both Jillian and Mine Shaft. Any free second I had was spent with Jillian, because we knew our time together was limited.

Dane scheduled and confirmed the dates of our first tour. The studio was pleased with the returns from the New Year's Eve concert, and confident we could handle headlining a small Central American/North American tour over spring break.

For one short week, everything felt right.

It was Jillian's last night of vacation. Tomorrow we'd join the ranks of long-distance couples. With Jillian in my arms, I stroked a hand over her arm. "Are you happy there?" I asked, before all those miles separated us. I had to know if she still wanted it. Selfishly, I also wanted to know if her mind had changed because of me. That was my biggest fear. If she gave up on her dreams because of my selfishness, I'd walk away. It would be the most painful thing I'd ever have to do, like cutting out my own heart, but I wouldn't make her choose between me and her future. Her wants, her dreams, they were mine, too.

She remained quiet. *Has she fallen asleep?*

I leaned forward and peeked at her face at the same moment she lifted her head to look at me. A tired smile flashed, then disappeared. It was so late, and I knew she had a long day ahead of her, but I couldn't get enough. I wanted to bring that smile back and catch it on my lips.

I bent low and lightly pressed my mouth to hers, scooping her cheek into my hand. She relaxed in my arms, so warm and soft. Sweet torture.

Chastely kissing her, I imagined our bodies pressed together, skin to skin, nothing keeping us apart. I yearned for that day, but it was not now. I wanted Jillian in my bed for days, our lovemaking uninhibited by all the shit that had kept us apart...heartbreak, grief, time, distance. We wouldn't have to hurry...unless we wanted to. I'd take her slowly, memorizing every sound she made...the way her body fit with mine. Then, when our passion became too much, our bodies covered in sweat, our lovemaking would take on a fever all its own. It was one of the hardest fucking things I'd ever had to do, to not think with my dick, but with my heart. Jillian wasn't just any girl, she was *the* girl...*my* girl. I would not fuck this up. So every time I touched her it was a blissful agony.

She parted her lips and a breathy gasp filled the narrow space between us. I slipped my tongue into her mouth, caressing and savoring every part she offered to me. My body sank beside her, and I sealed my mouth solidly over hers, deepening the kiss.

Eager to touch her, I slid my hand from her face, down her neck and shoulder, working my way to the hem of the t-shirt she wore...my t-shirt. Our bodies so close, my hard-on pressed against her, perfectly aligned. *It would be so easy to slip inside her.* She moaned and my dick throbbed in response.

I flicked the hem up and sent my fingers underneath. Jillian rolled closer, her hands working through my hair. If she kept that up, I was going to fuck my gentlemanly resolve and take her now.

With my tongue slowly plunging a sensual rhythm in and out of her mouth, my fingers moved languidly up her rib cage, reaching the lacy bottom of her bra. I wanted that damn thing off. I moved my hand over her breast, cupping it before I traveled toward her back, seeking out the clasp. Jillian sucked in a breath, her fingernails scratching my bare skin as she moved them down my back. Finally locating what I was looking for, I expertly flipped each closure between my thumb and forefinger until they fell away. One. Two. Three. The straps loosened.

Jillian froze.

Panting, I pulled away just enough to see her eyes. "What is it, Bean?" I whispered.

She shook her head. Even surrounded as we were by the darkness of the early hour, I noticed a single tear fall from her eyelashes and slip down her cheek. With my right arm still trapped beneath her head, I removed my arm from under her shirt to catch the tear. "Baby, what's wrong?"

She shook her head again, more tears swimming in her dark eyes. "I love you so much, Griffin." Her voice sounded raspy and thick, like something was choking her from the inside.

"Shhhh," I soothed, rubbing her back on the outside of the t-shirt. "I love you, too." Whatever was distressing her, I wanted to take it away.

Her body shuddered and she took a deep breath. My arms tightened around her, pressing our noses together.

"I'm scared, Griff," she choked.

"Of what?"

"Of losing you, and…" She trailed off, almost like there was something else she wanted to say, but couldn't.

There was a pinch in my chest. I had the same fear. Since I was sixteen and almost lost her, I'd lived with that fear. "Jillibean," I said, pulling us both up. I leaned against the headboard, lifting her up and settling her between my legs. I smoothed her disheveled hair and forced her to look me in the eyes. "There is no way in hell you could *ever* lose me." Cupping her small face in my hands, I rested my forehead against hers. "I'm yours, body and soul."

"I know." She sighed and laughed humorlessly. "Things just start getting good with us, and I have to leave again."

"What are you talking about?" I smiled, running my hands over her head. "Things have always been good with us. And isn't it par for the course that our timing sucks, as usual?"

She cocked her head. "You have a point."

"But this time we have our inevitable reunion to get us through the long haul." I wasn't sure whom I was trying to comfort more, me or her. "Let's get some sleep," I said, sinking down onto the pillow. Jillian shifted beside me and used my chest as her pillow, rubbing lazy circles across my skin. Energy hummed inside me, her touch bringing me to life like an engine. If she kept that up, she wouldn't be getting any sleep tonight. I placed my hand on hers and she stilled. "Sleep, Bean. You have a long drive tomorrow."

"Ugh, don't remind me."

I chuckled. Her head bobbed up and down with the motion, and I wrapped her in my arms and closed my eyes.

* * *

Griffin...Jillian called to me like a siren called to a sailor. The heavy darkness hid her from my view, so I listened again...her faint voice so far away. She was always so far away from me.

Griff. She spoke again, louder this time. An angel's wing brushed across my cheek. "Hmm?" I answered, rolling onto my back.

Like a boat on the water, the bed shifted under me and my eyes flew open. I squinted against the brightness of the room, focusing on Jillian's smiling face.

"Good morning," she said cheerfully, then bent to kiss my forehead.

"What time is it?" I groaned, kicking my legs free of the blankets.

"Quarter to eight."

Like the sirens I'd dreamed about during the few hours of shut-eye I'd gotten, Jillian sat in front of me like a naughty golden temptress. Her tangled mess of pale-yellow hair was wild and sexy. Her lips were pink and still slightly swollen from the working over I'd given them. She was so fucking hot. I could only imagine what she'd look like after having me inside her all night.

My dick strained against my boxer briefs, pleading for me to be less chivalrous. Staring at her, I licked my dry lips, eager to get my hands on her again. I sat up and grabbed her before she could get away. She giggled and snuggled into me. "Good morning," I growled, kissing the top of her head.

"You're making it very difficult to leave," she said, laying her head against my chest. *Me? How am I making it difficult? I'm not the one who looks like I just climbed off the pages of* Maxim.

"Don't. Go back tomorrow." I held her tighter.

"I can't," she groaned. "It's going to take me two days as it is, and classes start on Monday."

Her hands ran over my chest, lighting fires I knew I'd have to extinguish later. "This fucking sucks." Trying to hide my frustration, I tossed my head back, knocking it against the headboard.

"Tell you what," she said, tapping my chest. "Why don't I get packed up at Jennifer's, and I'll come back here before I head out. You can get cleaned up. I'll be back in an hour, and we can say good-bye then."

"It's better than having to say good-bye now, I guess." Muttering, I planted my lips on her head again, intoxicated by the scent of her messy hair.

Jillian stretched out and gave me a quick kiss. That wasn't working for me. I grabbed her and pulled her on top of me, our bodies flush. I kissed her hard, tangling my hands in her hair. My tongue brushed against her lips, forcing its way into her mouth while her hands held my face to hers.

With her on top of me like this, my hands had easy access to her gorgeous little ass. I slid my palms down her back until they were full of her cheeks. I cupped them forcefully, pulling her upward. A tiny gasp fell from her lips and she rocked against me.

Dear sweet Jesus! I moaned, guiding her body in a maddening rhythm with my hands and mouth. I was so fucking hard. *No! I have to stop this. If I have her now, I won't be able to let her go.*

Reluctantly I took my hands off her ass and put them somewhere safer...maybe. Her neck seemed relatively safe. I lightened my lips, withdrew my tongue, and placed several tiny kisses on her mouth before pulling away.

She opened her eyes, looking a little drunk. "Something wrong?" she teased, knowing she'd nearly sent me over the edge with her little shimmy. Seeing her breathless and wanting didn't help matters.

My heart thumped against my rib cage. I pushed her hair behind her ears, and answered in that low, deep voice I use during concerts. I knew it drove women crazy. "Oh, trust me," I smiled wickedly. "Nothing's wrong." I placed my hands on the sides of her face and kissed her lightly, one more time. "Promise me something?" I asked.

She sat up and faced me, pulling her legs into a yoga pose that resembled a pretzel. My eyes were glued to her legs. Fantasies involving those legs twisting around my body flashed through my head.

"Anything," she replied, snapping me out of my arousing daydream.

"That you'll wake me up like that every morning."

She opened her legs and scooted onto my lap, straddling me. I was certain she felt my erection pressing right against her sweet spot. She rotated her hips and whispered against my lips, "I'll do better than that." A sinful grin spread across her face.

Fuck me! Now! Please!

A growl ripped from my chest. What a little vixen, teasing me like that. With my hands behind her head, I pulled her back down, and thrust my tongue back into her mouth before rolling on top of her. Then I stood up abruptly, leaving her panting on the bed. *Two can play at that game, sweetheart.*

My chest heaved. I couldn't catch my breath. Seeing her sprawled out and wanting me was too much. "I've got a cold shower I need to take," I said, breathlessly. "Go get your stuff from Jennifer's house, and get your ass back here. I don't want you making most of that trip in the dark." I offered my hand and she grabbed on. In one swift motion I yanked her to her feet, our chests pressed together.

"All right," she groaned.

Stepping around me, she stomped to the corner of the room and retrieved her purse from the floor. I followed behind her, opening the door.

Once we were downstairs, I wrapped my arms around her and

pulled her back to my chest. I traced feather-light kisses from her shoulder all the way up her neck. I blew a breath across her ear, then nipped at her lobe before I whispered, "Bye, Bean." I felt her body shiver. "See you soon."

She turned in my arms, facing me. Desire lit up her face. "See you soon," she said quietly.

Chapter Twenty-Nine

I watched Jillian get into her car, and then I shut the door. That cold shower was calling my name, but first I had to do something with all the pent-up energy coursing through my veins.

I ran up the stairs, taking them three at a time, before bounding into my room. The air smelled different…feminine. I took a big whiff and closed my eyes, allowing Jillian's lingering scent to fill my lungs. I let out a big sigh, content, and turned on as hell.

With my foot I began sifting through the clothes scattered on my floor until I found my favorite pair of gym shorts. Putting them on, I got comfortable on the floor and cleared a spot where I could pound out some push-ups.

Stretching out, I supported my weight in my hands, keeping my back straight and parallel to the ground. I began, pumping my arms up and down, fast and purposeful. I breathed in…and out. Sweat beaded on my forehead first. My biceps burned, but I kept going. I pictured Jillian lying beneath me, rewarding me with a kiss every time I came down. That was something we'd definitely have to try. "Forty…six," I grunted, pushing back up.

I welcomed the fatigue in my arms and chest. It felt good to expend some of the energy Jillian had fueled inside me. The exercise leveled my head.

When I hit fifty, I mixed things up a bit. I counted out twenty push-ups on my right arm, resting my left hand at the small of my back. My muscles shook with each ascent and decent, but I kept going, switching arms when I began a new set.

"Seventy-two. Seventy-three. Seventy-four," I counted aloud, thinking back to yesterday, when Jillian had said she'd move in with me when she came home for the summer. This spurred me on even more. I'd asked Jillian to live with me dozens of times, before Thor and I became roommates. But she'd turned me down each time, spouting some bullshit about not wanting to get in my way. As if she could. I often wondered if we would have ended up together sooner, had she given in.

But that didn't matter know. We were together and there was no way in hell I'd ever let anything come between us again.

With my last ten, I put my feet against the wall, focusing on my abs and chest wall. "Ninety-three…ninety-four…ninety-five…"

One hundred. Dripping with sweat, I dropped my legs and stood. I bounced on the balls of my feet and stretched my arms across my chest. I was breathing heavily, but relaxed.

Still stretching, I walked into the hall and pulled a towel from the closet, ready to hit the shower before Jillian returned.

* * *

I threw on a pair of black jeans and an old Beatles t-shirt and pulled my boots on before heading downstairs. I hadn't heard from Thor all morning, either he and Harper were holed up in his room or he was at her place. Didn't matter, though, we did our best to stay out of each other's way when there was company over.

Heading downstairs and into the living room, I snagged my six-string from behind the couch and started plunking out some different chords. My low E was way out of tune. I jacked around with the tuning pegs until the sound suited me, low and resonant.

Outside, a car pulled up. Setting the guitar aside, I peeked out the window. Jillian shut the engine off and climbed out, her body hidden beneath a bulky coat and scarf.

I pulled the front door open and watched as she made her way up my walk. When she was within my reach, I pulled her through the door, my mouth landing on hers before she could speak. I kicked the door shut and pushed my tongue into her mouth. My fingers made quick work of her zipper. With my lips still moving on hers, I yanked her scarf free and pushed her coat to the floor, snaking my arms around her.

Now that her skin was free from the bulk of her coat, I had access to her jaw and neck. A desperate need to taste more of her compelled me across the corner of her lips, to her jaw, and onto her exquisite neck. I was hungry for her. "Do you have any idea how long I've wanted to greet you like that?" My tongue teased, tasting. She tilted her neck, giving me more room to play.

"I can imagine," she whispered. "Is Thor here?"

"No. I haven't seen him," I said against her neck. I could feel her pulse quicken against my mouth. "Why?" It seemed odd that she'd be thinking about Thor while my tongue licked across her skin. I took her hands in mine, lacing our fingers together, and looked her in the eye, giving her my most wicked smile.

She shook her head and cringed. "I don't know…it would just be awkward if he walked in and saw us all over each other."

I laughed. "I've seen him all over plenty of girls. Payback's a bitch." Then I recaptured her mouth.

She pulled away and smacked my arm. "Watch it, Daniels. I'm not just any girl."

"Damn straight you're not." I said, all joking aside. I brushed the sides of her thick, long hair behind her ears. I was burning for this girl. I crashed my lips onto hers again, making sure she could taste me on her lips until May.

"I've really got to go, Griff," she said against my mouth.

I growled. "Damn it." I pulled away, but only fractionally. "I hate that you have to make the trip alone. Anything could happen." Her safety was always my first priority. I wasn't comfortable with or used to my strong, independent College Jillian. But I had to let her go.

She brought her forehead to mine, her eyes warm and sparkling. "I'll be all right," she reassured me.

"I know, but I still worry." I sulked.

"I'll check in every hour. It's too late for me to drive straight through, so I'll get a room."

I relaxed a bit, enjoying the gentle stroke of her fingers against my rough face. "That makes me feel a little better." I wrapped my arms around her tiny frame, trying to put off the inevitable as long as possible.

With her head against my heart, she kissed me through my thin shirt…right where I carried her.

I walked her to the car and kissed her deeply, one more time. She climbed in and started the car, pressing her palm to the window. I put mine on the window, too. She blew a few kisses, and I did the same. It hurt watching her leave. With each passing mile, I felt her absence more. *How many fucking days until May?*

Chapter Thirty

That's a wrap, boys," the director shouted. "We'll get this over to post. It'll be ready before you head out on tour."

I let my bass hang around my neck and bumped fists with Thor. Our first official music video was in the bag. We'd filmed it all over the city, despite the arctic temperatures. Today we were lucky enough to have shot indoors, the haunted Lemp Mansion being our final stop.

I took in the burnt-orange walls and ornate chairs that lined the hallway. I didn't go for all the hype when it came to haunted houses, but there was definitely an eerie quality to a house that had witnessed multiple suicides.

"Strange place," I said, shaking off the cold that emanated from the walls.

"Yeah," Pauly added. "When I was little, my pop brought me here when it was one of his weekends. Said it'd put hair on my chest if I made it through the night in the attic room."

We all looked up.

"Must've been fucking terrifying, dude. You're a damn hairy beast," Thor said.

"Yeah, it was." Pauly scoffed and pounded his chest. "I was a six-year-old sporting a rug on my chest."

We laughed.

"I'm hungry. Let's get our shit packed up and get some chow," Adam suggested.

"Dude, you're always hungry." I waved him off and lifted my bass strap over my head. Bending over, I carefully laid it into the gig bag, and my phone buzzed in my pocket.

Slipping a hand into my back pocket, I pulled it free. It was a New York call. Not a number I recognized. I slid my thumb over the lock and answered, thinking it was most likely Mine Shaft business of some sort. "Griffin Daniels."

"Hi, Griffin, it's Sarah, Jillian's roommate."

My heart stilled. *Was she hurt?* This wasn't good. It felt like I'd just swallowed a ton of bricks. Something had to be wrong. Why else would she call?

"Yeah?" I asked, warily.

"Sorry for calling, but I got your number off of Jillian's phone. Now, don't think I'm like some sort of stalker or something, but—"

"Sarah, is Jillian OK?" I asked, cutting her off.

"Oh, yeah. She's really good, actually."

I blew out the breath I'd been holding, and raked my hand through my hair. "Shit, you scared the fuck out of me. I thought something was wrong."

"No, silly," she admonished playfully. "I was just planning Jillian's birthday party. I know this is a long shot, but I wanted to surprise her and have you visit. You know, like you'd be her birthday present?"

That idea wasn't half bad. The wheels in my head were turning, trying to figure out a way I could swing a trip east. "Let me see what I can work out. I'll get back with you."

"Awesome. Thanks, Griffin. Sorry I bothered you."

I shook my head. "No, thanks for calling. It's a great idea."

"Talk to you soon. Bye."

"Yeah, bye." I killed the call and immediately pulled up my calendar.

Jillian's birthday was in a week, the twenty-fourth. We had no gigs scheduled, just rehearsals. If I could get out of town on her birthday, leaving before the sun came up, I'd be able to make a late party that night. I knew flying was out of the question, she'd kill me (since her parents' deaths were linked to airplanes, she never took to them), and it was way too cold for the bike. I'd have to see if I could borrow someone's car.

"Yo, Thor." He was walking toward the exit, helping carry Adam's drum kit to the truck. "You busy next weekend?"

He thought for a second and nodded. "Yeah, Harper asked me to be her plus-one at her friend's wedding."

"Shit." I took one of the cymbal stands from his hands and followed him outside.

"What's up?"

"I need to borrow a car. I'm trying to swing a trip east next weekend. It's Jillian's birthday."

Thor passed the stand off to a roadie in the back of the truck. "Sorry, man." He clapped a hand on my back.

I passed my stand over, too. "I'll think of something." No way was I missing Jillian's birthday.

* * *

Thor's car was a bust, but I had one other option. It would take some sweet-talking on my part to get her to agree, though. Once

I got into town, I pulled into the Starbucks parking lot and shut my bike off. Stepping off, I removed my new helmet. Despite its bulkiness it looked badass. Jillian had great taste. I'd only had one requirement, it had to be black. When she'd deemed this one "sexy" I was sold. Nothing beat the smile that spread across her face as she held the helmet in her hands at the checkout counter. Even though I'd put down five hundred bones to appease her, no price was too high to see her smile like she did that day.

I fit my helmet under my arm and hunkered down against the polar wind, beating a quick path to the door. Inside, the coffee-warmed air filled my nostrils. I pulled on the fingers of my thick gloves, freeing my hands so I could call my dearest sister.

I went to a table and sat down, yanking my phone out of my riding jacket. I dialed Ren.

"Hey, Bro, what's up?" she answered.

"You busy?"

"Actually, no. I'm just leaving work."

I heard the Miata's horn chirp in response to Ren's hitting the key fob. "Wrong answer."

"Huh?" she said, confused.

"You are busy. You're meeting me at Starbucks. I'm already here, so hurry up." I smacked my gloves on the table for emphasis.

"And why am I meeting you at Starbucks?" she asked warily.

"Do I need a reason to want to hang out with my big sister?" I laid the sugar on thick.

"I'll meet you, but I'm wise to your game, Daniels. You're up to something."

I smiled. "Love you, Sis."

"Yeah, yeah. Be there in ten."

"Cool."

I disconnected the call and slipped the phone back in my

pocket. Standing, I joined the short line. Glancing at the counter, I noticed the display of CDs. My eyes instantly fell to the grainy black-and-white cover art featuring Mine Shaft. I'd seen the physical CD at the studio, but not in a store. Adrenaline flooded my bloodstream and kicked my pulse into second gear. It was wild seeing all my hard work come to fruition, and it further justified my decision to put school on ice.

I laughed inwardly. I couldn't wipe the beatific smile off my face when the barista asked if she could take my order.

Grinning like an idiot, I ordered a black coffee for myself and Ren's favorite, a white-chocolate mocha with soy, no whip. I hoped that thanks to my Starbucks offering, along with a heavy dose of my little-brother charm, she wouldn't be able to say no.

"Your drinks will be ready down there." The barista handed back my card and pointed to the opposite end of the counter.

"Thanks."

I put my card away and slid my wallet back into the pocket of my riding jacket. Stepping down to the next counter, I waited for our drinks.

The barista working the espresso machines glanced at the name on the cup and looked at me. "Griffin?" he said, setting my coffee on the counter.

I scooped it up and removed the lid before sliding a sleeve over the hot cup. "Yeah, thanks." I hate lids on my coffee cups. I enjoy the smell of coffee as much as the taste.

"White-chocolate mocha too?" he asked, setting it down.

"Yep." I nodded, picking it up. I dropped Ren's cup into a sleeve, too.

"Have a good one, man," the barista said as I walked back to my table.

Lifting Ren's cup in thanks, I said, "You too."

Setting the drinks on the table, I pulled off my jacket and one of the extra layers I'd put on to ward off the cold. I plopped into a chair and wrapped my hands around the cup. Lifting it to my mouth, I inhaled the steamy, rich scent of plain black coffee. None of that froufrou shit Jillian and Ren enjoyed.

The door opened and Ren stepped inside. I lifted my hand, waving her over. Loosening the scarf around her neck, she joined me at the table.

She draped her coat across the back of the chair and took up her drink. "White-chocolate mocha, soy, no whip?" Her eyebrow shot up questioningly.

I winked. "I like the scrubs, Sis." Ren was a maternity nurse at Anderson Hospital.

She took a sip, her eyes glancing downward. "What? You don't like Dora the Explorer?" Taking another swallow, she sighed. "Ahh, that's good. Heaven in a cup." Relaxing into her chair, she cradled her coffee and smirked. "So, when do you want the car?" she asked.

I screwed up my face. "What?" *How does she know?*

"Cut the shit, Griffin." She smiled, pressing her lips to her coffee. "It doesn't take a genius to figure out you're planning a trip to see Jillian. Her birthday is next week."

I sat back and stretched my legs out, propping one boot on top of the other. An impish grin consumed my face. "Whaddaya say?"

She groaned. "When do you leave?"

"Next Friday." My fingers pulled at the seam of the sleeve, ripping it apart little by little. "I'll head back home early Sunday morning."

"Oh, all right," she whined.

I threw my hands into the air and pushed the chair onto its two back legs, raising my hands into the air. "And Ren comes through for her baby brother," I said a little too loudly. "You're a lifesaver."

"Yeah, well. Don't think you're getting off easy, *baby brother*." The way she said that scared me a little. "You owe me big-time."

I let the chair fall forward with a thud, righting it back on all fours. "Whatever you want. Name it, it's yours."

She pursed her lips, devising an evil plot, no doubt. "I don't know yet. I'll have to think about it." A throaty cackle echoed across the table.

"Seriously, though, Ren, thank you." I had the coolest sister. Even as kids we'd shared a special bond. But, like any siblings, we'd endured our share of battles, too. In the end, though, we had each other's backs.

"Yeah, yeah. Tell Jillibean I love her. I'm staying at Mom and Dad's while they're in Florida. The car'll be in the driveway."

"Thanks, Sis." I leaned across the table and kissed her cheek.

Taking a long drink of her latte, she sat back in her chair again. Her eyes scrutinized my face while her lips spread into a toothless smile. "I'm proud of you, Griff."

I raised an eyebrow, her random compliment throwing me off. "Where'd that come from?" I eyed her over the top of my coffee cup, taking a long drink.

"Your career is taking off and you've finally got your girl. It's cool seeing you get what you've worked so hard for."

"Yeah." I nodded in agreement. Now that Jillian and I were on the same page, everything felt…real.

"But," Ren said, pointing a finger at me. "When *I* manage to snag a hot doctor, and get myself a life, I'm gonna need my wheels, dude. If Jillian stays out there for three more years, you're going to have to suck it up and ditch the bike."

I cringed, pulling in a sharp breath between my teeth. "Nooo." I shook my head. "The bike stays." She was right, though. If things worked out for Jillian—and I prayed they would—I'd have to take the plunge and buy a car.

Ren took another sip and slammed her empty cup on the table. "But, until that hot doctor sweeps me off my feet, I have a date with Netflix." She smiled, stretching her arms out wide. "I'm beat. Babies are tough customers." She stood, pulling her coat from the back of the chair.

I followed her lead. I tugged my blue fleece jacket over my head and slipped on my black riding jacket. Once we were armed against the cold, I leaned down and kissed her cheek again. "Thanks, Ren."

"You bet." She wrapped her arms around my waist and squeezed. "Love you, Bro."

I circled her in my arms. "Love you, too."

She pulled away. "Oh, will you please call Mom? She's driving me batshit crazy. You need to set things right with her." She pointed a finger at me. "BEFORE you leave on tour."

I pointed back at her, clicking my tongue. "Yeahhh," I drawled. "About that..."

Mom had put on a nice show at Christmas, for Jillian's sake. But she'd taken my news about school hard. Sometimes it felt like she was living out her unfulfilled college dreams through Ren and me. Ren had followed the plan, which had kept Mom happy. I hadn't. And now I was the family fuckup in her eyes. How was I supposed to set things right with her when she was the one with the problem?

"Just call her, Griffin. Please? Get her off my back."

I groaned. "I'll see what I can do." I wasn't holding my breath, though. As far as I was concerned, she needed to call me.

"Thank you." She hugged me quickly this time. "Talk to you soon."

Once Ren was gone, I sent Sarah a quick text before I headed out into the cold. *The birthday present will be there Friday night.*

She responded quickly: *Perfect! ;)*

I smiled and walked toward the door. My next order of business would be assembling Jillian's birthday present. I already had the frames, I just needed pictures…which meant I'd have to pay Jennifer a visit.

* * *

I rang the doorbell and bounced on the balls of my feet to keep warm. Seconds later Jennifer pulled it open.

"Griffin," she said coolly.

"Hey, Jennifer. How's it going?" I continued bouncing, trying to keep warm. After the twenty-minute drive over, I was cold as hell, despite my layers.

Jennifer stared. No cordiality, no pleasantries…nothing but an empty, pissed-off glare. Damn, this woman brought new life to the term *frigid bitch*.

"Umm, Jillian's birthday is coming up. She has some pictures in a drawer upstairs. I'd like to take them to her, if it's not a problem?"

Not saying a word, she pulled the door open wider and stepped aside, granting me access. *Holy shit. No nasty remarks? No commentary on how my presence lowers her property value?*

"Thanks." I nodded in her direction and stepped into the house.

"Go on up. Take what you need." Without another word, she walked down the hallway. I'd expected her to follow me, to make sure I didn't pocket any of her precious belongings. I was floored…and a little unsettled by her behavior. This was not *typical* Jennifer.

I set my helmet on the floor. "Thanks," I called after her. She didn't acknowledge me, not that I'd expected her to. I shook my head and went to the staircase.

Beating a quick path to Jillian's old room, I grabbed the handle and opened the door. Inside, the faintest scent of Jillian's perfume lingered even after all these months. I closed my eyes and drew in a breath, letting it out slowly.

I opened my eyes and crossed the room to her dresser, knowing exactly where Jillian kept the pictures of her parents. The drawer on the top right-hand side.

The day she moved in with Jennifer, I'd helped Jillian unpack. I'd dumped a box of old photos into the drawer.

I pulled on the brass knob, sliding the drawer open.

It was empty.

In that moment my love for her was multiplied by infinity. She was the strongest damn woman I knew. As painful as it must have been for her, in a small way, she'd taken her mom and dad with her.

I pulled out my phone and texted her, *I love you*.

Pocketing my phone, I sighed, then turned to leave. I'd have to rethink my birthday present idea, now that the pictures I needed were with her.

When I reached the bottom of the staircase, I went to my helmet, picking it up.

"Find what you needed?" Jennifer asked, coming down the hall.

I stood and turned toward her. "No."

Jennifer wiped her hands on a dishtowel and shrugged.

"Thanks, though." I gave her a nod and left.

Chapter Thirty-One

I parked a few blocks from Sarah's boyfriend's townhouse, just in case Jillian came outside and recognized Ren's car.

I opened the door and climbed out, my phone in hand. Sarah wanted me to send her a text before I came in. *I'm here*, I typed and pressed "Send."

Her response came quickly. *Give me two minutes. I'll meet you at the front door.*

Cool.

I walked slowly, giving Sarah the time she needed to get things situated. Every step I took knowing Jillian and I were within feet of each other, as opposed to miles, my pulse sped up.

Reaching Brandon's brownstone, I climbed the steps just as Sarah opened the door. "OMG! Jillian is going to flip." Sarah came out on the porch and threw her arms around me.

Being that we'd only met one time before, in a very awkward situation at that, I found it extremely weird to be hugged by this chick. But I was pretty sure she'd consumed her fair share of liquid courage, which explained her overly affectionate behavior.

I patted her back.

Sarah let go. "So this is my plan. Jillian's in the basement right now, dancing. I'll sneak you down, but you have to hide until I give you the go-ahead. 'Kay?"

I stood and marveled at her. She talked so fast. "Lead the way." I gestured forward. *I just want to see my girlfriend.*

With a squeal she grabbed my hand and pulled me through the door.

Inside, the small apartment was crammed with wall-to-wall people. *Does Jillian know all these people?* Sarah still had ahold of my hand, pulling me through the crowd.

"Hey, you're Griffin Daniels, aren't you?" one guy said, pointing as I swept by.

Sarah whipped her head around and glared at the guy. "Now, now!" she scolded. "You'll ruin the surprise."

We barreled down the stairs and made an immediate left turn into a small bedroom. "Wait here." With a flourish she turned and ran into the other room.

I peeked around the doorway, scanning the crowd for Jillian. Across the room I saw her smiling and giggling, standing beside another girl. Jillian looked sinful, her hot-pink ensemble hugged every curve she owned. And with her rainbow-colored hair, she looked edible...my very own decadent cupcake. I bit my lip, hungry for her.

"Everyone," Sarah shouted from the front of the room. "Hello? Shhh!" She tapped the mic. "EVERYONE! SHUT THE FUCK UP!" she yelled.

The noise disappeared and no one moved.

Now that's a chick who knows how to work a crowd. I laughed.

"Thank you." Sarah smiled sweetly. "Today's a special day," she continued. "We're all here to celebrate my best friend's birthday."

Best friend. It felt odd hearing that someone else had assumed that role in Jillian's life. I hadn't really thought about what I was to Jillian. *Boyfriend? Best friend? Lover?* None of those labels defined my title. None of them was a strong enough noun to encompass what Jillian and I shared…what we were to each other.

I watched Jillian, her back to me. There were two labels I knew I wanted for us, "husband" and "wife." But that was for later. We had a lot of miles to span before I'd have the honor of being her husband.

Sarah raised her glass and everyone followed her lead. Jillian raised a half-empty bottle of tequila.

Fuck me. I tensed. I prayed no one had slipped her anything.

"Happy nineteenth, Jillian!" Sarah shouted into the mic. The crowd repeated her words and tossed back their drinks. Jillian poured herself a shot and threw it back. The DJ cued up "Birthday Cake" by Rhianna and everyone started bouncing to the rhythm.

Sarah handed back the DJ's mic and skipped back over to where Jillian and some other dude was standing. Sarah leaned in and whispered something into Jillian's ear.

Jillian said something in reply and gestured to the crowd with the tequila bottle.

Sarah whispered to Jillian again, this time waving me over to join them.

She didn't have to tell me twice. Three large strides, and I stood behind my girl.

Sarah backed away from Jillian, a gigantic smile on her face.

I'd waited long enough, damn it. I needed to touch her. I bent down and whispered, "Happy birthday, Jillibean," into her ear.

Slowly she turned around and lifted her eyes to mine. In one step Jillian was in my arms. She grabbed a fistful of my jacket, pulled me down to her level, and crashed her mouth onto mine.

My tongue licked across her lips, tasting tequila. Her lips parted and I tasted deeper. Our tongues melded together, making up for lost time.

Needing air, I pulled away slightly. I rested my forehead on hers, staring into her eyes. Finding the slow rhythm to the song pumping from the sound system, I swayed her in my arms as we both regained our composure.

"How did I not know about this?" she whispered.

"Sarah swore me to secrecy."

"So she's the mastermind?" She smiled and pulled her head away from mine, but she didn't move out of my arms. "How did you get away?"

"I told the guys I couldn't miss your birthday. Thor said he'd keep things going for the weekend."

She wrapped her arms around my neck and brought me close. "Remind me to thank Thor."

I smiled, kissing her again.

We continued to get reacquainted with one another. Jillian pressed her backside against me. My hands didn't waste a single moment exploring her incredible body. Our bodies melded together, swaying and dipping as the music pounded around us.

Heat encompassed us. I kissed my way down her neck, tasting her sweat-slicked skin. All my nerve endings reacted to her scent...her touch. She might have been drunk on tequila, but I was drunk on *her*. I moved my hands to the curve of her hips, brushing lightly across her ass. I needed to get her alone.

"Griffin," she sighed, turning around in my arms.

I took advantage of the new position and cupped each of her ass cheeks. Her ass filled my hands perfectly, giving me just enough leverage to boost her up, bringing her mouth closer to mine.

She moaned, and I couldn't resist biting the sound off her lips. My body responded to her every touch. I was so hard.

I pressed my lips to her soft mouth, giving her a couple of soft, tiny kisses before I latched on with the third. Our lips fully connected, and my tongue pushed into her mouth. The deeper my tongue slid, the more I pushed her up with my hands. No matter how hard I pushed, she wasn't close enough. *I want to be inside her.*

She gripped my shoulders, running her hands up my neck and into my hair, pushing my face closer to hers. Her tongue played with mine, driving me wild. Our chests vibrated with moaned ecstasies.

She slid her lips to the corner of my mouth…down my jaw…and neck, her tongue devoured me. My hands massaged her ass, desperate to get her closer. My dick strained against my pants.

"Jillibean," I breathed in her ear.

She kissed me again, her tongue flicking wildly against mine.

"Jillian," I said, into her mouth. I put my thumb and forefinger on her chin to get her attention.

She stopped kissing me and stared into my eyes. Desire pooled in her eyes. "Hmm," she said, licking her lips.

Fuck me. That was hot.

"Do you want to go?" I asked, my voice thick with want.

She nodded.

I wrapped my arms around her waist and we made our way through the crowded dance floor. I hadn't realized how many people were still down here, and I didn't give a fuck. All I wanted to do was get my girl alone and show her how much I'd missed her.

We made our way upstairs. Sarah stood next to a guy in the corner of the living room. "Sarah!" Jillian called over the loud music. "Sarah!"

Jillian looked back at me and smiled.

"Hey, guys," Jillian said, pushing through the crowd.

"Hey, you two," Sarah sang, winking at Jillian. "Did you enjoy your birthday present?"

Oh, she is about to.

"I still can't believe you two didn't tell me." Jillian playfully punched Sarah in the arm and turned to smirk at me. I pulled her back and kissed the top of her head before resting my chin atop her rainbow hair.

"It wouldn't have been much of a surprise if you'd known I was visiting." I pinched her side, and she squirmed against me, sending more blood rushing south.

Jillian stepped closer to Sarah and whisper-shouted, "We're going to bail."

"OK." Sarah winked. "Happy birthday, Jillian." Sarah pulled her into a hug, both girls swaying and giggling.

I put my hand at the small of Jillian's back to steady her. Sarah leaned in close and whispered something into her ear. They giggled again. I couldn't make out what she had said, but I was pretty sure Jillian and I had the place to ourselves tonight.

Jillian stepped back. "Thank you, Sarah. For all of this." She flung her arm out widely, gesturing to the whole room.

"No problem. I wanted you to have a good birthday."

"I did. Thank you." Jillian turned to the guy standing next to Sarah. "Brandon, thank you for everything."

"Sure thing, Jillian." He patted her back and Jillian nearly lost her balance again. "Whoa, there." Brandon clamped a hand on her shoulder. "Hey, man," Brandon said, looking at me. "You'd better get her home. It looks like she's enjoyed her birthday a little too much."

Jillian scrunched up her face. "I did enjoy my party, but I am fine." She giggled. "I am not drunk."

Yep. She was wasted. Brandon was right. I needed to get her

back to the dorm. I reached around Jillian and extended my hand to Brandon. "That's my plan," I replied. We shook hands. "Thanks for having Jillian's party, man."

"It's cool." Brandon patted my shoulder with his other hand.

Jillian and I turned to leave, and I wrapped my arm around her waist. Once we were outside, I led her toward Ren's car.

"Damn it!" she yelled, coming to an abrupt halt.

"What's wrong?"

"Sarah has my keys." She turned and started marching with a determined effort, back to Brandon's place.

I jogged up to her and grabbed her hand. "Whoa, wait up a minute. Sarah will bring your car back to the dorm in the morning. I have Ren's car."

"Ren's?" Jillian hiccupped.

"A thousand miles and January air don't make for a very pleasant trip on a bike. Ren let me borrow her car."

"Oh. OK." She shrugged, and her shirt fell off her right shoulder.

With my palm I pushed it back into place. "I'm parked over here." I wrapped her to my side, trying to keep her warm. "I had to make sure I parked far enough away so you wouldn't recognize her car."

When Ren's Miata was in sight, I pressed the key fob and it chirped to life. I opened Jillian's door and helped her climb in. Quickly I rounded the front, noticing Jillian had reclined her head and closed her eyes.

Pulling my door open, I asked, "Bean, you all right?"

"Mm-hmm." She nodded, not opening her eyes.

Worry settled in the pit of my stomach. *Was that tequila clean? How drunk is she?* Not only did I worry that she might have been slipped something, I also worried about alcohol poisoning. I laid my hand on her leg and squeezed. "We'll be back to the dorm in just a minute," I whispered.

Jillian rested quietly in the seat beside me, unable to point me toward the dorm. I was pretty sure it wasn't far from here, and I knew its general vicinity. I put the car in gear and headed in that direction.

I traveled toward campus, taking the turns slowly, for Jillian's sake. Each bump and jostle of the road made her groan. I glanced at her. Every so often she'd shift her head, trying to get comfortable.

All the times I'd seen Jillian drunk, there had been an underlying reason why she'd ended up that way. She always partied with the intent of getting drunk. It was a choice, never an accident. I wondered why she'd chosen to get wasted tonight.

I rolled through a stop sign, Jillian's dorm up ahead. Pulling into the back lot, I found a parking spot close to the building. Jillian murmured as I got out of the car.

Coming around to her door, I pulled it open. She rolled her head to the side, her eyelids heavy. She looked up at me. I extended my hand, giving her something solid to hold on to. "Come on, Jillibean." I kept my voice soft, comforting.

"I...can't...move," she mumbled.

"Take my hand, Bean." She slipped her palm into mine. It was sweaty and cool to the touch. "Ugh," she moaned. Then, like someone had injected her with a syringe full of adrenaline, she sat up straight, her eyes wide.

It scared the shit out of me. "Bean?" I said, crouching beside her.

Her hand went to her mouth, and even in the dark, I saw her skin go from ivory to a dull green. I reached into the car and angled her body toward the parking lot. "Let's do that out here, baby," I said comfortingly.

She leaned toward me and I scooted to the side, clearing space between us. I held her hair back as the tequila made its reappearance.

When her stomach was empty of the poison, she sat back in the seat, exhausted. "Ugh," she moaned again.

"Come on, Bean." Gently I slid my arms around her back and under her legs. I stood, cradling her in my arms.

Like a rag doll, she rested against my chest. "I've always got you, love."

Chapter Thirty-Two

With Jillian in my arms, I had to finagle my way into her purse, which was sandwiched between our bodies. I felt around inside until my fingers touched her dorm access card. I pulled it free. Swiping it over the magnetic card reader, I waited for the light to turn green and the lock to click free.

Shifting Jillian's weight onto one arm, I pulled the door open, kicking it wider with my foot. I let out a heavy breath, putting my arm back beneath her. It wasn't that she was heavy, I just didn't want to drop her.

Jillian lived on the third floor, so I set off for the stairs, careful to keep my footsteps slow and light. It was an easy climb. I kept my eyes on Jillian most of the way up, hoping I wasn't jostling her too much.

Finally I made it to her floor. I opened the steel door with ease and made my way to her room. Once again I had to fish her room keys out of her purse.

I slid the key into the lock, felt the tumblers click into place, and pushed the door open. Carrying Jillian across the threshold of her dorm room, I peeled back the blankets on her bed and gently laid her down.

I watched her for a second, sleeping soundly. Her breaths full and even. *In…out…in…out…* A steady rhythm. A rhythm I'd used to write many a song.

Her hair was a tangled mess of colors against the white of her pillow. Usually her golden features reminded me of an angel's, but tonight she was a fairy. I cocked my head, considering the thought. "Yeah, a fairy all right. A punk rock fairy." I smiled. My beautiful, cute, comatose punk rock fairy.

I went to her drawer in search of something more comfortable for her to wear. I came away with a tiny pair of shorts and a little tank top. I'd seen her wear similar stuff to bed, so I hoped it was OK.

I knelt beside her. How was I going to get that dress off? It clung to every gorgeous part of her. *Damn.*

She probably couldn't hear me, but I walked her through what I was going to do. "OK, Bean." I let out a huge breath. "I'm going to get you into something more comfortable. Bear with me."

Carefully I pinched the bottom of her dress and drew it up her body. With all the fantasies I'd had about undressing this girl, in none of them had she ever been unconscious. I bunched the fabric in my hands and kept pulling.

Jillian moaned and rolled to her side, facing the wall.

Shit. That didn't help.

"Fuck it." Being gentle was getting me nowhere. I stood up and just yanked the dress the rest of the way off. Jillian didn't even flinch. I tossed the dress onto the floor. Had this been a situation where Jillian was a willing participant, I would have taken time to appreciate the sexy black lingerie she wore. But I couldn't do that to her.

I made quick work of pulling on the skimpy tank top. I guided her head through the opening, then her arm. Pulling the shirt down to cover her breasts, I rolled her body to face me, and fitted her other arm through the tiny straps.

Shirt. Done.

I picked up the shorts and stared at them. "No way." I shook my head and tossed them over my shoulder. "Sorry, Bean. Panties it is." Not that I was complaining.

I yanked the covers from the foot of the bed and pulled them to her neck, kissing her on the forehead. "I'll be right back. Gonna get my things from the car." I kissed her again.

Before I left the room I patted my back pocket, checking to see if I still had her access card. *Yep.* I opened the door, the keys still in the lock. I snatched them back and headed to the car for my bag and Jillian's birthday present.

I wasn't gone long, and was back in her room for the night. I searched through her closet for an extra blanket, and ditched my pants and shirt. I climbed over Bean, careful not to wake her. I spread the blanket out over my body and sat up. It only covered my stomach and the upper portion of my thighs. "What the hell kind of blanket is this?" I shook my head and rolled onto my side, spooning Jillian. I kicked my legs, trying to send some of the material to my feet. It was useless. Instead I opted for burrowing my feet beneath Jillian's, huddling against her for warmth. I flexed my arm around her and closed my eyes, happy to be at her side.

* * *

I felt the small bed shift. I craned my neck, peering over my shoulder. Jillian was sitting up. I gave her a lazy smile and blinked away sleep, flipping my body around to look at her. "Morning, Bean," I rasped, my voice thick with sleep.

"Morning," she whispered.

I yawned and stretched my arms above my head. "How are you feeling?"

She wrinkled her nose and stuck her tongue out. "I've been better."

Even hungover she was beautiful. "Sorry. I bet you're hurting." I sat up slowly to keep from jostling the bed.

As she rolled onto her back, I noticed her eyes dancing over the ink on my chest. It was such a turn-on.

"Griff, I'm so sorry."

I eased next to her. I loved when she used my arm as a pillow. "Sorry? Why are you sorry?" I placed my hand on her belly, drawing slow circles across the top of her shirt. When I was a kid, Mom always rubbed circles on my belly when I was sick. Somehow the leisurely movement magically erased the unsettled feeling in my gut. I wanted to do that for her now.

She drew a hand over her face. "Not exactly my finest moment."

My eyebrows pulled up. "Really? It's not the first time I've seen you drunk."

"I know," she sighed. "But you drove all the way out here, and I had to go and get fucked up. I was pissed that I had to spend my birthday without you, so I planned on drowning my sorrows in a bottle of tequila. Our time together is too short for me to be passed out during any part of it."

"Tequila. That explains it." I brushed my hand over her face. Strands of her Skittle-colored hair fell away, tickling my arm.

"Explains what?" she asked.

"The puking."

She cringed. "Oh, dear Lord. I didn't. Please tell me I didn't."

I wrinkled my face.

"I don't remember shit about last night," she whined, throwing her arm over her eyes.

I wrangled her closer to my side. My thumb moving lower on her stomach. Finding skin, I traced lazy circuits up and down her midriff. "You don't remember anything from last night?" I crooned. The memory of her tongue in my mouth stirred things.

She shook her head.

"Nothing?" I drawled.

"Griffin…" Panic rose in her voice. "Please tell me we didn't."

Oh. God no. I didn't think she'd jump to that conclusion. I didn't mean to scare her. "No, no, no." I shook my head. "We didn't. But…" I played with her hair, letting each color fall between my fingers. Her hair was so silky. It resembled a Kool-Aid waterfall pouring down over my hands.

"But?" she sputtered.

I pulled my mouth into a wicked smile. "You don't remember attacking me on the dance floor?"

"I attacked you?" she shrieked.

I shrugged. Messing with her was fun. "It's OK. I sort of attacked you back, so it wasn't all one-sided."

"Were we alone?" she cringed.

I shook my head slowly, for added effect. A sinful smile spread across my face. I shouldn't be teasing her right now. But damn, her embarrassment was too fucking cute.

"Ugh!" she screamed, rolling toward me. She buried her head against my chest. "How bad was it?"

"Well, there was lots of tongue, some moaning, ass-grabbing—"

"Stop." She cut me off. And I had just been getting to the good part. "Just stop. I get the picture." She shook her head.

"Do you remember now?" I asked, rubbing her back.

"No." Her words were a muffled blaze of heat against my skin.

"That's too bad," I groaned seductively. "It was so fucking hot."

She lifted her head and glared at me indignantly. "Why did you let me attack you? You were sober!"

"I really missed you. When you stick your tongue in my mouth, my self-control goes out the window. Sorry, Bean." I laughed. "However, I am sorry that you don't remember it. It was by far the best kiss I've ever had. I guess we'll just have to do it again."

"This fucking sucks. Apparently we kissed the hell out of each other last night, and I can't remember even the smallest peck." She pointed her finger at me and pursed her lips. "That will never happen again."

"What?" I sat up quickly and Jillian's head fell to the pillow. But right now I didn't care about that. *She wasn't going to kiss me anymore?* That was un-fucking-acceptable.

She yanked the pillow from beneath her head and smacked me with it. "I didn't mean the kissing, you idiot."

"Phew," I sighed, "you had me worried. I've waited a long time to do that, and I am not about to stop." I grabbed the pillow out of her hands and tossed it on the floor.

Lying beside me she looked up, all humor gone from her face. "I meant that I am never getting trashed to the point that I can't remember kissing you. I will remember ever single one of our kisses from here on out, and that's a promise."

"Well, enough talking. Let's start making some memories you'll remember." I leaned down just as Jillian squirmed her way out of my grip and slipped to the floor. She pressed her finger to my waiting lips.

"Hold that thought. From what you said I did last night, I need a few moments in the bathroom. I'll be right back."

Like a shot, she was up off the floor. "Hurry up, I have a birthday kiss to give you. I promise you'll remember this one," I teased.

She squealed and grabbed her bathroom stuff, shutting the door behind her. Apparently the promise of kissing me was a hangover cure.

Chapter Thirty-Three

I felt Jillian's stomach gurgle while I was on top of her. "You're hungry," I said, against her lips. "Your stomach sounds pretty pissed."

She smiled and I couldn't resist. I devoured it, sealing my mouth over hers.

"I'll order a pizza. I don't want to leave," she said when I let her come up for air.

With my long arms, I reached over us and pulled her phone from the desk. Jillian ordered quickly, then snuggled back into my arms so I could kiss her some more.

As we lay side by side, our foreheads touching, Jillian beamed. "This has been the best birthday ever."

I wrapped my hands around her folded ones and traced over the thin skin of her wrists with my thumb. She never seemed to mind when I did this, but I often worried that my callused fingers were too rough.

We were quiet for a moment, each of us caught up in the thrill of the other. "I haven't had a chance to give you your gift," I said quietly.

"Are you kidding? You're here. That's beyond enough."

I smoothed her hair back and smiled. "Of course I got you a birthday present." *She is so silly*. I placed a featherlight kiss on the tip of her nose. "But before I give it to you, I want you to keep an open mind."

I felt her tense in my arms. "What did you do, Griffin?" She pushed against me and sat up, crisscrossing her legs. I did the same, mirroring her, then reached for her hands.

I stared into her eyes, like black holes, praying they'd swallow me up and keep me for a lifetime. "It's nothing big or extravagant, but when I saw them, I thought of you…and us."

Her eyebrows pulled together in confusion. "What does that mean?"

I lifted my leg over her head and stood. I walked to the closet and reached up, moving a few things out of the way. While she slept off her birthday party, I'd hidden the frames.

"What are you looking for?" she called from the bed.

Just then her phone rang. Frantically Jillian patted the blankets until she pulled it free. "It's probably the pizza guy."

Damn it.

I backed away from the closet.

"I'll be right down. Thanks," Jillian said, ending the call. She smiled. "I was right, it's the pizza."

"Perfect timing," I mumbled.

She hopped off the bed and skipped toward me. "I'll be right back." Before she opened the door, she snaked her arms around my waist and yanked me down to her face. "You're acting very strange," she said, pressing our noses together. "You don't need to worry. Whatever you got me, I know I'll love it. I've never disliked a present you've gotten me." Then she kissed me…hard. I felt better. If my kisses cured hangovers, then hers were the cure for nerves.

* * *

Waiting for her to return, I fell onto the bed. It whined in protest under my large frame. I ignored it and threw my arm across my face.

The door kicked open and Jillian said, "Dinner is served."

"You OK?" I heard her ask.

I sat up and plastered on a confident smile. I was getting nervous again. I needed her to kiss me. "Yeah, I'm good."

She pulled open a drawer and dug out paper plates and napkins. "So are you going to give me my present?" she asked, opening the pizza box.

"Let's eat first. I'll give it to you later." I pushed off the bed and picked up a plate as I looked into the pizza box. "Pineapple? Seriously?"

"I only ordered it on my half, not yours." She tilted her head, giving me a cheeky glare.

I wrinkled my nose. "Your taste in pizza is hideous."

We sat on the floor, each enjoying our personal half of the pizza. I was so hungry. I folded the slice in half and consumed it in three bites before powering down another.

"Ahh, that was fantastic," Jillian sighed.

"Mine was fantastic…not so sure about yours," I mocked.

She snatched a piece of pineapple sitting in the empty box and popped it into her mouth. "You don't know what you're missing."

"I've watched you eat pepperoni-and-pineapple pizzas for what…thirteen years now? If I haven't indulged in your exotic taste in pizza yet, I think it's pretty safe to say that I don't believe I'm missing much."

"Your loss," she said, standing up. She tossed all the trash into the pizza box and walked it to the trash can beside the door. I watched as she stood on her tiptoes, glancing into the closet for her gift.

I got up and stretched, my mouth pulling into a yawn. I gave in to my laziness and flopped onto the bed. Amused by her eagerness, I got a kick out of watching her peek into the closet.

Jillian brushed her hands together, dusting off pizza crumbs. "So, when do I get my present?" she asked, wringing her hands together greedily.

"Your present, huh?" I sat up with a grunt and took two large strides to stand next to her, in front of the closet. I circled her in my arms, pressing her back to my chest. "I will give you your birthday present on one condition." I nipped at her ear and rocked her from side to side.

"What?" She looked up at me over her shoulder.

"You can't hide them."

"OK? But that's a silly condition. Why would I want to hide something you got me?"

"I'll explain once you open them." I tickled her sides and she tried to squirm away.

"Got it," she laughed, breathing faster now. "Now give me my present, damn it!"

I kissed the top of her head and stepped to the closet. Behind several smaller boxes, I'd hidden the wrapped frames. Turning, I presented them to her.

With my arm around her waist, we walked back to the bed. "Do you remember the day you moved in with Jennifer?" I asked as we sat down.

"Yes," she groaned. "She wasn't very happy to have me there and she made sure I knew it."

I scooted us back so we rested against the wall. "But I was there to help you." She dropped her head against my shoulder and my heart jumped.

"I remember. She loved that, too."

"It was fun to get her riled up." I laughed at the memory. "I remember unpacking a box with pictures, and you just lost it. It scared the fuck out of me. I didn't know what to do. I tossed the pictures into a random drawer and went to you."

"I didn't want those unpacked and when I saw them…"

"I know," I whispered, brushing my fingers over her pink cheeks.

"You wouldn't let me go until I stopped crying."

"You cried so much back then. I wanted to help, but I was…" I exhaled.

"You were only sixteen years old," she countered. "You were just a kid, too. I don't know many sixteen-year-old boys who would have put up with a broken teenage girl."

God. How do I convey to this woman how much she's always meant to me? I pulled her onto my lap. "You weren't just some broken teenage girl. You were my girl. The girl I promised to make happy when she was sad." I squeezed her tightly. She was the girl who inspired me to be better…to follow my dreams. "I tried to make you happy, but I failed miserably."

"Griffin, why are we talking about this? Can't I just open the gift?"

I shook my head. "Hear me out, please. I've got a point, I promise.

"Before your parents died, you loved to take pictures. Especially with your mom and dad. But once they were gone, that little girl wouldn't smile for the camera anymore. Anger and sadness wiped away the happiness of the little girl I used to play with when she'd visit her grandparents." I took her shoulders, forcing her to look me in the eyes. "I want to see that happiness on your face again." My eyes roamed over her face. "Open it."

At first she didn't move, just stared at the glittery paper I'd used. Then, very slowly, she began sliding her fingers to the edge. As she peeled back the paper, the two wooden frames came into view. She ran her fingers over the tattooed wood, spelling out the word "Promise." Then her gaze focused on the picture inside the frame. It was of the two of us. Dad had taken the picture at her going-away party, the night before she left for school. I loved that picture. Her smile could set the world on fire.

She glanced up at me, her fingers still tracing the letters. "This is perfect."

"Look at the other one." I nodded to her lap.

She placed the top frame underneath, giving her full attention to the second. It was identical to the other, except for the engraved word. This one said "Forever." "Promise" and "Forever"…our words. "This one's empty?" She held it up.

"That one is for your parents." I smoothed a hand over her head. "About a week ago, I went over to Jennifer's house."

"Wha—"

I held up my hand, cutting her off. "I knew those pictures I'd thrown in the drawer five years ago would probably still be there. I went to Jennifer's and asked if I could look for them. Surprisingly, she let me. When I pulled the drawer open, it was empty. You had packed them up and brought them with you." I smiled. "You kind of foiled my plan, but I was so happy that you were brave enough to bring them with you."

She gave a little grunt. "Not that brave." She pointed to the closet. "They're still packed in there."

I took both frames and laid them on the bed in front of us.

Pointing to the one that said "Promise," I said, "This is you and me. We have the promise of a happy future ahead of us." Then I pointed to the empty frame that said "Forever." "This one needs a picture of you and your parents. They're a part of you, and are with you forever."

Without a word Jillian launched herself off my lap. "Where are you going?" *She hates them. I fucked up.*

Jillian turned and walked to the closet. Bending down, she pulled a huge box out. I got off the bed to help her, but she put her hand up. "I got it," she croaked.

I understood. This was something she had to do on her own. Giving her space, I sat back down and watched her pull the box over to the bed. She plopped beside me and we both stared at the box. "They're in there." I could tell she was on the verge of crying, her voice thick with unshed tears.

"Are you going to open it?"

She nodded.

I leaned behind her and pulled a pen off the desk. I handed her the pen. Wrapping her fingers around it, she poked it through the tape stretched across the flaps. She ran the pen down the seam, and the tape split in half, the flaps popping up. I put my hand on her leg. She wasn't alone in this.

Jillian pulled the cardboard back and hesitantly reached into the box.

She pulled out a plain black frame. Inside, a little Jillian was sandwiched between her mom and dad. The smiles on their faces were beautiful and heartbreaking. I put my arm around her, and she looked up at me with so much love, I feared my heart would stop.

"Thank you," she whispered.

Chapter Thirty-Four

I helped Jillian exchange the old frame for the new one. She got up from the bed and set them side by side on her dresser.

I patted the bed. I needed her beside me. I scooted closer to the wall and opened my arms wide. She lay down next to me and my arms were around her in an instant. "You're amazing," I whispered in her ear. I also took the opportunity to press tiny kisses along her jaw and down her neck. Her skin blazed against my mouth. Incendiary. Jillian shifted slightly and I took advantage, climbing on top of her. I pressed my body to hers.

Her breasts teased me, spilling over the top of the little shirt I'd put on her last night. *Fuck, that is hot.* I moved lower, wanting to taste a part of her that had been off-limits to me until now.

The moment my tongue plunged between her peaks, Jillian placed a hand under my chin, drawing my eyes back to her face. My shoulders heaved. *I want to make love to her. I want to fuck her. I want to bury myself in her. I want to kiss her in places she's never been kissed before. I want to devour her. I want… her.*

"Griffin," she exhaled, drawing me back to her lips. *Does she know what I want? How much I want?* She kissed me with a greedy, hungry passion. We were all teeth and tongues.

My hands slid over her waist, grabbing the stretchy material and bunching it between my fingers. I'd dressed her last night, but now it was in the fucking way.

Jillian pressed her hand against my fist, stopping me from ripping her shirt off. I looked at our folded hands lying on her stomach, and then back into her eyes. They burned darkly, the brown completely consumed by the fire between us. "Griffin," she breathed again.

"What?" My chest heaved.

"Make love to me." Her eyes held mine, begging for me to oblige.

She loosened her grip on my fingers and pushed my hands down the length of her torso. Beneath me she bunched the white tank top in her fingers and pulled it over her head.

I loved this woman. "Jillian…," I whispered. I held her eyes, wanting to bask in the glory of her almost-naked body, but I was scared to. *Is she ready for this?*

She rose, supporting her weight on her elbows. Our faces millimeters apart. "I want this." She flattened her palm against my chest. "I want you," she demanded.

I moved my hand down her flexed arm, giving her a little push. She fell back onto the pillow.

With each inhalation her breasts swelled over the cups of her bra. My eyes traversed the hills and valleys of her lithe body, zeroing in on the white scars. Countless slashes covered her torso. In my hands she was a broken china doll. Though time had glued her back together, the cracks were still visible. Each fissure was a reminder of my failure. *Why didn't I catch her when she fell? I could have saved her from all that pain… all those cracks.*

"Griffin," she whispered.

My eyes left her skin. "Bean…" My hands slid from one crack in her skin to the next, counting how many times I'd let her down. I didn't deserve her. "I'm so sorry," I muttered quietly.

"Sorry?" A look resembling fear washed over her face. "Why are you sorry?"

So pissed at myself, I sat up and whipped my shirt off, throwing it across the room. Jillian flinched beneath me. I caught my right bicep in a white-knuckled grip with my left hand. I pressed five fingers into my skin, wanting to inflict even the smallest amount of pain on myself. I'd let her down. I'd broken my promise to her. I deserved to feel pain.

"Griffin?" Her eyes glistened with unshed tears.

She pushed against me, trying to wriggle her way out from underneath me. "Let me up," she demanded. "Damn it, Griffin! Let me up." She clenched her teeth and beat on my chest with her fists.

I snapped back to reality, refocusing my eyes on hers. "Jillian, what's wrong?"

"Nothing," she grunted, trying to push me way. "Just let me up."

Immediately I rolled off her, my back hitting the wall with a thud.

Beside me Jillian frantically searched for her shirt, holding an arm over her chest. Once she'd located her tank top, she put it on and fell onto Sarah's bed.

"Jillian?" I spoke quietly. I didn't know what had elicited her reaction. Why she felt the need to put distance between us…I loathed distance. Whether it was hundreds of miles, or just a couple of feet, Jillian belonged in my arms.

I got up and joined her on Sarah's bed, pressing her back to my front. I smoothed away some strands of her rainbow hair, the ones that stuck to my face. "Bean?" I whispered in her ear. "I'm sorry."

"I get it, Griffin, you don't have to explain. How I ever expected another person to want me...I'll never know," she choked.

What? She thinks I don't want her? This crazy talk ends now.

I gripped her shoulder and forced her to roll over. "You think that's what I'm sorry about? Jillian Helene Lawson," I scolded, cocking my head to the side. "Come on, you know me better than that." My eyes searched her face. Her eyes were glassy, and I could see the sting of rejection reddening her cheeks. "Do you remember when I got this?" I pointed to the scripture binding my arm.

"Yes." Her voice cracked. "Junior year."

I nodded. "I got this right after I found out what you were doing to yourself. I hated the fact that I couldn't take your pain away." I brushed her cheek with the back of my hand. "I felt powerless. There was *nothing* I could do to help you, and I *hated* that. My own powerlessness made me sick. I was your best friend, and I couldn't save you."

She shook her head. "Nobody could, Griffin. The voices in my head were so much easier to believe—their lies so much more convincing than the truth."

"When I got this tattoo, I made a promise to myself and to you. I would *always protect* you, *always trust* you, *always hope* for you, and *always persevere* for you." Each time I spoke, I pointed to the matching phrase on my arm, driving home the point. "This is what love means to me. That's why I got this, a physical reminder that I would never give up on you...or us."

"What about this?" She touched the words "Never fails"—the ones I hadn't mentioned.

I looked her in the eyes. "To remind me that failure wasn't an option. I wouldn't ever stop trying." I hoped she knew how serious I was. "Jillian, I had no idea. I didn't know how much you were hurting. Each one of those scars represents a time that I didn't protect you." I pointed to my tattoo again. "I feel like I failed you. Something love isn't supposed to do."

Her features softened. "Griffin." She kissed me gently. "You couldn't have saved me. I had to do that myself. But if you hadn't been by my side through all of that, I wouldn't have survived. You didn't fail me. You found me dying on the bathroom floor. You forced me to get help even when I didn't want to. You took whatever wrath I unleashed on you and willingly stood by my side. I'm here, wrapped in your arms...*because* of your love for me. I don't deserve it, but for some reason you think I do." She blinked and a small tear rolled down her cheek.

My fingers lingered at her waist until I couldn't take it anymore. A need so fierce ripped through me, I had to show her how desirable she was. But before I had the chance to act, Jillian pulled her shirt off, pushed me onto my back, and straddled me.

Whoa.

Air rushed from my lungs. I drank in her body, admiring every part of her. I traced the scars. She shivered under my touch. "Jillian," I said, "I promise I will always protect you." I rose, bringing my lips to the scar just above her left breast. "I promise I will always love you."

I kissed every scar, a symbol of my love and devotion to her.

She arched her back as I worked my way across her chest. "Make love to me...please," she begged.

I flipped us over, resting my weight on top of her. "I want nothing more than to make love *with* you, Jillian. But, when I do make love *with* you, I plan to hold you hostage in bed for several days. I don't want to wake up tomorrow and have to leave your side. Our first time will be perfect." I dropped my mouth on hers before she begged again. If she pleaded again, I wouldn't be able to say no.

"I promise," I whispered into her mouth.

Chapter Thirty-Five

By the time I got back from Rhode Island, I barely had time to piss. The next two months were chock-full of rehearsals, appearances, interviews, photo shoots, gigs, and anything else that would boost record and merch sales while we were on the road.

I was thankful for the distraction. There were 102 days separating Jillian and me. If I didn't stay busy, I'd lose my mind. And for this very reason, I didn't mind that Thor was knocking on my door at five thirty in the morning.

"Yeah?" I lifted my head and stared at the closed door. I'd gotten in late and hadn't slept worth a damn.

"Up and at 'em, bro. Interview with *Rock Review* in an hour." He pounded my door with his fist, then clomped into the bathroom, shutting the door.

My head hit the pillow. I stared at the ceiling for a moment, then growled. Scrubbing my hands over my face, I threw my body into a sitting position. "I'm up."

I had a feeling the next 102 days would be marked by the small victories, each of them bringing Jillian one step closer to home.

Showered and dressed, Thor and I made record time into the city. We were meeting Pauly, Adam, and the journalist from *Rock Review* at the Lounge in Ballpark Village.

Thor parked his Charger in one of the garages near the stadium and we hoofed it to BPV. He lit a cigarette and took a drag. "So." he blew out a puff of smoke. "Jill won't be back until May?"

I turned to glare at him. *Way to rub salt in the wound, dick.* I pulled the collar of my leather jacket closed and nodded. "Yep."

"Harsh."

I kept quiet. I didn't want to talk about it. I needed to stay focused on my distractions.

* * *

"So, guys." The reporter leaned in and smiled. I stared at her cherry-red lips. It was hard not to, they were like a bull's-eye in the center of her coffee-colored face. "Any significant others?" Her voice squeaked at the end of her question.

We glanced at each other. I knew Thor wasn't about to bring up Harper, and there was no way in hell I wanted to complicate Jillian's life by having her name plastered everywhere. And I was fairly certain Pauly and Adam weren't seeing anyone exclusively. I spoke up for all of us. "We'd prefer to keep our personal lives private."

She frowned. "That's too bad. There are hundreds of ladies out there that would like to know if they've got a chance."

Jesus. What happened to focusing on the music?

Pauly raised his hand, flashing her a smile from beneath his dark beard. "I don't know about these fuckers, but I'm always willing to give the ladies a chance."

The reporter, I forgot her name, scribbled and clicked furiously on her tablet. "Perfect. Perfect," she sang.

Pauly sat back and stroked his beard, eagerly anticipating the onslaught of female attention.

Her eyes flicked back to us. "Well, boys, I think I've got enough." She rested her palms flat against the table and smiled. "I'll let you know when it goes to print."

She stood, and we all stood after.

"It was so nice to meet you. I love the album." She offered her hand to me with a kind smile. I shook it gently before she went on to Thor, Adam, and Pauly.

"Thank you," I said. "It was our pleasure."

She gathered her things and shouldered her purse. "You guys are going to be huge." With a wink she turned on her heel and made her way to the exit.

Adam punched Pauly in the shoulder. "Ow," he howled. "What was that for?"

"You don't say that kind of shit to a reporter. Even I know that." Adam had a point.

Pauly lifted his chin. "I know those two don't want the publicity. But"—he looked at Adam—"you'll be begging for me to share the wealth."

"Well, yeah," he agreed.

"Dude," I broke in. "From here on out, we've got to keep interviews strictly business. We want people to take us seriously, it's got to be about the music."

"Griff's right," Thor said to both Pauly and Adam. "Stop thinking with your dicks."

Frustrated, I ran my hand through my hair. "Look, it's done. Let's just agree that interviews from here on out will be about the music."

Pauly rolled his eyes. "Yeah, whatever, dude."

I longed for the early days. When it really had been about the music. "Rehearsal later," I called over my shoulder, as I walked to the exit.

* * *

January and February were gone faster than one of Pauly's one-night stands. Tour prep had been insane, but now everything was ready. Our flights were booked and we headed to Cozumel tomorrow. Our three-week, ten-city tour kicked off there, then we hit the road: Playa del Carmen, Cancún, South Padre Island, Dallas... The list went on and on.

Adam and Pauly were hitting the bars tonight, Thor was hanging with Harper, and I opted to stay in, hoping to catch Jillian. We'd had so little time for each other.

Reclining in my favorite chair, I hit the FaceTime app and Jillian's number. My iPad gave a high-pitched chirp, waiting for Jillian to connect the call.

Then her face filled the screen.

"Jillibean," I sighed, and ran a hand through my hair. Her mouth parted into a toothy smile.

"Griffin." Her shoulders relaxed as she spoke my name.

I'd have given my right arm to kiss that smile. "Damn, I miss you." I scratched my face and settled back. "Whatcha up to?"

Jillian flipped the camera view, showing me a partially dressed mannequin. Then she flipped it back to her face. "Just sewing. Story of my life. What are you doing?"

"Missing you."

"I miss you, too. But hey, your tour starts tomorrow. Aren't you excited?"

Honestly, I wasn't. Don't get me wrong, I loved playing with the guys. I loved the music. But the whole *rock star* business was taking its toll on me. Photo shoots, interviews, I just wasn't sure I was cut out for it.

"Not really."

"What do you mean?" she mumbled, pulling something from between her lips.

I squinted, trying to figure out what she was doing. "What is in your mouth?"

She lowered her head for a second and came back up, smiling. "Sorry, they're pins." She held a small silver object up to the camera. "I was in the middle of pinning this fabric on the dress form when you called."

She was so busy. I shouldn't be bothering her. "I'm sorry, Bean. I'll let you go."

"No!" she shouted. "Don't you dare hang up." She pointed a finger at me and scowled. "I am very good at multitasking. Besides, you're getting on a damn plane tomorrow. You know how I get when people I love fly."

I did know. After what happened to her parents, she hated airplanes and wanted nothing to do with them. "I do." I nodded. "But it's only a six-hour flight. I won't be up there too long."

"The second your feet hit the Jetway is already too long, if you ask me." Her lips turned down and all I could think about was how they tasted.

Damn, she's hot when she pouts. In my head I pictured those pouty lips kissing their way down my chest. *Lower…and lower…*

"Bean," I said, my voice thick.

"Yeah?"

"You're in your room, right?" I hoped she was alone, because there was something I needed her help with.

"Yeah. Why?" she asked, taken aback by my sudden change in demeanor.

With one look she'd made me so hard.

"Are you alone?"

"Griffin?" She pulled an eyebrow up. "What are you suggesting?"

I sat up, my face filling her screen. I wanted her to see the desire on my face. "I want you, Jillian. But right now I can't have you. So…" I trailed off, letting her absorb what I meant. "Go lie down, Bean," I nudged.

Comprehension dawned on her features and she nodded. Her cheeks grew more flushed by the second. I watched the background shift as she walked to her bed.

The last time I'd had phone sex was in high school and, at least to my knowledge, Jillian hadn't ever. I'd have to walk her through it.

I watched Jillian climb into bed, aching to join her. Today she wore her hair natural, a long golden curtain fanned out around her head like a halo. I got up from the recliner and walked down the hall toward my room.

Mounting the stairs, I unbuttoned my fly, giving room to my growing erection.

"Griffin," she said breathily. "I've never done anything like this." Her voice was shaky. "This is so embarrassing," she laughed shyly.

I grabbed the knob to my door and pushed my way inside. "I'm right here with you, Bean. It'll be fun, you'll see." I kicked my door shut and went to my bed. "Are you comfortable?"

She nodded.

I liked that I could see her. The iPad brought a whole new level to phone sex. Seeing the flush on her cheeks was sexy as hell. I could get used to this.

I settled on my bed, resting my iPad against my drawn knees. "Close your eyes," I commanded.

She complied.

"I want to touch you so bad," I crooned, making my voice raspy and thick. "Do you feel my hand on you, Bean?"

With her eyes falling closed, she nodded again. Her lips parted slightly, and I could hear her breathing, slow and shallow.

"Show me," I whispered.

Jillian tilted her iPad, showing me her free hand. She drew lazy circles across her stomach, on top of her shirt.

I needed to feel skin. I moved my hand to my chest, imagining it was hers. "Jillian, I can feel you…running your hands over my chest…fingering my ink. Can you feel my hands? Your flat stomach, smooth under my fingers."

Her breath hitched. Her fingers were under her shirt now. "God, Griffin," she sighed. My beautiful girl was getting into it now.

"Your breasts…let me feel them," I begged.

Jillian shifted, then lay back down, her shirt gone. Filling my screen, her glorious tits heaved up and down. My hands longed to be filled by them. I fisted my right hand at the fantasy.

I imagined burrowing my fingers beneath the lacy material and shoving her breasts in my hands…my mouth. "Jillian, you have the most incredible body."

I lifted my ass off the bed and pulled my pants lower, kicking them to my ankles. "I want to feel *all* of you." Desire caught in my throat.

I watched her hand travel lower. In my mind I was kissing my way there. "Talk to me, baby," I coached, needing to hear the want in her voice.

Her fingers slipped inside her shorts. "Griffin, do you feel me? I'm so…" She hesitated.

I grabbed my dick for her, sucking in a breath. "You're what? Tell me," I begged through clenched teeth. I needed to hear her say how wet she was for me. "You're so what, baby?"

My hand moved faster, spurred on by her shallow breaths.

"Wet. God…," she moaned. "I want you inside me."

Fuck. Fuck. Fuck.

My hand moved double time. I wanted to thrust into her so badly. "Soon, baby," I crooned. I was so close, but I had to hold off. I wanted to watch her come apart first.

On the screen I watched her body arc with pleasure, her mouth opened wide. I wanted to shove my tongue inside. "Griffin," she called.

"I'm so hard for you, Jillian," I moaned with heady need. "Come for me, baby."

And then she fell apart. Her head pressed into the pillow, her eyes squeezed shut, her body shuddered, and she growled my name. It was the most erotic thing I'd ever seen.

"Jillian…" I clenched and my release came hard and fast. Stars burst against my clouded vision and every bone in my body turned to liquid.

For the longest time, we lay quiet. I listened to the glorious sound of her satiated breathing. It was beautiful.

She was beautiful.

When she regained the ability to speak, she said, "Griffin."

"Yeah?" I replied.

A smile worthy of a vixen spread across her face. "That was fun."

I love her. I smiled, too. "Damn straight."

Chapter Thirty-Six

Under the white-hot lights, sweat rolled down my temple. I'd already ditched my shirt half an hour ago. The sun beat down, glistening off the crystal-blue ocean. Despite Mexico's humidity—which rivaled that of home—outdoor venues on the beach kicked ass. We were down to our last two songs in Playa del Carmen, then we boarded a bus to Cancún.

As Adam counted us in, "One, two, three, four!" I mentally prepared for the next song. This one hurt every time I sang it. I walked my fingers over the strings of my bass and pressed the mic close.

> *Starving. Drunk. Don't give a fuck.*
> *Bleeding. Dying. Come back crying.*
> *Spin you around. Hold you down*
> *Don't play dead, it fucks with my head.*

The angry bass line burned in my fingers. My heart pumped the song through my body, recalling a time when fear and hatred ruled my emotions. When I'd found out Jillian was cutting herself, I was so angry with her…and terrified. But as angry as I'd been at her, I'd been furious with myself. *Why didn't I know? Why didn't I help her?*

Being a sixteen-year-old kid, hormones raging, I couldn't fathom what Jillian was feeling, why she inflicted pain on herself. My only from of reference was how music made me feel. To me, music cut as deeply as a knife.

The pounding drums, driving guitar riff, and dissonant keys represented a whip striking flesh…my flesh. I wanted to feel just a fraction of what Jillian had felt. Yet I still knew it wasn't even close. So by the end of the song, it had morphed into something penitent. I needed her forgiveness. I'd let her down.

> *Remorse. Regret. I can't forget.*
> *Forgive me yet?*
> *Silence. The clock ticks loud.*
> *Forgive me yet?*
> *Silence…*

On the next beat, our hands quieted our instruments and we froze. The wild crowd stilled. No one moved. No one breathed. Then, keeping my voice low and quiet, I delivered the last line, unaccompanied.

> *Don't play dead, it fucks with my head.*

The audience exploded.

For all the pain and sadness this song fostered within me, it was one hell of a crowd-pleaser. This song was our third single and by far our heaviest hitter.

To keep the crowd hot, Thor threw in some power chords. Over his guitar I said, "*Gracias*, Playa del Carmen. *¡Eres hermosa!* You're beautiful!"

The stage lights went dead, and we walked offstage. Thor's guitar's reverb continued to sound. Electricity sparked in the air, and the crowd buzzed like a live wire.

After playing three shows in Cozumel, and two in Playa del Carmen, we were seasoned veterans.

Our encore was quick and we put a wrap on Carmen.

"Great show, guys." Leo held out his hand for one of us to shake. Thor obliged. "Best one yet."

Still out of breath from the last song, I answered heavily, "Yeah, the audience was into it."

"Well," Leo said, dropping Thor's hand. "Cancún is going to rock."

"Hell yeah." Adam nodded in approval.

Leo pushed his glasses up on his nose and lifted his chin, acknowledging Adam. "Bus pulls out in thirty, gents."

I slung a towel around my neck. "We'll be on it."

The second Leo was out of earshot, Adam turned to me. "I don't think that dude likes me."

"Why do you think that?" While I waited for him to answer, I gathered my personal belongings.

Adam thought about it for a second and shrugged. "Just a vibe."

"Well, whatever it is, keep playing like you did tonight, and he's going to love you." I pulled a clean t-shirt out of my bag.

"How so?" Adam asked.

Pushing the shirt over my head, I stretched my arms through. "Because you'll be making him a shitload of money. We've got a bus to catch, dude. Let's hit it."

Shows might not always start on time, but damn, the tour bus was never late. Within the hour we'd be in Cancún.

* * *

The last three weeks passed by in a blur, like the Mexican landscape outside the tour bus window. I was dog-tired and missed Jillian something fierce. We hadn't talked since I'd left home, so the memory of our last conversation was what got me through the lonely nights in my hotel room.

Pauly and Adam were in their tanned, beach babe glory... especially Adam, who had recently broken up with Trina for the second time. At least Thor was miserable, like me. He was missing Harper.

Today's show was no different from the others. I'd gotten so used to prepping that I didn't need to think about it anymore. Using a small window of time while the opening act was onstage, I grabbed my iPad to FaceTime Jillian.

"Griffin!" she yelled.

I smiled widely. *God. She is beautiful.* "Hi, Bean."

"Where are you guys now?"

My screen froze as she said the last word, her lips forming the most perfect o shape. *Damn it! Why did the screen have to freeze now?* A message flashed on my screen: *poor connectivity.*

Then her face moved and she was back with me. Mexico didn't offer the best wireless services.

I shook my head and shouted. The band onstage was settling into its groove. "We're in Cancún."

"Awesome. It looks like you're getting some sun."

I glanced down at my arms. They were a little tanner. "Yeah, most of our shows have been open-air venues." I was anxious to get back to the U.S. We were far enough apart, I didn't enjoy adding more distance between us. "We're headed back to the States in a couple days. We've got shows booked in Texas, Oklahoma, and Missouri before we get to come home."

"You're a busy man." She nodded.

I walked to the cabinet where my bass was stored and pulled it out.

"What are you doing?" she asked.

I held my bass up to the screen. "We've got a show in twenty minutes. I'm just getting things together."

There it was again, her vixen smile. "That one's cool, but I much prefer its likeness on *you*," she said, wagging her eyebrows.

I got really close to the screen and whispered, "And I like when you *play* that one." I kept my voice dark and insistent.

Her cheeks flushed. "I miss you," she breathed.

I couldn't avoid the rush of blood heading south. "It's been too fucking long." I nodded in agreement.

Behind me Pauly rested his thick beard on my shoulder. "Hi, Jillian," he said, "you better be sweet-talking this dude." Pauly turned and looked at me. "He's feeling left out."

What? I shot him a pissed-off glare. "Shut the fuck up." I planted a palm to his face and pushed him off me. "Don't listen to a thing he says, Bean."

"Why are you feeling left out?" she asked.

Pauly jumped back in front of the camera, pulling at his chin. "There's a lot of tail here, girl. But no worries, your boy is behaving himself."

"Fuck, man. Back off," I yelled, knocking Pauly out of the way.

"Bye, Jillian," he shouted, stumbling away laughing. *I did not hit him hard enough.*

I righted the iPad, centering my face. "I'm sorry." I ran a hand through my hair.

She smiled sweetly. "It's OK. He seems to be enjoying himself."

"Let's just say Adam and Pauly are taking full advantage of spring break." I rolled my eyes.

"Adam? What happened to Trina?" she asked.

"She dumped his ass. She said he was a hothead, and she was tired of his outbursts."

She nodded in agreement. "He doesn't seem too broken up about it."

"Not in the slightest," I chuckled.

Jillian sat on her bed, brushing strands of hair behind her ear. "And Thor?" she asked.

I climbed the metal stairs, preparing to go on. Peeking at the audience, I saw the sun beat down on a sea of caramel-colored people. The stagehands waved us over. "Nope. He's still into Harper. Hey, Bean, I've got to go, they're calling for me."

"Oh, OK." She sounded sad. "Good luck. I love you."

"Promise?" I smirked.

Her smile brightened. "Forever."

"I fucking love that." I shoved my hair off my forehead. "I love you, Bean. Talk to you soon."

"Soon." She kissed her fingertips and pressed them to mine. So close, yet so very far away.

Chapter Thirty-Seven

Sixteen days.

Sixteen fucking days until Jillian came home. I missed her so much. Anger roared in me like a beast.

Even after talking to her, I couldn't mute the fury inside me. Frustrated by everything keeping us apart, I let my emotions get the better of me, and I launched my phone across the room.

The second it left my hands, I regretted it. "Shit!" I stared at the lifeless remains, not caring if the neighbors heard me through the paper-thin walls.

I needed to get out of here. Clear my head. Grabbing my keys and helmet, I raced out of the apartment. Straddling my bike, I focused on the back door. I hadn't locked up.

Screw it. If I didn't leave now, my fists would serve as hole-punchers for the paper walls.

With my bike between my legs, some of my anger quieted. I turned the key in the ignition and tromped on the kick starter. The engine roared to life beneath me, and I disappeared into the darkness.

Usually I wrote the best songs when I was angry. Mine Shaft might be looking at another number one.

I drove out to a secluded stretch of road, one that went on for miles. A road where I could open my baby up and let her fly. Being from a rural farming community, an abundance of secluded roadways came to mind.

The darkness swallowed me. I even considered taking off my helmet to feel the warm spring air on my face, but thought better of it. I couldn't do that to Jillian.

The rhythmic pulse of the road beneath my tires stirred a song inside me. I always heard the bass line first, followed by Adam's drumbeat. Once the music was straightened out in my head, then I could focus on the lyrics.

Lyrics. Goddamned lyrics. Since Jillian left in January, everything I'd written had been utter shit. Hallmark card shit.

I knew what I needed…Jillian.

Despite the heavy darkness, my headlight cut a small path ahead of me. The road's curves remind me of Jillian's curves—smooth, inviting, and beautiful. I envisioned my hand trailing over the contours of her hips and waist, traveling upward to her breasts. The thought of her breasts sent blood rushing elsewhere. I felt her flesh in the palms of my hands, and I squeezed the throttle, trying to bring my thoughts back to reality.

With the growl of the engine, I refocused my attention on the image of her face—much safer. *God, I miss her.*

With that thought, the hint of a verse began to work itself out in my head: *Caught in the dark. Can't see my way out. Not even hope leaves a mark. But it isn't until I get to the end of the road that I figure out, I can't go back.*

The song's skeleton took shape just as the clouds opened up above. Glancing at my speedometer, I eased off the gas just a little. *Damn it.*

My headlights shone on the rain-slicked road as I took the next turn and doubled back toward my apartment. I thought about stopping at Ren's place, it was closer, but I wanted to get home and flesh out the lyrics. Thankfully, these back roads were pretty much deserted at one in the morning.

I leaned into the next curve and came across a family of deer in the road. As I approached, I expected the lights from my bike to spur them to one side or the other, but as I got closer they showed no signs of moving.

With less than fifteen feet separating me and them, I slowed, coming to a stop. I dropped my feet to the wet asphalt. The expression "like a deer in the headlights" finally made sense. Eight eyes stared fearfully at the grumbling machine between my legs.

I lifted the face shield of my helmet and yelled, "Move it! Go on. Get!" They didn't move.

Shit.

I stretched my head up to the sky, rain pelting the patch of skin my shield usually covered. I blinked rain out of my eyes and flipped the mask back down. Inching forward, I revved the engine, thinking it would startle them.

Nothing.

I was so close now, the female's head was within my reach.

The rain sped up and the deer slowly came out of their stupor. But then all four turned their heads away from me, in the other direction. A loud screech sounded out of nowhere and headlights came barreling toward me.

For the deer, I wasn't the most dangerous encounter—that was the car all five of us were about to be hit by.

I hopped back on my bike and revved the throttle. My back tire fishtailed on the slick road and struggled to find traction. "Fuck!"

My muffled expletive was enough to send the deer scampering

out of the road, but I was stuck and the oncoming car approached fast.

I struggled to right my bike, but the rain wouldn't allow it. Before the speeding car slammed into me...before I had a chance to come to terms with the fact that I was about to die...time froze. I was a deer in the headlights. In my mind's eye the car slowed down, *Matrix*-style.

Then I was airborne.

Before my eyes closed, Jillian's smile flashed in my head, then shattered into a million pieces.

Chapter Thirty-Eight

Locked inside my own head, I couldn't escape. Memories kept me company. Music filled the lulls. And then there was Jillian.

When the memories and music quieted, I could hear her. I listened to her beg and cry, over and over again.

Why couldn't I wake up? I wanted to.

We'd just found each other. Our song wasn't supposed to end like this.

Wake up, Griffin.

I'm trying.

I love you, Griffin.

I love you, too, Bean.

You've never broken a promise to me, Griffin.

I know.

Don't you dare start now.

I'm sorry, Jillian.

Chapter Thirty-Nine

Two months later...

Smoothing my left hand up and down the fret board, I hugged my guitar close. Closing my eyes, I positioned my fingers for a simple G chord. Third fret, sixth string... second fret, fifth string... third fret, first string. It was all up there, my brain retained every ounce of music theory I'd learned over the years.

I depressed the strings with my once-nimble fingers and strummed with my right hand. The chord bellowed, awkward and unsteady. I tried again, achieving the same result.

Come on, Daniels. This is the easy shit. I shook out my hands and placed them back on the frets, opting for a C chord this time.

I strummed and the chord wobbled.

"Shit." I tossed my guitar to the opposite end of the couch and sat back with a huff. Frustration coiled in my muscles. Why couldn't I get these simple fucking chords? My brain knew what to do, why wouldn't my fingers cooperate?

For weeks I'd heard the same goddamned advice: *Give it time.* Brain injuries weren't like broken bones. There was no cast to wrap around my head to make my brain transfer data to my fingers any better.

Countless doctors and therapists had applauded my recovery, saying how lucky I was to have no serious permanent damage. None of my motor faculties had been affected, save one. I couldn't play like I used to. But my medical team remained confident that I'd continue to improve. Their favorite line was *Give it time*.

I blew out another breath and glanced at the ceiling, hearing dull thuds coming from upstairs. What was Jillian doing up there?

Curiosity got the better of me. I pushed off the couch to join her upstairs just as my phone buzzed on the glass coffee table. Reaching down, I scooped it up. My doctor's name flashed across the screen. What did he want? Had I forgotten an appointment?

I swiped my finger across the screen. "Dr. Adler?"

"Hello, Griffin. How are you today?" he asked jovially.

Instinctively I ran my hand over the right side of my head, where a small hole had been drilled into my skull. "Feeling good. Thanks."

"Good. Glad to hear it. No headaches? Dizziness? Blurred vision?"

I shook my head. "Nope. Haven't had a headache in two weeks or so."

"Wonderful. I was just in the office making some follow-up calls, wanted to check in."

"Thanks, I appreciate that. Feel like my old self. Still working on playing, though. The dexterity in my fingers isn't like it used to be." I tapped my big toe against the leg of the coffee table while I lamented my shitty guitar playing.

"Oh, give it time."

Of course.

"It's only been a couple months," Dr. Adler continued.

"Sure thing, Doc."

"Any other concerns?"

I shook my head. "No, not really."

"Good. As long as you continue feeling all right, you can head back to work, to the gym, whatever you did before the accident."

A jolt of excitement went through me. I'd been holed up in the apartment, bored stiff. Freedom sounded incredible. "Really?"

"Yes. But with an increase in activity, it is possible you could experience some negative side effects. If the headaches return, or you start to feel worse, call me immediately."

"Absolutely. Thank you, Dr. Adler." I smiled. More pounding came from upstairs. I looked upward, excited to tell Jillian my news.

"But Griffin—"

I started for the kitchen on my way to the bedroom. "Yeah?"

"No driving. Not for four more months."

I gritted my teeth together and scowled. *Damn it*. "All right."

"Call if you need anything."

"I will. Thanks, Doc."

"Take care, Griffin."

The line went dead.

Tossing my phone on the table, I ran up the stairs, taking them three at a time. With my bed rest lifted, I knew exactly how I wanted to celebrate.

In the bedroom Jillian stood near the dresser, admiring the pictures she'd placed there. She hadn't noticed me coming up the stairs. Standing in the hallway, I crossed my arms and watched a smile bloom across her face. I fell more in love with her. I could write a million songs about that smile and it still wouldn't be enough.

I stepped into our room just as she backed up, bumping into me. She looked over her shoulder and mumbled, "Sorry."

Not wasting a minute, I slid my hands over her arms, pressing her against me. I enveloped her body with mine, resting my chin atop her head. "You busy?" As I brushed my fingers over her soft skin, she sighed and relaxed against my chest.

"Not really," she replied dreamily.

My hands paused on her shoulders, and I took the opportunity to spin her around. I pulled her close and latched my fingers, resting them at the small of her back. She lifted her chin, fixing me with a breezy smile. "Already redecorating, huh?"

Jillian cocked an eyebrow and looked around the room. "Well, this place could use the help of a good designer."

"Anyone come to mind?" I swayed her gently, unfolding my hands. I slid them down her backside.

Looking thoughtfully at the ceiling, she played along. "Hmm, maybe," she simpered, biting the corner of her lip. "I think she prefers clothes to bedrooms, though."

Oh, really, Jillibean? I was confident I could change her mind. I matched her playful grin with my own. "Know what I prefer?"

She shook her head. "Uh-uh."

I inclined my head, my lips right at her ear. With a breathy rasp, I whispered, "I prefer bedrooms and no clothes."

Her body shuddered against mine, capturing the attention of my dick. I couldn't wait any longer.

Since my accident, any physical activity that increased my blood pressure had been off-limits. Not that it had stopped me from trying to convince her I was well enough to have sex. No matter how many times I'd sent my hands traveling over her body, or pushed a kiss beyond a PG rating, Jillian had made me behave. She'd forced me to be the model patient, which was no easy feat.

But I'd been pardoned. No more sleepless nights reciting base-ball stats when Jillian snuggled up beside me. Nothing stood in our way now.

"Griff…" She shook her head. "I'm not so sure…"

I could see the trepidation in her eyes. "Jillian, I got the all clear from my doctor today. As long as I'm not in any pain, no headaches, I can resume my normal level of activity."

"Really?" Her eyes flashed.

I nodded.

"Griff, that's great news." She stretched up on her tiptoes and kissed me.

Lifting my hands from her ass, I caught her face in my palms. Slowly I brushed my lips over hers, licking the seam of her mouth before I drew back. Resting my forehead against hers, I fixed her with a heady gaze. "I want you, Jillibean. I promise you, I'm fine." My thumbs traced light circles over the flush of her cheeks. "These last eight weeks…hell, these last six months have been excruci-ating." My knees almost buckled with how much I wanted her. I couldn't wait any longer. "I *need* to be inside you." My voice scratched its way out of my throat.

Jillian sucked in a breath and stared. The worry reflected in her eyes just moments ago ignited into passion as her lips curled into a sinful smile. "And that's right where I want you," she breathed.

"Fuck." Her words were my undoing. I slammed my mouth onto hers. I wanted to devour her. To taste and touch every part of her body at once.

I caught her lip between my teeth, sucking it into my mouth. The sweetness of her lip gloss slid over my tongue, making me crave more of her. I pushed my tongue inside, tasting deeper.

With my arms circled around her neck, I flexed my biceps, needing her closer.

"Make love to me," Jillian spoke against my lips.

I drank her words. She didn't need to ask twice. I slid my hands down the length of her spine and gripped her tiny waist in my palms. Bending my knees, I lifted her off the ground.

Jillian's legs wrapped around my waist as she threw her arms around my head, her tongue moving wildly against mine. I held her tightly, supporting her weight in my arms.

Taking a few steps toward the bed, I leaned down and placed her on the mattress. Slowing my lips, I pulled away. Jillian stared up at me. Our eyes locked for a second before I trailed over every part of her body. Sprawled in front of me, she was the best gift I'd ever been given.

I was determined to memorize her every feature. It'd taken us so long to get to this point, I wanted to remember everything. The way her sun-yellow hair fanned out against the dark-gray sheets on the bed…the desire and heat that pooled in her cheeks and burned in her eyes…her breasts rising and falling with each wanting breath…the way her flimsy dress bunched at her hip, teasing me.

Setting my hands at her knees, I pushed them up her thighs. Her soft, warm skin beneath my fingers drove me wild. My eyes found hers again. "I'm tired of being apart, Jillian."

I loved her soul-deep, and I wanted her to feel it.

With a nod she whispered, "Me too."

I smiled wantonly, impatient to get her naked. "Did you make this?" Fingering the hem of her dress, I slid my hands beneath the silky fabric.

Jillian shivered at my touch. "Mmm-hmm."

My dick strained against the zipper of my jeans, begging to be freed.

Continuing my ascent of her legs, I lowered my torso to hers.

Coming close to her lips, but not touching them, I breathed, "It's my new favorite."

Jillian sat up and rocked her body from side to side, working the dress over her hips, across her breasts, before pulling it off completely. She tossed it over my head. "I was never fond of it," she said, kissing my lips and flopping back onto the bed.

Fuck me. I was out of my league with this girl. "Jillian," I stammered. "You are so damn sexy." I smiled, taking in her gorgeous body. As I smoothed my hands across the skin of her ivory shoulders, her warmth soaked into my fingertips. I skimmed downward, filling my palms with her breasts, knowing that would be my undoing.

I groaned against my hardening erection. The clothes needed to go.

Shuffling back a step, I stood and grabbed the back collar of my t-shirt, ripping it over the top of my head. Keeping my eyes on Jillian, I unbuttoned my jeans, lowered the zipper and stepped out of my pants in record time.

As she watched me undress, her eyebrows shot up. It was the sexiest, cutest damn expression I'd ever seen. I loved her eyes on my naked body.

I stepped toward her, my skin tingling with anticipation. I pressed my hands to the insides of her knees, opening her legs as I slowly climbed on top of her. Working my palms over her shoulders, I lifted her from the mattress. She still wore too many clothes for my liking.

Drawing a sensual trail down her back, my thumb and forefinger flicked open the closures. Gently I lowered her back onto the bed, peeling away the pink bra that stood between me and her beautiful tits.

I flung the bra aside and pressed my mouth to her collarbone, working my way lower. With each kiss my tongue tasted her glistening skin. I wrapped my lips around her left breast, flicking my tongue against her nipple. She arched her back, pressing herself more fully against my mouth. If she kept that up, this wouldn't last very long.

I pulled in a breath, my nostrils consumed by her scent. It was a potent, lusty mix of her delicate perfume and arousal. "Flowers and the ocean," I exhaled over her skin. I couldn't get enough of her.

As I continued exploring her body, kissing…tasting…smelling…Jillian ran her hands through my short hair, over the muscles of my back, kneading her fingers over my skin.

I rested my chin on her breasts and looked into her dark eyes. "I love you, Jillibean," I rasped.

"I love you," she whispered back.

I smiled. Turning my head, I pressed my ear right above her left breast, and listened. "I could listen to your heartbeat all day long."

Keeping my ear to her heart, I guided my right hand up her arm, extending it above her head. With our fingers laced together, I moved my left hand southward, dipping my fingers just inside the top of her panties, eager to get them off. But first I wanted to watch Jillian come apart at my touch.

"Hmmm," I sang. "You're changing the beat, Jillian. Much more syncopated." A throaty laugh escaped my mouth.

Jillian's right hand pressed harder into my back, begging me for more. I slipped my fingers lower at the same time I planted my lips back onto hers. She was so wet…so ready. My dick throbbed, jealous of my hand. My tongue licked across her lips and she opened to me in more ways than one. I kissed her deeply.

Her legs spread wider at my touch. I circled over her slick folds, making her breath come harder, faster. She moved against my fingers, and I felt her pulse quicken. "I've written songs about you," I said against her mouth. "But your heartbeat right now has to be the damn sexiest, most gorgeous song I've ever heard."

I slipped one finger inside her, letting her get used to having me there. She moaned, working her body in time with my hand. Then I slid in a second, moving them in a rhythm that had her panting.

"Oh…my…Griffin…," she cried.

I watched her come apart. My fingers might struggle to play instruments, but they knew exactly how to play Jillian. And that was all I needed.

Jillian opened her eyes, love blazing from her dark irises.

Want coursed through my veins. I needed to be inside her now. I peeled her panties down her legs, taking them away as I stood.

Jillian propped herself on her elbows, still breathless. "What's wrong? Are you OK? Are you hurt?" she asked, panic rising in her voice.

I laughed, holding up my index finger. "Relax, Bean." I stepped to my nightstand and pulled open the top drawer. Tossing aside a couple of pieces of crumpled paper, I searched for my box of condoms. It'd been a while since I'd needed them.

Pulling one free, I turned my attention back to Jillian, holding the foil wrapper between my thumb and forefinger.

Understanding dawned on her face.

I bit the corner of the wrapper and ripped it open. As I rolled the condom over my length, I kept my eyes on Jillian. She watched me intently, her cheeks burning with desire.

I slid back between her legs. I put my hands on her shoulders and pushed her onto the bed. Brushing the hair from her face, I asked, "Are you sure?" I wanted her more than I needed air. But if she wasn't ready, I'd wait.

I searched her face. Then she nodded, breathing out a breath. It was music to my ears. I leaned forward, our bodies pressed together. Kissing her softly, I aligned myself to her.

Jillian's arms looped around my neck and she pushed her tongue into my mouth. Fire lit beneath my skin, and I couldn't take another second of separation.

I pushed inside her.

My body sang. My eyes closed, overcome by her warmth. I'd dreamed of having her in this way, but nothing compared to the real thing.

We were together. Nothing separated us anymore.

I moved slowly, acquainting our bodies. Knowing this was Jillian's first time, I didn't want to hurt her. Unhurried, I pushed and pulled. We fit together perfectly.

I committed the feeling of her to memory. My hands roamed over her body. I kissed her mouth…her jaw…the place below her ear that drove her wild. Jillian groaned in response. I loved that I did that to her.

Smiling, I moved faster. I grasped her hands, locking our fingers together above her head. She squeezed my hands and her muscles clenched. "Griffin," she moaned.

Hearing my name fall from her mouth nearly sent me over the edge. I thrust harder, pressing farther inside her. My tongue shoved into her mouth and she bucked her hips.

"Ahhh…Jillian," I sighed. Letting go of her hands, I propped my arms at the sides of her face, locking her beneath me.

Jillian dragged her fingers over my sweat-slicked skin. I hadn't thought it was possible to get any harder, but I did.

"Griff!" Jillian screamed.

I held her face in my hands. "I'm so close…," I muttered, my lips grazing her jaw. Jillian's fingernails dug into my shoulders. My muscles rippled in response. I knew she was close. "Come for me, Bean."

I thrust hard…twice…three times.

Jillian closed her eyes and arched her back, synching her movements with mine.

Then she clenched around me. So tight. She drew in a breath, and I watched her come undone. Stunning and fucking hot as hell.

I pushed into her again…and again.

Pleasure, like none I'd ever experienced, shot through my veins. A hum reminiscent of feedback buzzed in my ears, and I was lost. My body quaked, and I fell against Jillian with a sated grunt.

Together we caught our breath. I rolled off her, stealing a kiss as I propped my head in my hand. Staring down at her, I couldn't help the wicked smile pulling at the corners of my mouth. Her hair was a tangled, well-loved mess and her lips were swollen. I brushed some knotted strands away from her face.

I was so gone for this girl. I always had been, but now it was so much more. It was the history, the now, and the future…the whole song we'd written together. "Sorry, Jillibean, I lied."

She scrunched her face. "Huh?"

"Remember when I told you I'd planned to hold you hostage for days?" I said, smoothing my hand over her soft hair.

She licked her bottom lip and sucked it into her mouth. I was hard in an instant.

"Yeah."

I shook my head. "Try forever."

Jillian's smile turned into a peal of laughter. "Promise?"

"Damn straight." There was no going back now. I leaned in close and claimed her mouth, ready for the encore.

Epilogue

In the distance my eyes fell on her silhouette. Against the backdrop of a burnt sky, she sat on the rocky beach facing the water. On a warm Friday in May, I was surprised to see the park so quiet. But then again, that's why Jillian enjoyed coming here. It was peaceful.

I killed the engine and pulled the keys from the ignition. Before stepping out of my car, I scooped up the little black box sitting on the passenger seat. I tucked it away in the glove box. That was for later.

Pushing the Challenger's door open, I stepped out quietly. I hit the key fob, locking up the car, and headed in Jillian's direction. Gravel crunched under my boots as I walked across the weathered rocks. A light breeze blew inland off the rippling water.

With the sun setting behind us, I made my way to the beach. As I sat down beside her, that familiar burn in my chest returned. A flame in my heart, and she was the acolyte.

I nudged her with my shoulder.

"You found me." She took her eyes from the water, piercing me with a dark stare. She smiled.

"Always." I bumped her with my shoulder again, then reached around, drawing her to my side.

We'd spent many quiet hours on this beach listening to the water lap at the shore, breathing in the ocean.

After my accident three years ago, I'd been in a bad place. That summer had not been a happy time for us. Even though I'd made an almost complete recovery, I still couldn't play the way I used to. Without music I was lost and angry.

Music had always been an outlet for my emotions. What I couldn't express verbally, I could always say in a song. But then I couldn't look at my bass or guitar. In my head I knew how to play, I just couldn't transfer the information to my fingers. Even the simplest rhythms fucked with me.

The doctors said the same thing...*give it time*. I didn't have time. Amphion wanted their badass rocker, but that wasn't me anymore. I couldn't play. And I was pissed. Most often Jillian was at the receiving end of my petulant attitude.

I was the worst fucking patient. The day she made the decision to put design school on hold to help with my recovery was a wake-up call.

In that moment I realized what a selfish bastard I'd become. All the years I'd pushed her away and robbed us of our time together had been for nothing.

I sobered up.

She had to go back to school. She'd done so well, accomplished so much. I'd become what I feared the most...an obstacle in the way of her dreams.

I had to pull myself together, not just for Jillian's sake, but for mine, too. My ability to play music had been the only casualty of my accident. I didn't have the dexterity or fine motor control to play my bass like I used to. It was one of the hardest things I'd ever had to do, bow out of the band I'd helped create. But I was only bringing the guys down.

After I'd helped them audition new bassists, I stayed on as Mine Shaft's songwriter, and helped Leo in the production booth. Yet I still felt like something was missing. I needed a backup plan.

Luckily, Leo had some connections in Boston, at the Berklee College of Music. I jumped at the opportunity. Not only did they offer a degree in production, Boston was only an hour from Providence.

My decision to return to school even helped repair the strained relationship I had with my parents, especially my mom. When she'd thought she might lose me, our disagreement about my future hadn't seemed so significant anymore. But that didn't stop her from squealing with joy when I told her I was giving school another go.

Now Jillian and I were both facing graduation…and our future.

"What brought you out here?" I asked.

This place had become Jillian's retreat, a place to center her thoughts and listen to her heart.

She lifted her chin to look at me. "I got a job offer today."

"Really?" I sat forward, angling my body in her direction.

Pushing a strand of hair behind her ear, she nodded. "Mm-hm."

"Bean, that's fantastic." I hugged her. "Where? Who for?"

She pulled away, giving me her full attention. "New York. Kate Spade."

New York. The place where her parents had died. To most fashion design graduates, a job offer in New York City was a big deal. But all Jillian saw was loss.

"Bean," I sighed. "If there's one thing I've learned in these last three years, it's that life's too short not to try." I scooped her tiny hands into mine and squeezed. "No matter how worried, scared, hurt, or pissed off you are, you have to try. For so many years, I was too scared and worried that I'd complicate your carefully planned dreams. I pushed you away, and we were both miserable. Had my accident been five months sooner, and I hadn't survi—"

"Griffin," she interrupted, shaking her head. "Don't."

"But don't you see? We would have missed out on this." I lowered my chin and used my thumb and forefinger to lift hers. I kissed her lightly, trailing my fingers over her collarbone and up her neck. "And this." I pressed us closer, deepening the kiss. My tongue pushed past the seam of her lips, and I drank her in.

I cupped her cheeks in my hands and pulled away, resting my forehead to hers. I stared into her eyes. "Jillian, don't let this opportunity pass you by. We'll conquer the city together."

Her lips slowly turned up at the corners, then touched her eyes. "You'd go with me?"

I pulled away and shook my head, taken aback by the question. "What the hell kind of question is that? Of course I'd go with you."

She put her hand on my thigh. "What if you find a job somewhere else?"

"Don't worry about me. I'm pretty sure there are a lot of opportunities in the New York music scene." I picked up her hand…her left hand, placing a kiss right where her graduation present would sit tomorrow night. "It's you and me, Jillibean. Forever." I leaned in and kissed her again. "And that's a promise."

Please see the next page for an excerpt
from Jillian's side of the story

Across the Distance

Available now

Chapter One

The tape screeched when I pulled it over the top of another box. I was down to the last one; all I had left to pack were the contents of my dresser, but that was going to have to wait. Outside I heard my best friend, Griffin, pull into the driveway. Before he shut off the ignition, he revved the throttle of his Triumph a few times for my sister's sake. Jennifer hated his noisy motorcycle.

Griffin's effort to piss Jennifer off made me smile. I stood up and walked to the door. Heading downstairs, I slammed the bedroom door a little too hard and the glass figurine cabinet at the end of the hall shook. I froze and watched as an angel statuette teetered back and forth on its pedestal. *Shit. Please don't break.*

"Jillian? What are you doing?" Jennifer yelled from the kitchen. "You better not break anything!"

As soon as the angel righted itself, I sighed in relief. But a small part of me wished it had broken. It would have felt good to break something that was special to her. Lord knew she'd done her best to break me. I shook off that depressing thought and raced down the steps to see Griffin.

When I opened the front door, he was walking up the sidewalk with two little boys attached to his legs: my twin nephews and Griffin's preschool fan club presidents, Michael and Mitchell.

Every time I saw Griffin interact with the boys, I couldn't help but smile. The boys adored him.

I watched as they continued their slow migration to the porch. Michael and Mitchell's messy white-blond curls bounced wildly with each step, as did Griffin's coal-black waves, falling across his forehead. He stood in stark contrast to the little boys dangling at his feet. Their tiny bodies seemed to shrink next to Griffin's six-foot-four muscled frame.

"I see that your adoring fans have found you." I laughed, watching Griffin walk like a giant, stomping as hard as he could, the twins giggling hysterically and hanging on for dear life.

"Hey, Jillibean, you lose your helpers?" he asked, unfazed by the ambush.

"Yeah, right," I said, walking out front to join him. I wrapped my arms around his neck and squeezed. I took a deep breath, filling my lungs with the familiar scents of leather and wind. A combination that would always be uniquely *him*. "I'm so glad you're here," I sighed, relaxing into his embrace. I felt safe, like nothing could hurt me when I was in his arms.

Griffin's arms circled my waist. "That bad, huh?"

I slackened my grip and stepped back, giving him and the squirming boys at his feet more room. "My sister's been especially vile today."

"When isn't she?" Griffin replied.

"Giddy up, Giff-in," Mitchell wailed, bouncing up and down.

"You about ready?" Griffin asked me, trying to remain upright while the boys pulled and tugged his legs in opposite directions.

"Not really. I've got one more box to pack and a bunch to load into my car. They're up in my room."

"Hear that, boys? Aunt Jillian needs help loading her boxes. Are you men ready to help?" he asked.

"Yeah!" they shouted in unison.

"Hang on tight!" Griffin yelled and started running the rest of the way up the sidewalk and onto the porch. "All right guys, this is where the ride ends. Time to get to work." Griffin shook Michael off his left leg before he started shaking Mitchell off of his right. The boys rolled around on the porch and Griffin playfully stepped on their bellies with his ginormous boots. The boys were laughing so hard I wouldn't have been surprised to see their faces turning blue from oxygen deprivation.

Following them to the porch, I shook my head and smiled. Griffin held his hand out and I laced my fingers through his, thankful he was here.

"I'll get the trailer hitched up to your car and the stuff you have ready, I'll put in the backseat. You finish up that last box; we've got a long trip ahead of us." Griffin leaned in close and whispered the last part in my ear. "Plus, it'll be nice to say *adios* to the Queen Bitch," he said, referring to my sister.

"Sounds like a plan." I winked. "Come on, boys." I held the door open and waved them inside. "If you're outside without a grown-up, your mom will kill me." They both shot up from the porch and ran inside.

"Giff-in," Michael said, coming to a stop in the doorway. "Can we still help?"

Griffin tousled his hair. "You bet, little man. Let's go find those boxes." Griffin winked back at me and the three of them ran up the stairs.

I trailed behind the boys, knowing that I couldn't put off packing that last box any longer. When I got to my room, Griffin held a box in his hands, but it was low enough that the boys thought they were helping to bear some of its weight. "Hey, slacker," I said to Griffin, bumping his shoulder with my fist. "You letting a couple of three-year-olds show you up?"

"These are not normal three-year-olds," Griffin said in a deep commercial-announcer voice. "These boys are the Amazing Barrett Brothers, able to lift boxes equal to their own body weight with the help of the Amazing Griffin."

I rolled my eyes at his ridiculousness and smiled. "You better watch it there, 'Amazing Griffin,' or I'll have to butter the doorway to get your ego to fit through."

Still speaking in a cheesy commercial voice, Griffin continued, "As swift as lightning, we will transport this box to the vehicle waiting downstairs. Do not fear, kind lady, the Amazing Barrett Brothers and the Amazing Griffin are here to help."

"Oh, Lord. I'm in trouble," I mumbled. And as swiftly as lightning (but really not), Griffin shuffled the boys out of the room and down the stairs.

I grabbed my last empty box and walked across the room to my dresser. I pulled open a drawer and removed a folded stack of yoga pants, tees, and dozens of clothing projects I'd made over the years. Shuffling on my knees from one drawer to the next, I emptied each of them until I came to the drawer I'd been dreading. The one on the top right-hand side.

The contents of this drawer had remained buried in darkness for almost five years. I was scared to open it, to shed light on the objects that reminded me of my past. I stared at the unassuming rectangular compartment, knowing what I had to do. I said a silent prayer for courage and pulled open the drawer.

Inside, the five-by-seven picture frame still lay upside down on top of several other snapshots. I reached for the stack. The second my fingers touched the dusty frame I winced, as if expecting it to burst into flames and reduce me to a heap of ashes. Biting my lip, I grabbed the frame and forced myself to look.

There we were. Mom, Dad, and a miniature version of me. Tears burned my eyes. My lungs clenched in my chest and I forced myself to breathe as I threw the frame into the box with my yoga pants. I pulled out the rest of the photos and tossed them in before they had a chance to stab me through the heart as well.

Downstairs I could hear the boys coming back inside, and then footsteps on the stairs. Quickly I folded the flaps of the box and pulled the packing tape off the dresser. With another screech I sealed away all the bad memories of my childhood.

"Well, my help dumped me," Griffin said, coming back into my room alone. "Apparently I'm not as cool as a toy car."

Before he could see my tears, I wiped my wet eyes with the back of my hand, sniffled, and plastered on a brave smile, then turned around. "There. Done," I proclaimed, standing up and kicking the box over to where the others sat.

"You OK?" Griffin asked, knowing me all too well.

"Yeah." I dusted my hands off on my jean shorts. "Let's get this show on the road." I bent down to pick up a box, standing back up with a huge smile on my face. "I'm ready to get to college."

* * *

Griffin took the last box from my hand and shoved it into the backseat of my car. "I'll get my bike on the trailer, and then we'll be ready to hit the road." He wiped his upper arm across his sweaty forehead.

I looked into his dark eyes and smiled. "Thanks," I sighed.

"For what?" With a toss of his head, he pushed a few errant curls out of his eyes.

"For putting up with me." He could have easily gotten a plane ticket home, but he knew how much I hated airplanes. The thought of him getting on a plane made me physically ill.

He swung his arm around my neck, squeezing me with his strong arm. "Put up with you? I'd like to see you try and get rid of me."

With my head trapped in his viselike grip and my face pressed to his chest, I couldn't escape his intoxicating scent. Even though it was too hot for his beloved leather riding jacket, the faint smell still clung to him. That, coupled with the heady musk clinging to his sweat-dampened t-shirt, made my head swim with thoughts that were well beyond the realm of friendship.

I needed to refocus my thoughts, and I couldn't do that pressed up against him. I shivered and pulled away. Taking a step back, I cleared my throat. "I'm going to tell Jennifer we're leaving." I thumbed toward the house.

He scrutinized my face for a minute, then smirked. "Enjoy that. You've earned it."

I turned on my heel and let out a deep breath, trying desperately to rein in my inappropriate fantasies.

Months ago our easygoing friendship had morphed into an awkward dance of fleeting glances, lingering touches, and an unspeakable amount of tension. I'd thought he'd felt it, too. The night of my high school graduation party, I went out on a limb and kissed him. When our lips met, every nerve ending in my body fired at once. Embers of lust burned deep inside me. I'd never felt anything like that before. The thought of being intimate with someone made me want to run to the nearest convent. But not with Griffin. When our bodies connected, I felt whole and alive in a way I'd never felt before.

Then he'd done what I'd least expected...he'd pushed me away. I'd searched his face for an explanation. He, more than anyone, knew what it had taken for me to put myself out there, and he'd pushed me away. Spouting some bullshit about our timing being all wrong, how a long-distance relationship wouldn't work, he insisted that I was nothing more than his friend. His rejection hurt worse than any of the cuts I'd inflicted upon myself in past years. But he was my best friend; I needed him far too much to have our relationship end badly and lose him forever. Regardless of his excuses, in retrospect, I was glad I wouldn't fall victim to his usual love-'em-and-leave-'em pattern. Griffin was never with one girl for more than a couple of months; then he was on to the next. That would have killed me. So I picked up what was left of my pride, buried my feelings, and vowed not to blur the lines of our friendship again.

Climbing the steps to the porch, I looked back at him before going into the house. Griffin had gone to work wheeling his bike onto the trailer. His biceps strained beneath the plain white T he wore. I bit my bottom lip and cursed. "Damn it, Jillian. Stop torturing yourself." Groaning, I reached for the doorknob.

"Hey, Jennifer, we're leaving," I said, grabbing my car keys from the island in the middle of the kitchen. She sat at the kitchen table poring over cookbooks that helped her sneak vegetables into the twins' meals. Poor boys, they didn't stand a chance. Jennifer fought dirty…she always had.

"It's about time." She turned a page of her cookbook, not even bothering to lift her eyes.

"What? No good-bye? This is it, the day you've been waiting for since I moved in. I thought you'd be at the door cheering."

Usually I was more reserved with my comments, but today I felt brave. Maybe moving to Rhode Island and going to design school was giving me the extra backbone I'd lacked for the last twelve years. Or maybe it was just the fact that I didn't have to face her any longer. Judging from the look on Jennifer's face, my mouthy comments surprised her as well. She stood up from the table, tucked a piece of her shoulder-length blond hair behind her ear, and took a small step in my direction. Her mannerisms and the way she carried herself sparked a memory of my mother. As Jennifer got older, that happened more often, and a pang of sadness clenched my heart. Where I'd gotten Dad's lighter hair and pale complexion, Jennifer had Mom's coloring: dark-blond hair, olive skin. But neither of us had gotten Mom's gorgeous blue eyes. The twins had ended up with those.

With the couple of features Jennifer shared with Mom, though, their similarities ended. When Mom smiled, it had been kind and inviting. Jennifer never smiled. She was rigid, harsh, and distant. Nothing like Mom.

Jennifer curled her spray-tanned arms around my back. I braced for the impact. Jennifer wasn't affectionate, especially with me, so I knew something hurtful was in store. I held perfectly still as she drew me close to her chest. The sweet, fruity scent of sweet pea blossoms—Jennifer's favorite perfume—invaded my senses. For such a light, cheery fragrance, it always managed to weigh heavily, giving me a headache.

Jennifer pressed her lips to my ear and whispered, "Such a shame Mom and Dad aren't here to see you off. I'm sure *they* would have told you good-bye." She slid her hands to my shoulders and placed a small kiss on my cheek.

And there it was. The dagger through my heart. Mom and Dad. She knew they were my kryptonite. For the second time in less than an hour, I felt acidic drops of guilt leaking from my heart and circulating through my body. But what burned more than the guilt was the fact that she was right. It *was* a shame they weren't here. And I had no one to blame but myself.

I held my breath while my eyes welled up. *Not today, Jillian. You will not cry.* I refused to give her the satisfaction. I stood up taller, giving myself a good two inches on her, and swallowed the lump forming in my throat. She was not going to ruin this day. The day I'd worked so hard to achieve.

"Ready to go?" Griffin said, coming around the corner. "The boys are waiting by the door to say good-bye."

Jennifer stepped away from me and gave Griffin a disgusted once-over. "And yet another reason why I'm glad Jillian decided to go away to school," she said. "At least I get a respite from the white trash walking through my front door." Piercing me with an icy stare, she continued, "With the endless parade of women he flaunts in front of you, the tattoos, the music"—she scowled—"I've never understood the hold he has on you, Jillian." She stifled a laugh. "Pathetic, if you ask me."

Griffin took a step in her direction. "Excuse me?" he growled, his expression darkening. I knew he wouldn't hurt her, but he was damn good at intimidating her. He wasn't the little boy who lived next door anymore. He'd grown up. With his deep voice and considerable size, he towered over her, the muscles in his arms flexing.

She shuffled backward. "Just go." With a dismissive flick of her wrist, she sat back down at the table.

"Yeah, that's what I thought, all bark and no bite." Griffin pulled on my arm. "Come on, Bean. You don't have to put up with her shit anymore."

I glanced back at Jennifer; she'd already gone back to her broccoli-laced brownie recipe. Griffin was right; I wouldn't have to put up with her shit while I was away. But he was wrong about her bite. When he wasn't around to back her down, she relished the chance to sink her teeth into me. It hurt like hell when she latched on and wouldn't let go.

We walked down the hallway. Michael and Mitchell were waiting by the door. "I need big hugs, boys," I said, bending down and opening my arms wide. "This hug has to last me until December, so make it a good one." Both of them stepped into my embrace and I held on to them tightly. "You two be good for your mommy and daddy," I said.

"We will," they replied.

I let go and they smiled. "I love you both."

"Love you, Aunt Jillian," they said.

"Now go find your mom. She's in the kitchen." Knowing the boys' penchant for sneaking out of the house, I wanted to be sure their mother had them corralled before Griffin and I left.

I stood back up and looked into Griffin's dark eyes. "I'm ready." I tossed him the keys.

"I'm the chauffeur, huh?" Griffin smirked, pulling his eyebrow up. He opened the door for me and I stepped out onto the porch.

"You get the first nine hours; I'll take the backside." This time he gave me a full smile. *What would I do without him?* On the porch I froze. It finally hit me. What *would* I do without him? Sure, I wanted out of Jennifer's house, but at what expense? Couldn't I just go to the junior college like Griff and get my own apartment? Why had I made the decision to go to school eleven hundred miles away? How could I leave him—my best friend?

The lump in my throat had come back but I forced the words out anyway. "Griff…" I sounded like a damn croaking frog.

Griffin wrapped his arms around me. "Yeah?"

"Why am I doing this?"

"What do you mean? This is all you've talked about since you got the scholarship."

"I know." I sniffled. "But I don't know if I can do this. We'll be so far apart."

"Uh-uh. Stop that right now. I am not about to let you throw away the opportunity of a lifetime just because we won't see each other as often. You're too talented for Glen Carbon, Illinois, and you know it. Now go, get your ass in the car." With his hand he popped me on the backside, just to get his point across.

I jumped, not having expected his hand on my ass. My heart skipped and my cheeks flushed. "Hey!" I swatted his hand away.

"Get in the car, Jillian."

Damn, I already miss him.

Acknowledgments

All thanks and praise to my Lord and Savior, Jesus Christ, through whom all things are possible.

I finished book two. Wow! If it weren't for the love and support of my family, I wouldn't have gotten through the first draft of this novel. Thank you! Love and hugs, Boo and ReeShee!! And a special thank you to my husband for answering all my questions about the bass and guitar, and even patiently trying to teach me how to play the bass. I suck. I know. I'll stick to playing the piano!

Endless thanks to my amazing agent, Louise Fury. I'm so grateful to have you in my corner, championing my stories, and helping me grow as a writer with each new book. Working with you is a dream come true!

I'm also thankful for Team Fury, especially Lady Lioness. Once again, thank you for all your help and splendid ideas. I do a happy dance when my inbox pings with an edit letter from you! Infinite thanks!

To my brilliant editor, Megha Parekh, at Grand Central Publishing. I love working with you. Your insightful edits push me to be a better writer. Thank you for all you do to help my books land in the hands of readers!

My publicist, Fareeda Bullert, thank you for answering all my questions and leading readers to *Across the Distance* and *Can't Go Back*. I'm extremely grateful.

To my cover designer, Elizabeth Turner, for giving Jillian and Griffin their faces. *Across the Distance* and *Can't Go Back* are beautiful, and I love them! Thank you!

And to the rest of my publication team at Forever Yours, your tireless dedication to *Can't Go Back* means so much. Thank you for helping make *AtD* and *CGB* the best they can be.

NAC: Marnee Blake, Diana Gardin, Ara Grigorian, Amanda Heger, Sophia Henry, Jamie Howard, Kate L. Mary, Laura Salters, Annika Sharma, Jessica Ruddick, and Meredith Tate, you are all phenomenal! From Facebook parties to endless comment threads, I love hanging out with you ladies and Yoda. My dear friends, thank you for everything you do to support me! I love our group!!

SS Crew: Heather Brewer, Cole Gibsen, Emily Hall, Sarah Jude, Jamie Krakover, Shawntelle Madison, L.S. Murphy, and Heather Reid, thank you for helping this newbie out! I love you all dearly!

And a huge THANK YOU to the readers and bloggers who read, promoted, reviewed, and loved Jillian and Griffin!! Thank you for dedicating your time to reading my stories and telling others about my books. I can't wait to share more stories with you!!

About the Author

Marie Meyer was a language arts teacher for fourteen years. She spends her days in the classroom and her nights writing heartfelt new adult romances that leave readers clamoring for more. She is a member of RWA and the St. Louis Writers Guild. Marie's short fiction won honorable mentions from the St. Louis Writers Guild in 2010 and 2011. She is a proud mommy and enjoys helping her oldest daughter train for the Special Olympics, making up silly stories with her youngest daughter, and bingeing on weeks of DVR'd television shows with her husband.

Learn more at:

MarieMeyer.com

Twitter, @MarieMwrites

Facebook.com/MarieMeyerBooks

www.ingramcontent.com/pod-product-compliance
Ingram Content Group UK Ltd.
Pitfield, Milton Keynes, MK11 3LW, UK
UKHW021150020325
455674UK00006B/99

9 781455 590971